I0590973

NICARAGUA
WAY

Nina Serrano

This book is a work of fiction. Any references to historical events, real people, or real places are used fictitiously. Other names, characters, places, and events are products of the author's imagination, and any resemblance to actual events or places or persons, living or dead, is entirely coincidental.

Print Book ISBN: 978-0-9618725-7-1

eBook ISBN: 978-0-9618725-8-8

Estuary Press
P.O. Box 577
Oakland, CA 94604

Cover Art by Anthony Holdsworth
Cover Design by Adrian Arias
Book Design by Paul Richards

To the activists for peace, social, and
environmental justice the world over and
the people of Nicaragua and the United States

For Paul Richards, for all the reasons

Contents

Part One

San Francisco

1

Closet Secrets

"I love San Francisco in September," Lorna shouted out alone in the car through the open window to the blue sky and late afternoon sunshine. It was Sunday in September of 1975. Lorna headed for Eddie's house at the edge of the barrio in the San Francisco Mission District. It had been a year since she had visited her old friend, and she was both excited and nervous. It seemed they had always danced around each other, attracted, but unwilling to get involved. At least, Lorna had been unwilling. Eddie was married and she drew the line at married men. Although she had been a single mother for more years than she cared to remember.

The past year had changed little in Lorna's life. She had hoped a year in Madrid, working with Chilean refugees from the 1973 fascist Pinochet coup, might have produced a true-life companion. But she had come home from that human rights job as she had left, a woman alone, solely herself and her teenage daughter, Rini, short for Irene.

And now Rini was beginning her freshman year at the University of California in nearby Santa Cruz. Lorna had driven her down just the day before with her embroidered elephant duffle bag and all her gear.

Lorna's red Datsun remembered the way to Eddie's as if it were on autopilot. Eduardo "Eddie" Flores was a Nicaragua-born artist and activist in San Francisco's cultural scene. She and Eddie worked together in the San Francisco Community Arts Program, a City agency, and were also buddies in many Latino cultural and political organizing campaigns.

Lorna reminded herself that she had to leave early to prepare for her first day back at work at the Community Arts

1

Program in a year. Eddie's house hasn't changed, she thought. His stucco house was built over a garage, offering heartbreaking views of San Francisco Bay and the Bayshore freeway. Pink geraniums overran the front yard on the right. To the left, pre-Columbian figurine clay faces peeked out from under green sword ferns. They seemed to Lorna to be gods, peering at her through the fronds, protecting her now and Rini on her first day at college.

She rang the familiar bell, tucking in her tummy and standing a little taller, remembering the many times she had stood on this very spot, waiting for Eddie to open the door. She had thought life would all be over by forty, but here she was, forty-one and still intact. Men on the street still looked at her, though she had been trained not to look back. The rosy tan she had acquired in the Spanish summer was not about to fade in a San Francisco September, when beautiful Indian summer was just beginning.

Eddie must have run down the stairs because he arrived at the door instantly with the chimes still sounding upstairs as he reached out to hug her. Eddie swept her into his arms, engulfing her with his warmth and spicy Florida Water scent, the same after-shave her beloved grandfather, Gabriel Almendros, had used.

Eddie stepped back. "Let me look at you!" he said.

"Do I pass muster?" Lorna asked.

"You look great! Fantastic."

"You look good yourself, Eddie." He was of medium height, light brown skinned, but with unexpectedly light green eyes, a trim mustache, and kinky waves in his dark brown hair. He exuded physicality, charisma and vitality.

"Strong!" she added. He was even more muscular than she had remembered.

"Strong me no strongs, Lorna. I'm a regular Hercules," he said, falling into their personal code talk.

"I've been studying martial arts and jogging in Dolores Park with a backpack full of books. There's a battle ahead of us, you know."

"Rini gave me your mysterious message," said Lorna. "She said you didn't want to discuss it on the phone. So here I am."

"Yes, so here you are, more beautiful than ever," said Eddie, appreciatively.

"Well, I'm all ears," Lorna said, thinking he was still a flirt and hadn't changed.

"Ear me no ears," said Eddie, slyly looking her over. "How was a whole year working on human rights?"

"Man, invite me in," said Lorna. "I don't want to tell you the whole story standing here on the doorstep. Rini and I just got back. Yesterday, I drove her down to UC Santa Cruz with all her stuff, a real college student!"

"Great! So you're free now. No more mommy duties."

"Those never end," said Lorna. "You'll find that out one of these days." Eddie and his wife, Maria, had little ones, ages three and five.

"I may, or I may not, things are getting unpredictable," said Eddie. "But tell me, how did the work go? Your letters were so few and far between, I never really knew exactly what you were up to over there." He spoke over his shoulder, as he led her up the indoor stairs.

"But I wrote you," she protested. "I was helping political prisoners get out of Chile and into Spain. Pinochet has imprisoned and tortured so many. But I'll tell you more when I can sit down."

"So come on up." He climbed the stairs two at a time. Lorna followed, competitively trying to keep up.

The delicious smell of frying onions and garlic filled the small kitchen. Maria was hovering over a steaming pot and a sizzling pan. Even with her face moist and her hair pulled back, Maria was a sexy gorgeous woman, in her early thirties, wearing tight jeans and a clinging blue shirt. Gold bracelets jangled on her brown wrists, as she flipped a pork chop with a two-tine fork.

"Hey, Maria!" cried Lorna, moving to give Maria a hug. But the younger woman stepped away, barely looking up.

"I'm an empty nester now, Maria," said Lorna, hoping to combat Maria's coldness and dispel the threat that Maria might be feeling. "I drove Rini down to Santa Cruz yesterday to start her freshman year. I'm going to be at such loose ends. I don't know what I'll do." Lorna hoped this appeal to their common motherhood might soften her.

"Oh, you'll figure out something," said Maria, coolly. She lowered the gas flame under the pan. "I've got to finish making dinner before my sister brings the kids home. Gordita started preschool last week and Claudio is in kindergarten now. Thank god they're gone, at least some of the day. If I were you, Lorna, I'd be feeling damn lucky!"

So much for the common bonds of motherhood, thought Lorna.

Maria turned all her attention back to her steaming pot.

"Well, you're looking very fit, Maria," Lorna said, trying again.

Maria hardly glanced up. "I work out at Ben Wu's with Eddie."

Eddie was watching with a broad smile, oblivious to the tension between his wife and Lorna.

"We're all getting into shape," he laughed. "We're all getting ready for the struggle." He seemed very cheerful. "Come, come, come, let's sit down in the living room. You've got to tell me everything," he said to Lorna, as they walked out of the kitchen, leaving Maria alone at the stove.

The living room walls were a pale orange above a dark wood wainscoting. Windows were open to the warm September breeze. A row of brightly colored new silkscreen prints running the length of the wainscoting caught her attention and made her realize that Eddie had been working a lot. Eddie took a seat on the sofa, and pulled her down next to him, so close their thighs were touching. Lorna tried to move apart discreetly but found herself trapped by the old, soft spongy cushions.

"So, Eddie, what is this about the struggle that everyone's getting ready for? Is it what makes you think that things are unpredictable?"

"Wait," Eddie said. "First you. Tell me about Spain. What did you do?"

"What did I do?" sighed Lorna. "Oh my god, there was so much. I couldn't keep up, really. Pinochet has taken so many victims. Everyone who was even remotely part of Allende's government is dead or disappeared or fleeing. We were trying to find housing for the Chilean refugees, find them work, and help them find out what had happened to those left behind. There are posters everywhere in Santiago, of kids. *¿Dondé están?* People are in hiding until they can get smuggled into the embassies. Then, they get out any way they can. The military totally dominates Chile. Books are being burned. Censorship is everywhere. The slightest utterance seemingly critical of the military is considered treason."

"Yes, I know," said Eddie, gravely.

"To be honest, Eddie, I didn't do enough compared to what was needed. But they gave me an award in a ceremony just before I left. I read my poem to Neruda in this huge, elegant old theatre, the Teatro Alcazar. There must have been a thousand people in the audience. Not for me. I was a small part of it. But for the cause, a fundraiser. Quilapayun accompanied me. Have you heard them? It was exciting, to read before so many people. But I feel guilty, I didn't deserve it. Thousands of Chileans are still in prison or exiled or disappeared."

"Wow, Quilapayun," repeated Eddie, sounding impressed.

"Yes, like Inti-Illimani. Musicians, Chilean *folkloristas*. So now I'm home and Rini's in Santa Cruz. I'm all alone, and I hate it"

"Not alone, Lorna. A woman like you is never alone. Unless you want to be."

Lorna sighed, ignoring Eddie's flirting and looking up at the row of silkscreen prints hanging against the orange walls.

"Are those new, Eddie?! I love them! Such vibrant colors. Are they all of Nicaragua?"

Eddie looked pleased. "Yes. They're the new ones, from my

'Memories' series."

Lorna stood up, wanting to get away from the warmth of Eddie's thigh against hers. In one print, two women in red and green skirts washed clothes beside a river. Children splashed in the water alongside, while a hen pecked at seeds on the river bank under the shadow of three palm trees. Another print depicted a familiar male with a strong martial face and high cheekbones, wearing a white Stetson hat. Beside him, barely coming to his shoulder stood a woman with a white flower in her hair.

"Isn't that Sandino?" said Lorna. "My grandfather had his framed portrait in our living room. *El General de Hombres Libres/The General of All Free Men.* Who's the woman next to him? Is she wearing the *sacuanjoche* flower? They look like such a romantic couple."

"You're right. It's the national flower of Nicaragua. That's Augusto Sandino and the woman is his true love, the telegraph operator Blanca Arauz."

Lorna was surprised. "Blanca Arauz? My grandfather told me Sandino's true love was Teresa Villatoro from El Salvador. My grandfather met her once in Managua. He said there was a long scar on her face, but she was still very beautiful."

"Teresa Villatoro was one of his lovers. She was wounded in a skirmish while visiting Sandino at his headquarters, El Chipote." Eddie paused, and added, "Well, a revolutionary leader has many loves. He belongs to the people. Who knows which one is the true love? He can't belong to any one woman."

"Who?" asked Maria suspiciously, entering the room carrying a tray of chips, guacamole and two beers. Lorna felt uncomfortable being served like one of the boys. Like one of the superior beings, not expected to serve, but to be served. She didn't drink beer and tried to avoid chips.

"I was telling Lorna I would like to find a picture of Teresa Villatoro to make a silkscreen of her. Sandino's true love may have been this Teresa Villatoro, not Blanca Arauz, the telegraph operator."

"True love? Hah!" mocked Maria. "As if you knew anything

about it."

"I just want to create art, *amorcita*," said Eddie, smoothly. "Lorna's *abuelo* believed Teresa Villatoro was Sandino's true love. My friend, *Coronel* Viglieti mentioned this woman Teresa Villatoro also. She may have been with Sandino when Somoza murdered him. I want you to meet the *coronel*," Eddie said, turning to Lorna. "He's a great old man. He fought with Sandino. And he lives right near you. He has a great appreciation for beautiful women." Eddie's green eyes shone happily.

"The dirty old man, always slobbering over me," snorted Maria, as she set the food down with a slight slam.

"As you are beautiful, *Amorcita*, he always comments on it," said Eddie. He gave Maria a gentle slap on her well-formed rear as she headed back to the kitchen.

He turned back to Lorna, "Speaking of the murder of Sandino, you know, no one has ever found Sandino's body. It's rumored Somoza had him decapitated in order to deliver his head to Washington, DC, as a sign of loyalty to the Americans."

Lorna shuddered.

"Well, it's never been proved, but a lot of Nicaraguans believe it."

"Eddie, you've become so scholarly. You're just full of history's little known facts."

"If they're little known facts, it's only because we live in a Euro-centric society," said Eddie. "If Latin American history were taught in our schools as thoroughly as European history is taught, American school children would know the lives of all the Latin American liberators, and the names of the Indigenous peoples. Hell, they might even speak some of the Indigenous languages." He leaned forward. "I'll have to show you more of my new work, the prints from my 'Liberator' series. I begin with Anacaona. She's the Indigenous Taíno woman who fought against Columbus on the island of Hispaniola."

"A woman hero? Eddie, You're coming around at last."

"Hero me no heroics, Lorna. The truth is I hardly have any time left for my art. I'm too busy with real life."

"You mean your family?"

"I mean the big picture, Lorna. The big global screen. But let's not talk here. This room might be bugged." He rose, pulled Lorna up by her arm, and propelled her into the bedroom.

"Eddie, stop this! Maria's in the kitchen."

"She won't mind. Come. Maria knows this closet is the only place that isn't bugged," he urged, tugging her with one hand into the closet. Lorna found herself squeezed between silky dresses and wooly coats, smelling of perfume, personal odors, and moth-balls. She tried not to tread on the shoes under her feet. It was very dark and she could barely see.

"You're crazy, Eddie," she said, her voice muffled by the clothing. "I can't believe I am really following you into your closet! I've followed you a lot in the last few years. Here I'm back less than a week, and I'm following you again!"

"This isn't about following me, Lorna," he whispered, "although I'm flattered that you think you can't help yourself! We'll discuss that another time. I promise you! I'm just being cautious about unwelcome electronic ears." He put his fingers very gently on her eyelids. "Close your eyes. When you open them, you'll be used to the dark."

Lorna obediently closed her eyes and immediately felt the bristles of Eddie's mustache and two warm lips pressed against her.

"Stop it, Eddie!" she said.

He laughed. Lorna heard a rustling, and then a thump. "OK, you can open your eyes."

Eddie was holding a very large gun by the barrel with the butt on the floor.

"Isn't she a beauty, Lorna? She's an AK-47."

"What are you doing? Put that thing away," she said in alarm. "Is that even legal?" she asked.

"It's almost legal. I have to get around to registering it." In the dim closet light, Eddie slid one hand down the barrel.

"My sweet honey and I will be inseparable. *Dulce*, I call her."

"Great, you've given up womanizing for gun collecting."

"Not given up women, not at all. This gun is for the revolution. As Sandino said, 'As long as Nicaragua has sons who love her, and will take up arms to defend her, she will be free.'"

"For god's sake, Sandino lost the revolution fifty years ago!"

"Lorna, Sandino never lost! It's still the revolution, and it's happening all over again in the Segovia Mountains right now. The sons of Sandino are creating the *Hombre Nuevo*, Lorna. Che Guevara's socialist vision of the New Man goes beyond the ordinary capitalist man. The New Man works for the common good. To fight the revolution, the New Man is a man of iron, a man of steel. Totally committed. So I've joined the Sandinistas. Our local organization is called Nicaragüense Comité Cívico. We support the *Frente Sandinista de Liberación Nacional*, the Sandinista Liberation Front in Nicaragua. We usually just say *Frente* or FSLN or 'The Front.' Our San Francisco headquarters are here in the Mission. You see now why I had to pull you into the closet. If the CIA gets wind of this...." Eddie was grinning with pride and pleasure.

"Well, that kiss attempt wasn't part of *el Frente*," objected Lorna.

"Maybe not, but it was fun, wasn't it?"

They stood silently in the dark. Lorna could feel Eddie's breath on her cheek. She wondered if he would try that again. But now he seemed preoccupied with his enormous weapon and delighted in shocking her.

Eddie had always been passionate about politics. But an AK-47 and armed struggle worried her. She hadn't heard talk about Sandino since her grandfather's many stories of Nicaragua in her childhood. Now, according to Eddie, there were guerrilla camps in the mountains, and Eddie had acquired a rifle to use in the revolution.

Lorna flashed back to the day before when Rini had introduced Lorna to her new college roommate, Sally. Rini said, "My mom's grandfather was from Nicaragua." Lorna was surprised Rini was thinking about her great-grandfather, whom she had never met. He had died decades before.

Rini's roommate, Sally, was a lively young woman, tall, with long limbs and animal grace. "Have you been to Nicaragua?" Sally had asked Rini.

"No," Rini had said, "But I'm going to. I want to experience my ancestors' country." That had startled Lorna also. Rini had never shown an interest in Nicaragua before.

"My great grandfather raised my mom after her Nicaraguan mom and dad died in a car accident. But later, he died too, while she was still a kid. Then she was adopted by this American couple, but she never really felt comfortable with them. You didn't like them, did you, Mom?"

Lorna wondered if she was going to tell her whole life story to this stranger. "We were different, but I was grateful they took me in," said Lorna, awkwardly. "And how about you, Sally? Where are you from?"

"My family goes back to the first settlers in Jamestown, Virginia." The young woman's air of pride was annoying.

Lorna had been unkind, saying, "The fascinating thing about the Jamestown colony is that half of the first families of Jamestown came out of London's Newgate prison. It was either relocate to Jamestown or face the gallows. It was also the first landing place for slave ships with captive Africans."

Rini had looked at her mother, horrified, but if Sally was deflated by this, she did not show it.

Rini had quickly changed the subject. "My own parents are divorced," Rini had volunteered. Lorna had felt a stab of guilt.

"Oh, so are mine," Sally had offered, airily. "Mom's been married four times."

Rini eyes had widened. "That's a lot!"

Eddie's insistent whisper broke Lorna's reveries.

"Lorna, I can hear you thinking. Talk to me."

"I have a fear of guns, Eddie," Lorna said. "Violence solves nothing."

"The violence of the dictator Somoza's ruling class has to

be challenged by those oppressed by that violence."

"We don't agree on this. I'm closer to being a pacifist, Eddie. Anyway, I'm thinking about Rini, and about Sandino, about my grandfather and my childhood. It makes me lonely again. I'm feeling as if time and space have collapsed together."

"Time and space are too big for me, Lorna. I'm focused on one small Central American country barely the size of Oklahoma and the *Frente Sandinista de Liberación*. The *Frente* has been around for decades, really. It sprang up again after the Cuban Revolution in 1959. But I only got involved a year ago."

"How did you get involved?"

"Remember the Managua earthquake three years ago? The huge relief effort here in the Mission? I had lost touch with the Nicaraguan community, but then I helped my mom organize a clothing drive. The scandal hit just after you left. We found out Somoza had stolen the money, the food. Hell, he even stole the blood we donated. The entire Nica community in San Francisco was enraged."

Eddie moved the AK-47 up and down for emphasis. "I met some guys involved in the Sandinista movement, and I started meeting with them regularly. Mundo and Anibal. One day, a wounded *compa* from the *Frente* in Nicaragua arrived. Arnoldo. Then our group became four. We may be small, but never underestimate what a small group can do. Last December, thirteen guerrillas stormed the house of the minister of agriculture in Managua, during a Christmas party honoring that sonofabitch Shelton Turner, the American ambassador, and took everyone hostage. They demanded the release of our political prisoners, the founders of the FSLN. Somoza let the Sandinistas out of his prison and they flew to Cuba. Let me tell you, we're galvanized, Lorna. Nothing is going to stop us!"

"So you're all men?" Lorna asked.

"In Nicaragua, there are women in some of the guerrilla camps. But right now, here in the Mission, we're all men. But you'll see, women will join us. Arnoldo is our leader. Now, all

I do is eat, drink, and sleep this revolution. You see, Lorna, what happened in Chile is part of the same story. It's all one story of a criminal US foreign policy toward the Third World, the Southern Hemisphere. Pinochet could never have succeeded without aid from the CIA. It's all one revolution. This one is our revolution, Lornita. Because of our Nicaraguan roots. It's yours and mine. Our Nicaraguan revolution."

Memories of Abuelo, her grandfather, whirled through Lorna's head. She shared his reverence for Augusto Cesar Sandino and felt she belonged to something that had started long before she was born.

Lorna pulled herself together, "I don't like looking at that gun. It's making me very nervous."

"Not a problem," Eddie said, placing the weapon back into the recesses of the closet. He opened the door for Lorna to step out.

The world turned very bright. Lorna blinked. "I could feel the ghost of my grandfather in the closet, Eddie. I have goose bumps on my arms. What you're saying scares me."

Eddie continued, no longer whispering, "Come with me to headquarters. We rent a little storefront. We call it El Chipote, named after Sandino's headquarters. I'll introduce you to the *compas*. There are twelve of us now. Yes, don't even ask. They're all men. I told you, it won't stay that way. That's why I'm talking to you, Lorna. I know you. We need a woman like you, and you'll help us. I know that. The harder Somoza comes down on the Nicaraguan people, the bigger and stronger our San Francisco exile community becomes."

Lorna shivered. "The hairs on my arms are standing on end. Mentioning El Chipote brings back Grandfather's old stories. They're coming alive," she said. "Like I'm moving into the past, only I'm really moving into the present or maybe the future."

Walking back toward the kitchen, Eddie spoke to Maria. "I need to take Lorna down to headquarters," he announced. "Tell the kids to save some dinner for Papa."

Lorna could see her, framed by the doorway, at the stove. Eddie bent over his wife and kissed her lingeringly on her neck and Lorna thought she caught Maria's look of suppressed anger, finally succumbing to resignation to Eddie's domineering but sensuous ways.

To stay out of their way, Lorna turned to inspect Eddie's new prints of brown-skinned women washing clothes in the river. They are beautiful, she thought, with the little ones splashing in the water beside them. One woman could have been Maria. Lorna felt so different from this image. She wasn't the kind of woman that could just cook for a man, do his bidding, his laundry and raise his kids. She expected more for herself. Her year in Spain showed her she was an American. Eddie was different, being born and raised until he was five in Nicaragua. Her Nicaraguan roots had faded growing up in Chicago after Grandfather died and Jack and Ella adopted her. She hardly even spoke Spanish until it came back when Eddie got her involved with *La Raza* organizing in San Francisco.

Eddie came into the living room wearing an army jacket and a beret. "Let's take your car. I'm ready."

"I hope I am," said Lorna, rubbing the goose bumps.

2

El Chipote

Eddie jumped into the passenger side of the red Datsun. Lorna was already behind the wheel.

"Where to?" asked Lorna.

"Just go down the hill. El Chipote is on Twenty Second off Valencia."

As Lorna headed downhill from Bernal Heights, they caught a view of the Mission District below, and over to the hill where Lorna lived, and above to Twin Peaks, framed against a horizon banded with pink and red.

"You know, Eddie, your talk of Sandino makes me sad. My grandfather, who raised me, died when I was eight. I never got over missing him and now I'm separated from Rini. Separations are hard for me. They make me feel lonely all over again."

"Lorna," said Eddie, "you won't have a minute to be lonely. I've been telling the *compas* all about you. Your amazing skills and your stature in our community as a writer and organizer are well established and we need you. Not to mention you are easy to look at. And on top of that, helping us will bring you full circle back to your roots."

"It's thanks to you, Eddie, I'm in touch with my roots. You got me to drop my married name, start using Almendros again, and start working in the San Francisco Latino community. But I hate war, Eddie. I believe in a non-violent approach to social change."

"Wars of liberation are forced on us, Lorna. We don't seek them out. But I'm not asking you to fight. We need you to work with a group in Washington, DC, pushing for congressional hearings on Central America. They want to stop military aid to the Somoza dictatorship. If it weren't for US military support, Nicaraguans could rise up against Somoza and win."

"Mmmm..." said Lorna, dubiously, remembering the AK-47 in the closet.

"Look, it's the same struggle today as it was in your grandfather's time. We are fighting the son of the Somoza your grandfather opposed. And we are the sons of Sandino. It's the same struggle like the coup in Chile. The US is propping up Somoza. The Sandinistas can't succeed while Somoza's army is funded with US tax dollars. You're an American, Lorna. You're even a former city PTA president. You brought the arts and poetry into the schools again. Now, we need a mass movement of Americans pressuring Congress to stop military aid. Someone like you who knows how to organize a campaign in San Francisco arts and education communities and beyond."

"Why me?"

"Lorna, you're perfect for it. You're an American citizen, but you understand Latin America. Now that Rini's away at college, you can fill your life with the Nicaraguan cause."

"Wait a second, Eddie..."

"Let me tell you about the D. C. group," Eddie hastened to add. "It's run by a woman, Jeannie Giacomelli. Jeannie started as a graduate student working with the Washington Office on Latin America. Then she and some Quaker friends formed this group that deals specifically with Nicaragua. They call it Non-intervention in Nicaragua, NIN, named after the earlier organization from the twenties and thirties when all kinds of prominent American intellectuals protested the US Marine invasion of Nicaragua. You'll be carrying their banner."

"American intellectuals like who?"

"Poets and writers like Sinclair Lewis and Edna St.Vincent Millay. Jeannie's group wants to form chapters all around the country, but especially in California because of our large Latino population, to push Congress to end the military aid.

You could pull together the San Francisco group. Anyway, Lorna, there's no shooting involved." Eddie looked at her expectantly.

"Eddie, I'm a poet. Community organizing will zap all my energy."

"Don't underestimate your abilities. People know you in our community. They know your poetry. They love you. You speak Spanish. It's why I'm taking you to El Chipote."

"At least I won't have to kill anyone," she said.

Lorna became quiet, thinking about her grandfather and how much he loved Sandino. Supporting the Sandinistas seemed right. Following Eddie might dash her hopes for her poetry. The work in Spain was so demanding that it left little time for writing. Now Eddie wanted her to take on this new cause.

"I don't know if Arnoldo will be there tonight," Eddie was saying. "He's the only one who speaks good English in the group. The rest of the *compas* come from the urban proletariat."

"You never used to talk about the urban proletariat."

"I never used to take weekly political education classes, Lorna. A lot has changed for me while you've been gone. Reading and studying are the duties of every revolutionary. I've been reading Marx and Lenin, a chapter here, a chapter there. Pablo Neruda and Nicaraguan poets like Rubén Darío and Ernesto Cardenal and especially the writings of Che. Che Guevara and his talk of the new revolutionary man, 'The true revolutionary is guided by great feelings of love.' That's Che."

"I'm impressed with your reading list," Lorna said.

"I'm learning so much, Lorna. All these years I've called myself Chicano. I'm not Chicano. I'm from Nicaragua in Central America. I'm a Nica. Chicanos are *Mejicanos*. Latinos are lumped together. We don't stand up for our own diversity. Now, I'm celebrating my Nica self. I'm not a hyphenated American minority. I'm part of my people in exile. After my father left us, my mother couldn't feed us. So she loaded us kids on a bus to the land of opportunity where she was told the streets were paved with gold. Only it was a long, long, bus ride away, and the streets weren't paved with gold. Not for her, Lorna."

"The great gold myth. Grandfather believed America's streets were paved with gold, too. He learned the hard way."

"Yes, my friend, I'm filling the big gaps in my soul. I've been away in *Gringolandia* too long, forgetting the motherland. Now I am sucking at her breast." He looked over at Lorna. "Hah, I made you blush!"

"So how's your mother? Is she on this revolutionary course too?"

"No, she thinks it will lead to trouble for us back in Nicaragua. She's doing her own thing, anyway. She's taken up witchcraft."

"You're kidding."

"You know, herbs, candles, rituals, healing. The Caribbean folks in the hood have been influencing her. This Afro-Cuban guy, *Chocolate*, he calls himself, owns a *botanica* shop. He sells things for casting spells. She likes him."

"Does Beatriz think she's really a witch?"

"She calls herself a spiritual counselor who performs healing ceremonies and gives advice."

"I thought Beatriz was Catholic."

"The Spaniards forbade Indigenous religions, so we used Catholic symbols, but we were still worshiping our own spirits. Everywhere in Latin America the Catholic saints absorbed aspects of the Indigenous deities."

They turned onto Army Street from Peralta, heading toward Twenty-Second and Valencia Streets. "I'm not sure what's in this spirituality stuff for me," admitted Eddie. "But I notice an influence in my art. I just finished a silkscreen of Rubén Darío's head. I tried to put his soul into the eyes, and an aura around his hair." Demonstrating, Eddie's hand stroked the strands of Lorna's hair. "See, I can feel your aura right now."

Lorna moved her head away. Eddie had a disturbing habit of letting his touch linger.

"Sorry, Lorna, I forget how cold you Americans are. You Americans hate being touched."

"Eddie, what you do is sometimes inappropriate," Lorna countered.

"Inappropriate?" Eddie tossed the word back at her, and Lorna felt foolish but also annoyed. "I'm not being prudish. It is just very annoying."

Eddie smiled.

Lorna found a parking space right in front. A small storefront was squeezed between a Chinese restaurant and a jewelry store with *Joyeria* painted in gold on its small cluttered window.

Eddie jumped out and ran over to open her door.

"Welcome to El Chipote, *Compañera* Lorna," he said, bowing dramatically.

Lorna was astonished as she looked in the window. "Oh, look! There's my book, *Ancestors/Antepasados!* I'm so thrilled. I am touched. This is the first time I have seen it on public display. Rini and I left for Spain right after the release party."

"Touch me no touches," Eddie grumbled, but he was smiling.

Above her book hung a silkscreen of Rubén Darío's head in Eddie's unmistakable bold style. Underneath simple lettering read, "Father of Latin American Literature." Alongside was a black and red poster of Sandino in his wide hat, leaning on a long rifle. A copy of a newspaper was also handsomely displayed.

A cowbell hanging from the inside door knob clanged as they entered. The headquarters, El Chipote, consisted of an old couch, two desks, and folding chairs set out on a scarred but shining clean linoleum floor. The blue and white Nicaraguan flag hung high on the wall. Under it was pinned a huge map of Nicaragua at eye level. A door led to a lighted back room from which Lorna could hear the rhythmic hum of equipment rumbling and clanking. Two men emerged from a back room.

"*Compas*, I've brought *Compañera* Lorna Almendros," Eddie said in Spanish, gesturing towards the two men. "This is Anibal," Eddie said to Lorna. Anibal was thin, in ironed blue jeans and ankle boots.

"We've heard so many wonderful things about you. I am honored to meet you!" Anibal said.

The other man was stocky, with a strong torso, short legs and curly hair. "I am Mundo," he said. He had crooked, discolored teeth, she noticed, as he flashed her a smile, and a flat, flared nose. "We've been awaiting your arrival. We hope you will agree to help us."

Lorna cast Eddie an accusing look, but he only smiled back at her innocently.

The rumbling and clanking stopped, and a third man emerged from the back room. He had a high forehead on which a thin white scar ran from the corner of his eye up into his hairline. He had pale skin and large brown eyes. His light auburn hair was like her own.

"Arnoldo," said Eddie, "is in charge of political education and editing our newspaper."

"*La Gaceta Sandinista,*" said Arnoldo with pride. "Did you see the copies in the front window?"

"I did. Very impressive," said Lorna.

"I've heard a lot about you, *Compañera* Lorna. We've been waiting for you to return. I knew we would be allies." He reached for her hand, and as she extended it, he brought it to his lips. "We read a translation of your fine magazine article on the international solidarity movement."

Lorna hoped she wasn't blushing.

They were standing close to the map of Nicaragua, and Arnoldo pointed to the slimmest part of the country. "You see here, how the Atlantic and Pacific are almost joined by these lakes, Lago Colcibolca and Lago Xolotlán?" He traced the expansive blue bodies of water on the map. This is where your robber barons, the Rockefellers and Vanderbilts, wanted to build a canal. They needed a quick and easy route to California's gold mines," he said with a bitter laugh. "Starting with the conquistadores, the lust for gold has always brought the foreigners."

Now Arnoldo pointed toward the border with Honduras.

"This is where our movement is concentrated, *compañera*. In the Segovia Mountains, especially near and around the town of Palacaguina. We have a song about it. '*Cristo ya nació en Palacaguina*,' by Carlos Mejía Godoy. It brings the nativity story into the brewing revolution."

"How does it go?" asked Lorna, always eager to learn a new song.

Mundo, Eddie, and Anibal joined in as Arnoldo sang a few lines.

> Christo ya nació en Placaguina
> del Chepe Pavon y una tal Maria...

"Bravo, bravo!" cheered Lorna. "You have a nice voice," she added, to Arnoldo.

"I sang in prison, to keep up my spirits, and the spirits of the other *compas*."

Lorna tried not to look at the scar over his left eye. She realized that Arnoldo was the Sandinista that Eddie had mentioned, who had come from Nicaragua to mobilize their group.

Now, Arnoldo was pointing out the sparsely populated autonomous regions. "They're all tropical rain forest and wilderness. Most Nicas speak Spanish, but here on our Atlantic coast, the people speak English."

"I never heard of English-speaking Nicaraguans," Lorna said.

"Probably because they're Black," interjected Eddie. "Never underestimate the power of racism."

"Our eastern seaboard was colonized by the British," Arnoldo was saying. "There, Black people escaping slavery in the Caribbean islands intermarried with English and Irish pirates, as well as the Indigenous Rama, Sumo, and Misquito Indians. It's an isolated zone, very hard to reach. Once a week, a ferry, the Bluefields Express, heads out there. Our ferries are not like ones here going to Alcatraz, Tiburon or Angel Island. Picture a very old, small boat stuffed with people, packages, babies, chickens, a goat, and huge baskets covered with cloth or plastic. In the rainy season, storms may wash a few passengers overboard. But for people from Bluefields, it's worth the risk to go home."

Arnoldo turned away from the map. "I'd give anything to go home right now, feel the heat and the rain make puddles up to my knees. I would never again complain about mud and dust. I would kiss the ground in front of my mother's house. But there is work to be done here, *compañera*. We need the good people of this country to raise the awareness of their Congress."

Standing in El Chipote, Lorna vividly recalled Grandfather's stories of his faraway homeland Nicaragua. He had told her of tropical rain puddles up to his knees, always using that phrase, and ancient preserved footprints of giants trying to flee the volcano. She was so young when he died. It made the past so mysterious. Grandfather used to say, "Only the past is dark." Lorna had wondered about that as child, afraid to fall asleep, afraid of the Chicago dark. Sometimes she had thought the present was also dark. Abuelo had returned to Nicaragua when Lorna was eight because he had inherited a house, telling her he was coming right back. But he died in Nicaragua and never returned. She still had the deed the lawyer gave her when she reached her eighteenth birthday. The house was in a village called Pueblo Azul, which she had never been able to locate on a map.

She snapped back into the present at the sound of Eddie's voice.

"What's the matter with you two? Where's the funeral?"

"In the heart," Arnoldo answered, very quietly.

Anibal interrupted, changing the mood. "Come and see how we produce *La Gaceta Sandinista*." He motioned toward the back room, where, their old friend, a Multilith 1250 offset printer stood. She and Eddie had christened the old machine "Black Beauty" and forgiven it all its faults.

"Eddie, that's Black Beauty!" Lorna exclaimed.

Anibal touched a switch, and Black Beauty sprang into action, clinking and rattling, shooting sheets of newsprint into a bin at one end.

"Right after you left for Spain," Eddie explained, "our grant ran out. So that magazine issue of *Cantinflas* with your article on the international Chilean solidarity movement was our final issue. We donated our left-over resources to El Chipote to print the *Gaceta Sandinista*."

"We published everything on that machine," Lorna said fondly. "But didn't Black Beauty always require someone under it with a wrench to keep it running?"

Arnoldo pulled the wrench out of his pocket. "It still does," he said, smiling. Then he pointed to stacks of bundled newspapers lined up along the walls. Some looked like back issues, and others appeared fresh and ready for imminent delivery. "The *Gaceta* is sent monthly to the Nicaraguan exile communities in the Mission, Los Angeles, Costa Rica, Mexico, and everywhere we can," Arnoldo explained.

"Who does the writing?" asked Lorna.

"We get clandestine material from Nicaragua, from other exiles in Mexico, and we also write a lot here. We receive stories from all over," said Arnoldo.

"So, who's paying for all this?" Lorna dared to ask.

"We ask for donations from the Nica community. There are thousands of Nica immigrants in the neighborhood now. But basically we pay for it ourselves. We pay the rent out of our own pockets, the utilities, and phone. Each of us kicks in money every month. We'd like to publish in English as well as Spanish, and we'd love to go weekly. So much is happening. There's news every day. But we need help. There are only twelve of us."

Mundo stood with his thumbs in his belt. "It's been hard to find jobs, *compañera*. Anibal works in a restaurant. I do deliveries for a dry cleaning store. Arnoldo is a banquet waiter."

Eddie picked up a sheet flying out of the machine. At the top was a black-and- white photo of a small boy shining the boots of a huge US Marine. "Look at this," he said, showing it to Lorna. "Washington denies it, but this picture proves we're right."

Arnoldo stepped closer, pointing at it. "The United States denies it has a military presence in Nicaragua. But US Marines train Somoza's personal army, the *Guardia Nacional.* This photo is eyewitness evidence that the US Marines are there, training the *Guardia Nacional* in torture," said Arnoldo, bitterly.

Now Lorna understood his scar. Arnoldo persisted, "This is why we wanted Eddie to bring you here, *Compañera* Lorna. You must organize the Non-intervention in Nicaragua chapter in San Francisco. We must end the US-sponsored brutality in Nicaragua."

"I'm not sure I'm right for this. I've never been there." Lorna felt herself floundering.

"You are a Nicaraguan, *compañera* Lorna. You carry the spirits of your ancestors. We have read your poetry. You have heard of the corn goddess? You carry the spirit of the corn goddess, Xilonen."

"My grandfather told me about the corn goddess. I pretended to myself that the Xilonen was my mother." Lorna was shivering. Something about his words seemed so right.

"Be, indeed, the daughter of the corn goddess, Lornita," said Arnoldo, holding her eyes with his. "Embrace Nicaragua as your mother and help us free her. We are willing to give up our lives for this mother. We need to reach the conscience of Americans, *compañera.*"

Eddie spoke stepping between them. "Somoza doesn't have the support of the people. Without the US, his regime would collapse. The NIN group in Washington DC is pressuring for a congressional hearing on Central America."

Mundo interjected, "San Francisco needs a group to pressure Congress in the same way."

Arnoldo continued, "Fifty years ago Americans like you, intellectuals, famous writers, formed the first Non-intervention in Nicaragua."

"I'm hardly a famous writer."

"You are extremely well known in our community," said Arnoldo.

"You would be perfect for this, Lorna," Eddie concurred.

Then Mundo turned to Lorna, "Compañero Eddie tells me you live near my uncle. Do you know him? Coronel Viglieti? He fought with Sandino."

"Sandino was killed in 1934, the year I was born. There can't be many of the original fighters left. They would be as old as my grandfather."

"He is *muy viejo*," agreed Mundo. "But he still likes the pretty ladies."

Meanwhile Eddie had found five bottles of Coca Cola in the refrigerator and passed them around.

"Let's drink to the *compañera*," he laughed. "I think she's deciding to join us."

"To Lorna, and to the revolution," Anibal declared, holding up his bottle.

The men all raised their bottles. "¡A *la Compa Lorna, patria libre o morir!*"

How could Lorna back out now?

3

Lonely Night

Lorna drove back to her flat as the streetlights came on. Eddie had stayed at El Chipote to help the *compas* with the paper. She recalled how she had missed her home at the top of Hill Street during her year in Spain. It was a magical spot, with views out across the city in three directions. Lorna had found the apartment when the neighborhood was unfashionable. Actually, it still was, although gentrification in Noe Valley was starting to creep down the hill. She parked, banking the front wheels sharply against the curb to prevent rolling on the steep slope, and got out and stretched. The block was lined with bottle-brush trees with their cylindrical fuzzy red flowers. Purple bougainvilleas and late roses tangled over front yard walls. It was a street of solid Victorian houses. A few were grand, with three stories and round towers projecting upward from the corners. Most of them were modest, one-story Victorians with windowed bays looking out on the street, and their small front yards filled with euphorbia and rosemary. Lorna had always wanted a round room. Down the hill she heard the clang of the nearby 'J-Church' streetcar.

She opened the door to the building and was climbing the stairs when the phone rang inside the flat. Pushing open the apartment door, she rushed in to answer it, thinking it might be Rini.

It was Eddie. "So are you going to do it?"

"Eddie, for heaven's sakes, I just saw you ten minutes ago. Give me a break. Let me think about this."

"Don't think about it, Lorna. Just follow your heart."

"Right now, my heart is missing Rini," said Lorna.

"You'll get over that, Lorna."

"Goodbye, Eddie," Lorna said, pointedly. She set the receiver in its cradle, and within a second the phone rang again.

"Stop, Eddie! Please," she snapped. "I told you I wanted some time to think!"

"Hi, Mom," Rini chirped. "Hey, what's going on? Think about what?"

"Rini! I was just telling Eddie how much I missed you."

"Eddie? Why are you still bothering with him, Mom?"

"Don't start that again," said Lorna. Rini didn't like him. No matter how many times Lorna had explained how Eddie had encouraged her poetry, involved her in the Latino arts world, and designed the cover for her book, Rini still resented him.

"You know he's important to me, Rini," Lorna said, carefully.

"No, Mom. Eddie's important to Eddie," said Rini.

"Please, Rini, let's not go through all that Eddie stuff again."

"OK, OK, Mom. Look, please do me a favor, will you? Can you look for my old 'Freedom and Independence for Vietnam' T-shirt? I saw a notice for a campus meeting, in two weeks. They want to raise funds for a hospital in Vietnam to compensate for war damages. If you find it, can you mail it to me? I want to wear it for the meeting."

"OK. I start work tomorrow. Can you take the bus up this weekend? I need to talk to you. Something has come up, something Eddie wants me to do, and I don't want to discuss it on the phone."

"Mom! Stop this mysterious talk! You're starting to sound just like him. Anyway someone wants to use this phone. I'm on that pay phone down the hall in the dorm. Be sure when you call, to let it ring at least twelve times because it takes a while for someone to answer it. Good luck back on the job. I've got to go, now."

"Will I see you next weekend?"

"Yes, I'll take the bus up."

She hung up the phone, and the apartment seemed suddenly very quiet.

Lorna made herself a cup of tea and settled herself in the overstuffed brown chair with its wings and padded arms, next to her table lamp and radio, in front of the view. Soft music accompanied the quarter moon. It was higher now, the sky dark, and small lights sparkled on the East Bay hills as she looked over the Mission toward Potrero, and out towards the bay, with Oakland and San Leandro twinkling distantly across the black water.

The visit with Eddie to El Chipote had brought back such intense memories of Abuelo. The last day she saw her grandfather, she had been leaving for summer camp. "I am going to Nicaragua to look at my house," her grandfather had told her. "I promise to be back in fourteen days, Lornita. I'll be back before you are home from summer camp. I'll be waiting for you." But every day, swimming, chasing butterflies, watching fireflies, singing around the campfire, Lorna had missed him. Every night she wished on a star for Abuelo to be there. Then one morning, as Lorna was braiding leather strips for a belt, she was called into the camp director's office. Her grandfather had died. Lorna could hardly breathe. By bedtime, she was crying hysterically. "Abuelo! Aaaabueloooo!" Her body had ached from crying. The pain of loneliness became her constant companion. She was instantly adopted by an American couple, Grandfather's dentist and his wife, Jack and Ella Elliot. The loneliness continued through all her years with her adopted parents, and her college years at the University of Chicago. It didn't end until fifteen years later, in 1957, when she married Rini's father, and became part of a family again.

She had met Rini's father, Carl Sevens, while she was a graduate student in comparative literature at the University of California in Berkeley. Carl had been a graduate student in political science there. He was intellectual and intense, with heavy black-framed glasses. As a student leader, his self-confidence was charismatic. He was totally fearless, left-wing, and skillfully argumentative. Their romance began inside the Ban the Bomb movement against atomic war. They married at the Berkeley City Hall and, a year later, having moved to a cramped apartment in San Francisco, Rini was born. Lorna's bonding with Rini solidified her feelings of belonging.

They had been married five years when they attended their first meeting against the escalating war in Vietnam. It was in 1963 at the North Beach apartment of Bob Stern, a friend of Carl's. Eight activists crowded into the living room. Bob started it off, declaring, "There's been a civil war going on in Vietnam ever since the French defeat in 1954. The US has picked up the ball that the French dropped and now the Vietnamese people are fighting against escalating US intervention. Kennedy has increased draft calls. We have to stop the draft and US intervention in Vietnam!" Lorna knew about nuclear bomb testing in the Pacific but she had never heard of Vietnam.

"Where's Vietnam?" Lorna had asked.

"It's called Indochina on the map," Bob had answered condescendingly. Soon after, Carl and Lorna joined anti-war protests at San Francisco's Civic Center, carrying signs that said "Stop the undeclared war in Indochina. Stop the killing." Their movement began to grow. Lorna wrote press releases and went to meetings, while Rini played on the floor with her dolls. Carl traveled to give speeches and wrote articles for the alternative press. Once the military draft became a big threat, the whole nation was aware of the war. But while Lorna's political life heated up, her marriage to Carl was cooling. They were always quarreling.

"You compete with me for leadership, Lorna," Carl had accused. "You don't know how to fight and I do. You're going to lose this battle."

Not long after, Carl left Lorna for Bob's girlfriend and they moved to New York City. Lorna was left alone, with a four-year-old child to raise. She and Rini became the family.

Now, sipping her tea, listening to music on the radio, Lorna was alone again. Only this time, she thought, she was not twenty-eight. She was forty-one. Her sense of absence and loss lingered in the shadows. When she finally went to bed, the low radio voices mixed with her dreams. The old loneliness ebbed and flowed. She didn't turn off the light or the radio until morning.

4

Congressional Hearing

Nine months later, Lorna stood at the boarding gate at the San Francisco airport with Rini and her roommate Sally, on her way to the June 7, 1976 congressional hearings in Washington, DC.

Helen Hart was rushing toward them. Helen was Lorna and Eddie's boss at the San Francisco Community Arts Program. Four years older than Lorna, and her best friend, Helen was striking. Her face was like English porcelain, with milk-white skin that could freckle. Her pale-blue eyes were sparkling, and her straight light brown hair hung soft and silky on wide shoulders. Her strong legs showed beneath her mini-skirted business suit as she hurried down the hall.

"I made it!" Helen said breathlessly. "There's half an hour until you board." Her full bosom peeked out from under the low cut silk blouse and form fitting jacket. Helen stood very straight, exuding a slight bossiness and certainty. She was known to be "a good organizer" in liberal City Hall politics. But there was that unexpected, irreverent sparkle in her eye, and always a subtle subtext (Let's do it!) with a readiness for adventure, any adventure, which endeared her to Lorna.

Around them, passengers for Pam Am's nonstop flight to Washington's Dulles Airport waited for the boarding call. Rini and Sally stood out in their youth and freshness. Lorna had grown fond of Sally. She was a good influence, supporting Rini's focus on her studies. They had both come to see Lorna off.

"Sally," said Rini, "This is my mom's friend, Helen. She's almost like an aunt to me."

"Hi, Auntie Helen," said Sally.

"Hi, Sally. I have heard so much about you," answered Helen. "I am so excited that you girls are going to transfer to San Jose State next year to complete a degree in engineering. That's so smart. So many women major in English, and the only job they can find when they get out is secretary to some male executive. Will you girls have to give up your cottage in Santa Cruz?"

"No," said Rini. "We've talked about that. We love living in Santa Cruz. We'll keep the house and commute to San Jose. It's a commute, but we want those engineering degrees and some hard-core skills under our belts when we graduate."

"That's my girl, Rini. You take after your mother," said Helen hugging Rini. "Nothing stops her either. When Lorna first told me about the Non-intervention in Nicaragua group Eddie wanted her to form, I had my doubts. But now I am part of it and here she is, just six months later, on her way to the Congressional Hearings. Eddie's pretty persuasive."

"Don't let's talk about Eddie," Rini groaned.

"Eddie is a good friend, Rini," said Lorna defensively. "He's set this whole thing up. He even said there is a chance I might be asked to testify before the committee. He'll meet me at Dulles and drive me to Jeannie Giacomelli's. Eddie's arranged for me to stay with her. She's with the national office of Non-intervention in Nicaragua."

"I just hope he manages to show up," Rini sniped.

"I'm so impressed," said Sally. "You'll be covering the story for *Bulwark Magazine* and you might even testify. You're my hero, Lorna. I mean, my she-ro."

Helen pulled six manila folders from her attaché case, being brisk and business-like. "Just don't lose these, Lorna. These have all the background information you'll need for your article and if you're asked to testify," she admonished and then gave her a bag of corn chips. "Just for fun" she added.

Lorna stuffed them all into her colorful Mexican string bag.

Helen regarded her a bit skeptically. Lorna was wearing an embroidered peasant blouse, a ruffled skirt, and sandals. "I do wish you had a real briefcase, Lorna, something other than that silly Mexican marketplace bag. And that outfit. You know, DC is very conservative. I hope you've brought a suit along."

"I'm going on behalf of the people of Nicaragua, Helen," said Lorna. "They don't wear suits, and neither do I."

"What about that linen blazer..." Helen looked worried.

"She looks great!" said Sally, quickly interrupting. "She's perfect, just as she is."

"We're your cheering squad, Mom," offered Rini.

"Boarding for flight 103 to Washington DC at gate 4," announced a loud speaker.

Rini handed Lorna a red leather notebook. "A present from Sally and me, for you, Mom. Be sure to write down all your profound thoughts!"

Lorna kissed Helen and her young cheering squad and minutes later was in the air. Outside the small window, thick bits of fog and cloud streamed by, obscuring the view of the bay. Turning to the first page of the notebook, she wrote, "US House Subcommittee on International Organizations Hearings, June 8-9, 1976: Human Rights Abuses in Central America." Under that, she wrote '¡Patria libre o morir!' She thought of Abuelo and the corn goddess, Xilonen, and then wrote, "Whether God exists or not, Xilonen is with me."

Six hours later, the plane touched down, and there was Eddie, his green eyes gleaming, waiting among the crowd at the arrival gate. As she got closer, he grabbed her and gave her a full-body hug, smashing his lips down on hers. She was enveloped with sensations of hard muscle, mustache, and Florida Water.

"Whoa!" Lorna warned, but it was useless.

Eddie was full of news and full of life, as he drove them the twenty-six miles into the capital. Now he was telling her about the noticias on Spanish language TV. Eddie reported, "Somoza won't allow Pedro Joaquín Chamorro to leave the country. He doesn't want him testifying at the hearings."

"Who's Pedro Joaquín Chamorro?"

"The most popular man in Nicaragua," answered Eddie. "Chamorro is the editor of the daily newspaper, *La Prensa*. Actually he's very rich, and totally bourgeois, but he opposes Somoza, and Nicaraguans admire him for that. This censorship will make Chamorro more popular than ever. They're sending a liberation theology priest in his place. He's bringing testimonials from peasants and poor people in his parish. They're all in Spanish. You and Jeannie will have to translate them tonight so we can hand them in first thing tomorrow morning. We're going to be up against the machinations of the pro-Somoza lobby, a couple of corrupt dogs if ever there were any."

"Who exactly are you talking about?" asked Lorna.

"Couple of congressmen. Charlie Wilson of Texas. Johnnie Murphy of Staten Island. Both totally in Somoza's pocket."

As they crossed the Potomac, Lorna could follow the water's powerful current moving downstream far to the east through a landscape very unfamiliar to her. The soft, green rolling hills of Virginia seemed bathed in a kind of moisture emanating from the ground, a bright mist making the landscape shimmery and luminescent. Washington was a low city, no more than three stories high, and Eddie spun her around town, quickly pointing out the White House.

"The White House!" Lorna blurted out, her heart lurching.

Eddie gestured toward the Mall with the Obelisk visible high above the feathery green of the early summer foliage and the white marble dome of the Capitol rising at the far end.

"That's where you'll be tomorrow," Eddie said.

"I might be speaking truth to power," she said, remembering the new pale green summer dress she carefully packed just in case and the two-page plea she wrote on the plane in case she had to testify before the congressional committee.

Despite her dislike of her government's foreign policy,

Lorna felt a thrill to be there. The Federalist and Neoclassical architecture of the capital was so beautiful. This was her country. She felt buoyed by a sense of belonging and her small role in history.

Their destination was Dupont Circle, where Jeannie Giacomelli had an apartment in a three-story brownstone. Eddie parked and they walked up to a second floor apartment and knocked on the door. Jeannie was a slim and rounded Italian-American, with dark brown eyes, and a friendly, intimate style of speaking. Lorna liked her immediately.

"How did you get involved in this?" Lorna asked her after Eddie left and they settled in. Jeannie had prepared hero sandwiches and a big pot of coffee, and they were sitting at her kitchen table.

"I did field work for a year in Central America as an undergraduate.," said Jeannie. "It was heart wrenching to see the incredible poverty of the people, and the obscene wealth of the upper classes. Then in grad school I met some Quakers from Philadelphia. They'd been going to Central America for years doing literacy work and running health clinics. We learned about the original Non-intervention in Nicaragua group in the twenties, and I started to understand the historic role of the US in this suffering. I decided to pick up where the original NIN left off. I began speaking, writing, and raising money, and found I was good at it. First, I worked with the American Friends Service Committee here in Washington and with all kinds of other church groups. Then I continued to develop NIN after I got hired as a part time congressional aide and later as staff for the Washington Office on Latin America, WOLA, which has played a major role in forcing these hearings on human rights in Central America. Now I am working full time for NIN. How about you?"

"Our San Francisco group began as a Latino arts collective, mostly fired up about the whole issue of civil rights for Latinos. Did you hear of *Los Siete de la Raza?*" Jeannie shook her head, no.

Lorna explained, "The city accused seven Salvadoran

immigrant teenagers in San Francisco of murdering a policeman. The whole community was enraged. We believed they were framed. Defending them got us started organizing the barrio. Initially in that work, I was Lorna Sevens. I still used my ex-husband's last name, even though we'd been divorced for years. When Eddie learned I was born Lorna Almendros, and my parents were Nicaraguan, he was so excited. He appealed to my Nicaraguan roots and it resonated with me. I took back my name, and got rid of the Sevens."

"Maybe that was about time?" said Jeannie, with a wicked smile.

"You can say that again," Lorna affirmed. "Then last fall, after I came back from a year working with Chilean solidarity groups in Spain, Eddie helped me see that this Non-intervention in Nicaragua work was the necessary next step in empowering the community to speak truth to power. And in six months our group has really grown. The Reverend Don Crane joined recently. He was with the original NIN back in the twenties. And we are trying to get some labor people. My daughter and her roommate have started a chapter at their College."

"Eddie mentioned what good work you've done. He's been really busy since he got here keeping us connected with Nicaragua. All very hush hush." Jeannie said. "Tell me more about Eddie."

"I've known Eddie for years but he doesn't tell me everything. He's secretive because of the nature of the clandestine work in Nicaragua." She paused and added, "And . . . he loves drama."

Jeannie lifted her eyebrows.

"To be honest," Lorna said, "he gets a kick out of cloak and dagger. My daughter thinks he overplays that hand. But he's passionate about the cause and he's a serious silk-screen artist."

"Well, he's pretty cute," said Jeannie with a smile.

"He's married," said Lorna.

"Aren't they all?" Jeannie sighed. Pointing to the dining room table, she said, "We've got a sheaf of testimonials to translate before eight tomorrow morning. Let's do it."

"Let's do it," said Lorna.

The two women spread the papers out on the dining room table, surrounding themselves with Spanish/English dictionaries, Spanish-only dictionaries, English-only dictionaries, an English thesaurus, and yellow legal writing pads. Lorna picked up some manila folders that were filled with pastoral letters from priests and bishops in Nicaragua. The contents were disturbing. Twenty-four people disappeared from the town of Sofana in the province of Zelaya. Three large new graves in Sofana; four large older graves nearby. Six people murdered. Over one hundred people disappeared from the province of Matagalpa. The lists of the dead, the disappeared, and the tortured seemed unending. Lorna and Jeannie worked until long after midnight.

At eight the next morning Eddie stopped by to pick up the translations.

"Meet me outside room 2200 in the Rayburn House Office Building at one-thirty," he said. "By the way, Lorna, I've seen the schedule. You won't be testifying."

"I won't?" Lorna tried not to let her disappointment show. Quickly, she began planning how she could integrate her two-paged plea into the text of her unwritten *Bulwark Magazine* article.

Eddie continued, "The line-up is the congressman from Staten Island—a real Somoza buddy, let me tell you. Then us, the Central American human rights contingent. Tomorrow people from the State Department will testify. That will be a joke. And some professors from Syracuse and SUNY Potsdam. The committee isn't interested in our grass-roots activism. They want to hear from the so-called experts."

At one-thirty Lorna and Jeannie stood at the entrance to room 2200 with Eddie and a man Eddie introduced as Father Fernando from Nicaragua. "Father Fernando is one of the liberation theology priests," said Eddie. "He believes the New Testament calls for a society in which there are no rich or poor."

The priest, a man close to fifty years old, had black hair and wide eyes, giving him an alert, kindly look. He was barely taller than Lorna. He wore the banded collar and black jacket of a cleric. "Thank you for translating the testimonials," he said to the two women. "Eddie delivered them this morning, and they will form an important part of the record."

"Lorna Almendros is a poet, Father" said Eddie. "A poet and a Nicaraguan-American. She's a good translator."

"My brother is a poet," said the priest. "He will be very pleased to learn an American poet translated these materials." At that moment the massive oak doors opened, and Father Fernando walked forward to take a seat in the first row, while Lorna, Jeannie, and Eddie took seats at the back of the wood-paneled room. A table with two chairs sat before the members of the committee.

Chairperson Congressman Donald M. Fraser of Minnesota called the meeting to order. "Because of time constraints," he said, "we will hear first from the Honorable John M. Murphy of Staten Island." A jowly individual, clean-shaven with bright blue eyes and carefully trimmed hair, took a seat at the table.

"The Castro regime has taken dead aim at Nicaragua since 1962. Cuba is bent on turning it into a pro-Communist satellite in the Caribbean," he testified. "On December 27, 1974, a dozen thugs, armed by Castro, stormed a farewell dinner being given for the American ambassador. After murdering the minister of agriculture and three guards, these thugs took the remaining guests hostage and made outrageous demands. You ask about martial law in Nicaragua? Yes, Somoza has declared martial law, and he is within his constitutional rights to do so. Nicaragua faces aggression by these Communist insurgents supported by Cuba."

Congressman Murphy wiped his sweaty brow, and continued. "Here are four killings, a matter of record, by a political terrorist group supported by Fidel Castro. To date there have been no deaths in this vein that can be found perpetrated by the government of Nicaragua. Yet the

Washington Office on Latin America makes these irresponsible charges. They shed crocodile tears over alleged and unproven abuses, yet ignore such an atrocity."

To Lorna's surprise, the chair then recognized Congressman Ed Koch of New York sitting near him on the congressional panel.

"Jack," said Koch, "you personally know Somoza, having served with him at West Point. Is that not true?"

"Yes and he is a family friend. We were in grammar school together. He's a great guy. Speaks beautiful English. He's a true friend to the United States."

Jeannie whispered, "He's a true puppet."

The hearing continued and when Murphy finally stood up to go, it was Father Fernando's turn to sit at the witness table.

"Nicaragua serves as Somoza's private plantation," Father Fernando began in his heavily accented English. "The Somoza family owns sixty percent of the agricultural land, the transportation, and even the factory that sells the government bricks for paving the roads, while my parishioners live in the most impoverished and brutal conditions. We endure arrests of clergy, union, and opposition leaders. Torture. Disappearances. Sometimes whole villages or communities are annihilated. This murder is perpetrated by Somoza's military and para-military, all paid for by US taxpayers. In the past fifteen years the Somoza family has received twenty million dollars in military aid from the United States of America. Three million of that is for arms purchases and one million is for training programs for the National Guard, the *Guardia Nacional.* But the problem is that while Nicaragua has lots of military aid money, we have no external enemies, despite what Somoza's friends may say." He looked around to see the impact of his words.

When Father Fernando's eyes lit on Lorna and Jeanne, Lorna nodded and smiled. Jeanne gave him a thumbs up.

The priest continued, "Somoza's American friends present him as the Central American bastion against Communism. But, he is actually the contrary. Regimes such as Somoza's promote communism among the people. As long as there are dictators who take away freedom, who keep their citizens hungry, malnourished, and poor, there will be Communism in our region. Not even with all the military power of the United States will communism be avoided in our countries under these conditions."

Father Fernando slid out the testimonials from their manila folder. "There are concentration camps in Siquia, Amatillo, Ococona, Waslala, Rio Blanco, and Cuscawas. Peasants who are sent to these camps never return. At Lomas de Panecillo in León, many families are in jail and subjected to brutal treatments. Their only crime was organizing to defend themselves against high-ranking officials of the *Guardia Nacional*, Somoza's police who wanted to take over their small plots of land. Are these so-called Communists? Their crime is to refuse to sell their property to these members of the *Guardia Nacional*."

Congressman Fraser frowned. Lorna squeezed Jeannie's arm remembering how only hours before they had translated these words.

Father Fernando read aloud a list of individuals who had been disappeared from Sofana during three days of February 1976. He read a pastoral letter from the bishop of Zelaya dated May 20, 1976 and read aloud from the testimonials of those who had been tortured. He recited a list of Guardia Nacional officers who had ordered violations of human rights.

"There is no freedom of speech in Nicaragua," Father Fernando said in conclusion. "Civil liberties are totally curtailed and those who dare to speak in opposition to Somoza are arrested, tortured, and disappeared."

Lorna watched Congressman Fraser shaking his head. Then, Congressman Ed Koch spoke again.

"Is it not true, Father, that Pedro Chamorro, the editor of *La Prensa*, the national newspaper of Nicaragua, speaks out frequently in opposition to Somoza? He continues to speak out, and he is not in jail. So how can you state that civil liberties are curtailed in Nicaragua?"

"Pedro Chamorro is a very wealthy man, Congressman," responded Father Fernando. "Yes, he does speak out against Somoza and he is not in jail. At least not at the moment. You will note I have introduced a sworn statement of Pedro Joaquin Chamorro's concerning the human rights violations he observed while being held at *El Modelo* prison on February 11, 1976. But in Nicaragua we have a saying, *neither the rich nor the clergy go to jail.* You may note that I also have been free to speak out. In Latin America, we have a tradition that universities are sanctuaries, akin to a church, perhaps because almost all Latin American universities were founded by the Jesuits. So the list of persons missing, assassinated, tortured, and disappeared that I am presenting to you represents poor persons, farm workers, and labor organizers. You notice that Chamorro is not in jail. But, still, Somoza forbade him to leave Nicaragua to address this body."

"I simply wanted that point to be clear," said Koch. "Somoza does not go after those very few who are wealthy and powerful. I am not concerned with US military assistance given to counteract a security threat. But the military assistance given to Somoza has been used to arm Somoza's police for the indiscriminate repression of the population, based only on their assumed complicity with subversive groups."

The chair then called Dr. Rene de León Schlotter of Guatemala, a leader of the World Union of Christian Democrats, to join Father Fernando at the table. As Dr. Schlotter took his seat, Lorna drew a line in her notebook at the end of her Father Fernando notes. She wrote down Schlotter's name, but she knew nothing about him.

Dr. Schlotter began his remarks by saying, "Mr. Chairman, let me refer to another aspect of Central American politics. The violent situation in Guatemala is directly attributable to the movement for national liberation against the government of Anastasio Somoza Debayle, and those who have helped to establish him as dictator of Nicaragua and would-be dictator of Central America. Since 1974 I have been pointing out the grave danger to the whole of Central America that is represented by the increasingly powerful presence of General Somoza. Somoza is far more than a dynasty that has continued, without interruption, ever since it took power with US help in 1937. Somoza is also a style of government, that includes fraudulent elections, limits on political opposition, corruption, repression in both the political and the economic realms. When I denounce the Somoza-ization of Central America, what I want to point out is the clear and present danger that this kind of regime could become permanent in Central America."

Lorna wrote a note to herself to research Somoza's impact on the rest of Central America.

Dr. Schlotter continued, "Somoza personally owns large ranches in Costa Rica and he is the owner of the ferryboat line across the Gulf of Fonseca, whose success is due to artificially maintained hostilities between Honduras and El Salvador. In my own country, Guatemala, he has holdings in a number of different companies and enterprises. He has an increasingly powerful presence in the political and economic life of five countries."

Congressman Koch jumped in again, "Father Fernando, on a scale of one to ten with Chile being the most repressive at number one and Costa Rica perhaps not being repressive at all, at number ten, where would you place Nicaragua in terms of oppression?"

The priest took a deep breath. "I believe this question has little significance and importance for us. We have not come here today to determine who are the champions in violating human rights in Latin America. I do not know how many people are killed in Chile. I know that, with North American assistance, Somoza killed one hundred and fifty persons during three days in February in Zelaya. I do not know how Congressman Murphy can testify as he did earlier. He does not know Nicaragua. He knows the castle of the dictator, and he has false information from both General Somoza and the US Embassy in Nicaragua. I have not come here to ask anything of the United States. I only ask that you allow us to solve our own problems. We do not want you to celebrate the bicentennial of your independence, while you prevent us from realizing our own by helping dictators such as Somoza."

Jeannie whispered, "Ed Koch is pretty amazing to even hold these hearings. He's very interested in human rights."

"Shhhh," cautioned Lorna, who was riveted by the testimony she was hearing. There was so much she did know, but so much more she was learning for the first time. Her new red notebook was filling up.

The hearings continued for two more days. It was wonderful for Lorna to hear dissenting voices in front of the US Congress.

On Thursday morning, Jeannie drove Lorna to Dulles Airport. Again Lorna marveled at the hot humid East Coast summer. How green it was, how damp, with its own gentle beauty. As Jeannie pulled up to the departure curb, she turned to Lorna. "I don't know when we'll see each other again, but this has been wonderful, Lorna. We will remain connected in our hearts."

Lorna leaned over to hug and kiss her new friend. "I only hope we made a difference."

At the airport, Lorna purchased both the *New York Times* and the *Washington Post* and devoured them. There had been protests in Managua because Somoza had denied Pedro Joaquin Chamorro's exit visa to testify at the hearings. But there was little about the actual testimony at the hearing, or the reaction of the committee members. She tried not to feel discouraged.

5

Computer Art, a New Idea

Back in San Francisco three days later, Lorna was working on the article for *Bulwark Magazine*. It was not going well. Her fingers were streaked with white-out from making so many corrections. She could not stop thinking about a phone call that morning with Helen. Lorna had been complaining about Eddie's flirting and how easily he let her be bumped out of testifying before the committee.

"You're too critical," Helen had said. "You expect men to have no faults. If I had your standards, I wouldn't have had my last two weddings." Helen was now on her third marriage, to a lawyer named Larry Hart. Lorna thought, for herself, she wouldn't want a guy like him. But Helen had been willing to settle for a tall somewhat overbearing man, with a good income, who adored her. Well, that was pretty good, but what could they talk about in the morning? Helen was lively and chatty, but Larry Hart? He'd sit and read the newspaper, while Lorna and Helen talked. Now the phone was ringing again. It was Eddie himself.

"I want to meet at El Chipote. There's something I want to ask you, but not on the phone."

She was getting used to his conspiratorial, secretive behavior.

"OK, I need a break from this damn article. I'll walk down the hill and meet you in fifteen minutes. Can you give me a ride back up the hill? I shouldn't be away from this article for too long."

"If you don't mind a lift on my motorcycle. Maria has the car. She's taken the kids shopping."

It was a pleasant walk down the hill to *El Chipote*. Lorna

always enjoyed the walk, passing well-groomed homes and front yards of her neighborhood that gradually gave way to the working-class hardware stores, plumbing outfitters, nail shops and taquerías of the Mission.

At El Chipote she found the latest pages of the *Gaceta Sandinista* taped to the plate glass windows. "US Congress Hears of Central American Human Rights Abuses," read the headline. Lorna opened the door. The little cowbell announced her entrance. But no Eddie. His motorcycle wasn't parked in front. Then Arnoldo emerged from the back room.

"Welcome, compañera." Arnoldo took her hand and kissed it. "Eddie called. He'll be here in a minute."

The bell jingled again and in walked Eddie, wearing his black leather motorcycle vest and riding gloves. He peeled off the gloves and loosened the vest. Strands of colored beads peeked out of the neck of his Sandino T-shirt.

"I am flying to Los Angeles tonight to meet with the Los Angeles *compas*," said Eddie. His mustache bristled as he kissed her cheek. "Remember we talked about possibly setting up a Los Angeles NIN group and you said you would discuss it with your NIN group here?"

Lorna nodded and said, "Yes, we discussed it at our steering committee meeting the other night. People got excited. They all had contacts, friends and relatives in LA. And we made a list."

"So can I give this list to the LA *compas* so they can get started?" Eddie said.

"Yes, I have a copy here. We'll call them in advance to let them know someone will be contacting them."

"Great! I wanted all the names, but I didn't want Big Brother listening on the phone," Eddie said.

Lorna waved her hand cavalierly, "Let them listen all they want. NIN is going on the radio. The more people who hear about what's happening in Nicaragua, the better."

"Brave words, Lorna, but when the FBI comes to your door, you may feel differently."

Lorna fumbled in her purse for the list which was copied

on the back of an old tattered flier with lipstick stains on it. She looked at it with dismay, and said, "Sorry it's such a mess. There is so much work and so few of us and I'm hitting a wall trying to write this article about the hearing."

"So how many are you now?" asked Eddie.

"Six on the steering committee. Helen Hart, of course, you know. Francisco Disdier, the young installation artist. He calls himself the Cisco Kid. The poet, John Hersh who you already know. And Reverend Don Crane who was with the original NIN in 1927. He's almost eighty, and so active and spirited. Joe Schneider from the San Francisco Labor Council came to a few meetings. Also, a student from San Francisco State, Omar Martinez has been attending. He's quiet, and very thoughtful, but he's leaving after the next meeting to go to grad school in Texas. And then there's me, of course. So when Omar goes we will be only six. How will we ever get it done?"

"Double that number and you're in. Look what Fidel Castro did with twelve. And Jesus only had twelve, although one was traitor."

"No traitors in our group. We are six fearless souls speaking truth to power, the power of the military industrial complex," Lorna said, mockingly. "We've been invited to be interviewed on Mama O'Ryan's radio show. She suggested we put fliers up around the neighborhood urging people to listen. I was hoping you would design the flier for us."

"I'd love to but I can't. I'm flying to Los Angeles tonight and I'll be gone a week."

"I'll ask Reverend Don," she said. "He mentioned he knows someone who designs fliers using a computer."

"Computers and art? That's a contradiction in terms," said Eddie. "Art requires soul. Computers are for zombies. Computer art. What a bad joke."

After a pause, Eddie asked, "When's the radio program on?"

"In two weeks."

"So I'll listen when I get back. Drop off some of the fliers here. The *compas* can help post them around the neighborhood. Good work, Lorna."

"I don't know. I get discouraged. A lot of people I talk to don't even know where Nicaragua is."

"They'll find out," said Eddie. "You can bet on it."

He slipped his motorcycle gloves on his square, strong brown hands and one long fingernail. "So we're bookin'?"

"OK. Let's go," said Lorna.

At the curb, Eddie straddled his bike. Holding his shoulder for balance, Lorna threw her leg across the backseat and grabbed his waist. "I'm nervous, Eddie. With all the hills in San Francisco, gravity may pull me off."

"Just hug me tight with your thighs."

"Oh, right." Just what she was afraid of.

Eddie shouted, "Hang on!" and they were off, with wild turns around the corners, Eddie dipping the cycle low to the ground. "Having fun?" he yelled back.

"Not yet," said Lorna, fearfully.

"Just hold on tight!"

At the top of Hill Street, Eddie roared to a stop. "Maybe it will be better for you to walk from here because it's so steep." Letting go of Eddie, she slid off the motorcycle. Saluting smartly, he roared away. At her door, Lorna climbed the long flight of stairs up to the apartment. So lonely, she thought, glancing at Rini's room. Empty, of course. Rini's only here some weekends. Lorna's worktable with its drafts and notes confronted her, a chore she was in no mood to return to. Picking up the phone, she dialed NIN's newest member.

"Hi, Revered Don. We've got a problem. Eddie's taking off for Los Angeles, and we need some artwork for the flier we talked about. But we need it by Thursday. Can you ask your friend, the one with the computer?"

"Today's Saturday," he answered. "Thursday doesn't give him much time. But I'll phone him and call you back."

Fifteen minutes later the phone rang. Lorna was expecting Reverend Don, but this was a different voice. "Hello, may I speak to Lorna Almendros?"

"This is Lorna speaking."

"This is Luis Jaramillo. The Reverend Don Crane told me your group needs a flier. I can probably help you. Reverend Don has been talking to me about what's happening in Nicaragua. He's a very interesting man. It sounds like he's been involved for half a century."

"And now you're offering to design us a flier, and you don't even know us? See what fifty years of organizing experience can do?"

Luis laughed. He has a nice laugh, Lorna thought.

"You're right. I will need to know the particulars," Luis said.

They agreed to meet the next morning at the little café near El Chipote, Cafe Rendezous.

The next day, Lorna arrived at Cafe Rendezous a few minutes early and busied herself working on questions for Mama O'Ryan to ask for the radio interview. When she finally looked up, she saw a nice looking brown-skinned man with straight dark hair standing in the café doorway. He wore a tooled leather Western belt, and carried a well-worn leather bag. His height filled the doorframe. His dark eyes swept the room. Ah! This had to be Luis Jaramillo, she thought.

He walked over to her table. "Lorna?" He had a tanned face with crinkles at the eyes, a slightly receding hairline that gave his brow a high, intelligent look. Close up she saw his hair was chestnut brown.

She nodded.

He extended his hand. "I'm Luis Jaramillo," he smiled warmly.

"Luis?" She said, taking his hand. It was strong and firm, in a way that made her aware of her rings but not hurting, just comfortable. "It's a pleasure to meet you. Please have a seat."

"Thanks," he said, pulling out a chair. "So Reverend Don says you need graphic art for a flier. Tell me again what you want."

Lorna described the upcoming radio show. "But I have

trouble understanding how a computer can make art," she added.

"Digital art? It's been around since the early sixties. An engineer at Bell Laboratories by the name of Michael Noll is usually credited with creating digital art. He recreated a painting by Piet Mondrian using a computer. He did such a good job that a lot of people couldn't tell which was created by Mondrian and which by the computer. Of course Mondrian's art was relatively simple. Repetitive patterns are easily expressed mathematically. Noll has a fascinating piece in which waveforms are generated as parallel sinusoids with a linear increasing period. . . ." He stopped in embarrassment.

Lorna was confused. Luis looked at her with concern.

"Sorry," Luis said, laughing at himself, "I get carried away sometimes. I'm a nerd, I admit it. Gadgets and gizmos fascinate me. I love to take things apart to see how they work. But I'm sorry for going on like that."

"I get worried when I think a man is declaring his superior intellect. My ex-husband did that. He had more degrees than I did, he remembered more facts, and he thought he should win all the arguments. I hated that. I vowed never to be in that situation again, that's why I never want to remarry."

Now Lorna stopped in embarrassment. Why in the world was she telling a man she had only just met about ex-husband and that she didn't want to get married. She had hated Carl's constant putdowns and was determined not to allow herself to be overwhelmed by a man's IQ and verbal skills since it always translated into an attempt to dominate her intellectually. But why was she saying this to a stranger?

"I hope I'm not acting like your ex-husband, Lorna," said Luis. There seemed to be a smile in his eyes, but she couldn't be sure. "Along with my technical side, I have an artistic side, and they've been at war most of my life. It was a big conflict for me, growing up. Would I become an engineer? Or would I follow my heart and become an artist?"

"Where did you grow up?" Lorna inquired.

"We were poor, growing up in New Mexico. I was good at

math. I got scholarships, and I ended up with degrees in electrical engineering. But when I saw Doug Englebart's 1968 demo at the Fall Joint Computer Conference at Stanford, I was wowed! It was the mother of all demos. He showed that computers could increase our collective intelligence to solve social problems ranging from environmental threats to wars. Computers allow people to work together from all over the world in a communal interface. I love this new technology. I was so inspired, I moved to California where the action was. I saw the possibilities of a collaboration of art, engineering and technology for a better world."

Lorna responded. "I didn't know about any of this and it's all happening only an hour away."

"Damn, I'm babbling again," he said laughing. "Telling you my whole life story. Sorry,"

Quickly Luis pulled out a drawing pad from his leather bag. "So please, tell me again exactly what you want."

Lorna described the upcoming radio show and what an opportunity it was for them to get the word out. Luis sketched, his head nodding and his tongue showing under his upper lip in concentration. Then he pushed the pad toward her. Strong pencil strokes of differing thicknesses and at various angle created a militant fist, holding a radio microphone. The sketch was angular, yet dynamic and lyrical.

"I like it," said Lorna. "But how are you going to do this on a computer?"

"Most computers are room-sized monsters used in Defense Department programming, but my buddy and I at Stanford found something much smaller. I can create this graphic on the computer as a line drawing and fill it in, and then I'll print it out in black and white. I could have it ready by Wednesday night."

"You're fast," said Lorna.

"Consider yourself lucky that I'm not doing 3-D animations and raster drawings. When I get into something, I can't put it down till I finish."

"Not me. I'm easily distracted." Lorna thought of her

unfinished article.

"Not so easily, from what Reverend Don says. Not only have you founded the San Francisco Non-intervention in Nicaragua group but Reverend Don says you're a published poet. I take poetry seriously. I'd like to read your book."

"I'll give you a copy, if you'd like."

"Like? I'd love it."

Lorna hoped she didn't look as embarrassed as she felt. "So, how did you meet Reverend Don?" she asked to hide her discomfort.

"He and I struck up a conversation at a copy shop," laughed Luis. "He was probably printing some of your publicity pieces, and I was running off copies of a design. I learned he's been active for decades in Central American issues. Me and my family have been involved in the land grant movement back home in New Mexico."

"You mean the Mexican land-grant heirs trying to get back their lands?" Lorna asked. "I read about Reies Lopez Tijerina and the New Mexico court house raid. The United States totally ignored its side of the 1848 Treaty of Guadalupe Hidalgo."

"Yes, exactly!" he said, excitedly. "Our family goes way back on our land. My parents and older brother still keep our little ranch going."

Lorna thought he was easy to talk to, now that there was no more talk about the parallel sinusoids.

"Actually," Luis was saying, "the land-grant movement is not about private ownership of land. Because according to earlier Mexican law, this land couldn't be bought or sold. It was to be held in common by the people. The old *ejido* system. In New Mexico we still have communal ways of irrigating our lands."

"My family lived off the land in Nicaragua," Lorna said. "But now the flower pot on my back porch is as close as I get to nature." She was thinking of Abuelo, his house and land he'd left her to go deal with.

"All this land is really stolen from the Native peoples," Luis said. "They have the good sense to realize that no one can own the earth. She's our mother."

"Mother Earth," repeated Lorna.

Luis added, "The communal aspect of computers for doing intellectual work is what attracted me to Englebart's theories and drew me to California."

"For me, it was graduate school and the San Francisco Beat poetry scene," Lorna said.

When they finally stood up, Luis promised to deliver the fliers to their Thursday night meeting at Cisco Kid's studio. On Thursday night, the fliers caused quite a stir at the steering committee meeting, as did Luis' presence.

Luis and Reverend Don Chase walked in together. Luis carrying the box of fliers and quietly setting them on a clear space on Cisco's work table. Reverend Don, with his bushy white brows and thinning white hair, introduced Luis Jaramillo to the group. Pointing to the box he announced proudly, "All designed by Luis on a computer."

Luis smiled modestly, looked around at everyone, and nodding in greeting, opened the package of five hundred fliers. The fliers glowed, printed on bold neon yellow paper. The militant fist holding the microphone was in the shape of black lines and cubes. Under the image was the date and time of NIN's interview, with the call letters of Mama O'Ryan's radio show.

"Bravo! Bravo!" cried John Hersh, the poet. Hersh was Lorna's age, large and lanky, fond of French berets and Gauloises cigarettes, and wrote strong poems. Several of his books were on the shelves at City Lights Book Store in North Beach, even though he was new on the San Francisco poetry scene. "Bravissimo, Luis. All this without the cutting and pasting of the original designs, the trips to the printer, and the waiting for publication." He patted Luis on the back enthusiastically.

"Inspired," said Lorna. She felt Luis's gaze fall on her, approvingly. He seemed so pleased that she was happy with what he had done. She could feel herself smiling under his glance.

Francisco Disdier, whom they called Cisco Kid, an intense and talented young man in his early twenties, looked around at his sculpted pieces in various stages of assembly. "I should check out your computer stuff, Luis. I feel like I'm slipping behind the times," he mumbled.

"You'll get your chance, Kid," said Reverend Don. "I invited Luis to join our steering committee."

"Welcome, Luis!" said Helen "We so need you!"

Everyone joined in the welcoming. Joe Schneider shook Luis's hand enthusiastically.

Omar, the student, nodded his silent consent shyly. It was his last meeting.

"Hmmm," Lorna observed. "So now we are seven. *Los siete.*"

"On the steering committee just like that?" asked Luis looking confused. "What will the membership think?"

"There is no membership," said Cisco Kid. "When we need troops for an action or campaign we put out a call, and anywhere from forty to two thousand people turn out. Depends."

Hersh further explained, "We're a steering committee with broad outreach into the solidarity, progressive and anti-imperialist community. People know us and support what we are doing."

"Thanks for accepting me," Luis said humbly. Everyone cheered.

Cisco Kid put up the water for coffee and tea. Lorna began setting up the cups. Luis appeared at her side, "Lorna, I want to make amends for how stupidly I behaved at the café, going on about technology and leaving you feeling intellectually oppressed."

Lorna, although surprised, instantly responded, "No, I'm the one who needs to apologize. I was so strident, being so politically correct."

"No, Lorna, you are just perfect." Luis said.

Still smiling the next morning, Lorna wandered into Helen's office at the Community Arts Program. As always,

Helen looked dressed for success, ready to meet with the mayor if she had to, in a white bow-tie blouse. "What's up, Lorna?"

"Want to take a coffee break? I just thought it would be fun to post-mortemize about last night."

Helen slid into the blue jacket on the back of her chair ready to march out in her sensible stacked heels to their favorite Civic Center café. "We're outta here," she said, throwing the receptionist an "If anyone calls, I'm in a meeting until ten."

At the café, they settled in with lattes and girl talk. "Luis fits in so naturally with our group and good looking too," observed Helen.

"He has a very steady feel to him," Lorna readily agreed.

"His marriage is kind of unusual," confided Helen. "She's a high-powered civil rights attorney and was reassigned to the Los Angeles office. They have no kids. She's only home every other weekend."

"And how did you find all this out?" Lorna asked in dismay.

"Asked."

"Ah," Lorna's voice went flat and her coffee cup rattled in the saucer. "I'm more than a little disappointed that Luis is married."

6

Red-Haired Poet

Lorna watched darkness come early through the windows at the Community Arts office. It was November 1978. Helen Hart's corner office blazed with fluorescent light. Lorna walked from her desk in her cubicle to Helen's open door. Behind Helen, a dark window faced the black night, punctuated with the lights of the Civic Center. Helen's short-skirted brown business suit and ruffled shirt bustled with purposeful energy as she pushed a drawer closed and stuffed a folder into her attaché case.

"Will you close up?" Helen asked. "I'm meeting Larry for dinner in Chinatown. How come you're working so late?"

"Eddie wants me to pick someone up at the airport. It didn't make sense to go home first. I thought I'd stay and send out a press release for the Nicaragua poetry benefit."

"Who's reading?" Helen inquired, walking into the hallway, carrying her coat.

"We've got Ferlinghetti, a Nuyorican poet, Avotcja, a bunch of other high profile local poets, and this Nicaraguan poet he's asked me to pick up at the airport, Rosalea Bandera, and me. Eddie is the MC, of course."

"And you?" said Helen. "As if you weren't important. If it weren't for you, there wouldn't even be a poetry benefit for Nicaragua, Lorna."

"It was Eddie's idea."

"Aren't they always Eddie's ideas? You're the one who makes it happen. So what are you going to read? Have you decided?"

"Maybe the poem for my grandfather in my book, *Ancestors*. But that poem makes me feel so vulnerable. Maybe 'The Day the Vietnam War Ended' or the one I read with Quilapayún when I was in Spain, the one about Neruda."

"So," began Helen, "is Rosalea Bandera some famous Nicaraguan poet I've never heard of?"

"I don't know if she's famous. All I know is she's a red-headed Nicaraguan poet. She's coming for the reading, then she has an important meeting with the *Gaceta Sandinista* staff. Eddie asked me to put her up. I'm happy to do it. The apartment feels so empty with Rini gone."

"Rini's been gone two years, Lorna. Aren't you used to her being gone yet?"

"I love the semester breaks when Rini is home," said Lorna.

"Maybe you shouldn't have dumped that professor you were dating," Helen poked.

Lorna was annoyed by this reminder. "We had absolutely nothing in common," she said, a bit stiffly. "He was a pompous bore."

"I thought he was amusing enough that time we all had dinner together. At least he was more fun than the piano tuner."

Lorna winced. "OK, I admit the piano tuner was a mistake."

"As I have mentioned before maybe your standards are impossible, Lorna. You set the bar so high, no man could meet it." Helen scooped her car keys from her purse. "I've got to get going. Larry's waiting for me. Thank god for Larry, saving me from single-girl loneliness."

As far as Lorna was concerned, silent, grumpy Larry was even more pompous than the professor.

"Go! Enjoy Chinatown! I'll turn off all the lights," Lorna said, in a bright, false tone. Helen kissed her friend on the cheek and departed.

Helen's remarks had played on Lorna's vulnerabilities, leaving her too agitated to work on anything. She walked around the office shutting off lights, upset again with herself for allowing her old anger at Carl's high-handedness and desertion to keep her from moving on. Every time one of her little attempts at a romance failed, she got mad at Carl all over again for leaving her. She always maintained her "official line" with Rini, never calling him a braggart or deserter. Lorna had said to her, "No reproaches. None. Your father did what he had to do, and I did what I had to do." Being a good mother to Rini had not helped Lorna move past her resentment. Loneliness was filling the office. It was time to go.

Lorna arrived at the airport early and took a seat at gate 3 to await the mysterious red-headed poet. She used the time to work on a report for Jeannie Giacomelli's national Nicaragua Network newsletter. She and Jeannie were in frequent contact. The NIN San Francisco chapter had grown. Local elected officials were responding now to the Non-intervention in Nicaragua movement. There were perhaps thirty to fifty thousand Nicaraguans in the Mission District these days, some of them voters. That usually got the attention of the politicians. House members from California had read NIN statements into the Congressional Record. The movement was growing as the US ramped up its military presence in Nicaragua.

Lorna's life was full of meetings and more meetings. There was always something to do, some meeting to attend and seldom a peaceful moment for her poetry. But the muse required time for reflection. And reflection time made her feel alone. So she rushed out to meetings just to be with people. She wondered if Rosalea Bandera would understand, as a poet and an activist, about this conflict. Eddie liked to say that after the revolution, there would be plenty of time for musing the muse. But he found time and energy for his art right now.

Lorna always wrestled with the question of what Abuelo would want her to do. Abuelo, like her parents and Eddie, were Nicaraguans in exile. Lorna was not. She could assume that her work for Nicaragua was the work they wanted her to do. Would Abuelo understand that she was not doing this just for Nicaragua but also for her own country? She wanted her own country to act right.

The flight from Miami arrived, and Lorna stood up.

Passengers spilled out of the Jet-way. She saw young couples with children and old people, many carrying bulging plastic bags, but no red-haired poet in the throng. Lorna wondered if she had been given the correct information. Maybe it was a different flight, or a different day.

The last person off the plane was a large stylish woman in a pant-suit and a wide brimmed hat. A leather messenger bag was slung over one broad shoulder. She must have been six feet tall. The woman walked toward her.

"Lorna Almendros?"

Her hair had been piled up under the hat. Now as she removed it, coppery hair tumbled down around her shoulders. The statuesque woman was in her early thirties with clear hazel eyes. Her posture and bearing showed strength and balance. Lorna blinked at Rosalea's presence, startled by the bright, exploding confidence in her step and the delight-in-living smile.

"Rosalea!" exclaimed Lorna, giving her a hug and a kiss on the cheek. "Do you have much baggage?" Lorna asked in Spanish.

"No, just this carry-on," replied Rosalea, in English. They chit-chatted about the flight as they moved toward the parking garage where the red Datsun awaited them.

"Have you eaten, Rosalea?"

"Not since Miami. They serve the best Cuban food in the Miami airport. Better than in Cuba."

"Oh, you've been to Cuba?"

"We've all been to Cuba, Lorna." Lorna wasn't sure what that meant. Rosalea continued, "If we're going to make a revolution, it makes sense to visit a country that's had one."

"I'd love to visit Cuba, but the US State Department doesn't allow Americans to travel there."

"How strange, *compañera*. I think of *los Estados Unidos* as exploitative and aggressive toward other nations, but very good to its own people. I guess I was wrong. We Nicaraguans are kept so underdeveloped, thanks to centuries of American interference, that I'd never guess that they would limit their own citizens from traveling to Cuba."

Lorna was silent. Even though they were both on the same side, when her country was attacked, she resented it.

"I can feel you bristling, *hermana*. What's the matter? You must know you live in an imperialist country."

"Yes, but as an American, I struggle against imperialism and hate injustice," Lorna said. "We're not all cut from one cloth. I may hate US foreign policy, but I still love my country, and want to change it." There, she had said it.

"Of course. I apologize. Forgive me, Lorna. I work with too many men. They don't bother with the niceties of feelings."

On the drive into the city, Lorna described the work of the Non-intervention in Nicaragua group. She told Rosalea about Reverend Don and the other steering committee members. Rosalea seemed especially intrigued by the technological skills and knowledge that Luis was contributing. "I have heard about computers in Nicaragua," Rosalea said, "but I have never seen one."

Rosalea described the struggle in Nicaragua. How buoyed the spirits of the Sandinistas had been when Edén Pastora, known as Comandante Cero, had led a group that took over the National Palace in Managua, and captured everyone present. They had demanded the freedom of Tomás Borge, now the sole living member of the original *Frente* group, $500,000 in cash, and a plane to Panamá.

"A woman, Dora María Téllez, was one of the comandantes." Rosalea said. "We were galvanized by that. They held fifteen hundred congressional delegates captive with a band of twenty-five *compas*. It was incredible. They escaped unharmed. Somoza was forced to fly them to Panama." She turned to Lorna. "I feel guilty, leaving the front for this trip to San Francisco. A coalition called *los doce*, a group of twelve, including some of our people, is demanding Somoza's removal. We're winning, *Compañera* Lorna." Lorna's spirits rose.

On the way to Lorna's flat, Rosalea was all exclamations of wonder, at the steepness of Hill Street. "*Ay ay ay ay ay!*" she cried, as Lorna's little Datsun slowly crawled up the hill. Once inside she marveled at the spectacular night views from the large windows. She admired everything. The disordered books, the Navajo pottery, the Mexican rugs and healthy plants.

Lorna put on a kettle and the two women settled in for tea and talk.

"So, you have a *novio*? A boyfriend?" Rosalea asked.

"I was dating a professor from San Francisco State. But he wasn't political. He wasn't involved in our movement. He was just too dull."

"And there's no one else? A life without a *novio* isn't healthy."

"You go straight for the vulnerabilities, don't you, Rosalea?" said Lorna.

Rosalea smiled her delighted, infectious smile, pleased that Lorna had her number. She enjoyed emotional combat, Lorna could see.

"I do go straight for what you call the vulnerabilities," Rosalea said. "I'm practicing the habit because this revolution doesn't give me much time. I meet people. We share experiences that bring us together quickly. Then I never see them again. Why bother with superficial politeness? I trade it for truth, at least when I care about a person, and I try not to waste my time with people I don't care about. I've only just met you, but I think I care about you, Sister Poet."

Lorna smiled, pleased that this woman saw her as a sister soul.

After their tea, Lorna showed Rosalea the bathroom and turned on the hot water to fill the tub. Then she poured in bubble bath, making mounds of pink foam.

"*Ay ay ay*, hot water, it's been years since I've had a hot bath. In Nicaragua, only the most expensive *gringo* hotels have hot water."

"Enjoy it!" said Lorna, handing Rosalea a towel. She pointed to her shelf of beauty ointments, rose soap, Oil of Olay, cucumber cleansing mask, and coconut body lotion. Most were presents bought at the health food store from Rini and Helen on her last birthday.

"Help yourself!" It amused Lorna to ply the no-nonsense poet with her little luxuries. Rosalea seemed very pleased.

"Oh, I will be so beautiful!" she laughed.

Lorna laughed too. "Take your time. I'll get some dinner ready."

In the kitchen, Lorna saw her own distorted reflection on the shiny frying pan lid. Her face stretched awkwardly, as in a carnival fun mirror, but her expression was pink and happy. She got the rice going and made a salad while she sizzled onions, garlic, celery, and tomatoes. Then she added black beans flavored with a splash of wine and hunks of pork sausage, and served it with a warm loaf of San Francisco sourdough French bread.

Rosalea emerged from the bathroom with the towel wrapped turban-style around her head, wearing one of Lorna's bathrobes. Lorna was struck again by the vitality in the way she carried herself, the total clarity of her expression.

Rosalea wolfed down the meal with the appetite of an Amazon.

"As good as the Cuban food in Miami?" teased Lorna.

"Better, *amiga!*" laughed Rosalea.

After the meal they moved to the living room. Lorna had set out several thick red candles on candle holders of different heights. Their flames reflected in the big, dark windows, through which the lights of San Francisco sparkled. The women took seats on the old sofa and Lorna poured wine, using two Waterford crystal glasses still left over from her wedding presents.

"*Bienvenida,* Rosalea." The glasses rang with a icy clear note as they clinked.

"What a beautiful view you have!" said Rosalea. "Your apartment is so clean. So silent. It is very peaceful here."

Lorna nodded.

"To the longest revolution . . . the revolution within the revolution, the women's revolution," said Rosalea. They clinked again. It seemed to Lorna that the glasses rang a long,

long time.

"So, Rosalea, tell me about your poetry. What kind of poetry do you write?"

"Who told you I write poetry?" demanded Rosalea.

"That's what Eddie said," she answered. "You are not a poet? You're here to give a poetry reading, as well as consult with *Gaceta* staff."

"Yes, I am a poet, or was, in my other life," said Rosalea. "The revolution doesn't leave much time for poetry. I smuggled some poems I wrote in prison to Arnoldo in the men's section. Maybe he saved them and showed them to your friend, Eddie."

"Why were you were in prison, Rosalea?"

"Somoza's government wanted vengeance. A member of a wealthy family, joining the Sandinistas? To them I was a class traitor. They wanted to teach me a lesson I would not forget. Prison. Humiliation. Rape. Torture, You know, Lorna, I come from an old and wealthy family in León. My parents gave me everything, including an education. And this red hair! But in giving me my education, they inadvertently gave me the gift of an independent mind. The Roman Catholic Church glorifies motherhood and the adoration of the Virgin. In Catholic societies like Nicaragua, that's the only role an upper-class woman is supposed to fulfill. Motherhood, the truly honorable and respectable role. We women who reject that, who try to take a part in public life, who speak out, they call us whores, lesbians and loose women. That's why the *Guardia* raped me while I was in *El Modelo*."

"That is so awful, " said Lorna, the shock showing in her voice. "How do you survive something like that?"

"I don't know, *compañera*. We have no choice. We have to find a deeper, inner strength that allows us to survive and to serve a purpose larger than we are. We serve Nicaragua itself. The people. We serve the revolution and freedom."

"And your poems are about revolution and freedom?"

"I write about love, Lorna. It allows us to survive beyond torture and its scars."

"I'd like to hear one of your poems."

Rosalea straightened up, closed her eyes. After a moment, she recited:

> My poems are born in the manger
> where I hid for three days
> when the *Guardia* looked for me in the city.
> They broke Cecelia's arm
> because she didn't know where I was,
> or so she said, despite the pain.
> My poems incubate
> on the long walk up the mountain
> where I declare myself a *guerrillera*
> in Sandino's armed struggle,
> and I lean toward the sun.

There was a silence. The candles flickered and flared. Before them, small lights sparkled down in the Mission and on Potrero Hill and across the Bay to Richmond and Oakland.

"You know your poems by heart, Rosalea. I admire that."

"Nicaraguan poets always recite their works from memory. We learn to declaim poetry as children. Any Nicaraguan can recite to you from Rubén Darío."

"My grandfather used to recite Rubén Darío." Lorna searched her memory bank, hearing Abuelo's dear old voice and recited:

> Eres los Estados Unidos, eres el futuro
> invasor de la América ingenua que tiene sangre
> indígena, que aún reza a Jesucristo y aún habla en
> español.

"All Nicaraguans know that poem," Rosalea said. "Nicaraguans are poets and guerrilla fighters. I am both. I have learned to shoot. I've learned to walk long distances. I've learned how to be hungry. Many women have joined us, Lorna. Every time I return to the mountains, the number of women has grown. And we are changing the consciousness of the men. A young *compañera* was told to wash the clothes of the male *compas*. She told them, 'I came to fight. Wash your own clothes.' They locked her up in a homemade brig, but she still refused to be their laundress. Finally they had to give up. They let her out. They washed their own clothes after that. Today she's leading a troop. *Una comandanta.*"

"Don't you find most men are *machistas*, even the most idealistic ones?" asked Lorna. "My ex-husband had no use for a woman's intellect."

"Yes, many men. But women are rising," Rosalea continued. "For example, last year, three Solentiname Island women captured the army headquarters at San Carlos for a short time. Some of the sisters weren't even armed. But news of it has spread and Nicaraguan women all across the country are inspired. An anti-Somoza women's group is forming. *Asociación de Mujeres ante la Problemática Nacional.* AMPRONAC. The male *compas* are critical of them. They call it an organization of middle class ladies. But I'm proud of my *compañeras* in AMPRONAC. Those women actively support other women."

"There's something I want to ask you about, Rosalea. I find this revolution is consuming all my time, when I'm yearning for more time for writing. How do you deal with that conflict?"

"I hear you, *amiga*. But if I had more time, would I write? Hmm . . . What would I write about? Would I write a poem about a cocktail party? 'In the room the women come and go/Talking of Michelangelo,' to quote T.S. Elliot." Rosalea paused briefly. "It's the struggle that gives me the images and compresses the words. I'm not interested in writing poems for scholars to ponder. I still write a little, whenever the inspiration strikes and time allows. I just try not to suffer over it." Rosalea leaned forward intently, swirling the wine in her glass and looking into it, as if she saw events and images swirling there as well. Her long coppery hair swung forward when she moved.

"Last year, Somoza lifted the three-year state of siege. Popular opposition rose up almost immediately, like a genie out of the bottle. But the assassination of Pedro Joaquín Chamorro last January provoked the general strike. Now everyone is demanding Somoza's resignation."

"There was a big protest when Somoza refused to allow Chamorro to attend the Washington DC congressional hearings two years ago," Lorna commented.

"This time it was not a matter of letting him leave the country, or not. This time Somoza arranged Chamorro's murder. Everyone knows it. Bankers, the priests, and the Catholic schools . . . everyone! By February, it was total popular outcry. The Left and Right were outdoing each other staging funeral events. It was a farce, Lorna, if there can be anything comic in such a sad struggle that costs so many lives. The bankers were preaching non-violence, all the while nominating themselves for president. They were confident the next election would be rigged, just as all the previous ones had been. Ultimately the people took the lead. We burned down Somoza's blood bank where he was selling the blood of the children and the poor. Crowds formed a blockade spontaneously, so his fire brigades couldn't save it."

"It sounds like we're winning."

"We can defeat Somoza militarily. We're arming and training anyone who is willing to wear the red and black scarf. We say, 'You can be a Sandinista.' There's no ideological test, or class purity test.   Neighborhood by neighborhood, rebellions arise. We'll rid ourselves of the Somoza family rule," Rosalea said, quietly.

She was staring into her glass. "We Sandinistas will be leading that struggle, women as well as men. The question is, what will happen when we win? How will we protect our victory? How will we remain democratic? There will be attacks, covert attacks. Many people will die. There are already those I'll never see again. Pinochet's coup in Chile haunts me. Pinochet was backed covertly by the CIA.

Sí, siempre es los Estados Unidos,
el invasor, futuro y presente, de la América ingenua que
tiene sangre indígena . . .

Rosalea's voice trailed off quoting another piece of Rubén

Darío's poem.

"Eddie says the situation in Nicaragua is explosive. He says the question is, who will lead the popular opposition, the old-guard 'loyal opposition,' the old Conservative party of bankers and business-men who have always opposed Somoza? Or the Sandinistas?"

"Is that what Eddie says? You're always quoting Eddie. Who is he to you? He sounds like your lover."

"He's not my lover. We've worked together on political causes for years. I owe him my *Raza* consciousness."

"*Raza* consciousness?" asked Rosalea.

"It's the movement for Latino civil rights," replied Lorna. "*La Raza* speaks out against the racism in our country against Latinos. They're calling us 'Hispanics'. For a long time, racism meant only the plight of African-Americans. But now Latinos are getting organized. We have suffered discrimination also, and we're demanding equal rights. We're promoting our *La Raza* culture, even though we are of different national origins."

"OK, so he developed your consciousness, so what? If he hadn't, someone else would have."

"When I came back from Spain, I followed Eddie into the Nicaraguan cause."

"This could be dangerous, Lorna, letting someone lead you like that. Especially a man."

"I'm aware of that, Rosalea, but he doesn't take no for an answer. He doesn't know how domineering he is."

"So," said Rosalea, suddenly mischievous. "Not a *novio*, only a friend. Not a lover, but you jump at his beck and call. Pour me some more wine. Tell me more about love in San Francisco! Clearly I don't understand it!"

Lorna opened up to this new friend. The breakup with Carl. His rivalry with her at meetings, putdowns at home and finally having an affair with Bob Stern's girlfriend and moving in with her. How Abuelo had left for Nicaragua and never returned. Her adoption by Jack and Ella and her struggle to learn their English-speaking, middle-class ways. How Rini had been the one person in her life who needed her and would not desert her. How Rini's going off to college felt like abandonment, even though Lorna knew this was silly, because, of course, independence was what she wanted for her daughter. She even went so far as to confess, after a second glass of wine, that sometimes she was attracted to Eddie. But she had very strict limits about married men. And even if he hadn't been married, his obsessive womanizing made him out of the question.

"There's another man in our group I am seriously attracted to, but . . . he's married too," Lorna admitted.

"The man with the computers?" Rosalea asked.

"How did you know?"

"It was obvious from the way you talked about him."

Rosalea spoke of her first *novio*, who had not understood the revolution. He had been a member of her class, and when she had broken off the engagement, her father had been enraged. Her second *novio* understood the revolution very well, but only as a man's game. Handsome, passionate, courageous—but he did not accept Rosalea as his equal. "Although we seemed equal in height," Rosalea had giggled, "I was in fact slightly taller."

"When my revolutionary *novio* died," said Rosalea, "I decided I'd had it with *novios*. Until a man could accept my strength, intelligence, and courage, I would do without romantic commitment. That was where I am now. That does not mean, Lorna, that I am a nun. I am not living in a convent. I do as the men do. If an attractive man is willing . . . ?" she shrugged. "No emotional involvement. You know, Lorna, do as they do. Use them and throw them away, like a Kleenex, no?"

Lorna shook her head. "A human being, even a faithless man, is more than a Kleenex."

And so, the evening passed magically, with talk of politics, poetry, and love.

Their visit was rocked the next morning, on November 18, when the *San Francisco Chronicle* headlines screamed about the mass suicides at Jonestown, Guyana. Over nine hundred members of the People's Temple in the Western Addition, led by San Francisco minister Jim Jones, had been found dead at a farm in their communal enclave in remote rural Guyana. Many Bay Area politically progressive families had followed Jones there to be free of racism and injustice. And then, they voluntarily drank Kool-Aid laced with cyanide. Even the children. It was a jolting shock.

The city was still grappling with the bewildering insanity of it when the Monday following Thanksgiving, Dan White found his way into City Hall and murdered Mayor George Moscone and City Councilman Harvey Milk, the first gay elected official. Nicaragua became a more distant reality, as Lorna tried to absorb the incomprehensible violence emanating from her own city.

"It seems like our world is falling apart, Rosalea," Lorna said through her tears as she wept. "The murderous events of the past weeks have shaken everyone."

"Oh, Lorna. I am so sorry. I know how this feels," Rosalea said, embracing her. "The mass suicides are incomprehensible to me. But homophobia I understand. It's a disease like male chauvinism. Something I fight relentlessly against in our movement at home too. We have so many battles to wage at once."

The next day, Lorna drove Rosalea to the airport. She had attended many meetings with the *compas* from El Chipote and with the others who had driven up from the Los Angeles branch of the Sandinista groupings. Their poetry reading had gone well, an enjoyable moment in her whirlwind visit.

"I hate saying good-bye to you Rosalea. I've only known you two weeks, but I feel so strongly connected. So inspired by you."

"And thank you, *compañera*, for your great kindness to me. You have a very loving heart."

Sadly, Lorna watched Rosalea enter the airport, with her high-style jacket and messenger bag. She wasn't wearing the big brimmed hat now, and her red hair streamed down her back. A prayer rose up in Lorna's heart. Be safe, my friend.

Be safe.

For weeks after Rosalea left, Lorna searched the *Gaceta Sandinista* pages for news of her. There was none.

7

Arrested and Gone

Two months later, Rini was helping Lorna prepare for the NIN bulk mailing party. The January, 1979 winter sun shone through the dining room window and, in the far distance, the peak of Mount Diablo poked up above streaks of clouds.

Lorna's heart burst with pride as she regarded her twenty-one-year-old daughter. Rini, now a confident young woman, athletic and tall, with thick honey-colored hair cascading down her back. Tonight she was wearing jeans and a Guatemalan peasant blouse with colorful embroidery at the neckline.

"Did I tell you we took over the corner of Mission and Twenty Fourth Street?" Asked Lorna, as she lay out forks and knives.

"What do you mean, 'took over'?" Rini asked, carrying plates from the kitchen.

"Last Saturday afternoon we renamed that corner 'Plaza Sandino.' We used a bullhorn and an electric amplifier to spread our message. We had music and poetry; we burned *copal*. About two hundred people attended our ceremony. Imagine, we used to have picket lines of only seven! We chanted, '*Que se caiga. Que se caiga. Que se caiga, Somoza.*' Let him fall. Let Somoza fall."

"Mom, that's great. I don't mean to change the subject, but I hope I didn't put the *nacatamales* up too soon. They smell like they're ready."

"Well, turn the stove off and keep the steamer lid on to keep them warm. They'll be fine. Everyone will be here soon. When I told them you were here for the weekend to make Nicaraguan tamales, they couldn't wait to sign up for the bulk mailing party."

Rini laughed. "Gotta motivate them politicos some way. Let's have some music, Mom. Mind if I put something on?"

"What are you thinking of?" said Lorna, on her guard.

"Oh, I thought maybe the soundtrack from 'Saturday Night Fever,'" said Rini. "Or how about the Bee Gees 'Stayin' Alive?'" She snapped her fingers, "Stayin' alive, stayin' alive."

"Oh my god, no," said Lorna, but her beautiful daughter was already fussing with the stereo. To Lorna's immense relief, she heard that Rini had selected Carlos Santana's "Black Magic Woman." Carlos Santana had been a neighbor of Eddie's on Bernal Hill, back in the old days. Eddie himself was expected shortly.

"Just teasin' you, Mom," called out Rini, as the doorbell rang. Lorna pressed the door buzzer.

Now Luis was running up the stairs with a brown paper bag in his arms. "Soda! Beer! Bubble water!" He kissed Lorna on the cheek. "You look lovely," he said. "Where shall I put these?"

Before Lorna could answer, the bell rang again. Cisco Kid and Hersh were heading up the stairs with cardboard cartons of letters, fliers, and envelopes. Reverend Don was right behind them with two shoe boxes of zip code stickers, rubber bands, and stamp pads. "Put the mailing supplies in the living room," Lorna said, "and food things go in the kitchen."

For the next half hour members of the San Francisco Non-intervention in Nicaragua group and a few friends streamed into the flat, with Rini and Lorna taking coats to the bedroom, and directing people to the *nacatamales* and other refreshments on the dining room table. Finally everyone except Eddie had arrived, and Lorna helped herself to one of the *nacatamales* and took a seat on the sofa. Luis filled a plate and sat next to her.

"Rini's *nacatamales* are different from the tamales we make at home in New Mexico," said Luis. "We use corn husks, but she's used banana leaves. Did Rini learn to make these from you?"

"No way!" said Lorna. "I hadn't tasted a *nacatamal* for thirty years until today. My grandfather used to buy them Saturday mornings and we'd eat them all weekend. After he died, I tried to make them, but I couldn't get them right. Rini's roommate has a Nicaraguan boyfriend, and he's been showing the girls how to make *nacatamales*. Rini is so excited about the fact that she is part Nicaraguan. She's really into her ethnic roots these days. You'd think her father never existed!" Lorna said this with a laugh.

"You sound a little bitter, Lorna," Luis said with a chuckle. "I hope some day you find a man worthy of you. And of Rini," he added. Lorna noticed he laid his arm along the top of the sofa behind her. It was not touching her shoulders, but had it dropped an inch or two, his arm would have encircled her.

"Not bitter," Lorna said. "Just a realist."

"Reality is an ever-moving target," said Luis.

"You're really into philosophy today," said Lorna.

"Am I not always?" said Luis.

Was it Lorna's imagination, or had the long arm slithered closer to her shoulders?

Reverend Don stood up and tapped a glass with a spoon. "OK, gang, time to start our bulk mailing project. The important thing is to keep the fliers in zip-code order. Separate each zip code and kept them in numerical order. Then, we put on color-coded stickers on the rubber-banded bundles we create. We can't let the mailing labels get out of order!"

"Keep them in order!" reiterated Hersh. "I spent two nights typing those labels."

"OK, all right already," said various voices. "Tell us what you want us to do."

Rini cleared away plates, while Hersh and Reverend Don laid out the supplies on the dining room table. Lorna stood up. Time to get to work. Before she could take a place with the others, the phone rang.

A familiar voice was on the other end. "Lorna, it's me, Eddie."

"Eddie? Where are you? We're getting started already."

"I'm in jail in Los Angeles."

"Jail?" Heads turned. Her voice must have hit a squeaky high note. The room fell silent.

"Who is it?" Rini whispered.

"Eddie," Lorna mouthed. Speaking into the phone, she asked, "What happened, Eddie?"

"I got stopped for speeding. While the cops were writing out a ticket, one of them saw *Dulce* in the back seat."

"*Dulce?*"

"Come on, Lorna. My gun, I never got round to registering it. It's a chicken shit charge. Pure bureaucratic bullshit. No problem. I'll be out by Monday."

The group in the dining room had heard only "Eddie," "jail," and "*Dulce,*" and it was unlikely they knew what to make of *Dulce,* but already Luis had moved across the room and stood beside her.

Luis whispered to Lorna, "Does he need a lawyer?"

"Do you need a lawyer?" Lorna asked. Is Luis is thinking of his wife? she wondered. But Jennifer doesn't deal with criminal law.

"No the *compas* here in L.A. took care of that," Eddie said.

"What about bail?"

"They're taking care of that too."

"So what are you doing down in LA when we're having our big bulk-mailing party right this minute?"

"I'm down in LA because I'm mobilizing the LA *compas*, Lorna." Eddie sounded a bit defensive; he wasn't used to such a sharp tone from her. Out of the corner of her eye, Lorna saw Rini giving her a thumb's up.

"The L.A. community needed me. It's not just about Northern California, Lorna. The whole other half of the state is here. Well, with my arrest, they most definitely did get mobilized."

"You didn't register your gun? And now you're in jail?" said Lorna, critically. "Well, everyone in the NIN group is here. How can we help?"

"Maria needs support," said Eddie, relieved. "I told her you would call," he continued, his voice losing its pleading tone and becoming, as she usually heard it, cocky and self-assured.

"That's all you need?"

"That's all I need," said Eddie. "I've got the rest of it covered."

OK, I'll call Maria right now. Good luck. We're thinking of you. Bye."

Lorna hung up. She had not forgotten the coolness Maria consistently showed to her. She relayed the news to the group.

Rini snorted. "Mr. Macho Man strikes again. He's the only one I know who would get into a jam like that."

Reverend Don shook his head. "That stop may not have been as random as he thinks."

"Lorna," said Luis, "this sounds serious."

"Very serious," added Joe Schneider.

"Eddie says it's a minor bureaucratic problem. He just wants me to call Maria. He doesn't sound frightened," said Lorna.

"I'll bet he's pleased with himself," chimed in Rini, "creating another exciting disaster to disrupt everything. Always the center of attention."

"Tell Maria," urged Reverend Don, "we're ready to help in any way."

Obligingly, Lorna dialed Maria's number. A child answered.

"Hi, sweetheart. Is your mother home?" asked Lorna.

Maria's voice came on the line. "Hello?"

"Maria, it's Lorna. Eddie just phoned us from Los Angeles."

"I'm afraid, Lorna." Maria's voice was trembling. "Remember the Nuyorican independence fighter? Lolita Lebrón? She went to jail when her daughter was a child. Now she's a grandmother, and she's still locked up. I'm afraid they're going to keep him."

"They're not going to lock Eddie up, Maria. He hasn't done anything. It's just a little mix-up," said Lorna, soothingly. "He assured me he has a good lawyer."

"I told him not to take that gun, but he insisted. He never listens to me. I get feelings about these things. Sometimes I sense them before they even happen."

"Eddie said it's just a bureaucratic thing, Maria."

"Eddie says a lot of things."

"You sure have that right," said Lorna.

"But he doesn't know everything. I've lit the candles his mother gave me for protecting a loved one."

"I have some of those candles too. I'll light one," Lorna said, remembering Eddie's mother, Beatriz, with her Cuban voodoo amulets and charms. She recalled the day she and Eddie had gone to the *botanica* store. Statues of saints and the Virgin Mary stood alongside black wax candles. Little packets of who-knows-what were labeled with names like Mojo and Seventh Sun. Lorna had joked that maybe there should be a little packet labeled Macho, but Eddie didn't laugh. He had been preoccupied with the crystals and potions.

"Lorna, I'm trying to be brave in front of the kids, but I'm frightened to death. He's so reckless. I just don't know what to do," Maria said.

"Do you want me to come over?"

"Can you?" asked Maria, gratefully.

"I'll drop by later. Maria, he'll be all right. Let's hope he gets out by tomorrow. Eddie always lands on his feet."

"Feet of clay," echoed Rini from her chair. The group continued slapping on address labels and adding stickers, but everyone seemed more subdued. Rini had changed the music. Now it was Jimmy Cliff's album, *The Harder They Come*, "Many Rivers to Cross" was playing, and Lorna heard the words "and I can't seem to find my way over."

That evening, Lorna visited Maria at the little house in Bernal Heights. There were deep circles under Maria's eyes. Together they lit one of Beatriz's sacred candles. Maria brought a glass of water from the kitchen and set it next to the candle. Lorna was happy to see there was no trace of resentment between Maria and herself.

"Beatriz says to keep a glass of water next to it." Maria said, looking at the burning *copal* in an abalone shell in the kitchen.

"I'm clearing the room of harmful spirits," Maria

continued. "I'm invoking the lost Indigenous civilization that lies here, under our feet, in the Mission."

"May the ancestor spirits protect him," said Lorna thinking of the little gods poking their faces through the sword ferns in the front yard.

"Eddie always has to do his own thing. He doesn't listen to anyone." Maria complained.

For the first time, Lorna thought, she and Maria were pulling together.

At home, later that night, Luis phoned. He wanted an update. Lorna reviewed her visit with Maria while hearing Jennifer's voice prompting him with questions in the background. Lorna was pleased that Luis had spent the afternoon with them even though it was one of Jennifer's weekends at home.

Tuesday morning Eddie breezed into the Community Arts Program office. He exuded his usual bravado. "See? I'm a free man. The Los Angeles *compas* got off their butts. They were slowed down at first because it was a weekend, but they phoned the congressional aides first thing Monday morning, until they located some of the big boys. Congressman Ron Dellums put a word in for me, too. They released me yesterday. Just like I predicted."

"Predict me no predictions. Our years of outreach paid off." Lorna said. "People have finally heard of the Nicaraguan struggle. Helen was a star player with her San Francisco City Hall connections. They used their contacts too and really came through."

"Thanks," said Eddie. "It was great that you enlisted the support of the Mayor's Office. I feel in top form but I feel the work I'm doing here in California will continue without me. These L.A. people are operating on all cylinders. Now I want to get into the real struggle as soon as possible."

"You mean war?" Lorna asked.

"War me no wars. I mean liberation. I'm taking *Dulce* to the place where she belongs."

Lorna followed Eddie to the copy machine. Eddie placed

a document in it and closed the lid, hardly able to contain his excitement. "Things are really heating up in Nicaragua, Lorna. There are uprisings in towns and cities all across the country. And Somoza? He imagines he can bomb the people into submission. I don't intend to miss the big moment."

"Somoza is desperate," agreed Lorna.

"Do you know Somoza's slogan? 'Easter week without Sandinistas.' But ours is:'Every home a *Sandinista* barrack.'"

"Do you know what's happening with Rosalea Bandera? I never see any news of her in the *Gaceta*. Nothing."

"I'm sure she's fighting bravely," said Eddie. "News from the front lines has to be scarce. So don't worry because you haven't heard anything."

"I am always worrying about her," Lorna replied.

"I told you about the three tendencies in the *Sandinista* Directorate?" Eddie interjected excitedly. "The communiqués we're getting now indicate they're moving toward unity. I'll be joining them the minute they unify. *Pronto*."

"I don't understand the differences between the various factions."

"They are not factions; they are tendencies."

"Excuse me, *tendencies*. Whatever that's supposed to mean."

Eddie's eyes were shining. "The tendencies are beginning to negotiate with each other. With unity, comes strength, and with strength, comes the final offensive! This year, 1979, is the year we're going to win."

"So the differences between these tendencies are . . . ?"

"All the tendencies are part of the Sandinista revolution. But my group, the *Terceristas*, the Third Force, represents the insurrectionary tendency. We just keep fighting to bring Somoza down. We don't emphasize ideology; we emphasize winning the military battle. The other two tendencies are divided ideologically. *Tendencia Proletaria* upholds the central role of the urban proletariat and the labor unions. The other, the *Guerra Popular Prolongada*, sees a prolonged struggle led by the peasants in the countryside."

"All these tendencies just mean more fighting and killing?"

Lorna murmured, turning away.

"Yes, but we'll be united in our common efforts. Just imagine the urban underground, the peasant organizations, the labor unions, and all the various guerrilla groups in the mountains, all of them under one command. We already have the people's support. What we need is unity in our leadership. That's how we will lead the masses to victory."

"I know you've been training for a long time. Still, it frightens me to think of you actually in Nicaragua, fighting."

"It's the bottom line. We can't create a new society without bringing down the old. I'm ready to leave the information and propaganda wing behind and enter the real fray. You know me, I'm a hands-on guy."

"When will you leave?" asked Lorna, looking back at him anxiously.

"As soon as I hear that the directorate is officially united, I'm gone."

"What about Maria and the kids? Your job?"

"Job me no job, Lorna. Our job hours are already reduced. Cultural Arts will probably fall to the Proposition 13 budget cuts. Me? I choose history. Maria's strong. She knows I have to live out my destiny. We agree on that. She's committed to this struggle too."

The copy machine was spewing out Eddie's last page. "I'm out of here. Talk to you later on the phone."

"So Somoza's days are numbered?'" she asked as he walked away.

"You got it!" said Eddie, triumphantly over his shoulder, as the door closed behind him.

Two weeks later, on the Tuesday night Eddie was to leave for Nicaragua it was raining. Lorna, unaware, sat by the window watching the rain. At seven p.m. the telephone rang.

"How much cash can you raise tonight?" asked Eddie. "I need a thousand, at least. It has to be cash; no checks. I'll come by about eleven to pick it up."

"Why so much money?" she asked, already dreading the answer.

"I can't say why on the phone," said Eddie.

Lorna understood why. Eddie was on his way to join up with his guerrilla mountain team. She had $67.50 from returning Rini's coat to Macy's. She needed to keep the change at least for parking in the morning. She dialed Helen and got her husband, Larry. Their relationship was what Lorna thought of as a third-party connection. They both related to Helen, and each heard about each other almost everyday. Yet Lorna and Larry rarely talked directly.

"Hi Larry. It's Lorna. Is Helen home?"

"She's at a meeting of the Arts Task Force to discuss budget cuts for arts programs. She never gets back early from those. It will have to wait until morning."

"It can't wait, Larry," she said. She took a leap. "Larry, I need to ask a big favor. I need to raise some cash by eleven tonight. No checks. It wouldn't be a loan. Can you help me?"

"Eddie's been here and gone. We seem to be the first ones he thought of."

She hadn't mentioned Eddie, but clearly, she didn't need to.

"Helen emptied her purse and convinced me to unload my wallet. I know I'll never see the money again. Five hundred buckeroos we coughed up. I'll have to go to the bank in the morning. Eddie has Helen wrapped around his little finger. He told her he's leaving the job at Community Arts. That's all the notice she gets. 'I'm leaving and we need cash.'"

"But, Larry, Helen understands." Lorna said.

"That's what gets me. Helen just hands it over. Then she insists I give him money, too. Eddie's into dangerous things, Lorna, and you know it. I'm sorry he's dragged Helen and you into it, and I'm glad he's leaving."

"We're all fighting for the same things. We're all on the same side."

"Yeah, I know," said Larry. "There are only two sides. One's black and the other's white, right? You guys just don't seem to understand gray."

When Lorna set down the receiver, she began calling the

NIN phone list numbers to activate the solidarity network. She couldn't reach Luis, Hersh, or Cisco Kid, but she left messages. Reverend Don answered and set about calling his church contacts. She reached Joe Schneider, who said he would call his labor buddies and leave the money at Reverend Don's right away. Within the hour, Lorna went to Reverend Don's to pick up the money he and Joe had raised. At eighty, Reverend Don no longer drove. She was relatively dry when she got back as the rain had lightened. She was kicking off her shoes and hanging up her damp coat when the phone rang.

"Hi, Lorna, it's Luis Jaramillo, here. I can bring you $500 cash. I'll be right over."

He arrived soaked as the rain had increased again. "Heavens, did you walk over?" Lorna exclaimed when she saw him. She knew he lived in North Beach, near Hersh.

"No, I drove. But I parked a couple of blocks away," said Luis, setting five hundred dollars in an envelope on the dining room table. "Lorna, this includes some from Hersh and his poet friends. But most of it is from my business. I'm working against a deadline tonight so I can't stay." They hugged hurriedly and he was gone down the stairs.

When the doorbell rang again at eleven thirty, Lorna was ready. Putting the money envelop in her jeans pocket, she ran down the stairs. Eddie stood before her, his green eyes gleaming with excitement.

"Look out for Maria, the kids and my mom." Eddie said. "It's now or never, Lorna," When she handed him the envelope, he stuffed it into an inside pocket of his camouflage jacket. "¡Patria libre, o morir!" He reached forward impulsively, smelling as always of Florida Water, and crushed her to him, his body lean, hard, and hungry.

"Thanks and pray for me, you beautiful corn goddess you," said Eddie.

And he was gone.

8

Hairpin Mechanics

Rini took the bus up from Santa Cruz the following Saturday. Lorna met her at the East Bay terminal. Rini, hip-looking, in jeans, boots, and a tight black jacket, was wearing her blonde hair in a disheveled, sexy look.

"My daughter, Marilyn Monroe, studying engineering," Lorna proclaimed proudly, giving Rini a big hug.

"Good to see you, Mom. I have so much planned for this weekend. Can I use your car? I could drop you off and be back in time for dinner. But then I need it again to go out tonight," said Rini.

Lorna had a cold, so being dropped off at home was just fine. That night, Lorna cleared the table while Rini washed dishes. She pulled a fresh tissue from the box on the table and sneezed.

"So, Mom, congratulations on your new job. That didn't take long."

"Luis knew some of the faculty at the New College of California. They were looking for someone to teach cultural arts with an emphasis on Latin America. He put in a good word for me. I jumped in. I think I'm really going to enjoy it."

"Cool. But don't you feel bad about leaving Community Arts? First Eddie, and now you? How does Helen feel?"

"Well, her job is safe. After the mayor's budget cuts, I could see the writing on the wall. And we discussed it. I did Helen a favor by leaving. At least she doesn't have to lay me off." Lorna took another tissue, sneezing again. "Oh, Rini, It's so terrible. Now that Eddie's left, all I can think about is Nicaragua. Arnoldo's friend from the *Gazeta*, Tomás, left just a month ago, and was hit with a grenade and died. I ran into his mother at the supermarket. She was devastated. I am so worried about Eddie."

"Mom, if I know anything about Eddie, he'll be fine. He's a survivor. How do Eddie and the other volunteers get into Nicaragua?"

"I'm afraid to ask," answered Lorna. "It's safer not to know. They must walk over the mountains from Honduras or through Costa Rica."

"Probably, the fewer people who know, the better," agreed Rini. "But that's a lot of walking, Mom."

"I think about them all the time. Especially the poet I told you about who stayed in your room, Rosalea Bandera. When I'm working on a poem, all comfortable sitting on the sofa here, I imagine Rosalea, sitting on the hard, cold ground in some guerrilla camp, scribbling in her little notebook. We have it so easy. But at least, finally, there's some rippling of consciousness in Congress. The *New York Times*, at last, acknowledges there's a civil war going on in Nicaragua."

"I met this really interesting woman, Mom, when I stopped by El Chipote this afternoon. There were fresh flowers on the desks. You know those guys. Cleanliness, but no aesthetics. I asked who brought in the flowers, and they introduced me to the new woman from Nicaragua. Her name is Maria Rosa. I think she's been around a while; her English is so good." Rini threw the dishcloth over the faucet and took a seat at the dining room table across from her mother.

"I was telling Maria Rosa about last year when the school newspaper wouldn't print my Nicaragua article. The student editor said the revolution in Nicaragua was an attempt by Cuba to import Marxism into Central America. He implied everything I was writing was all Commie hype and propaganda. He says I was making it up. Then this month the same dude calls me back. He remembers my story and wonders if I wouldn't like to update it, and resubmit. Interesting, huh?"

Lorna sighed. "Yes. That's good. Interesting. But when I think of Eddie and the others in danger on the ground there,

I get scared."

"The other engineering students think I'm really weird paying attention to Central America. I liked working on the Nicaragua article. Sally's Nicaraguan boyfriend, Julio, gives me a lot of information."

"So how did your blonde Mayflower roommate come by a Nicaraguan boyfriend?"

"Well, Mom, she met him in her women's studies class."

"No!"

"It's funny, Mom. He said he and his buddy signed up for a women's studies class because they wanted to meet women!"

"Oh my god!"

"Well, it worked. He met Sally. Anyway, he's really interested in feminism and the Equal Rights Amendment, and all that. He probably knows more than I do about Elizabeth Cady Stanton and Susan B. Anthony."

"It's ironic. Your blue-blooded roommate, Sally, with an immigrant."

"Yes, I've seen her go through so many changes. Two years at Santa Cruz and now San Jose State have really opened her eyes to all kinds of social issues. Julio's family aren't Somoza fans. Julio says there is almost complete political opposition to Somoza." Rini pushed back her chair. "I gotta go get dressed. I'm checking out this new salsa club with some friends, now that I don't need fake ID to get in."

"It's ten o'clock at night Rini. Isn't it late to be going out?"

"Mom, it's Saturday night. Nothing even starts hopping until eleven."

"Where do you get so much energy? You even find time for good grades."

"I feel like I've got a fire under me, Mom. I have a brain and I want to use it. Can you imagine the kind of electrification projects I could work on in Nicaragua? Julio tells us what a struggle it is for poor people to get clean drinking water."

"Rini, you sound like you want to go there."

"Maybe I do, Mom."

That Monday, the steam from the bubbling soup pot fogged the windows of the Cisco Kid's studio. Damp tendrils of Lorna's hair curled down onto her forehead. A portable heater hummed on and off.

"Your chicken soup is ready, Cisco. It's a sure cure for your flu," Lorna said.

"You are an angel of mercy!" Cisco cried down from his sleeping loft. "I'll sculpt you in stone, marble, or granite." Unshaven and uncombed, he climbed down, in a mismatched set of sweats, a knitted longshoreman's cap, and a scarf.

Lorna set a bowl on the cluttered table. "Inhale the steam first!"

Cisco obeyed. "Now I can breathe a little. Thanks," he sighed. He sipped a few slow spoonfuls. "It's so wonderful the way our group takes care of each other. Luis came yesterday with vitamin C. Reverend Don brought me the heater. Today you, with the soup."

A ringing phone interrupted Cisco's soup therapy. "Hersh? Sure! Come on over." He turned to Lorna. "Hersh is coming over to read me his new poems."

"What are they about?" asked Lorna.

"Love! Hersh is in love."

"Do I know her?"

"It's that new woman, Maria Rosa, at El Chipote. She's running the show right now."

"Rini's talked about her, but I haven't met her yet. I'm planning to go over there this afternoon."

"She's all Hersh can talk about." Cisco said, blowing his nose.

"Knowing Hersh, she's young and beautiful with long flowing locks."

"Not young, she's your age."

"Cisco, you are busted, caught red-handed. You think I'm old?"

"No, no, no! I don't know how old Maria Rosa is," Cisco said, defensively. "Anyway, Hersh has only been in love for a week."

"Well, maybe I'll meet this ancient heartbreaker. This Maria Rosa. After I leave here, I'm going to El Chipote to check the news. I've been so worried. I think about Eddie and Rosalea Bandera all the time."

Cisco climbed back up to his loft, and Lorna finished washing the sink full of dishes. As she let herself out, she shouted up to the loft. "A week's too fast to fall in love."

Now more interested than ever, Lorna hurried over to El Chipote. The storefront window delighted her with its new display of the latest issues of *La Gaceta Sandinista*. The copies were laid out around a potted aloe vera plant on a straw mat beneath a large red-and-black Sandino silkscreen Eddie had printed before he left. The cowbell rang as she entered, and a small group of men and one young woman looked up. They were busy erasing something on a stack of bright yellow fliers. Rafa was the only person Lorna recognized. He was a slim young man who had recently come to San Francisco to fill in for his uncle Mundo, who had left with Eddie's group.

"*Buenas tardes*," she said to the group. "I am Lorna Almendros. I don't think I have met most of you."

Rafa jumped up. "Let me introduce you. *Compas*, this is our great collaborator, Lorna Almendros. She founded the San Francisco Non-intervention in Nicaragua group, NIN." He named off the people at the table.

"So what are you doing?" Lorna asked.

"We crossed out an endorsing group on this flier by mistake. Well, it wasn't exactly by mistake, but then we learned we had to include them after all," Rafa replied.

Lorna picked up a flier. Gay Activists Latino Alliance had a line through it. "What happened?"

"We were embarrassed to have homosexuals on our flier," said Rafa.

"It's a disgrace to have Sandino's picture and our name on the same page as that of the homosexuals," said one of the other young men.

"The Sandinistas need all the support they can get. The Gay Activists Latino Alliance supports self-determination for

Nicaragua. Isn't that the important thing?" said Lorna.

"God made it so that only a man and a woman can produce a child," said the young man.

"Well, the corn goddess made it so we would all love one another," she retorted.

"The corn goddess? Who's that?" asked another man.

"Just another way of thinking about God," Lorna replied, not ready to discuss the female nature of the universe.

Rafa explained, "Maria Rosa insists we leave the homosexuals in. She says without their support, we won't get anywhere in San Francisco. That's why we're trying to erase all the lines. We have to put the group's name back."

"I've come to meet this Maria Rosa." Lorna said. "And to hear the news. Has anyone heard from Eddie since he left?"

They shook their heads.

"Maria Rosa's in back," Rafa said. "Come, I'll introduce you."

Two shapely legs in striped socks and tennis shoes were sticking out from under Black Beauty. There were sounds of tinkering.

"Maria Rosa!" called out Rafa. "Lorna Almendros has come to see you!"

The legs inched forward, followed by the body of a small woman who extricated herself from under the machine. She came up to Lorna's nose. She had a little cat face, a pointed chin and a broad forehead supporting a crown of braids. Her black hair was streaked with silver. Maria Rosa wiped her hand on her ironed jeans before extending it for a warm handshake.

"Thank you, Rafa," Maria Rosa said as he left. She sent a radiant smile to Lorna. "Hello, Lorna Almendros!"

Lorna noticed the three heavy silver rings on the woman's right hand, and a beautiful green stone set in silver on her left. Although apparently mechanically inclined, the newcomer clearly had a sense of style. She spoke a very clear and precisely enunciated Spanish, very different from the slangy Spanish of the male *compas* who hung out at El Chipote. Lorna guessed that despite her mechanical gyrations under the machine, Maria Rosa gave the impression of an educated woman like Rosalea.

"I've been wanting to meet you, Lorna. I'm so impressed with all you've done with the Non-intervention Group. It makes a huge difference." Her accented English was very fluent.

"And I've heard so much about you," said Lorna. "Everyone is telling me what a good organizer you are, how you've breathed a new spirit into El Chipote."

"Would you like to have coffee?" asked Maria Rosa. "I could use a break."

"Is Black Beauty fixed?" worried Lorna.

"I fixed it with this!" said Maria Rosa, laughing. She held up a U-shaped hairpin and then fastened it into one of her braids. "The right twist of a hairpin may hold things together for decades!"

Maria Rosa gathered her purse and the two women walked headed out, with Lorna taking bigger steps to keep up with Maria Rosa who was skipping lightly ahead. It had become darker now.

"Let's walk up Twenty Fourth Street," said Maria Rosa. "My favorite coffee shop, Cafe Rendezvous, is right up the hill." After a brisk climb, they pushed open the door to roasted coffee smells, the hiss of a Faema espresso machine. "Now this," she said with a sweeping gesture, "is what I'd call a café."

They ordered at the counter and took seats at a table against the wall. Two men played chess at a table by the window.

Lorna studied her new friend with fascination. She was bright, with quick, graceful feline movements. Her round brown eyes were set evenly under delicately arched eyebrows. She talked rapidly, gesticulating with her small hands, and Lorna admired the big green ring on her left hand. It looked expensive.

Maria Rosa saw her looking at it. "This? You are surprised to see a Sandinista woman wearing jewelry? It was a present from my godparents for my *quinceañera*. Actually my godfather lives here now, in the Mission. You may know him. Coronel

Vighlieti. He is very old."

"Coronel Vighlieti? Yes, my friend, Eddie Flores, took me to meet him. He was very gracious. And very old but very lively—he must be in his nineties."

"Then we will visit him together sometime soon," said Maria Rosa.

"I'd like that. The ring is very beautiful," said Lorna.

"It is very beautiful, it is a peridot. It is my birthstone. I keep it for now, but I may have to sell it someday, who knows!" she laughed. "It is good to have something in reserve."

"Let's hope that doesn't happen," Lorna responded.

"Ah, but your daughter Rini is so charming," Maria Rosa continued. "I met her a few weeks ago. Irene. What a lovely name. It comes from the Greek, eirene, as you know. It means peace. Your daughter talks about you so much. She's so proud of you."

"Thank you. I usually hear nothing but criticism from her. So what did Rini actually say about me?"

"How proud she is of you for forming the Non-intervention group. She also told me about your work in Spain to save Chilean political prisoners. But she seems proudest of all that you're a fine poet.

'Only the past is dark.
The future always shines bright . . .'

"I love those lines. I found your book in the office," said Maria Rosa.

"You did?" said Lorna. "How nice! I didn't think anyone really read it. I had no idea Rini would praise my poetry."

"I gave my mother a hard time, too. It's the way of children. Now I'm raising my sister's children, Pedrito and Luisito. They came to us in Nicaragua and then moved here with my mother and me. They would ask when their mother was coming back. Now they avoid mentioning her."

"Why did she leave them?" quizzed Lorna.

"There was no choice. My sister's husband Nando was involved in the 1974 Palace commando action. He was arrested and thrown into *El Modelo* prison where he was tortured. He died there a few days later. They came looking for Hilda. She had to go underground or be killed."

"How did you and your sister get involved with the Sandinistas?"

"Maybe you've heard of AMPRONAC? My sister and I joined with other educated women to try to reform *Somocismo*. But with our brains, it did not take long for us to see that no reform was possible, given what Somoza was doing to our country. The man was a thug. Nando was a poet, and a Sandinista. It wasn't long before he had converted both of us."

Lorna thought of Rosalea Bandera. Her story had been similar. Even members of the middle class now were coming to the side of the Sandinistas.

"How often do you hear from your sister?"

"Not often. My sister is a *guerrillera* in the mountains. From time to time a letter comes, wrinkled inside another envelope, postmarked from strange places. My sister carries the letters around for weeks, until someone comes through who can mail it for her. She writes the boys little stories."

"They must love that," said Lorna.

"No. They show little interest."

"They're hurt. It must be hard for them to understand," sympathized Lorna.

"She's been away from them for five years. Her children are orphans."

"So you don't have children of your own?"

"No, my husband died before we could have children. I was hoping to be a doctor, but I dropped out to work as a medical researcher while he completed medical school. We were postponing having children until he finished his education. Then he got involved with the Sandinistas. One night the *Guardia* found him as he was removing a bullet from a *compa's* shoulder. They shot Antonio in the head. Then they shot the *compa*."

Lorna was silent.

"Now I teach health education classes in Spanish and translate for patients at San Francisco General Hospital. I try to make myself useful. Tell me about yourself, *hermana*," said Maria Rosa, calmly.

"My parents were from Nicaragua, but I barely knew them. They died in a car accident when I was three, and my grandfather raised me in Chicago. He filled my head with stories about Nicaragua. I loved him dearly and I still miss him."

"That's why you're helping us?"

"That and Eddie. He' so committed. He can talk me into anything."

"Eddie is very persuasive. Your friend, Hersh, was telling me how much you've done with NIN. It's been so very important to us. The US Government props Somoza up, but we're out in the open now, closer to winning every day. One of the San Francisco *compas* in Managua now, Arnoldo, has been selected as part of the Group of Twelve. *El Doce.* They have been charged to negotiate with Somoza and present our demands. You know Arnoldo?"

Lorna remembered him well with the white scar on his face, who had served time in Somoza's prisons. "Yes, he led the political education here at El Chipote for years."

"I hear you're preparing a national conference in San Francisco with NIN groups from all over the country."

"The work is exciting," said Lorna, "and frightening at the same time."

"Yes, the revolution is exciting. The day-to-day running of a government will be another matter. But I hope for the best, or even better than the best."

That made Lorna laugh. "Maria Rosa, what could be better than the best?"

"You know, Che Guevara didn't want to help build the new society," Maria Rosa said. "Governing was not his thing. Revolution was. So he left Cuba to encourage revolutions elsewhere in Africa and South America. A Cuban poet told me Che's life itself was the poetry. *El poeta eres tú.* Making the revolution is poetry. What comes after can be tedious. But it's necessary. That's what I see. *Compas* like Eddie and the others, they love the revolution. Off they go with machine-guns and a head full of dreams. But sooner or later it comes back to the boring task of governing."

"I wonder if the Sandinistas will be up for that," ruminated Lorna.

"*Hermana*, that's where I see the contribution of us women. We know the long, patient haul of child-raising. We know how to work, day in, day out, for an outcome that is so long in coming, the raising of a child. It will be our responsibility to find roles in the new government, and to make that new government work."

Lorna said, "Yes, I hope a woman like you will be in the Sandinista government leadership."

Maria Rosa laughed.

"I love how long we can sit here with one cup of coffee," said Lorna. "No one bothering us. I feel like celebrating! Do you like chocolate, Maria Rosa?"

"Chocolate? I love chocolate and romance. Equally."

"Then I'm getting us some Black Forest cake. The treat's on me," said Lorna.

Lorna carried two orders of chocolate cake from the counter back to their table. "So, I know what you think about chocolate, but I'd like to hear your thoughts on romance. So what about romance, Maria Rosa. Any theories?"

"Theories, yes, I have a few, but actually I'm more of an empiricist." Maria Rosa stabbed the cake with her fork and poised a delicate mouthful at her lips.

"I thought as much," laughed Lorna. "So you like our *Compa* Hersh?"

"I only met Hersh a few days ago. First in the morning at El Chipote and then later that afternoon at my apartment. He met my family."

"That was fast."

"In the revolution, you have to be fast. Sometimes there is no time."

Her words made Lorna think again of Rosalea Bandera.

"Hersh is a fine man. But he cannot come first with me. I have to do as my conscience dictates. It may appear as sacrifice, but it is the only way I can live. I am taking care of my nephews."

"Have you heard from their mother recently?"

Before Maria Rosa could respond, Rafa stepped into the café. He hurried up to their table. "Here you are. I knew you'd be here. Black Beauty is stuck again."

"Luckily I have another hair pin." Maria Rosa turned to Lorna. "I have to go. This was fun. I'm so glad to have met you."

"Let's do it again, soon."

"We shall. Give my regards to Rini."

The two women kissed, on either cheek. Maria Rosa smelled deliciously of roses.

Lorna understood why Hersh was so smitten. She had found herself a new friend.

Five days later the phone was ringing in the middle of the night. "Lorna, it's Hersh."

"Hersh. Why are you calling at this hour? It's after two a.m.," groaned Lorna.

"Maria Rosa. Someone's thrown a fire bomb into her apartment."

"What?" she shouted, now wide awake. "Is everyone OK?"

"No one's hurt, but the place is damaged. They have to get out."

"Are you there now?"

"Yes, I am. The police just left."

"Do they know who did it?"

"If they do, they're not saying. We think it was Somoza supporters. *Contras*. The children and Maria Rosa's mother are going to Reverend Don's place, but it's very small. Could I bring Maria Rosa over to your place?"

"Don't you want to put her up?" Lorna inquired.

"She'd be welcome, but Maria Rosa doesn't think it would

be proper."

"Oh my god, proper at a time like this."

"Well, you know what she's like. She has very strict standards. So, can I bring her over?"

"Of course, Hersh. Eddie mentioned the contra threats against the Los Angeles group."

"The cops don't get it or don't want to get it," he replied. "We'll be right over."

Lorna put on her robe and wandered into the dark, cold kitchen. Turning on the light, she put on some water for tea. As she waited for the teakettle to boil, she sat down at the kitchen table and pressed her face into her hands. Her heart was beating loudly, upset that the war was reaching up toward them, in the Mission, their sanctuary, where they offered safety to others.

The bell rang as the water came to a boil. At the foot of the stairs, Maria Rosa's round brown eyes had a dazed look. She was carrying her briefcase and her purse. Tall, lanky Hersh was beside her, carrying her small overnight bag, with his arm around her back.

"Come in, come in," said Lorna. She padded down the staircase in bare feet, taking the overnight bag from Hersh. "I've made some tea. Come on upstairs."

"I'm going to go," said Hersh. "The cab's waiting. Call me if you need me, but I think you're safe for now. I'd like to smash those cowardly bastards. An eye for an eye."

"Victory and the rule of the people will be our revenge," said Maria Rosa. "They know we are winning. This attack is a sign of their desperation."

"I'll come by in the morning," said Hersh, heading back to the waiting cab.

Lorna led Maria Rosa to Rini's room. Except for Rini herself, on occasional weekends, the last person to stay in that room had been Rosalea Bandera. Lorna was still without news of Rosalea, although months had gone by. As she glanced at Maria Rosa's stricken face, the image of the large, big-boned poet seemed to enter the room. Rosalea had been twice the size of tiny little Maria Rosa. Such an indomitable force. Yet Maria Rosa had her own kind of strength, Lorna could see.

"Set your things down and come into the kitchen. I've made us some tea."

Seated at the kitchen table, Maria Rosa visibly relaxed. She placed her small hands around the belly of the teapot, warming them. "This smells so good. My mother used to make *manzanilla* tea for us when we were children."

"How are your nephews?"

"They were frightened at first. But going to Reverend Don's house in the middle of the night is an adventure for them." Maria Rosa fell silent for a moment, closing her eyes. Then she opened them, and looked at Lorna. "The *Guardia* kept coming around looking for my sister. There was always heavy surveillance of our house. They figured Hilda would come back to see the children. She didn't because she knew she couldn't. They followed us everywhere we went. We would only get my sister's occasional letters. Finally my mother couldn't take it any more. She was seventy and it upset her too much. North American friends arranged for us to come here to San Francisco for safety. Now they bomb our house."

"They could have killed you," said Lorna.

"Yes, but I think they just wanted to scare us. To let us know that they know where we are. As if that will stop anything. I'll be back at work in the morning. All I need is a few hours sleep. The new issue of the *Gaceta* comes out tomorrow."

"You're going to El Chipote in the morning? It could be dangerous for you."

"I don't want to give them the slightest satisfaction. They want to intimidate us, and I won't let them. The Sandinistas are winning and there's no room for fear."

"I still remember the deep loneliness when Abuelo never returned from Nicaragua. It still haunts me. Those poor little boys. They must feel terrible," said Lorna.

"When victory comes they'll have a mother again," asserted Maria Rosa.

Maria Rosa stayed with Lorna for a week. When the

apartment was repaired and things had settled down, she moved back home.

9

Birds

Spring came with beautiful May weather. Lorna and Luis were alone in Cisco Kid's studio finishing up a big mailing. Luis gathered up his papers, smiling. "You go on ahead, Lorna. I'll lock up. Cisco gave me the keys."

"Thanks. I'm giving a final exam today. Thank heavens Cisco's studio is right around the corner from the New College. Eddie's mother, Beatriz, wants me to take her shopping in Chinatown Saturday morning. I had told her I would, but yesterday my car died on the way to school. Right in the middle of a crosswalk. The garage across the street from school towed it off the crosswalk for free."

"Free?"

"Well, free to get it off the street, but there's a hefty hourly charge to fix it. The worst of it is, I won't have a car till Monday."

"Hey, could I drive you and Mrs. Flores to Chinatown Saturday morning?"

Lorna was surprised. Luis had mentioned at the Tuesday night steering committee meeting that Jennifer was flying up from L. A. for the weekend. He had seemed excited about their weekend plans. Luis shrugged and seemingly read her mind. "Just in case you're wondering, Jennifer's not coming this weekend after all. She's got a really big case pending. There's too much work to do down in L.A."

"I'm sorry. I know you were looking forward to going out," Lorna said trying to keep her voice neutral. Actually she was pleased to think he might be free.

"I'd love to escort you ladies," Luis said "What does Mrs. Flores want from Chinatown?"

"Birds. She wants birds. Eddie's mom is into spiritualism...like Santería. I hope you're not shocked. She is going to perform a ceremony for Eddie's safety."

"You mean voodoo?"

"Sort of," said Lorna, not wanting to go into a big explanation.

"Well, I figured it wasn't Unitarianism," said Luis.

"She needs live birds. Still want to take us?"

"I'm intrigued," he said, looking into Lorna's eyes. "More than ever."

The next morning at eight, Luis rang Lorna's doorbell. And then rang it again. Rini, in a bathrobe and fuzzy slippers, buzzed him in. With long strides Luis came up the stairs as Rini was grabbing Pobrecito, her tabby cat who was trying to slip between her legs and flee to freedom. Rini, Sally, Julio, and the kitten were all squeezed into Lorna's flat for the weekend.

Lorna watched Luis come into the kitchen carrying a wax paper bag.

"See, I bought you *pan dulces*," he said. "Where's the coffee? Do we have time to eat them?"

"Well, we don't have to hurry," Lorna greeted Luis. "Beatriz just phoned. She needs a little while longer. Usually that's at least an hour and a half. And the coffee's made."

Sally and Julio appeared, followed by Rini, and the five of them settled in at the dining room table.

"Where are you two going so early on a Saturday morning?" asked Rini.

"We're taking Eddie's mother to Chinatown. My car's in the shop all weekend, so Luis's driving us," Lorna explained.

"In the shop all weekend?" Rini whined, in a slightly outraged voice. "We were planning to use your car to go to a concert in Marin tonight."

"Oh, how nice," said Lorna. "What if I had been planning to go somewhere?"

"You always go over to Helen and Larry's on Saturday nights. I figured we could drop you off and they'd bring you home." Rini said.

Lorna felt uncomfortable that Luis was hearing about her unromantic Saturday nights.

"What's the concert?" Luis asked.

"Michael Franks!" crooned Sally.

Luis looked totally uncomprehending. "Don't feel left out, Luis," said Julio, breaking into the conversation. "I never heard of him either, except these two play his tape over and over."

"And you play *Inti-Illimani* over and over. It's like living in the Andean highlands," retorted Sally.

"In Nicaragua, my uncles are all *músicos* and they all play the guitar. My dad plays marimba and accordion. Our whole family loves the music of the *cordillera*," Julio defended himself.

Sally took Julio's hand. "I'm dying to visit Nicaragua and meet your musical family. I never wanted to go some place so bad."

"I want to go, too," declared Rini eagerly. "Mom's told me so many stories about Pueblo Azul and her grandfather. I really want to check it out."

"That's odd," reflected Lorna. "That's the first time I've heard you say that."

"You can come and visit me at the Revolutionary Ministry of Rural Electrification, Mom, if they create such a thing."

Julio raised his juice glass, "*¡Patria libre o morir!*"

After breakfast, Luis and Lorna jumped into his Volvo and headed to Beatriz Flores's house in the Outer Mission, a working-class district south of the Mission. Beatriz was in her sixties, with dyed black hair and heavy make-up. With her strong perfume and shiny clothing, she looked dressed for night-clubbing rather than a Saturday morning market outing to Chinatown. Eddie's high school graduation photo was framed on the living room mantel, looking much the same, young, handsome, and invincible. Beatriz led them upstairs to the room that had once been Eddie's. A large altar covered with a gold cloth stood against one wall, and on it was a vase of tall peacock feathers. "This is where I will do the ceremony," she announced.

"What kind of ceremony?" asked Luis.

"A ceremony for protection for Eddie and the *compas*," answered Beatriz.

Lorna looked to see if Luis was uncomfortable. But he seemed fine and soon they were on their way to Chinatown. "I'll drop you ladies and go park," said Luis as they arrived in the crowded Grant Avenue commercial district.

Waiting on the sidewalk for Luis, Lorna watched Beatriz make her way into a shop where dozens of live birds enclosed in slatted wood boxes fluttered. Lorna could smell the birds even on the sidewalk. After pointing, shouting, and arguing, Beatriz emerged triumphant with three paper shopping bags full of pigeons, bumping and fluttering against the bags. Down the street Lorna saw Luis's tall figure approaching. He was so much taller than the other shoppers.

Luis carried Beatriz's lively bags through crowds of tourists, leading the women to where he had found a rare parking spot on Grant Avenue.

Beatriz sat in the back seat with the birds. "They're dancing in the bags," she said, happily.

As they got back on the freeway, a bag ripped open, and flapping, squawking pigeons, with their legs tied together, filled the back seat of the little Volvo. Luis hurriedly rolled up the driver's side window.

"Shut the windows!" he commanded. Lorna wound her passenger side window closed with one hand and nervously shooed away the escaped pigeons with the other.

Beatriz was sputtering, "¡Ay, *Dios mío!*" as she tried in desperation to corral the birds.

Lorna turned awkwardly in her seat as she waved her arms to help shove the pigeons out of the front seat area. "I hope they don't poop," she wailed. Luis grabbed a squirming pigeon while driving. "I caught it," he yelled triumphantly, and tossed it over his shoulder into the back seat. Beatriz herded the birds into the corner next to her.

Luis flung his sweater that was sitting on the front seat

between him and Lorna into the backseat. "Tie them up in it," he instructed Beatriz, and somehow she managed to snare them, tying the sleeves around them.

They were all three laughing hysterically by the time they arrived back. Beatriz slipped out carefully, without letting a pigeon escape, carrying the sweater-wrapped bundle and two bags of squawking and wiggling birds into the house.

Lorna turned her head. The backseat of the Volvo was adorned with pigeon droppings. But instead of being furious, Luis was wiping tears of laughter from his eyes.

Beatriz returned with damp cloths and a spray bottle, and dabbed at the mess in the back of the car. "I will wash your sweater, Luis," she said. "I am truly sorry for what happened."

As they drove away, Luis looked at Lorna. "What exactly will happen to these birds?"

"They will be part of the ceremony," Lorna snickered, demurely.

"You mean like virgins on the pyramids?" he chuckled.

"I mean sacrificed. The birds will meet their sacred destiny. Their lives will be exchanged for Eddie and the other *compañeros*."

"And then pigeon stew?" laughed Luis.

"I don't know," said Lorna, recomposing herself.

"I am used to animals," Luis said. "You were scared of those birds."

They fell silent driving back toward Hill Street. The windows were open to air out the car. Luis checked his watch. "We're just a few blocks away. Want to detour and see my new office?"

"Sure," said Lorna, always happy for a good detour. They pulled up in front of an old warehouse, on a street with repair shops and bars.

Luis unlocked a big metal door, and then a second door half way down the first floor hallway.

"This is my new lab," he said as they entered a big room with windows into a shared rough patio. Several half-assembled computers were sitting on a table, with wires in many colors dangling from their interiors. Large spools of colored wire hung neatly from racks attached to the wall.

Luis smiled as he turned on a computer. "I could show you how to use one of these. It would make it easier for you to revise your poems."

"I'm not very technically minded," she said uncertainly.

"It's very simple," he told her, rolling out a chair for her. She sat down hesitantly.

"Go ahead. Try it. Write me a poem."

Lorna looked up. "I don't write poems on command," she said, but she saw the twinkle in his eye.

"OK," Luis said. "I'll write one then, and if it's terrible, you can take over."

Luis rolled his chair in and wrote:

> I saw the birds bring confusion,
> but I cling to my illusion,
> The wise man knows that feathers flutter.

"The wise man?" said Lorna. "Is this the *I Ching* or something?"

"Or something," laughed Luis.

"Well, why is it always the wise man?" said Lorna.

"So you change it," he challenged.

She rolled her chair in and put her hands on the computer keyboard for the first time.

> The wise woman avoids disillusion
> Flies without confusion
> Finding feathers falling from her heart.

He laughed, rolling his chair in as she rolled hers out.

Lorna was having trouble even recognizing Luis this afternoon. The silliness he had slipped into, when the pigeons escaped, had only taken a greater hold on him. They were both giggling like teenagers.

"Luis," she said in a mocking professorial tone, "a poem should be about something. It's not just word play. I hate poems that don't mean something, or make no sense."

"Well, Lorna," he said equally professorially, "as

Shakespeare advised Cervantes, this computer could be a useful tool for you. So roll your chair next to mine and let's begin." Sitting by her side he patiently guided her step, by step, through typing out and printing their document.

"Wait till Rini sees this. I've entered the electronic age!"

"Come on, Lorna. Let's celebrate! We'll go to dinner, and then drive those kids to the concert in Marin. Michael Franks? Never heard of him. We'll see what the youth are up to nowadays. We might even like it."

10

Changing Tide

The little red Datsun tooled south down Highway 280, zipping and passing other cars, bouncing with the exuberance Lorna was feeling this summery June morning. Soon Rini would graduate and come home. At the thought, the red Datsun leaped forward of its own accord. Rini's four years of college were almost over!

Lorna pulled up in front of the wood-frame cottage, with its sagging porch and weathered, creaking boards, jumped out and rang the bell. The front door was open but the screen door was locked. Loud music in Spanish streamed through the open screen and out into the street. Lorna rang the bell again, this time holding it down, one thousand and one, one thousand and two, counting out five seconds, not knowing if anyone inside would even hear it over Mercedes Sosa's powerful Contralto. "*Cambia, todo cambia*" Then she saw Rini approaching the door, carrying a telephone with a seemingly endless cord dragging behind her. She was wearing blue-jean cut-offs and a faded T-shirt, and her hair streamed down her back. Lorna felt the familiar tug at her heart at the sight of her daughter. In Lorna's eyes, no other young woman in the universe possessed so much inner luminosity.

Rini popped open the door and nodded to her mother, without interrupting her phone conversation. "OK, I just wanted you and the committee to be the first to know. But now, my mom's at the front door and I have to go. *Hasta la vista.*"

"Uh, sorry, Mom!" laughed Rini. "How was your trip?"

"I'm so excited. My baby is graduating college and coming

home!"

"Graduation is exciting, Mom. But I have even more exciting news."

"Turn down the music, please, Rini, so I can hear you."

"OK, come on in the kitchen. Have a seat. I'm just warming up the eggplant I made last night. Want some?"

"Smells good. So what's your news?"

Rini took a deep breath. "Mom, I'm trying to be calm, but . . ."

"But what, Rini?" Lorna felt a stab of alarm.

"Look, it's something very good, Mom. I'll just give it to you straight. Sally, Julio, and me are leaving for Nicaragua right after summer school ends in August."

"No! You could get killed!" Lorna's response was involuntary.

"Mom, I'm not going to get killed."

"I won't let you go," said Lorna, without thinking.

"I don't think you can stop me, Mom," said Rini, serving the eggplant.

After lunch Rini convinced Lorna to come with her for a beach run. Lorna's thoughts were still a confused jumble. One thing was certain. Lorna didn't want Rini to go to Nicaragua. It was one thing for Eddie and his buddies to take on this dangerous adventure, but her twenty-one-year-old daughter? Lorna could not accept it.

After jogging for a few minutes, Rini turned to her mother. "Do you want to take a break?"

Lorna spotted a bleached driftwood log and flopped down on it. "A mile is all I can handle."

"Sure, take a break, Mom." Rini ran in wide circles around the log, her feet barely leaving footprints on the soft sand.

In front of Lorna, a flock of sandpipers skittered toward the receding tide, as if they were all part of one body. Behind her, Rini was shouting out against the ocean's roar: "We're the class of seventy-nine! We love revolution, love, and music! Nothing can stop us! We're invincible!"

Each time Rini's youthful bravado rang out over the ocean's

roar, it hit Lorna like a breaking wave.

"Come sit down, Rini. Talk to me. I came to see you, after all." Lorna tried to adopt a restrained, motherly tone. "What do you plan to do in the middle of a war in Nicaragua, Rini?" Lorna asked, swallowing the urge to tick off the hundreds of reasons why she thought this was a totally insane idea.

"Mom. Everything I know and feel, I learned from you. A new world is being created in Nicaragua, and I have to be part of that. Me. Us. The class of seventy-nine. It may sound corny, Mom, but we really want to feed the hungry, heal the sick and smash imperialism. Fight for human dignity."

Lorna shifted uncomfortably on the log, trying to quiet her mind so she could hear Rini.

"There's a social, political, and military revolution going on in Nicaragua right now," continued Rini, "and I just have to be part of it. I'm an engineer, now, Mom, a real live engineer. I can dam up streams and make electricity. I feel so powerful. Let there be light and there was light. You know what I mean? Let there be electricity—and there will be electricity. I feel I can light up the whole Third World with hope, because I am Engineer Sevens and I can ignite the light."

Lorna could see that her cautious pleas wouldn't have a chance. Rini jumped up and ran toward the receding Pacific tide, waving her arms over her head, shouting crazily:

> I know all the words
> that rhyme with light
> fight, bright, height, right.
> For I am Engineer Sevens
> I can electrify the endless night
> to endless light

Rini had waded into the waves and now she came running back, and Lorna felt no more beautiful mermaid had ever emerged from the sea. Rini's blonde hair swung in the wind, and her lithe body danced to and fro in front of her mother.

Lorna, unable to restrain her fears, said, "Gertrude Stein type poetry is all very nice, Rini. But Nicaragua is incredibly dangerous. You saw what happened to that ABC newsman. *Gringos* aren't all that welcome in Nicaragua, no matter how good their intentions. The war may be almost over, but even after the Sandinistas win, Nicaragua will be incredibly volatile."

"Mom, I eat fear. If I waste all this learning on a job in a navy blue suit in a fancy engineering company, I'll miss everything. It will be too late to feel the pulse of history."

Lorna listened in resigned silence. She was reminded of herself. So headstrong. So convinced she was right. She couldn't muster an argument. She only knew she didn't want her baby to leave.

"I want to be where people are on the move, not on the money," cried Rini. "I have a vision. I want to carry the torch of my ancestors and make up for a hundred years of US colonialism. I want to contribute."

"But there are many ways to contribute, Rini," Lorna said, with motherly patience. "You don't have to risk your life on the front lines to make a contribution. Sometimes there are better ways, even if they seem less heroic."

"Oh, right, Mom. Well, that's not me." Rini brushed some sand off the log and sat down next to Lorna. She put her arm around her mother's shoulders. "I know you're worried about me. But I have to do this. I don't totally know what I'm going to do. But I'll find Great-grandfather's grave under the almond tree and ask him. He'll show me the way."

"Rini. You're not thinking rationally. Be serious," Lorna insisted desperately. Yet mention of Grandfather made Lorna's heart lurch. She knew this was just the kind of thing she would do herself.

"I can't let history pass me by. It's my destiny," insisted Rini, quietly. "I have to go, Mom."

"Be practical, Rini," Lorna pleaded. "Where are you going to stay?"

"We're going to stay with Julio's uncle in Managua when we get there. He'll put us up for a few weeks. We'll figure it out from there."

"I'll call Maria Rosa and see what she thinks."

"Don't call anyone, Mom. Please. We're on our own."

Lorna drew a big circle in the sand with her toe. She was holding back tears.

"We'll be fine, Mom." Rini said, awkwardly. "I hope you won't be too lonely."

On the trip back to San Francisco Sunday night, Lorna detoured past El Chipote. There were lights on and Lorna could see Maria Rosa in the front window, taping up the new issue of the *Gaceta*. Lorna parked and tapped on the plate glass with the car keys. Maria Rosa unlocked the door.

"So how was Santa Cruz?" asked Maria Rosa. "When will Rini be home?"

"She's not coming home, Maria Rosa," said Lorna. "She's decided to join the Sandinistas."

"Come sit down. Tell me about it."

Lorna spilled the whole story, her fears and Rini's determination.

"You will have to let her go," counseled Maria Rosa.

"Yes, but it's so dangerous," cried Lorna. "I don't know what's going on down there. We never hear from Eddie. I ask and ask and ask about Rosalea Bandera. Never a word. People get swallowed up in this revolution, Maria Rosa. I am so frightened for her."

One look at Maria Rosa's face and Lorna knew something was wrong. "What is it, Maria Rosa?"

"We do have news of *Comandanta* Rosalea Bandera. She was killed in the fighting in Matagalpa three days ago."

"No!" screamed Lorna. All her pent-up fears about the redheaded poet now mixed with her fears for her daughter.

"We got a call from the *compas* in Mexico City yesterday. There are very few details yet."

"She is too young to die," Lorna sobbed, not knowing if she was talking about Rosalea or Rini.

"Rosalea Bandera was from a very prominent, very conservative family," said Maria Rosa. "They must be so conflicted now. This is the cruelest part of war. It's almost over, yet it could go on for days, or months, taking those we love."

Lorna wept as wave after wave of loss swept over her. Maria Rosa handed her some tissues.

"Be strong, *Compañera* Lorna," she said. "Rosalea Bandera will live through our victory. The *Guardia* are defecting in droves. Even President Carter is distancing himself from Somoza. We are winning!" But Maria Rosa's voice was somber.

"Why can't the war just end?" Lorna wailed.

"Somoza bombs the civilians, and the killing goes on. Behind the scenes, there's political maneuvering. We know the US State Department is stalling. They won't give Somoza safe passage to Miami until they find a puppet to take his place," said Maria Rosa, bitterly. "The United States is engineering a coalition of anti-Somoza forces led by the very same conservatives who profit from US imperialism. They refuse to consider a government that includes the Sandinistas."

"I may never see Rini again!"

"The mothers in Nicaragua feel this way too. Somoza's bombs fall everywhere. But our revenge will be the day our people will live in peace."

11

Endings Create Beginnings

The Mission District was exploding with anticipation a month later. Euphoria was palpable in the air of the *barrio*. It was July 17, 1979. After many years of struggle, the exiles and immigrants of the Mission District knew for sure that the dictator was going to fall in hours or days. Every night the air was filled with the sound of car horns honking in caravans around the Mission District and improvisational musical groups playing at Plaza Sandino, chanting and singing the slogans and songs of the revolution. Lorna and the NIN comrades joined the jubilation in the streets night after night.

In the month following her late night conversation with Maria Rosa at El Chipote, Lorna had listened avidly to the news coming from the shortwave radio about Nicaragua. *Sandinista* troops were on the outskirts of Managua. Somoza had announced he was ready to leave but was waiting for the US State Department to arrange a safe-conduct for him to Miami. The State Department was stalling while they made a last ditch effort to prevent the total defeat of the hated *Guardia Nacional*. But, the Sandinistas, along with the Organization of American States, was having none of it.

Lorna met Maria Rosa at their favorite uphill café before joining that night's triumphant car caravan up Mission Street. Maria Rosa had pinned a fragrant white *sacuanjoche* flower into her black braids. It was imported from Hawaii from a fancy florists that morning as a *plumeria*, but it was the same flower. They had ordered mochas and Lorna was carefully eating the whipped cream off the top and licking the spoon while Maria Rosa talked.

"The provisional Government of National Reconstruction will not allow the *Guardia Nacional* to remain in place," Maria Rosa said. "Can Carter really believe they have any place in Nicaragua, after all we've seen in the past months?"

The ABC television correspondent, Bill Stewart, had been shot in the head by Somoza's henchmen in June. Another ABC cameraman had filmed the event and it had flashed around the world, horrifying those who were otherwise unaware of the struggles in tiny little Nicaragua.

Taking a sip of her mocha, Maria Rosa continued, reading from her article in *La Gaceta Sandinista*, "We demand the *Guardia* be abolished. We demand the Nicaraguan Congress hand over power directly to the National Reconciliation Government and our Sandinista Junta. We will hold the first free elections ever held in Nicaragua." Maria Rosa pounded the table with her fist, the massive green peridot ring flashing on her middle finger.

"Yes, but how long will it take and how many people will die?" Lorna asked. "Eddie and the other *compas* are still at war."

"Just a few more days," Maria Rosa was vowing. "We'll get that dog out of there, and if he doesn't go voluntarily, you can be sure he's going to be hanging by his ankles in the central plaza, for the whole world to see. We're winning!" cried Maria Rosa. "Our forces are so close to Managua, I can smell it!"

"Even the *New York Times* is advising President Carter to stay out of it," said Lorna. "I can't wait for the triumph and the end to the bloodshed."

Maria Rosa crumpled her paper napkin and stood up. "I'm ready to celebrate now," she said. Driving in Lorna's little red Datsun, they joined a long parade of vehicles festooned with garlands of flowers, Nicaraguan flags, and red-and-black Sandinista banners. Mission Street had a carnival atmosphere, with its flocks of pigeons, and its countless bystanders milling on the street. A man selling Mexican tamales from a tray attached to a shoulder harness was crying, "*¡Rico, rico, rico, rico, rico, lindo!*" His call trilled like a tropical bird song and he ended it with a long *liiiiiiindo!* Car horns honked rhythmically, and voices periodically were raised in cheers and shouts of joy. "*¡Venceremos! ¡Venceremos!*"

"My god, every Nicaraguan and every supporter of the *Frente* must be here in San Francisco tonight!" exulted Maria Rosa. She had rolled down the passenger side window and was waving to everyone they passed. "Actually, not every Nicaraguan is here," Maria Rosa corrected herself. "It sure looks like those *contras* are staying home."

Young Rafa, Mundo's nephew, was screaming deliriously from the back of a pickup truck just in front of them: "*El pueblo, unido/jamás será vencido!*"

"The people, united," chanted hundreds of voices in the answering call, "will never be defeated!"

The caravan was moving. Onlookers cheered from the sidewalk and waved from windows overlooking the street.

"If Rosalea Bandera was still alive," said Lorna, sadly, "I would be describing this for her in a long letter." Despite her happiness, a tear rolled down her cheek for all those who hadn't made it. She prayed silently for Eddie.

After the car caravan, Lorna dropped Maria Rosa off at El Chipote, and drove back to Hill Street.

Lorna walked in pleased to find Rini home as expected, for a visit. She was glued to the shortwave radio. "The Nicaraguan Congress met after midnight, Managua time," she reported. "I'm listening to the BBC. They've accepted President Somoza's resignation. He's on his way to Miami. But they've named a Somoza politician, Francisco Urcuyo, as the new president and he is about to give his acceptance speech! Goddamn! With the Sandinista army right outside the city, they find another puppet?"

"Shh!" Lorna cautioned, "I want to hear Urcuyo's speech."

Rini obediently quieted down, but after the short speech, Rini screamed at the radio, "You didn't even mention the Sandinistas or their call for a cease fire. Urcuyo, you won't last until morning!"

"You know, Rini, it's not safe to go down there yet," Lorna

said, soberly. "The killing will continue."

"I know, Mom," said Rini, absently.

"I wonder if you really know," said Lorna sadly thinking of Rosalea Bandera.

The BBC announced that former president Somoza had arrived safely in Florida.

The next night there was another triumphal car caravan. Lorna maneuvered the Datsun through a sea of honking autos and cheering, screaming bystanders, with Rini and the Cisco Kid in the back seat. On a side street, Lorna found Luis standing next to his Volvo as they had arranged. Luis jumped in to join them in the caravan and later to continue the celebration at Hill Street in front of the shortwave. Their spirits were euphoric from the rally, and everyone wanted to discuss what was going on.

Rini turned on the shortwave radio and sat cross-legged on the living room floor, taking notes. Her hair hung forward as she scribbled.

"What's happening?" asked the Cisco Kid. He lounged, skinny and intense, on the sofa, watching her.

Rini looked up, tossing her hair back, with a big smile. "Urcuyo has fled! The US embassy staff has been flown out also. The Sandinistas are demanding unconditional surrender. Victory is hours away."

By three in the morning on July 19th, still glued to the radio, they heard the BBC announcer report that Sandinista troops had taken Managua. Daniel Ortega and the *compas* had entered Managua on a fire truck to be sworn in at the National Palace. Over the static of the shortwave, the four listened to the cheering and screaming of jubilant, massive crowds almost three thousand miles away.

Rini and Cisco Kid jumped up, slapping their palms in high fives, running in crazy, exuberant circles around Lorna's living room, whooping and hollering. Lorna watched their antics. Happiness filled her heart. They had won.

"Please, please, dear God, let Eddie be safe!" she exclaimed.

Luis pulled her up to her feet. "Victory at last!" he cried, wrapping his arms around her. His arms were warm and strong.

"Peace at last," murmured Lorna. "Peace at last."

12

Suitcase to Suitcase

Within hours of the Sandinista victory on July 19, 1979, ecstatic joy swept through the community. Rafa, Maria Rosa, and four other *compas* from El Chipote had liberated the Nicaraguan consulate office on Market Street the next day. Lorna had seen Maria Rosa on the TV news during the take-over and had heard about her appointment as the new San Francisco chief consulate.

"It had to be done," Maria Rosa said, when a few days later, she and Lorna met at Café Boheme, just recently opened near El Chipote and the new Mission Cultural Center on Mission Street. The center's front window was covered with a huge mural of Sandino by artist Alfonso Maciel.

Maria Rosa's braids were interwoven triumphantly with red and black ribbons. As soon as they settled in with their foamy coffees Lorna said, "I saw you on the telly during the Nicaraguan Consulate takeover. We rushed down to join the support picket outside. It was the first time I ever used the new BART train. I have to admit it's faster than the bus."

"Just like I told you," Maria Rosa laughed.

Lorna clanked her spoon in applause on the side of her cup. "Congratulations, Madam Consul, on your appointment! You are perfect for the post." Maria Rosa flushed with pleasure.

"Now, tell me all the details. What happened up at the takeover?" Lorna demanded.

"OK," Maria Rosa said, taking a deep breath. "As soon as we learned Somoza's staff had fled the embassy in Washington, DC, and had taken all the cash, we knew we had to move fast. We had to get there before they did the same thing here in San Francisco. That money belongs to the people. Rafa gathered the six of us at the BART station and we rode downtown. We tried to look just like everyone else, except our hearts were beating so fast. We rushed into the building trying to act normal. I was wearing a suit. There were other passengers in the elevator. We just got off and walked to the glass door that read CONSULATE OF THE REPUBLIC OF NICARAGUA. We walked right in. Only two staff people were there. I tried to sound very official and said, 'You'll have to leave now.'"

"What did they do then?" Lorna asked.

"They became furious and tried to take the official stamp. I walked up to them and said, 'Put that down! It belongs to the people of Nicaragua now!' The woman shouted, "Dirty Communists!" But she put the stamp back in the drawer and left hurriedly with the older man. When we opened the cash box, it was empty. It's the same as Somoza looting our national treasury. They may have made off with the money, but we've got the power. I've been using that stamp all day, working there."

"Doing what?" Lorna asked.

"As soon as the US recognized the Sandinista government, *Nicas* have been pouring in to the consulate. They want to get their passports updated, they want news of their families, and to congratulate us. The *gringos* want entry visas. Rini got hers already."

At the mention of her daughter, Lorna's heart sank. "Rini hadn't mentioned the visa," said Lorna.

Maria Rosa continued, obviously proud and thrilled. "I am leaving for Managua with my mother and the boys in few days for the official Ministry of the Exterior swearing-in ceremony. I'll be back in a week."

"I am so happy for you, Maria Rosa. The news of Rini's visa is a blow. I've been trying not to face Rini's leaving."

"She is going to be fine, Lorna. The war is over," consoled Maria Rosa.

Two weeks later Lorna was driving Rini, Sally, and Julio to

the airport with a sinking heart, unable to believe that her beautiful, strong Rini was leaving her again. She had hoped to have her lovely daughter back home.

"Mom, don't look so glum! It's not like you'll never see me again," Rini said, ready for the trip, in blue jeans, her Guatemalan blouse, and a jeans jacket. Sally wore black pants and a red shirt, looking like a lovely blonde moth next to dark-skinned Julio. All three had big heavy backpacks stuffed in the trunk.

At the airport, Rini kissed Lorna good-bye. "Don't worry Mom, your grandfather will be looking out for me," Rini said. Lorna couldn't watch them board the plane without tearing up, suffering the pain of separation.

She drove back home. For the next two weeks, without a word from Rini, she was sleepless with worry. The word in the Mission District community was that, even though Nicaragua was getting organized, the situation was still wild and lawless.

It was mid August when Maria Rosa phoned to say she and the family were back. "I saw Rini in Managua. She gave me a package to give to you. Come on over!"

Lorna fairly flew down the hill to the darkening Mission District.

"How did Rini look?" asked Lorna when she arrived at Maria Rosa's apartment.

"Beautiful, Lorna. Although a little thinner."

"But Rini's never carried any extra pounds," Lorna exclaimed.

Maria Rosa smiled and continued, "She's very excited about volunteering in the Literacy Brigade until she can figure out how to put her engineering skills to work. The Literacy Brigade is the pet project of the priest you met in Washington, four years ago, when you attended the hearings. Father Fernando. All the youth are joining the Literacy Brigade."

Lorna thought of the priest with the deep-set eyes, whose brother was a poet, but her excitement at the moment was about Rini. "Doesn't she get enough to eat?"

"As much rice and beans as she can bear," said Maria Rosa. "Do you like my new Nicaraguan chairs?"

Lorna ran her fingers over the hand-crafted wooden chairs with their carved birds and flowers. "They're beautiful."

"The furniture was inexpensive, but I had to get a loan to afford the shipping. It was worth it. My mother loves them."

Suddenly a bird twittered and Maria Rosa pointed to a birdcage Lorna had not noticed. "Look at Pepito. I had quite a struggle getting this little *chicuyo* out of customs. Even with my diplomatic privileges."

"Even with your diplomatic charm!" corrected Lorna. "And your sister? How was she?"

"She's pregnant. She's on sick leave from the army. She's been told to spend the rest of her pregnancy in bed."

"How was it for the boys?"

"Fine," Maria Rosa sighed, as if something were not fine. "We decided they should come back with me and complete their schooling here. They need a firm grasp on reading and writing in English. Anyway my sister is in no condition to take care of them. But the boys are happy to be back in San Francisco."

Maria Rosa pointed at an object at the far end of the room. "OK, I've made you wait long enough. There's Rini's gift."

Lorna spied a cardboard suitcase with a rope tied around it. It reminded her of the cardboard suitcase her grandfather had taken on his fateful trip to Nicaragua but even older. Lorna ran toward it, untied the rope, sprung the lock open, and lifted the lid. The suitcase was overflowing with balled-up newspapers from which Lorna carefully unwrapped a rustic clay pot, adorned with a stylized jaguar.

"This looks like the jaguar embossed on Grandfather's old leather wallet. Rini used to play with it as a child."

Lorna was admiring the smooth feel of the baked clay, when a butterfly flew out of the suitcase. She gasped.

Maria Rosa started laughing in surprise. "A butterfly from Nicaragua! It means you are expecting a visitor." Then she paused. "Or maybe you will be the visitor."

Part Two

Nicaragua

13

First Visit to Ancestral Land

The new revolutionary Nicaraguan government was eight months old by January of 1980. Lorna, en route to Nicaragua for the first time, sat by the airplane window, straining to see the countryside below, the dark mountains, the green and yellow checkerboard fields. *Bulwark Magazine* was sending her on assignment to report on the Nicaraguan socialist experiment. Helen Hart sat on the aisle, and tiny Maria Rosa sat between them.

"Fire! The mountains are dotted with tiny fires!" Lorna exclaimed.

"Of course. It's dinner time. People are cooking," Maria Rosa explained.

The plane was descending. An old woman began praying aloud. At the final landing thump, a spontaneous cheer rose up from rturning refugees, immigrants, and exiles. The loudspeaker crackled. "You have just landed in the Augusto C. Sandino International Airport at Managua, Nicaragua. Do not stand until the captain has turned off the seat belt sign."

Ignoring this, the aisles immediately filled as passengers jostled to open the overhead compartments and take down their belongings.

The three women stepped out into tropical heat. Armed teen-age soldiers in military stances wearing fatigues were on the tarmac. Occasionally a military truck moved from one spot to another.

"Armed soldiers! I'm glad they're on our side," muttered Helen.

"Yes they are!" said Maria Rosa, proudly. "Don't worry. I

will get you through."

Lorna passed the young soldiers very quietly. The intense heat and humidity made the air shimmer. The terminal was cooler, but damp with a dusty metallic odor, as if an air conditioner were failing. Among the crowd waving from the terminal balcony, Lorna spotted a tall girl with honey-colored hair and a straw hat waving. Her heart lurched. "It's Rini!" cried Lorna, waving back.

Lorna and Helen stood in the line for *extranjeros*–foreigners– although Maria Rosa, with her diplomatic status, passed rapidly through immigration and customs. An armed customs agent ordered Lorna to open her suitcase. He pulled out items left and right. Lorna suppressed silent impatience. She felt the suspicion in his black eyes. Finally he nodded. She was free to put everything back in her suitcase and go on.

When they finally emerged outside the terminal, Rini and Maria Rosa were there, waiting with a cab.

"Rini! Please go with your mother and Helen to the house. I still have to deal with the diplomatic pouch. I'll see you there." Rini had been living with Maria Rosa ever since Sally and Julio returned to the US for graduate school at summer's end.

As they bounced down the highway, the sights of the outskirts of Managua streamed past them. Empty blocks of earthquake-devastated ruins gave the drive through the city an eerie feeling. Chipped stucco walls bore graffiti and slogans. *Afuera Yanqui.* Red and black Sandinista banners and placards. Yankee Go Home. Dogs, horse-drawn wagons, and occasional cows gave the capital city of Nicaragua a very rural feel. Military trucks filled with young men in camouflage clothing, holding rifles, kept passing them on the four lane road connecting the airport to the city. Family groups clustered around open cooking fires in empty lots, next to war-torn houses, often with a rifle-carrying youth in their midst.

Lorna paid less attention to these new sights and sounds than she did to studying her beautiful daughter. Rini had pulled her hair away from her scalp and tied it into a ponytail. Her face looked tanned. Older. Lorna saw that Rini was an adult.

Taking Rini's hand, Lorna asked, "So, Rini, what's my baby been up to?" Lorna was impatient for a long, intimate chat to catch up.

"Mom, I'm excited. I just got word I've been confirmed to work on the rural electrification project in Jinotega."

"Wonderful. But what about the literacy project you were working on?" asked Lorna.

"We've just completed Nicaragua's first botanical inventory, working with the *campesinos* to write down the names and descriptions of all the flowers, trees, and wildlife. The spirit here is incredible, Mom. The country is jubilant, but it's also in mourning. So many people died. There's probably not a single home that hasn't been touched by death. The war and the killing have affected everyone. And even the *Guardia.* We hated them, because we viewed them as Somoza's tool. But the fact is a lot of the Guardia were just young kids, like the Sandinistas. People have been so poor here; they've been willing to take any employment where someone promised to feed them."

Lorna looked out the cab window, Rini's words giving meaning to the passing view of smoke rising from cook fires outside small wooden shacks painted with Sandinista slogans.

Maria Rosa lived in Los Robles, a middle-class district west of the Carretera Masaya, where the streets were shaded by almond trees in blossom. The driver pulled up in front of a white stucco house with a red-tiled roof. Rini jumped out and ran up to the carved wooden door. She rapped the metal door knocker and after a while the door creaked open to reveal a small dark woman in an apron.

"Xiomara!" cried Rini. "I'm back with my mother and her friend, Helen."

The maid pulled the door wide open, and the taxi driver set the luggage in the tiled entryway. Rini paid him, and then followed Lorna and Helen into the dark interior. Lorna liked the house immediately. It was spotlessly clean, with tiled floors throughout. It emanated an aroma she couldn't totally place—a woodsy, almost patchouli-type scent, something herbaceous, but mixed with cleaning products. It was unfamiliar, but pleasant.

"Mom and Helen, this is Xiomara. She does the cooking and the cleaning."

Xiomara smiled. Like so many Nicaraguans, she needed dental work. She bowed slightly but she made no move to shake hands. Lorna realized that even in the revolution, there remained an unspoken caste system.

The house was a simple Spanish-style home, three bedrooms and two bathrooms, plus a small room and half-bath for Xiomara. The main room was spacious, with doors that opened onto an interior courtyard with a small garden and utility sink area for laundry. The house was filled with crafts and artifacts of Nicaragua, hand-woven rugs, a hand-carved table, woven wicker sofas and chairs. On the dining table, Xiomara had laid out a small feast.

"I asked Xiomara to go to the market and have something ready for us. Are you hungry?" asked Rini. A woven blue runner lay across the length of the dark wood table, set with baskets of *nacatamales*, banana chips, white cheese, shredded cabbage, papaya and watermelon. A pitcher of white *horchata* stood on the table surrounded by tall drinking glasses.

"It looks wonderful!" crooned Lorna.

Helen nodded. "We had some great Cuban food at the Miami Airport. But that was hours ago."

"Well, I don't know how this will compare with the Miami airport," said Rini, "Xiomara is a wonderful cook." By the time they took their places at the table, Maria Rosa walked in the door.

"I ran into Eddie at the Ministry," Maria Rosa announced putting down her briefcase. "He said that now that you are here, he'll arrange a little gathering for the old El Chipote crowd."

Rini announced, checking off, using her fingers, "Arnoldo's

on the staff of the National Directorate. Mundo's part of the Military Brass and he has a chauffeur. Anibal's an Air Force director. Maria Rosa is the San Francisco Consul. Damn, Mom, we might have Daniel Ortega's entire cabinet!"

"That will be quite a celebration," Lorna declared. "We don't usually know people in such lofty circles."

Helen added, "Because just a year ago, they were all waiters and dishwashers."

"So what is Eddie doing?" asked Lorna.

"He's still a lieutenant in the army, but he's working for the Ministry of Interior, in military intelligence," Maria Rosa said.

"Mission impossible, conspiracy, all that stuff," Rini added. "You can be sure he loves it."

"Actually, his work is very important," asserted Maria Rosa. "Some of Somoza's people are still here. They didn't all leave the country. Many of the *Guardia Nacional* have become counter-revolutionaries. *Contras.* Then, there are the usual CIA agents, and suspicious foreign visitors."

"Have you run into a lot of that, Rini?" Lorna was instantly concerned, remembering the customs agent with the suspicious eyes who had ransacked her bag at the airport.

"Well, it helps that in Nicaragua my last name is Sevens Almendros and I speak Spanish. Just like when we were in Spain. But, yeah. Sometimes."

"Nicaragua has enemies internally and externally," said Maria Rosa. "If Reagan wins in November, it will get worse."

"I can't imagine a grade-B Hollywood movie star as president," said Helen, nibbling a plantain chip. "It seems to me unlikely that he'll win."

"Well, you Californians elected him to two terms as governor," said Maria Rosa, tartly.

"I didn't vote for him!" cried Helen.

"I didn't vote for him, either! He created homelessness in California by closing the mental health hospitals. I can just imagine what will happen if he becomes president." cried Lorna.

"If Reagan is elected, he'll be a hawk. The people behind him are ugly. We'll need you to build a whole new Non-intervention movement," said Maria Rosa.

"Again?!" protested Helen. "I'm in the middle of a kitchen and bathroom remodel. We might even add a hot tub." She closed her eyes, shaking her head.

"Here in Managua, we're still trying to get clean running water to all our citizens," Maria Rosa said. She turned to Lorna. "By the way, I ran into a poet friend, Carlota Pérez, over at the Ministry of the Exterior. She's very interested in talking to you about solidarity work. Will you have time to see her?"

"Oh, absolutely!" said Lorna. "I'm here to talk to anyone and everyone, especially such a noted woman poet in such a flourishing poetry scene. I would love to interview some of the emerging poets from the rural and army poetry writing groups that I've heard are springing up everywhere to include in my article.

"Yes, Carlota is working with the first lady Rosario Murio," interjected Maria Rosa, "to set up international solidarity groups concentrating on culture. You know, they are both poets."

"I'm thrilled to see poetry playing such a role in creating the new society. I want to see all of this revolution for myself," said Lorna.

"Meeting Carlota will be a good start," said Maria Rosa.

"Yes, it will be my first interview and a great beginning. I've promised myself that before I go home, this *Bulwark Magazine* article will be ready for its final draft."

"I almost forgot, Lorna," Maria Rosa said, lifting her fork. "There's something else, a press conference at the Ministry of Culture at ten a.m. tomorrow about the new community cultural campaign. I put your name on the invited press list. I will schedule your date with Carlota after that."

"A press conference?" said Lorna. "You mean the same press list as the *Newsweek* and *New York Times* reporters?"

"Not to mention *Le Monde*, the *London Times*, and *Pravda*."

added Maria Rosa.

"Cool, Mom!"

"You never know where poetry and revolution will take you," said Maria Rosa.

"Go, Mom! Follow your path!"

Early the next morning, Xiomara had prepared breakfast for the travelers. Xiomara fascinated Lorna as she moved about the house with ease. Lorna knew that Maria Rosa had left the house in Xiomara's care when the family fled Somoza years before. Her presence kept the house from being looted during the chaos of the revolution and even now, when Maria Rosa was away at the Consulate in San Francisco so much of the time. She realized how much more than food preparation and house care Xiomara gave to Maria Rosa. Lorna devoured an omelet *queso frito*, and *gallo pinto*, along with a hot coffee and milk.

Lorna headed out into the blazing, blinding sunlight of a Managua morning. She fumbled in her purse for her dark glasses. She had dressed with care, wearing a beige linen skirt and jacket, over a simple sleeveless pink top, imagining she would be rubbing elbows with the international press corps.

Lorna had to take an expensive cab ride to the Ministry of Culture on the outskirts of town. The beautiful property used to be called *El Retiro*, and had been Somoza's private retreat on a hilltop overlooking a gorgeous view of rolling hills and a lake. The cab drove up a wide curving road, past tropical trees and fields to the charming main building with a covered portico held up by arched columns. A large bird cage housed a beautifully plumed and talkative parrot.

The press conference did not occur at ten a.m as scheduled. It was closer to noon when it began. Lorna didn't see anyone from *Newsweek* or the *New York Times*. She had been expecting world-class journalists in seersucker or wrinkled linen suits. Instead she looked around the room of mostly empty chairs with a few student-looking types with backpacks scribbling notes. They seemed younger than she was, in jeans and T-shirts.

Poet Lionel Ruben entered the room, and stepped up to the podium. "The revolution strikes a chord in the hearts of the people through words," said the prominent literary figure. "The success of the literacy project has created the possibility of developing writing workshops in rural communities and in the army to tell the people's stories. We are planning publications of anthologies of people's poetry and narratives. The art of Meso-America predates written history and we carry on these traditions. The only limits are the shortages of paper and ink caused by the US embargo." There was a question-and-answer period that lasted only ten minutes and the press conference ended. Lorna left feeling inspired, in spite of the lack of world media interest.

She caught a ride back to town with a group of Swiss backpackers, squeezing into the backseat of their rented car. As the sun rose higher and brighter she peeled off her jacket and shoved it into her bag. She gave them directions to the office of poet Carlota Pérez, her next meeting.

They dropped her off in a fancy neighborhood of now mostly abandoned homes nationalized by the new government. She walked up to the front door of a Miami-styled modern suburban house. A guard answered the door and took Lorna back to Carlota's office. Her office had a standing fan rotating back and forth, sending a cooling breeze Lorna's way every few seconds. An ornate heavy wood dresser held a tray with a pitcher of water and some glasses. Lorna became aware of how thirsty she was when Carlota Pérez stood up from her desk and offered her a glass of water.

"Thank you so much for coming. I've just started this post and everything is still very confusing. Maria Rosa tells me you are a well-known poet in San Francisco."

"She is very kind. I am a very minor San Francisco poet," said Lorna. "I am curious how you find time for your poems, doing this kind of work?"

Carlota smiled. "I am glad you had the opportunity to hear from Lionel Ruben about the community cultural campaign we have started. As for me, I have little time for poetry. I'm so busy with reports. What we need more than anything is for people to tell the truth about what's going on here," Carlota declared. "The Sandinistas are still being described in your US publications as tools of Cuba and the Kremlin. Taking orders from Moscow. That is so far from the truth."

"I am on assignment from *Bulwark Magazine* and it doesn't take that line," said Lorna. "It was founded in opposition to the Vietnam War, and it continues to give voice to writers who dissent from American foreign policy. I'm here to see for myself and to write my own story. I want to include what Lionel Ruben had to say."

"How wonderful that a US magazine like *Bulwark* exists," cried Carlota. "We hope journalists like you visiting Nicaragua will begin to give Americans a truer picture of what we are doing."

"The magazine has a very modest circulation," Lorna said, apologetically.

"Every journal counts." Carlota asserted. "We are so worried this actor Ronald Reagan may win the election and send in the marines again."

She leaned forward, looking directly into Lorna's eyes. "What I want to ask you is, will you to set up an artists and cultural workers solidarity organization in San Francisco?"

Lorna felt a slight shock, knowing from her work with NIN, what this request might mean. This was not just an interview. She should have known that Maria Rosa would have set her up.

Carlota continued, "We're organizing by sectors. Shoemakers with shoemakers. Or, like you, artists and cultural workers in solidarity with their Nicaraguan counterparts."

"You mean sending money?" Lorna laughed. "Artists never have money."

"Not money. Perhaps arranging cultural exchanges, people-to-people friendships. Maybe sending material aid like paint brushes, or holding exhibits of Nicaraguan art, or translating Nicaraguan poetry, and letting the world know about the cultural upsurge here. We need all kinds of support. We've started a national arts program through our new Ministry of Culture. As you know, the great poet, Ernesto Cardenal is heading that up."

Carlota planted her elbows on her desk and her chin on the heels of her hands, so that her fingers almost covered her eyes. She gave a deep sigh, shook her head, and then looked up. "We have got to do what we can to discourage an American invasion, Lorna."

"Does computer art count as cultural work?"

Carlota's eyes brightened. "Computer art would be thrilling!"

In a few minutes Carlota had Lorna committed. "OK, Carlota, I'll do it," said Lorna. It made sense. She had the whole Non-intervention in Nicaragua experience behind her. With Rini living here, Nicaragua was on her mind all the time, anyway. Lorna wanted to do whatever she could to keep an American invasion from happening.

At dinner that night at Maria Rosa's, Lorna described the press conference and her meeting with Carlota Pérez. Rini, Helen and Cisco Kid were there. Lorna was surprised to see how pale and tired he looked. She knew he had been in Managua for more than six months, painting murals with the *compañeros,* but he had also come down with hepatitis, a common disease in Nicaragua, although he was now recovering. Despite his illness, the Kid ran with the idea of the new cultural solidarity group.

"Let's launch the organization with a paint brush drive for *Nica* artists," Cisco suggested.

"Great idea, Cisco," said Lorna. "It'll be a good way for our new group to mobilize artists and art students."

"Not me," Helen begged off. "Today, I decided to change my life."

Everyone turned to look at Helen.

"This morning I met three Europeans wandering around the *Plaza de la Revolución,*" Helen explained. "We got to talking and decided to chip in and rent a car to visit the Masaya volcano. What an experience! We looked down into that explosive bubbling brew and saw little green parakeets nesting in its hot lips. Somoza used to throw his political enemies into that cauldron. Or so they say. I don't know what happened to me, but I knew right then that when I return to San Francisco, I'm going to run for city supervisor."

"Yay!" cried Rini, clapping.

"That's the most ambitious thing I've heard since Eddie told me he was going to Nicaragua to win a revolution," said Lorna.

"The primordial power of that volcano was very much like the violence that people use against one another. But the little parakeets co-exist with that, and stand for something else. Something more hopeful. I want to run for office because of what I'm seeing here. I want to use political power for positive change."

Lorna lifted her glass of water. "You'll be fabulous, Helen. Congratulations! Helen Hart for Board of Supervisors!"

Maria Rosa banged the table, Cisco beat his utensils together to join the cheer, and Rini put two fingers in her mouth and gave a loud Bronx whistle.

"Thanks," said Helen. "Hopefully, I can muster more support from City Hall for your cultural work than ever." She looked very pleased.

The next day Lorna met with Eddie at an outdoor terrace café overlooking *Laguna de Tiscapa*. She wore a white dress with an open stretchy ruffle neckline that she could push off her shoulders. Her reddish-gold curls were pinned up at the top of her head and her coconut shell earrings dangled.

Eddie slouched back in his chair, sitting across from her at a small table. He wore olive green fatigues with his .45 automatic pistol in its holster strapped to his thigh. His short-sleeved military shirt revealed smooth strong forearms. It had been a year since she had seen him. They had sat in awkward silence waiting for their food and drinks under a striped umbrella providing little relief from the heat. But now, their order had arrived and Lorna sucked the ice floating in her glass.

"So, Eddie, I see you don't have to keep your gun in the closet anymore," she said with a smile. "What happened to *Dulce?*"

"After the victory, I put her away. The Ministry issued me this .45. Unfortunately, it's very necessary the way things are right now."

"Is there any space in your life for your silk-screening these days?" asked Lorna.

He laughed. "No room. No supplies. And no time. Sometimes I doodle in my notebook."

"Well, Eddie, the truth is," said Lorna, "I am so glad to see you alive and in one piece. We worried so much about you. Maria, the kids and your mother miss you. You are looking really well."

"Even though I miss my family, I'm loving this job. I'm looking for a house so I can bring them here. But my wages are low and the work is 24/7. It hasn't been easy re-integrating myself into Nicaragua after growing up in the States. Some guys give me a hard time."

"You look great in a uniform," said Lorna, pushing her food around on her plate. It was too hot to eat. She was feeling uneasy sitting next to an armed man.

"You're looking fantastic, as always," said Eddie. His eyes slid appreciatively over her bare shoulders. He stroked the corner of his mustache, giving her a sidelong look. "So, you're here to write an article, Lornita?"

"*Bulwark* has me on assignment, Eddie. I went to the press conference yesterday with the poet Lionel Ruben," said Lorna. "It was inspiring. I thought I'd run into some big-name reporters, but there were none there. That was disappointing."

"Oh, you thought you'd run into Stephen Kinzer or Alan Riding?" teased Eddie, lifting his eyebrows.

"The way Maria Rosa described it, I thought it was going to be a big deal."

"For us in the revolution, it was a big deal. Too bad only a small-fry outfits like *Bulwark Magazine* covered it. I guess military news trumps everything. I was interviewed by *Time* magazine last week. The United States and Honduras are holding joint military exercises near our border. The reporter wants to talk to me again. You would be helping us a lot more, Lorna, if you could find a more important outlet for your story."

Lorna was stung. "Our readers are activists. I remember when you called *Time* magazine a CIA mouthpiece," she said.

"I remember when you were aiming for great visibility," Eddie countered.

"I want to encourage activists, intellectuals, artists and cultural workers. That's my audience," objected Lorna. "I interviewed Carlota Pérez yesterday. She's working to create a San Francisco cultural solidarity group."

"I'm glad I'm in the revolutionary military," Eddie interrupted. "I'm sick of working with artists and their elitist, neurotic ways. I had too much of it."

"But, Eddie, you were so good at mobilizing other artists and using your wonderful silk-screens for the movement. Since you left, we mostly relied on Luis Jaramillo with his compelling computer designs for our outreach."

"Computer art?" exploded Eddie in disgust. "It lacks the human hand. Computer art is nothing!" Eddie flicked his hand out in front of him dismissively.

"Luis puts his heart and his hands into his computer designs. And sometimes, I write my poems on a computer. We're even trying to get a computer lab at the college."

"Computers and robots don't interest me. I had lunch here just last week with Daniel," said Eddie, changing the subject.

"You mean the president?" Lorna asked, covering her hurt feelings.

"Yes, the president. He's asked me to take on some very important tasks because of my command of English and my contacts."

"Like what?" Despite herself, Lorna was excited for him.

"I am not at liberty to say. And anyway, like the *compas* keep reminding me, 'You wouldn't understand. It's a Nicaraguan thing.'"

Lorna couldn't ignore this slight. A flush rose in her face. "You've changed, and I don't think I like the new Eddie. What happened to my old friend, that guy in the closet?"

"I haven't changed," he replied. "You've never been easy to get along with, Lorna. You have a huge chip on your shoulder where men are concerned. You take offense very easily, and, to be honest, you don't really understand my goals and my mission. But, I'll tell you this much. Daniel has plans for me."

Now the smirk and the mustache-stroking irritated her more than the heat.

"Well, who do you think you are, Eddie?" snapped Lorna. "Who organized the Non-intervention Committee in San Francisco and helped get all that attention from Congress? Who stood by you and took care of Beatriz and your family when you had to run down to the *revolución*? Now you're acting like I'm a nobody. The outsider."

"Well, isn't that how it is, sitting here in a Managua café? This time you are the foreigner."

"So that's how it is?" Lorna fired back, trembling. "So now I'm material for one of your stupid intelligence reports for the Ministry. Will you title it, 'Conversation with a North American *Gringa?*' Not a Nicaraguan-American? Will you call me Sevens and not Almendros? We used to be friends and comrades, Eddie, or don't you remember?" Angry tears stung her eyes.

Eddie laughed. He placed his big tanned hand over hers. She snatched her hand away.

"We're still friends and comrades, *Compañera* Lorna," he said tenderly. "Nicaragua needs you."

"You dare to laugh? How condescending is that?" ranted Lorna. "I have a chip on my shoulder? I should be a *New York Times* reporter? Who elected you political commissar to make all these judgments? What happened to your love of art and culture? Did it ever occur to you that I am a poet and might have ambitions of my own?"

"Most middle class women do," said Eddie calmly. "'NOW for me'—isn't that the motto of you liberated North American feminists? You sound like a shrill liberal for the National Organization for Women."

"So! Now that you've given up art and culture, you're the expert on every social trend, including feminism?" she spouted off in one last attempt.

He stroked the corner of his mustache with his forefinger, frowning slightly, as if cogitating, then nodded his head slowly up and down with a sly smile.

"I think that's it, Lorna. I am the expert on every social trend." Eddie raised a couple of fingers, and the waiter hustled over. He pointed to their glasses, which were empty, and soon the waiter was back with a fresh soda and a cold bottle of Corona.

Lorna took a long sip of her drink. She really didn't want to have this fight.

"So, when do you think you'll hold the El Chipote reunion?" asked Lorna, trying to make a fresh conversational start.

"I think we're all too busy right now," said Eddie, airily dismissing the question.

Lorna turned her face away to hide her disappointment that he had issued an invitation, and then dropped it. She had been so looking forward to it!

Her anger would not go away. She was as angry with herself as she was with him. They lived three thousand miles apart, and she was still reacting as if everything he said was so damned important. As if he were still the leader. Like the Masaya volcano, her anger was rising but it didn't quite erupt. It just simmered and smoked near the surface.

Now Eddie placed his entire arm around her shoulders. "I know women are sometimes unreasonable when they're getting near the change."

"I'm not being unreasonable!" she shrieked, shrugging his arm off. People at other tables turned around.

"I rest my case," said Eddie. There was a moment of pulsating silence. Eddie wiped the beer off his mustache.

"Where will this unpleasant conversation end? Are you

going to kill off our friendship after all these years with your high-handed attitude? Really, Eddie, I just can't take it."

"Attitude me no attitudes, Lorna. Thanks for bringing my boots from my mother. A soldier can go only as far as his boots will take him."

"You're welcome. No problem," she said, seething.

Eddie signaled the waiter for the check.

"And by the way," Lorna added, "I forgot to mention that Helen Hart is going to run for City Supervisor."

As they stood up, two ragged children swooped in and grabbed the leftovers from their plates.

At dinner that night, Helen asked, "So, Lorna, did you see Eddie?" Lorna, Rini, Maria Rosa, Helen and the Cisco Kid were all enjoying one of Xiomara's meals at Maria Rosa's dining room table in Los Robles.

"Yes. We quarreled. It seems as if Eddie has demoted *Bulwark Magazine* and the San Francisco arts community. It was so different than my meeting with Carlota Pérez. She was eager to have us participate and was even impressed that we use computer art."

"But Eddie's such a darling," exclaimed Helen. "How could you quarrel?"

Rini snickered. "I bet it was easy, Mom."

"It was so hot.," complained Lorna. "He seemed so condescending. He laughed at me like I was a little nobody while he was Mr. Revolution himself."

Helen shook her head. "Poor guy. He was probably disappointed that you weren't more impressed. After all, he just won a war! Eddie's a very sweet guy. Look how well he treats his mother."

"And how badly he treats his wife!" Rini jumped in.

"OK, so he's not perfect," Helen conceded.

The phone rang and Maria Rosa pushed back her chair to answer it.

They could hear her voice singing out. "Hello, Luis! Yes, Cisco is here. He's improving. We're taking good care of him. He'll be back as soon as he finishes his mural."

The phone was passed around and everyone took a turn speaking with Luis. His voice was very loud and clear. Lorna was last. "It sounds as if you're right here, Luis."

"I'm in San Francisco freezing to death. Was it Mark Twain who said the coldest winter he ever spent was a summer in San Francisco? So anyway, how are you?"

She thought of the unpleasant afternoon lunch with Eddie but decided not to speak of that. "I've been busy doing interviews for *Bulwark*," she dodged.

"*Bulwark* is so lucky to have you."

Soothed by his words, the angry knot inside her loosened. Lorna described her meeting with Carlota Pérez and the new arts and culture solidarity effort, adding how interested she'd seemed about his computer art. "Cisco thinks we should kick off the new organization with a material aid campaign for sending art supplies to Nicaraguan artists."

"Well, count me in," announced Luis excitedly. "Everyone wants digital art now. I'll use my new software to design a flier for the artist supply campaign. A hundred winged paint brushes flying on a peace mission to Managua. So, does it look like this revolution is going to work?"

"People are excited. Every cab driver and marketplace vendor has a strong opinion. All of them different. But everyone's very nervous about the United States, especially if Reagan gets elected."

"What do you think if I pick you up at the airport when you return? I want to hear it all firsthand."

"That would be wonderful. I'd love it," Lorna said.

"Write a lot and take care of your health. Good-bye, Lorna. See you soon." Luis hung up.

Long after the call, Lorna and Rini prepared for bed.

"You know, Rini, in San Francisco, I'm always missing you. But now, in Managua, I feel homesick. Luis was talking about how cold it was there. I think I miss the cool fog."

"Maybe you miss him, Mom," Rini said, turning off the light.

Two weeks later at the San Francisco airport, Luis loaded

Lorna's bags into the trunk of his Volvo. They left the freeway at Army Street and drove uphill toward her neighborhood. Lorna surveyed the San Francisco landscape. Everything looked so familiar, so comfortable. She was glad to be back.

"Rini feels at home there in Managua. She doesn't want to leave. But for me San Francisco is home. Each street, tree, and shop we're passing holds some of my personal history. In Nicaragua, I never lost my sense of being a stranger. Although I did develop some new routines. *Café con leche* for breakfast, with *quesillas*, warm tortillas topped with a salted milky cheese."

"You're making me hungry. I came straight to the airport from work," said Luis.

"Let me treat you to dinner. It was so kind of you to pick me up. How about the Nicaraguan place on Mission Street?"

At the little hole-in-the-wall restaurant, *Trebol*, Luis was full of questions about Lorna's health, Rini, and her impressions of Nicaragua.

"So tell me about the cultural exchange group with Nicaragua?" he asked.

"It sounded easy at the moment when I told Carlota Pérez I would do it. But when I think about it, a lot of the people from our old group are gone or involved in something else. Hersh is in New York with no plans to come back. Reverend Don is working with a church group and Cisco Kid will be returning to Los Angeles once he's well. So who is there? You, me, and maybe Helen, pretty much."

"So we'll find new people," Luis said excitedly, spearing a bit of meat with his fork. "Let's begin with Cisco's idea of collecting paint brushes. I began designing the flier, after we talked on the phone. We can send it to art schools and college art departments to announce our first organizing meeting. Reverend Don thinks a few of the cultural types at the Council of Churches might like to work on this. I talked to some Latino arts organization people and they seemed interested." His enthusiasm grew. "I was thinking we might call the new group, 'Friends of Nicaraguan Culture.'"

Suddenly Lorna felt weary. She'd been traveling since before dawn. "Can I really do all this, Luis? I have to earn a living, write that article for *Bulwark*, and, oh yes, help organize Friends of Nicaraguan Culture."

Luis pushed away his plate. "No problem. I'm here. We can do it. With our combined energies, it's a piece of cake. After a good night's sleep, you'll see. Don't underestimate us, Lorna. So, how's Eddie?"

"Fine. He's into state security—very superior and secretive. He's trying to find a house so he can bring the family down. He put his art aside. We had an argument."

"He's one of the few real guerrilla fighters I know," Luis said, motioning for the check. "He adores you, Lorna. You'll see. You'll make up. We're all on the same side."

Lorna insisted on paying and they rose to leave. There were several scraps left on Luis's plate. Lorna remembered the faces of the Nicaraguan children grabbing the leftovers.

14

Seventh Visit

Six years later, in 1986, it was Lorna's seventh trip to Nicaragua, visiting Rini, representing Friends of Nicaraguan Culture, and reporting for *Bulwark* on the revolution's progress. Outside roosters were crowing, and the iron bells of Managua's Santo Domingo Church gonged a slow beat, then ended in a noisy, jangling torrent of sounds. Lorna's nightgown stuck to her skin, and a half-understood dream clung to her thoughts. Where was she? She remembered. She was in Los Robles, in Maria Rosa's house and it was almost time for the revolution's sixth anniversary. She stretched out on the narrow bed, a shaft of sunlight slanting through the window grill. Lorna smelled unfamiliar smells of furniture polish, bleached tiles, and the whole dusty, hot, fruity aroma of Managua wafting through the open window.

Lorna loved dawn's coolness. Often she awoke in time to catch her dream and mark the day's first reflections in her journal. But today the dream would have to stay lost. She had slept too late and now the sun dominated the morning.

Today Eddie Flores was driving her to her grandfather's village, Pueblo Azul. Eddie had been living in Nicaragua for the past six years. He'd found a house and brought the family down. But it did not take long for Maria to get fed up with his absences. She divorced him and returned to San Francisco with the kids. He had betrayed her too many times. He always had some sort of post in the government. Now he was working in public relations in the army press corps.

Lorna and Eddie had patched things up over the years as he had helped her with the work of Friends of Nicaraguan

Culture. He didn't come across quite as self-important to Lorna anymore. And he'd been very kind on this trip. Their old arguments seemed distant and no longer important. When she confided to him that she'd never been yet to Pueblo Azul, he offered to drive her. She had the deed to Grandfather's house with her, and she wanted to see it.

Lorna stretched, feeling her muscles and joints loosen in the tropical heat. It was already too hot to write in her journal, a blank book Luis had given her as a going-away gift. It had come as lovely surprise.

In no hurry to get out of bed, she listened to the roosters answer one another in the distance while thinking about her relationship with Luis. She and Luis had carefully kept each other at arm's distance. Their political work required sacrifice, and not messing up a *compañero's* marriage was one of the sacrifices. But having him as a friend was a blessing. Their Friends of Nicaraguan Culture meetings took up two or three nights a week and sometimes even a weekend afternoon. FNC, as they referred to themselves, had been hyperactively busy between organizing visiting delegations, exchanging art exhibits, and managing musical tours. Her two-year relationship with a union organizer had petered out, just like her earlier affair with the math professor before him. She never had enough time for them. Luis might have had the same problem of not devoting enough time to the marital relationship if it weren't for his wife, Jennifer, working in LA. Larry seemed to give Helen lots of space. The way he had come through for her during her two successful election campaigns made Lorna realize that Larry had been a better choice than she had given him credit for. Lorna lamented that there still seemed to be no one for her.

To escape her puddle of self-pity, Lorna stepped out of bed and peeled off her nightgown. Standing naked, she took solace in the fact that at fifty-two, she still had a strong body, full breasts, a slim waist and shapely legs. Vowing to keep up her fitness program, she picked up the twisted sheet from the bed and flapped it out, creating a breeze around her damp skin.

Maria Rosa shouted from the kitchen. "Eddie's here! And Xiomara has breakfast ready."

"I'll be right there after my shower," she shouted back, hurrying towards the bathroom.

Lorna had sorely missed Maria Rosa, who had been living full time in Managua for the last three years. The United States government had shut down several Nicaraguan consulates, including the San Francisco Consulate, in retaliation for the deportation of a US Embassy employee in Managua. The Sandinistas had accused him of being a CIA agent. Maria Rosa had been given three days to pack up her family and belongings, and leave. Before that Lorna and Maria Rosa saw each other almost every day. Now, Lorna and Maria Rosa saw each other once a year during her visits to see Rini in rural Nicaragua. Maria Rosa was more dear to her than ever for her loyalty to Rini, offering her a port in the storm whenever she needed it. It thrilled Lorna whenever Rini came to San Francisco, and she still hoped that maybe one day Rini would stay. Wrapping the sheet around her like a sarong, Lorna walked on bare feet over the cool tiles to the bathroom.

"Eddie," she stammered.

He stood in the bathroom doorway, crisp in his fresh khaki fatigues. His eyes traveled down her body, and her face burned. It seemed as if he could see through the thin sheet.

"I came early," he announced. "Lorna, don't you know you should never go barefoot? There are terrible worms in the tropics that enter through your feet."

"I overslept. I'll be ready fast," she replied.

She assumed he would step aside. He didn't budge.

"Lorna," Maria Rosa shouted from the kitchen, "do you want eggs?"

Eddie moved to let her pass, but her body brushed against his in the narrow passageway. Over the years she had deflected these moves with stern lectures about sexism and how married men should behave. But today she skipped all that and pushed past him into the bathroom, tingling from the slight touch of her breasts against his uniform.

Back in Maria Rosa's guest room, Lorna chose an outfit suitable for embracing her Nicaraguan heritage. She chose a white sleeveless blouse embroidered with colorful flowers along the border of its deep neckline and a calf-length white skirt that skimmed her hips. She pulled a hairbrush through her thick auburn curls and twisted them into a knot, with little tendrils dangling at the hairline. She was ready for Pueblo Azul, and she breezed into the dining room.

Maria Rosa and Eddie were already seated at the table. Through the open door, Lorna saw the leaves of the papaya tree and twining red-flowered vines. She smelled the wonderful jasmine, and other flower fragrances of Maria Rosa's garden. Little birds she did not recognize chirped from the vines.

"Mmm, smells wonderful!"

"Let's eat," said Eddie, pulling out Lorna's chair. "Your hair looks nice pinned up like that," he told her softly, almost whispering in her ear, so that his lips tickled the side of her neck. She could feel her belly and toes respond as she adjusted herself in the seat.

"Thank you," she said a bit primly and he sat down next to her.

Xiomara came in from the kitchen, carrying a small platter. "I made a Spanish onion and potato omelet."

"To friendship," Lorna toasted with her fresh mango juice.

"To friendship!" Eddie added, leaning forward so that his gun rubbed against Lorna's hip, hard and intruding.

"So you're headed up toward Pueblo Azul?" asked Maria Rosa. "Haven't there been some contra attacks up that way recently?"

"We know the *contras* are near there, but they're usually further north toward the Honduran border," said Eddie. "We'll be back before dark, so we should be fine."

After breakfast, Eddie held open the jeep door and Lorna climbed in, careful not to brush her white skirt against the muddy door. She placed her blue nylon bag containing a bottle of cold water that was still cool against her leg on the floor.

He gunned the motor and they took off over the cobblestones. "Did I tell you I've been translating poetry, for fun?"

"Don't you ever do silkscreens any more? They were so beautiful," said Lorna.

"No. Silkscreens need too much studio space, equipment and time." He patted his breast pocket. "I keep a little notebook in here. My portable studio, you might say."

"So what are you translating?" she asked.

"Open my breast pocket and take out my notebook," he instructed, keeping his hands on the steering wheel as they bounced down the street.

Lorna carefully lifted out a little black notebook.

"OK, now turn to the third page after my sketches. Read that aloud," he ordered.

Lorna dutifully found Eddie's English translation, entitled "Zero Hour by Ernesto Cardenal," and recited:

> Tropical nights of Central America,
> with lagoons and volcanoes under the moon . . .

"That's as far as I got. So what do think? I wish I had more time to finish it," he said excitedly.

"It's a great start." she said, "I've been translating a major poem by Lionel Ruben. I met him in Managua. Are you familiar with his poetry?"

"Of course, he is one of Nicaragua's great older and respected poets. I'd like to translate his poetry, too. He is someone I want to get to know, but I never have any time."

"So what work keeps you too busy for art and poetry?" she asked, returning the notebook to his pocket.

"I've taken on tedious tasks, necessary tasks, and too many of them. We all do. When we committed to revolution, we didn't think about garbage collection, water distribution, and commodity prices. The people want miracles and want them *pronto*. And now, thanks to Reagan and John Negroponte, we have the *contras* on our border. We fought and won one war, and now we're fighting another. The *contras* are waging a dirty, undeclared war, Lorna, and it's funded by the United States. We build a school and they burn it down. We build a hospital, and the *contras* burn that down. So the only way to keep from feeling overwhelmed is to move faster. The area I'm taking you to isn't the safest, you know. We have to leave before dark."

An hour later, Eddie turned off the highway on to a sandy red dirt road. Palm trees lined the road, and there were fields of cotton on either side. A wagon drawn by two horses approached them, driven by a woman and her husband with his arm in a sling. Soon Eddie and Lorna found themselves overtaking a truck with an open back where six men sat and stood, holding on as the vehicle lurched around potholes. They passed a woman in a tight yellow skirt riding a bicycle. At a fork in the road, Eddie glanced at a map drawn inside a matchbook cover.

"Where are we?" asked Lorna.

"We should be close," said Eddie.

Red dust rose and swirled from the truck ahead of them and crept into their noses, mouths, eyes, and ears. Eddie tied his handkerchief over his face with only his eyes showing. He looked like a bandit. The road was a narrowing cut in a thick forest that scraped the side of the jeep as they drove along.

Lorna coughed, and her eyes teared. "Can you see, Eddie?"

"Barely," he answered through the handkerchief. "Roll up your window!"

They both rolled up the windows. Still the onslaught of red dust seeped in.

Lorna shouted, "Do you think this is the right way? It almost isn't a road."

"I followed the map," he yelled. His voice was muffled by the cloth, and his teeth were chattering as the jeep bounced down the road.

Then around a curve, the road opened into a valley of green fields, flowering trees, and blazing sunshine. A cluster of small houses and a white stucco church stood at the base of a small, rounded hill. It seemed less than a town, but it was clearly a community.

Lorna looked down at her white skirt. It had turned a terracotta red.

Eddie wiped his hair, face, and mustache with his grimy handkerchief. "Wherever we are, I think this is it. I think we're in Pueblo Azul."

Lorna blew her nose into a wrinkled tissue. This wasn't exactly what she had been expecting.

"Abuelo used to say, 'One day, Lornita, we will sail on the Queen Mary through the Panama Canal and take the train with our own private suite to Managua. My cousin Achilles will pick us up with the wagon and two pinto mares and we will ride in style to Pueblo Azul. In the cool of the twilight, we'll listen to the church bells and watch the fireflies dance. One day, Lornita, you will see my village.'"

"We sure didn't come on the Queen Mary," said Eddie.

"I always pictured more of a town."

"So has Nicaragua disappointed you, Lorna?" Eddie asked.

Lorna blew her nose again and looked at her dusty cotton skirt.

"I came to check out Grandfather's stories. All this time I've clung to them, Eddie. They kept me company when I was lonely. They put me to sleep when I was afraid of the dark. I guess I built up in my mind an imaginary Pueblo Azul. This is . . ." she paused, "Well, different. I never thought I'd really ever be in Pueblo Azul."

In the distance, a man in a faded blue shirt and an old wide-brimmed straw hat was approaching them. He was riding bareback, guiding his horse with a rope looped around its head for bridle.

"So are you disappointed?" Eddie repeated.

"I'm confused. I'm trying to bring the stories together with reality."

The rider was almost upon them, a worn, weather-beaten man of indeterminate age. Now he slid off the side of the horse. "*Buenos días, compañero,*" he greeted, acknowledging Eddie's uniform and weapon, but ignoring Lorna.

"We're looking for the Almendros place," Eddie answered in Spanish.

The man frowned. "The Almendros place?"

"This is Gabriel Almendros's granddaughter."

For the first time, the man acknowledged Lorna with a brief glance, then looked down, as if an ocean of class and culture separated them.

"Where is the Almendros place?" Eddie asked again.

The man pursed up his lips and jerked his head to indicate one of the small houses. It was white with a metal roof, and was fenced in by a low outer wall that faced the road. Two large banana trees sprouted huge fronds in the front yard.

The rider suddenly asked, "*Comandante*, can my daughter and I get a ride in your jeep to Las Palmas?"

"OK. We'll be here a few hours," said Eddie. "What's in Las Palmas?"

"The new clinic," the rider said. "My daughter has a fever." He pointed to the house farthest to the right. "I'll be there with the child," he said. Then he mounted his horse and rode off.

Eddie and Lorna drove on toward the hamlet. "Subsistence farming," said Eddie, looking at the fields surrounding the car. "Red beans, yellow corn, cotton, and maybe a little cattle. It's the cotton fields that makes the air so dusty."

"I can hardly stand it. The closer we get, the harder my heart pounds," muttered Lorna.

Eddie drove up to the house with the banana trees and parked in front. A young girl who looked about seventeen emerged from the yard. She smiled shyly as she dried her hands on her apron.

"Hello, *compañera*. Is this the Almendros place?" Eddie asked politely.

The girl nodded. She had a round moon face and brown hair pulled back behind her ears. Thin silver hoops hung from her earlobes. She wore a green blouse, and faded pedal pushers.

Then she smiled again at Lorna. "You're all dusty, doña."

Lorna replied in Spanish, "This was my white skirt. Now

it's red." The girl giggled.

"I'm Lorna Almendros," she continued in Spanish. "Gabriel Almendros was my grandfather, and I've come to visit his home. This is my friend, Lieutenant Eduardo Flores."

"I am called Arminda," said the girl. "There's no one here but me and Doña Milagro. My husband is at the dam. Would you like some water?" She led them toward the well.

This was where Abuelo washed himself, Lorna thought. Glancing toward the banana trees, she could almost see Abuelo reaching for the hanging fruit. She looked around for the mango and papaya trees that he had talked about, remembering the way their juices had dripped down his chin.

"Are we related?" Lorna asked the girl.

"I'm not an Almendros and neither is my husband. My husband is the son of Doña Milagro. Arturo Almendros was her first husband."

"Is this lady my aunt, or something? Arturo Almendros was my great-uncle," declared Lorna.

"I don't think so," Arminda said. "Arturo Almendros was her first husband, but Doña Milagro was his second wife. When Don Arturo died, she married my husband's father."

"This is complicated," Lorna said. "I need to make some sort of family tree of all this."

An old woman's voice screeched from somewhere inside the house. "Arminda! Arminda! Come here at once!"

"So she's your grandmother?"

"No. She is my husband's grandmother. But his father is not Arturo's son. Doña Milagro was married before Arturo."

Lorna's head was spinning.

The shouts from the house grew louder. "Arminda! Arminda!"

"That's her," Arminda whispered. "Wait here," she said, pouring water from a clay pot near the pump into two tin cups for them. "I'll be right back."

"It's a soap opera, Lorna," Eddie commented.

Lorna gulped her water. "When Grandfather left for the States, he left his mother, Doña Rosa, his baby sister who is

146

my great-aunt Rosita Delia, and his younger brother, Arturo. Arturo's first wife had no kids."

"It's clear to me that no one in that house is related to you today. Yet, you have the deed in your bag," Eddie said. "This is going to be interesting."

"The land was left to Grandfather because he was the oldest. I remember when he opened the letter telling that his mother had died. It was the only time I ever saw him cry. His sister had married a Honduran and moved away, leaving my great-uncle Arturo and his family here. Arminda says that after my great uncle Arturo died, Doña Milagro, who was his second wife, remarried, and that husband is Arminda's husband's grandfather."

"Well I'll be damned," said Eddie, pressing both palms to his temples. "So the world turns, or something."

"It's perfectly clear," Lorna explained. "Arturo Almendros's widow lives here, with her grandson from her second husband. That grandson's wife--our lovely young Arminda, looks too young to be married," Lorna added. "I wonder if the old woman will want to talk to me."

"Well, she better want to. After all, you have the deed to their house and the land. You could claim the house, take possession, and then where would she be?"

"Grandfather loved this place," reflected Lorna. "He loved the sunset, when the birds perch in the trees."

Arminda emerged. "Doña Milagro says to come in. I told her you were related to the Almendros."

From within, a voice could be heard, "Arminda! What's keeping you? You lazy slut, I need my pills. You can bring the visitors inside."

"We're coming, doña, we're coming," Arminda shouted back.

"Arminda! Arminda! Hurry up!"

"Yes, doña. We're coming."

After the intense sunlight, the darkness inside the house left Lorna momentarily blind, and she reached for Arminda's hand for guidance. The small fingers gave a light squeeze back as Arminda led Lorna into the center of the room.

"Doña Milagro," shouted Arminda toward the back room, "the visitors are here."

Lorna's eyes slowly adjusted. So this was grandfather's house, the setting for all his stories! The earthen floor, swept clean, lay hard and compacted. A wooden table and five chairs with woven straw seats were placed at one end of the room, with two carved rocking chairs facing an old television set. Between two open windows a smaller table held a water pitcher and glasses.

"A penny for your thoughts Lorna," Eddie said.

"I was thinking about my parents, my grandfather, and all those who came before. All of them may have spent time in this room."

"You talk so different, Doña Lorna," said Arminda, gently.

"I'm not from here," Lorna replied.

"You're from Managua?"

"I'm from the States. My grandfather emigrated there with my parents a long time ago. He returned in 1943 for a visit and died here."

"I heard something about it but I don't really know. I thought I knew all the old stories. Doña Milagro talks about old times a lot. Maybe she'll remember. Here she is now."

A bent, elderly woman entered with determined, slow steps.

"Doña Milagro," Arminda said. "These are your visitors. They are relatives of your first husband, Arturo Almendros."

"Not me," said Eddie hastily. "I am simply accompanying my friend. She is the granddaughter of Don Gabriel Almendros."

"Is that so?" replied Doña Milagro, shrewdly eying Lorna up and down, then switching her gaze onto Eddie's gun. "Just what do you want?"

"Doña, all is well," answered Eddie with great deference. "We're here on a social call. This lady, the granddaughter of Don Gabriel Almendros, only wanted to visit her family's home."

"Is that so?" repeated the older woman. Her eyes narrowed

with suspicion, her body alert, poised to strike.

"Yes, I am Lorna Almendros. Don Gabriel Almendros was my grandfather. I wanted to meet you and find my family."

Doña Milagro sneered, "Your family! Cutthroats, whores, and villains, like all the neighbors." She pointed to Arminda. "Like the family of this slut."

Lorna was shocked. Nothing Grandfather had ever said had even hinted of such a monstrous person as this woman. Lorna quickly realized that he must never have met her.

Arminda didn't react to Doña Milagro's meanness.

"Serve my guests some *fresco de papaya*. They probably never get anything good to eat in the city."

"Of course, doña," said Arminda.

"I'll help you," offered Lorna. She followed the young woman out into the yard, leaving Eddie to charm Doña Milagro as best he could.

When they were out of hearing range, Lorna asked softly, "Arminda, how do you stay so calm? Is she always so mean?"

Arminda picked a heavy ripe papaya dangling from the tree. "Oh, she's not so bad. Her feet are probably hurting." The papaya was the size of a small watermelon.

"Arminda, there is something I want to know. My grandfather is buried under an almond tree near here," Lorna said. "Do you know where?"

Arminda shook her head. "I don't, but my great-grandmother, Doña Angélica, might."

"Could we ask her?" urged Lorna.

Arminda placed the fruit in a tin bowl. "If Doña Milagro doesn't need me, we can go see my *mama abuela*. It will cheer her. I miss her so much. Before I moved to this house, I used to rub her feet every night. Now there's no one to do that. I think that's why she's sick."

"Does she live nearby?"

"It's two kilometers from the banana grove. With the lieutenant's jeep, we can drive there very fast. But *Doña* Milagro doesn't like me to go there."

"Why not?" probed Lorna.

"Because Doña Milagro was in love with my great-grandfather. She says my great-grandmother stole him away. Doña Milagro says God is punishing *Mama Abuela* for that, by sending her rheumatism."

Lorna was disliking Doña Milagro more and more.

Inside Eddie and Doña Milagro sat side by side in rocking chairs. Doña Milagro was laughing, her eyes riveted on Eddie.

Eddie now jumped to his feet, his hands waving madly. "Yes, doña, there were millions of them coming at us. I had left my rifle against the wall, so I grabbed a sheet off the clothesline and howled like a ghost! I tell you, I scared them off!"

"Oh, you dear crazy boy! I'm laughing so hard, I'm crying."

Arminda had peeled, seeded, and chopped the papaya, and now blended the pieces with water, adding a touch of salt and a generous amount of sugar. She filled the pitcher and glasses, placing them on a tray.

Doña Milagro was still howling with laughter as Arminda served the drinks.

"Doña, I wonder if you know where Don Gabriel Almendros is buried?"

Doña Milagro frowned, "*Don* Gabriel? Never met him." Then she excused herself to Eddie. "I must take my nap." She hobbled out of the room.

Glad to see her go, Lorna turned to Eddie. "Eddie," she said, "Arminda thinks she can help me find Grandfather's grave. Her great-grandmother was living here when he died. She lives two kilometers away, and Arminda can show us how to get there."

"We'll have to step on it," said Eddie. "Remember, the old man wants us to take his daughter to the clinic before we leave."

Arminda hung her apron on a peg. "I'll need to use the toilet."

"Me too," stated Lorna and Eddie almost at once.

Arminda led them to the outhouse. Lorna went first. She held her breath, and tried not to look into the hole. Sitting, she found an old issue of the opposition newspaper, *La Prensa*, torn into strips. Using *La Prensa* for toilet paper meant this was not a Sandinista household. If it were, they'd use *Barricada*, the Sandinista newspaper. Maybe that explained some of the nasty old woman's outbursts. Her side had lost.

When Lorna came out, she headed for the sink by the pump and washed her hands and face. Later, Eddie stuck his whole head under the spigot and let the water pour over his hair, ears and neck. "Ah, that feels much better."

"God, I'm so gritty from the trip, " Lorna said. "Maybe I should do that."

"Sure. I'll help you," said Arminda. She cut off a piece of an aloe vera plant, picked up a spoon and scraped out the inside.

Lorna leaned over the sink and unpinned her hair, letting the water splash through her curls down to her very scalp. It was cold and wonderfully refreshing. Arminda's fingers massaged the aloe vera into her scalp like a shampoo and then rinsed it, directing the water here and there.

"That feels wonderful. Thank you, Arminda. I'm so refreshed," said Lorna. "My hair will dry on the ride," she said combing it out.

"We better get a move-on," said Eddie, "if we're going have time to find everything." He gestured to Arminda to get in.

"Since *Doña* Milagro is taking her nap now, let's just go," said Arminda.

The jeep bounced along the road, with Arminda in the backseat. Lorna saw no almond groves. After a half mile, Arminda pointed. "That's it. That house over there by the *jocote* tree. It has such pretty little yellow plums. This is my house, where I used to live with my family before I married."

Eddie pulled over and parked. Lorna noted large birds roosting in the trees, looking like a Christmas illustration of a partridge in a pear tree.

"Those birds look familiar. What are they?" asked Lorna.

"Those are called chickens and turkeys," said Arminda kindly.

Lorna was embarrassed to show her urban ignorance.

"Not all fowl are as tame as Mother Goose," teased Eddie.

Arminda looked puzzled. "Who is Mother Goose?"

"No one," said Lorna. "He's just being silly."

Arminda led them across the hard-packed front yard to a porch with three carved wooden rocking chairs and a small table.

"Mama?" called Arminda into the house. "Where are you? I've brought friends."

A woman came from around the back. She was carrying a baby and was followed by a naked toddler holding a half-eaten tortilla. She looked a lot like Arminda, although when she smiled, she had a missing front tooth. She didn't look much over thirty.

"Doña Lorna," said Arminda, "this is my mother, Dora Magallenes."

"I am so happy to meet you," said Lorna. "This is my friend, Eddie. Lieutenant Flores."

Dora nodded. "I was worried when I saw a soldier and a Jeep. Everything has been so unsettled. Welcome. My house is your house." She turned to Arminda. "Arminda, could you bring the guests some of the lemonade I made this morning?"

"I'll help Arminda," Lorna said, and quickly followed Arminda into the dark interior. It had few windows and no glass panes. Something made her feel sure that Grandfather had been here too.

"Mama Abuela," Arminda called. A tiny, frail old woman in slippers slowly made her way into the room. Her smile beamed from waves of folded wrinkles.

"Sit, Mama Abuela," she said, taking the older woman's arm and guiding her to a chair. "Doña Lorna, this is my *mama abuela*, Doña Angélica. Doña Lorna is the granddaughter of *Don* Gabriel Almendros."

"Oh, my goodness, are you Lorna Alma? My little princess, my heavenly girl?" exclaimed *Doña* Angelica. "Come closer. Let me have a good look at you. I can hardly see these days. Stand in the light." Lorna moved closer to the window.

"Oh blessed Virgin, thank you," said Doña Angélica. "I never thought I'd see this day. I had given up all hope. But the truth be told, you've always been in my prayers, dear child. Sit down beside me, my angel."

Lorna obediently sat. Doña Angelica beamed at her. "Gabriel spoke about you so much. He showed me so many photographs of you. There you were, as a baby with your parents, God bless them. He showed me your beautiful first Holy Communion dress, looking so sweet in your little white veil and shoes. How the dear man loved you."

"You knew my grandfather?" asked Lorna, her heart trembling.

"Of course. We grew up together. I am your father's godmother. I was heartbroken when they all left for the States. Now I amuse myself remembering the good times we had together. That's how it is when you're old; you remember the past. He died in this house."

Arminda returned with lemonade.

"Is he buried here under your almond tree?"

"Oh, may God forgive me! I never thought a poet would create a mess of history."

"What poet?" asked Lorna.

"I am the poet!" answered Angélica, sitting higher in the chair. "Maria Angélica Magallenes Polo."

"I'm honored to meet you," declared Lorna. "But I don't understand what you mean about poetry and the mess of history."

"I refer, Lorna Alma, to my poem about him in which I say he was buried under the almond tree," said the woman, proudly. "But I meant it poetically, not factually. Gabriel is actually buried behind the church. But since his family name means almond tree, in my poem I used the image to suggest Gabriel had returned to his roots. Perhaps this is how legends are born—when the truth of the poet becomes the truth that endures."

"I know what you mean, Doña Angélica."

"Not Doña Angélica, but Compañera Angelica. Like your

grandfather, I am a Sandinista through and through."

"So you and my grandfather supported General Sandino back in the 1920s way before the new Sandinistas were even founded in the sixties."

"Yes, these young ones. Carlos Fonseca and Tomás Borge. But Augusto Sandino himself fought for decades before his dastardly assassination in 1934."

"Grandfather used to sing songs about him."

"We knew General Sandino was right to keep on fighting. He did not give up like the others. My generation was thrilled by the Mexican Revolution of 1912, by Pancho Villa, and Emiliano Zapata. Now we have won and I will die in peace and happiness."

"Please don't speak of dying, *compañera*."

"What a blessing that you are here. This is the answer to my prayers. When your grandfather died, I wanted you here with me. I was raising my own grandchildren. It wouldn't have been any more work to have one more child. And now you are here. All grown up and lovely. I always pictured you in your little white dress."

"I am also a poet, Compañera Angélica. But I've never heard your poem about grandfather."

Angélica pulled up into a concentrated posture in the chair and recited:

> He's gone to the almond grove
> his wanderer's heart burst in joy
> at this homecoming,
> where his boyhood leapt and danced.

"I can feel Grandfather in this very room," Lorna said, taking Angélica's delicate hand. "He is present and enjoying our reunion."

"The last time I saw Gabriel," said Doña Angélica, "he asked how I found time to write poetry, what with the grandchildren, and managing the house and farm. I answered him with this poem I'd written when we were young."

> In the light of the present

> I will make poems
> until there is no more present
> until there is no more light.
> Only the past is dark.

Lorna blinked away tears. "'Only the past is dark.' That is what Grandfather used to say when I was afraid of the dark. For years, I couldn't decipher it. How could the past be dark when if we turned out the lights the present was dark?"

"You see what trouble we poets cause?"

Lorna laughed, and sniffled.

"Gabriel told me the sad story of your dear parents' accident."

Lorna's voice became very small. "Did you know them?"

"Your father was my godson. Your mother was from the North; a very pretty girl. Fair skinned, like you."

Angélica squeezed her hand with a grasp as fragile and light as a butterfly.

"Do you have children Lornita?"

"Yes, a daughter, Irene Gabriela."

"Promise me you will bring me your Irene Gabriela. Now tell me one of your poems before I rest. I'm afraid I'm very tired now."

"I know so few of my poems by heart," Lorna said. But then the words flowed out.

> Hope falls from me
> softly like autumn leaves from an autumn tree
> softly as the petals of a rose,
> an old one falls and a new one grows
> I was not born a stranger but became one
> searching through language for words
> for home / belong / welcome
> My tongue tasted /friend /teardrop/bee
> I will not die a stranger
> I light my life like a friendly beacon
> for only the past is dark

Angélica clapped her hands. "You used my line! You are

truly my little girl. Bring me your Irene Gabriela. Does she have children?"

"No."

Doña Angélica looked concerned. "Is she ill?"

"She's not ready to get married. I promise to bring her." She kissed Angélica and helped her up. "Thank you for these moments."

Eddie barged in. "We have to hurry. That guy on the horse is outside waiting. I'm on duty tonight, so we'd better go now."

"I hate to leave, but I'm coming back. This house feels like home," Lorna said to Angélica.

The horseman followed them a half mile back down the road to the hamlet of Pueblo Azul. The sinking sun reflected off high mountains to the east. The father tied up his horse, disappeared into one of the adobe houses, and re-emerged with a ten-year-old girl wearing a baseball cap. Father and daughter climbed into the back seat, where they sat in silence.

Lorna fell silent, also, reliving all she had experienced in the past few hours.

Eddie looked at Lorna, speaking in English, for privacy. "When we left this morning, I hoped we'd have more time for ourselves. But I'm glad you've begun to connect with your family here." He slipped Lorna a white *sacuanjoche* flower.

"Yes, it's been very deep," said Lorna. "Thank you for bringing me here." She tucked the flower behind her ear and inhaled its scent deeply.

Eddie's hand touched her knee and she didn't move away, unable to resist his sympathetic gesture.

The man in the backseat suddenly shouted, "*¡Aqui! ¡Aqui!*" pointing to the side road they were in danger of missing. Eddie did a wild left turn over rocks and ruts, driving up a little hill, to a recently built, wooden building emblazoned with a hand lettered sign, "Clínica Rosalea Bandera."

"Clínica Rosalea Bandera?" Lorna said out loud. Her heart lurched. "Rosalea would be so proud. This was what her struggle was about, healthcare for rural adults and children, practical things like a clinic out here in the countryside."

The young girl in the backseat broke her silence. "Rosalea Bandera was the first woman guerrilla to die in the fighting in our zone."

The father thanked Eddie before climbing out of the jeep with his daughter.

Eddie took a deep breath and turned to Lorna. "Alone at last," Eddie said.

Lorna was already climbing out of the jeep. "Eddie, I have to visit this clinic for a minute. Do you remember when you arranged for me to host Rosalea in San Francisco?"

"OK, but just for a minute," said Eddie, following her. "I have to be back for my shift. It's going to get dark soon, not really safe."

They greeted the militia guard standing sentry at the door. He wore jeans and a Miami Dolphins T-shirt, but carried an M-1 rifle and seemed tense. He said something to Eddie that Lorna didn't catch, as she hurried inside.

Following her inside, Eddie reported in a low voice, "He says there's been trouble since the clinic opened." Lorna looked around the large rough room with unpainted wood walls covered with posters of cartoon characters advocating hand-washing and boiling drinking water. A receptionist counter stood back from the entrance. Small triangle-shaped red-and-black Sandinista banners dangled across the doors like leftover party decorations. Women, sitting on benches and chairs around the walls, nursed their infants, while keeping an eye on their other children. Some of the women were young and looked worn. Many were pregnant.

As the sick girl's father spoke with one of the receptionists, the door behind the counter opened. A young, beautiful Black woman bounced out, wearing a white shirt, tight white jeans, and high-heeled sandals with a stethoscope dangling around her neck. Her ebony skin glowed and her hair puffed out in a soft Afro. She was holding a clipboard.

"Go home to bed for three days," the doctor said to a mother carrying an infant. "You need more rest." Lorna detected a Cuban accent.

Eddie bolted to the young doctor's side. "Hello, *compañera*. So you're one of the volunteer Cuban doctors I've been reading about? I knew Cuba was sending its medical personnel, but I didn't understand Cuba was sending us all its beautiful women."

Lorna was appalled at his boldness.

The doctor drew herself up, holding her head high as she looked at him. She seemed amused but hardly impressed by attentions from men. Her color, her high energy, her completely confident manner, set her apart.

"*Compañero*, we beautiful women of Cuba are here for solidarity with Nicaragua and its people. You should see the beautiful stitches I did today. And the beautiful medicines I prescribed."

The doctor winked at Lorna, a big warm conspiratorial wink. "Hello, doctor," Lorna responded. "I knew Rosalea Bandera."

"I'm honored to meet you," said the doctor, moving forward to shake Lorna's hand.

Eddie, staying hot on the doctor's heels, said, "I knew her too."

Before he could say anything more, a woman holding a squirming child on her lap cried out, "I've waited long enough. It's my turn to see the doctor."

"Certainly, *compañera*, go ahead," answered the Cuban doctor, cutting Eddie off and nodding good-bye as she motioned the woman into the examining room.

"Wait," urged Eddie to the doctor, "when can I see you again? Can you come to Managua on Sunday? There's a big party at the Ministry of Culture in the afternoon, and Grupo Mancotal and Los Compas are playing. I have an invitation for two."

"I don't have a ride," the doctor said, over her shoulder. She was about to close the door.

"I'll find you one! Meet me in the lobby of the InterContinental hotel at eleven thirty in the morning," persisted Eddie. He was shouting at her back as the door was closing.

The doctor put her head through the half-open door, laughing. "I'll ask my friend about transportation."

Back in the jeep, Lorna said, "I can hardly believe this doctor was actually falling for your routine, Eddie. Maybe doctors aren't as smart as they're cracked up to be. This one is so young, she must be right out of medical school." Lorna ripped the flower out of her hair and tossed it out the window.

"It's getting late," Eddie said, starting the jeep. "We better get a move-on."

Once on the road, they traveled in silence. The choking dust returned, and the road was hard to manage in the twilight. Eddie's hand reached out to the back of Lorna's neck. "Poor baby, you must be tired. It's been a long day. I'm sorry we never got to the graveyard."

Lorna moved his hand away briskly. "That's fine. I'll come back another day."

He dropped his hand to her thigh. "Maybe we could pull over."

She knocked his hand away. "In your dreams. Aren't you worried about getting back in time for your shift? Isn't it dangerous to be here after dark? I hope your little flirtation with the doctor hasn't delayed you too much."

"Lorna, I'm flattered. You're jealous."

"I am not."

"You're jealous. But don't be. The Cubans are doing so much to help rebuild Nicaragua. It's very important to make them feel welcome."

"Make them feel welcome?!" repeated Lorna, outraged. "You're incredible, Eddie. Just incredible. Who named you the one-man welcoming committee?"

"I can't help it, Lornita," said Eddie, apologetically. "She's wrapped like a curvy tamale. You know how I am."

Lorna found that even more irritating. "I do know how you are. That's why I'm so mad. Now watch the road. You're going too fast." They lapsed into silence again. It was after dark when they arrived. Maria Rosa was outside waiting for them.

"Eddie," said Maria Rosa. "*Comandante* Camilo phoned. He said to go to headquarters immediately. The contras have burned down the Rosalea Bandera Clinic."

"Oh my god. I hope everyone got out safely," said Lorna, engulfed by a giant wave of fear.

"It was after hours," said Maria Rosa. "But the night guard was killed."

Eddie nodded, his jaw clenched. "The bastards," he muttered. He brushed Lorna's cheek with his lips, jumped back in the jeep, and was gone in a cloud of engine exhaust.

Maria Rosa was shaking her fists, almost crying. "Every time we build something, the contras destroy it. Volunteers slaved to build that clinic. I gave a class in childbirth preparation there. It's been my dream to be able to give workshops in a free clinic, in a free Nicaragua. Who could believe a clinic could become a battlefield?" Maria Rosa looked at Lorna, now seeing the terracotta skirt, the dust on her arms and face. She ordered, "Go clean up, woman, you're filthy."

In the shower, red powder flowed down Lorna's arms in cool rivulets, pooling in pink puddles at her feet. She lathered her hair again and again, until the water ran clear. Toweling off, she reflected how her meeting with Doña Angélica in the afternoon seemed already part of the dark past. She prayed the Cuban doctor and all those people waiting in the clinic were safe. Rosalea Bandera's red hair burned in her memory, evoking her dread that the clinic might now be a mound of glowing ashes. "The past is dark and the present rages with pain," she murmured to herself.

15

Rebuilding

Two weeks later, Lorna was back in Las Palmas helping to rebuild the Rosalea Bandera Clinic. She was one of many volunteers working around the still-intact foundation of the burned out building.

"Get moving!" shouted Úrsula, the crew boss, in Spanish. She was a thick rough woman with a bulldog-like face, clearly used to giving orders. Lorna's eyes popped open. She was dozing, standing up with her chin resting on the handle of the shovel. She'd had precious little sleep for the past two nights, and now the heat and humidity in Las Palmas was unbearable. She was having trouble sleeping in a strange place. So, before falling asleep each night, she would translate a few more lines of Lionel Ruben's poem by flashlight in her cot.

She had met with the poet a few days ago through Carlota Pérez. Carlota and Lorna met for coffee so Lorna could fill her in on Friends of Nicaraguan Culture's activities. Carlota leaned forward over the table, and said, "My friend Lionel Ruben, a great poet of the older generation, just wrote a formidable epic poem about the planetary crisis. It is filled with the flora and fauna of Nicaragua, which is only now, since the revolution, being more deeply investigated and documented. Lionel is hoping it could be translated. Would translating the poem interest you? I can arrange a meeting."

"Yes. Definitely. I would love to meet him. I've heard him speak, but never met him," Lorna replied. They met the next day. He was a tall, white-haired man, dressed in a guayabera and an elegant straw hat. Lorna was thrilled to meet a poet of the stature of Lionel Ruben. She had seen him on her first visit to Nicaragua, but he seemed much older now. He handed her a folder containing several typed pages. "I hope you will like the poem," he said in a friendly but distant way. "It is my finest work."

Lorna accepted the folder, and said, "I am thrilled to translate this for you. I'll bring you a draft of my translation before I leave."

"Thank you," he replied, with a fleeting smile and invited her to bring it to his office in the Ministry of Culture.

Now she was dozing on her shovel after staying up translating his words.

"You're getting nowhere, *yanka*," Úrsula snarled. "Hand that shovel to Rabbit. You go help Frenchy distribute water."

Yanka. The word echoed in Lorna's head, setting off an inner rant about how demeaning it was. It was a derogatory word used in Nicaragua for over a century to describe wives of North American businessmen, plantation owners, diplomats, and marines. Lorna resented it being used on her, an internationalist solidarity worker who was breaking her butt. Someone named Almendros, whose family was from Pueblo Azul only a few kilometers away. She concluded that Úrsula didn't give a damn about being liked.

For the past week, Lorna and Maria Rosa had been part of a volunteer brigade to rebuild the Rosalea Bandera Clinic, although, to Lorna's disappointment, Maria Rosa had then been reassigned to a different project farther north, but she would be returning to this crew soon.

Relieved and resentful, Lorna handed the shovel to a thin young man, barely twenty. His fair skin had turned splotchy from the tropical sun. He looked embarrassed for her. Straightening her shoulders, Lorna trudged up the hill, tasting something salty, like sweat or tears, or both.

Frenchy, a volunteer from France named Carla, a very blonde woman, visibly pregnant, was pouring water from a big tank into buckets in a shady spot under a wide-canopied *guanacaste* tree.

Hi, Carla. Úrsula sent me here to help you. I'm Lorna. May

I have some water, please?

"Of course," smiled Carla, pouring water into a metal cup and handing it to Lorna.

"Thanks," said Lorna. "So when are you due?"

"Next month. I hoped my mother would come from France. But she's afraid of planes."

An English-speaking voice with an American accent interrupted them. It came from an old man walking vigorously toward them up the hill. "Got a cool drink, sisters? I'm hot and dry as a cactus," he said as he joined them in the shade.

With a smile, Carla filled another tin cup. "For you, brother."

"You sound French," he said.

"I am from Marseilles."

"*Enchanté*, madame. Jimmy Greene's the name; Abraham Lincoln Brigade's the fame, now with the International Longshoremen's Union in San Francisco."

"What is the Abraham Lincoln Brigade?" the Frenchwoman asked.

"Americans who fought in the 1930s during the Spanish Civil War. They called us 'premature anti-fascists' because the US didn't start fighting fascism until later when World War II broke out. A few of us oldsters are here now helping build the medical centers. Or rebuild," he said, looking around. "Damn shame when my own government destroys a health clinic. So what are your names, *compañeras*?"

"I'm Carla."

"And I'm Lorna, also from San Francisco."

"So what's little junior here?" he asked, pointing at Carla's belly. "Is he a Frenchman or a Nicaraguan?"

Lorna flinched; the question felt very rude.

"A revolutionary," Carla said. Lorna silently applauded her answer.

A second white-haired volunteer was trudging up the hill. He slowly lowered himself to the ground in the shade of the *guanacaste*. "Water! Give me water!" he said, crawling forward toward Carla, holding his hand in a comic beseeching manner.

The other three laughed at his theatrics. Carla poured a cup of water for the newcomer.

"Thank you, ma'am!" He slurped from the cup greedily. "So let me introduce myself. Name's Fred, Lincoln Brigade vet. And by the way, watch out ladies! Jimmy has a way with women!"

"I had a way," corrected Jimmy. "Don't get around much, anymore. If you know what I mean."

"What group are you with?" asked Fred.

"I'm not with any group," answered Lorna. "I came to Nicaragua to visit my daughter. She's working on a dam project in the north, near Jinotega."

"How long have you been working here?" continued Fred.

"This is my first week," answered Lorna. "It's hard though. I'm not used to manual labor."

"Ho ho," responded Fred. "At last! A bourgeois tells the truth."

"I'm a talk-and-write sort of person, not a lift-and-dig," said Lorna.

"Lift and dig? That's the story of my life. I went to sea at fifteen, started work as a longshoreman just in time for the 1934 San Francisco general strike, and I've stayed with the union ever since. I like hard work. Keeps me young. So I'm here on my vacation," said Fred.

"I'm surprised Úrsula isn't down on your case, Lorna. She don't put up with no softies," said Jimmy.

Carla listened with interest to the English conversation. "Oh, that Úrsula," she said in her French-accented limited English.

"Not to worry," said Lorna. "Úrsula's down on my case all the time. She wasn't happy with my ditch digging talents, so she sent me to help Carla."

Lorna spied young Marcos striding briskly up the hill. He was another of Maria Rosa's innumerable cousins. With his good manners and English, he had found a position in the Ministry of Foreign Relations helping to oversee the work of international volunteers. He was slim and earnest, wearing an unbuttoned short-sleeved white shirt that managed to look crisp even in the heat. He called out, "What's all this laughing about? Tell me, I need a good laugh."

"They're making fun of me," confessed Lorna. "I was so tired, I fell asleep on my shovel."

"You old people shouldn't work so hard," Marcos said, stepping into the tree's shade.

Stung, Lorna thought that surely he must be able to see that she was decades younger than these Abe Lincoln brigadiers.

Marcos continued on, "We worry you'll wear yourselves out. You *viejos* work so hard and fast."

Jimmy growled, "Don't worry about us. We've been working hard since before you were born. We'll rest when we get home."

"Rest is for the graveyard. This working is good for the soul. We're working for the people, not for some stinking capitalist," added Fred.

Marcos ignored their irritation and went on, earnestly. "We worry when we see you white haired people working so hard in the hot sun. Look at *Brigadista* Polly over there. Pushing the wheelbarrow nonstop since breakfast. I begged her to take a break, but she wouldn't listen to me."

"Polly was a nurse in Spain. She's like a tank. Don't try to argue with her. She'll roll right over you," said Jimmy. "That's the Brigade spirit!"

"Marcos!" Úrsula yelled. "There's someone here for you from the Ministry," she said in Spanish.

"Excuse me, *compañeros*," Marcos said in English as he was leaving. "I have to go. But please rest. You're not used to this sun. Take it slow."

"That's music to my ears," said Lorna.

"Music?" said Jimmy. He pulled out a harmonica. He winked at Carla, then played "*Après de Ma Blonde.*" Then he played a mournful "*La Vie en Rose.*" "Edith Piaf," he told them, then shifted into tune of the "Arkansas Traveler." From her station at the bottom of the hill, Úrsula must have heard the harmonica and laughter.

"Hurry up, *compañera*," she shouted up to Lorna. "Come back down here and help Rabbit carry these boards. Hurry up!"

"Oh, damn," Lorna said in English. "Just as I'm enjoying myself, the wicked witch finds me."

Jimmy gave her a hand as she struggled to her feet. "Don't worry, Sister Lorna. We'll talk again."

"You Abe Lincoln vets are good for me," Lorna said. She found herself running down the hill.

Rabbit was standing at one end of a stack of boards. Lorna squatted, taking the other end, slowly rising, and off they went on the rough, pitted ground, past rubble and supplies, to set them down near the foundation of the old clinic.

"What's your real name?" Lorna said to the young man. "Úrsula belittles people with her horrible nicknames."

"Tom, ma'am. From New Zealand, ma'am."

"You're really far from home."

"Not far enough," he said.

"I'm Lorna, from California."

Tom's face lit up. "When we finish building this clinic, I'm hitching to Honduras, then Guatemala, up through Mexico, and then to California. Can I stay with you, ma'am?"

This was unexpected, and before Lorna could frame an answer, she heard a woman's voice calling. "¡Oye, *compas!*" The accent was unmistakably Cuban. Lorna turned. The Cuban doctor was bounding up the hill toward another crew. Her tight white jeans were as spotless and dazzling as Lorna had remembered them. Even though Lorna had been told that the doctor had survived, this was the first time she'd actually laid eyes on her. She was so relieved. Lorna had worried that she had died in the explosion. On top of that, she felt guilty about her jealousy. She was grateful the doctor was safe and was glad to be in Nicaragua with the opportunity to help rebuild the clinic named after Rosalea. She rejoiced even under Úrsula's rule. A mean-tempered brute of a woman was her boss, but it's what she'd asked for. A revolution. Warts and all.

Úrsula's voice pierced her reverie. "Now what, *compañera?* You're staring into space again. Is Rabbit supposed to do the job all by himself?" She pointed irritably at the rest of the boards.

Lorna took a mollifying tone. "I'm sorry, Úrsula, I was just thinking about how amazing you are. How did you ever learn so much about construction?"

"You do the first thing, and that leads to the second, the second leads to the third, and so on. The first thing is to bring the boards from here to there," barked Úrsula. Clearly she wasn't having any of it. "We'll talk later," the crew boss said, walking away.

Lorna rankled under Úrsula's shouts and orders. She was a *Yanka* and nothing Lorna could ever do would please her. Lorna and Rabbit lifted another stack of boards, carried them to the foundation, and set them down. Carried another stack, walked them over, and set them down. That was the pattern of the afternoon. After many such trips, Rabbit asked, as if he had just remembered, "So can I stay with you when I come to San Francisco, ma'am?"

"You don't have to call me Ma'am. Please call me Lorna.'"

"I'm sorry. It's just a habit when I talk to older ladies."

"When are you planning to come, Tom?" Lorna didn't catch his answer, because Úrsula was shouting an announcement about a break.

Portable grills had been set up under the *guanacaste* tree where women warmed tortillas with white melted cheese and shredded cabbage. Carla handed out plastic bags of water, tied at the top with tiny straws sticking out. Lorna found herself behind Úrsula in the food line.

"So, Úrsula, what did you do before the Sandinista victory?"

"When the *Guardia* killed my parents, I ran away to the mountains and joined the *guerrillas*. They gave me a pair of boots and a gun. I learned to clean and shoot an M1 rifle. As I said, one step leads to another."

"Were you the only woman?"

"Not at all. Half of us were women. I was under the

command of a woman. Comandanta Rosalea Bandera. This clinic is named after her."

Lorna was stunned. "You knew Rosalea Bandera?"

"I fought under her command. I did not know her."

"So you fought near here?"

"A lot of us fought around here, *yanka*," said Úrsula. The line moved up. Úrsula did not seem inclined to talk further, and while Lorna was sorting out her wildly flying thoughts, she found herself at the head of the line, facing the food server, a short toothless woman.

"You want more sauce?" the woman asked.

"No, thanks," Lorna said, feeling the loss of her friend, the red-headed poet. If only Rosalea were here, alive and well instead of this troll of a woman, this Úrsula, who could have told her so much, but would barely speak to her.

She found a comfortable spot next to Carla, Jimmy, Fred, and Polly. Other gray headed vets Lorna did not know filled out the circle.

"Hey, kid, meet the folks," said Jimmy. "Attention one and all. Know ye that this beauty is Lorna Almendros from San Francisco. She's not with any delegation; she just wanted to help out. And she's come to Nicaragua looking for love. Any questions?"

"I have not come to Nicaragua looking for love," objected Lorna. She was laughing, but she wondered why he would even say that.

Jimmy shrugged, lifting his eyebrows, which seemed to say, really?

"Don't pay attention to those geriatric Lotharios," said Polly. "They'll say anything to try to get you to sign on for more volunteer work."

Jimmy pulled out his harmonica and blew a Bach fugue. Carla stretched out on the grass and rested her head on Lorna's lap. Her round pregnant belly rose like a volcano when she breathed.

"You Abe Lincoln guys make me feel young," Lorna said. "Everyone is so young in Nicaragua. I'm usually the oldest person around. My daughter says she feels old in Nicaragua and she's only in her late twenties."

"Hey, my daughter is going to be fifty next Thursday," said another white-haired vet. He had a British accent.

"Where are you from?" asked Lorna.

"From London. Retired docker and chairperson of the Nicaraguan Solidarity Committee. I'm also a Spanish Civil War vet."

Lorna caught another glimpse of the slim figure dressed in white, headed toward the water tank. "Carla, do you know that Black woman over there?"

"You mean the Cuban doctor? The one in the sexy white jeans?"

"What's her name?"

"Dr. Daisy Varela. She's wonderful. She saved my baby when I was spotting."

"She seems too young to be a doctor."

"The Cubans churn doctors out and send them off as a form of foreign aid. Daisy worked in Angola, as well. She's in her twenties. Like your daughter."

"I've never known a doctor to wear high-heeled sandals and tight white pants. She's so young, not like any doctor I've ever known."

"If your American doctors are as bourgeois as our French ones, she's probably not like any doctor you've ever known. She may be a doctor, but she's also a working class woman. In Cuba, medical schools are free. Revolution means all people can fulfill their dreams and potential, no matter what their origins. I want a world like that for my baby. Daisy must sense we're talking about her. She's coming our way," said Carla sitting up and waving to the doctor.

"*Hola, chicas,*" said Daisy. "How are you doing?"

All the vets stopped talking as the sexy Cuban came over.

Daisy extended her hand to Lorna. "I remember you. You're a friend of Eddie's. You and I met the day the clinic burned, remember? My name is Daisy."

"I'm Lorna Almendros. I'm so glad you're all right," Lorna

said, realizing that Eddie and the doctor were already seeing each other.

"Back to work!" shouted Úrsula and they all scattered.

16

Life of the Soul

That evening, Lorna stepped into an outdoor shower behind an improvised wall, hanging her clothes on a nail. She was grimy and sticky. Outside, Polly waited her turn. Lorna felt lonely without Maria Rosa there. This shower reminded her of summer camp, of how she felt when daylight faded and she would miss her grandfather so badly. She washed her hair quickly with cucumber shampoo she bought from a health food store near Luis's office back in San Francisco. Luis didn't think much of her cucumber shampoo, Lorna remembered. He claimed he didn't understand why a woman would want to smell like a cucumber. She had bought it anyway, in an act of defiance, feeling that she did not have to please him, or any man for that matter. After all these years, she and Luis had never made it past the flirtation stage. No wonder she felt lonely. A wry smile crossed her face as she reflected on the irony that Luis, who would have loved all this hard dirty work, was back home. And she, who suffered with all the dirty work, was here by herself. She slipped into her sandals and put on clean shorts and a T-shirt.

"The Jalapa group is returning tonight," said Polly, on her way into the shower.

"Oh, good. My friend Maria Rosa is part of that group."

As Lorna made her way on the short trail to the food line, she saw Maria Rosa, laughing, talking to a very tall man Lorna had not seen before. He was taller than anyone else in the crowd and from a distance appeared to be extremely handsome, with broad shoulders, and soft wavy black hair that curled at the ends. But then she lost sight of Maria Rosa and the stranger as they were quickly swallowed up by the groups of volunteers.

Lorna came upon Úrsula, who was supervising the food service. Since the brief conversation at lunch, she'd felt the very slightest softening in the crew boss's demeanor. "Who is that tall man, head and shoulders above everyone?" Lorna asked her.

"He's with the Ministry of Housing," Úrsula replied, turning her back on Lorna.

Walking along, Lorna recalled Helen's voice from an old conversation they had in San Francisco. "No, no, no! You can't use romance for escape."

Lorna had argued back, "Am I doomed to live without passion? What about love?"

"First, love yourself," Helen had said. "Then you'll find a real partner."

"I love myself plenty," she had said impatiently. "I treat myself to the little luxuries, like the cucumber soap, pretty hair bands, and sparkly earrings. Loving myself is not the problem."

Now Maria Rosa spotted Lorna and called her to join her in the food line. But the man wasn't there.

"*Hola, hola!* I want you to meet Guillermo Villanova. I was telling him about you, your grandfather, and the people you met when you were trying to find his house."

"The tall man you were talking to?" Lorna said, feeling suddenly shy.

Maria Rosa looked around and called out, "Guillermo!" and made space for him next to them in the line.

The tall man reappeared out of the crowd. He looked even more handsome close-up than from a distance. His black hair shone blue against his dark skin. His eyes seemed to penetrate deeply and, if you looked into them long enough, there was something to be found.

"Guillermo, I want you to meet my good friend, Lorna Almendros. Her grandfather came from Pueblo Azul."

"So this is the beautiful friend you were telling me about," he said, lifting Lorna's hand and kissing it. The grave expression of the mouth gave way to a devastatingly wide smile. "Welcome to Nicaragua, *Compañera*. Maria Rosa has told me so much about you." His baritone voice was mellow and low. To Lorna he look so young, like everyone in this country; maybe he was in his thirties at most.

"Guillermo is with the Ministry of Housing," said Maria Rosa. "He is an architect and an engineer."

"I'm neither an architect nor an engineer, but I'm getting a lot of hands-on experience in the building trades here," said Lorna. "It isn't easy."

"No, and we are so grateful when you *norteamericanos* volunteer to help," he said. "It's not easy. After six years we're still rebuilding what Somoza destroyed. Not to mention what your US-backed *contras* are destroying."

His reference to "your US *contras*" made her sad. She and others couldn't do enough to offset the terrible consequences of US policy in Central America.

"Welcome back to the land of your ancestors, *compañera*," he was saying. She could feel something opening up inside her, as he met her eyes with his searching and quiet gaze.

"Have you seen the ancient ones?" he asked, holding her eyes with his. "I'm referring to the huge stone statues as tall as I am carved to represent humans and animals, found around Lago de Cocibolca. There are similar statues at Nawawasito, in Chontales, and many more on the Isla de Zapatera. The richness of our culture is unimaginable."

"No, but I've heard about them," Lorna said.

"They are the legacy of our ancestors, but a legacy that is so poorly understood. How our ancestors used these statues is mysterious. Some believe they guarded sacred places used for worship or even for human sacrifice. Little research has been done."

"Human sacrifice," shuddered Lorna.

"*Compañera*, one way or another, human sacrifice has been a constant in Nicaragua's history. Consider how many people have died in our revolution. We are fortunate that these figures endure and that the Christian fathers did not find them, or surely they would have smashed them in their conquest. And even now we have to fear the rapacious international art market, and the museum anthropologists."

"I would love to see them," said Lorna.

"Perhaps we could go together," said Guillermo.

She looked at him silently, wondering if he was serious or not.

He went on, "I believe these statues are from our own Indigenous ancestors. But some anthropologists believe early African traders sailed to South America on the ocean currents, long before Columbus. They have found statues in Mexico with African features and claim ours are African too. Do you know the work of the Caribbean scholar Ivan Van Sertima? I have to ask myself, between the Euro centrists and the Afro centrists, where do we Latin Americans stand? Even our ancestors are stolen from us."

"My grandfather used to talk about the ancestors' footprints, fleeing the volcano, but I'd always thought that was a fantasy story for children."

"*Las huellas de Acahualinca* are no fantasy," said Guillermo. His eyes had not left hers. "Come with me. Let's go there."

Someone cutting through the line jostled Guillermo into Lorna. As their bare arms touched, a jolt passed from Guillermo to Lorna.

Maria Rosa stood up on her toes. "Can you see what they're serving?"

"I don't have to look," Lorna told her. "*Nacatamales* and shredded cabbage. We have the same menu every night. A lot of the volunteers feel bad that we're fed so lavishly while children go hungry."

"In Jalapa, we drank warm soda pop for three days because the contras had knocked out the electricity," said Maria Rosa. "The CIA and President Reagan should go without water. They might rethink their insane policies. Ah, but I hear Úrsula calling me. Keep my place in line. I'll go see what she wants."

Lorna and Guillermo moved closer. She noticed his cap of black hair, the silky ends curling at the back of his neck.

"Lorna, how long will you be here?"

"A few more weeks," she said, mechanically while her mind whirled on some other track entirely. "I'm waiting to see my daughter. She's an electrical engineer. She's been working on a little power plant and dam in the north, but she's coming down to Managua soon, so we can spend time together." She had put it out there. She was the mother of an adult daughter, a professional engineer, capable of making electrical power.

"Would you consider remaining in Nicaragua like your daughter, *Compañera* Lorna?"

His question caught her off guard. "You mean never leaving? I can't think about that. It's like trying to think about infinity."

"For me," said Guillermo. "The worst thing would be having to leave Nicaragua. The revolutionary process is too amazing to miss even one day. So tell me about your grandfather and your family. Where are you looking for your family?"

"I've been to Pueblo Azul. I met a very old woman who'd been a friend of my grandfather's. Doña Angélica. She is wonderful. She was godmother to my father. She attended my parents' wedding. The most marvelous part is that she is also a poet. She recited one of her poems to me."

"Your ancestors are here. Your daughter is here, Lorna Alma. What if you reconnected to your roots? Then would you stay?"

Lorna Alma is what Grandfather and Angélica had called her. "Do you believe in the soul?" Lorna asked.

"I believe the soul loves the body but leaves it. You can see the soul is gone in dead people, or even dead animals, or dead plants. The soul is the life force."

"And what about love?" Lorna asked, not believing she was having this conversation. She didn't have these kinds of conversations in English. Spanish seemed to lend itself more easily to soulful conversations. "I believe that love is a force too," she blurted. "Like a cloud that passes over us. Or maybe we walk right into it."

The smoke from the outdoor wood fires carried with it the smells of roasting banana leaves and meat. The food line began moving faster. Lorna moved up in the line to first place, with Guillermo so close behind her she felt his chest, his legs touching her.

"Is that so?" inquired the toothless woman, who was serving Lorna. She had placed a warm bundle neatly tied in a banana leaf on her plate. "I think two people fall in love when they're both lonely and horny."

The other servers laughed. Lorna felt a flush mount in her face. The word "horny" distressed her.

Guillermo moved up and extended his plate. "Thank you, *compañeras*, for your wisdom and your good food." He did not seem embarrassed.

Lorna took a seat on a stack of lumber, offering Guillermo a place beside her. She untied her *nacatamal* to find shredded beef, potatoes and carrots in savory sauce marked by the flavor of banana leaf.

"I'm fortunate to arrive at dinner time. I've had no lunch," Guillermo said.

"What brought you here?" asked Lorna.

"The *responsable* at a cooperative farm complained that a case of eight-penny nails had been delivered by mistake. They had ordered shovels. I remembered Úrsula needed those nails and that the Abraham Lincoln Brigade had donated extra shovels here. So I came to see if I could trade the nails for shovels."

"Oh, your nails are the answer to our prayers," said Lorna, hoping it was fate that really brought him.

"I also need to locate the Cuban doctor. Have you met Dr. Daisy?"

"A remarkable young woman," Lorna said, hiding her disappointment.

"Yes, we are grateful for all the medical assistance from Cuba," he said. "But had I known I'd be meeting you, I would have come sooner." Lorna smiled. "But if I had, I might have missed meeting you here on the food line. So it's all for the best. My streak of bad luck is ending."

"You're so young. I hope your bad luck has not been going on too long," Lorna said.

"Not so young. The war speeds things up."

"How old are you?" asked Lorna. She was being *gringa* direct.

"I'm thirty-eight. Does it matter?" He lowered his voice. "Death can come at any age."

Maria Rosa returned with a group of boys following her, the very oldest no more than fifteen, and most appeared to be younger. "Úrsula wanted me to take them to the bus."

"Our militia reserve unit has been called up," announced the oldest one. A chill passed through Lorna. They were too young even to shave. Through the tree branches, she spied a brilliant star and made a silent prayer to keep these boys safe.

After they walked on, white-haired Fred pulled up a plastic chair in front of Lorna and Guillermo. "Lorna, help me finish talking to this engineer about the shovels." Lorna translated a discussion between Guillermo and Fred.

Guillermo glanced at the luminous face of his watch. "*Compañera* Lorna, please translate that on behalf of the revolutionary people of Nicaragua and the Ministry of Housing, I extend heartfelt thanks and appreciation to *Compañero* Fred and the Brigade for their strong show of solidarity."

He turned to her. "And to you, *Compañera* Lorna, this one solitary Nicaraguan thanks you from the bottom of his heart, which he leaves in your good care until we meet again." He bowed slightly, then glanced again at the luminescent dial. "I'm late, and I need to be going. I'm expected in the capital tonight."

Lorna refrained from asking by whom.

"I'm leaving for Havana," Guillermo said. "To attend the Habitat Conference. May I contact you at Maria Rosa's house when I return?"

"You're going to Cuba?" asked Lorna.

"Yes. That's why I hoped to see the doctor. She has letters and photos for me to deliver to her family."

"Yes, by all means, contact me at Maria Rosa's," said Lorna happily.

"What did he say?" asked Fred, who had been listening.

"He said, 'Good-bye.' Even as she spoke, Guillermo had disappeared into the darkness.

The next day Lorna awoke feeling joyful. It was Friday, and the work shift lasted only until noon, when trucks would arrive to transport the volunteers back to Managua. She stretched luxuriously on her cot, looking up at the sky just beginning to lighten. In the trees surrounding the women's sleeping area, unfamiliar birds were chirping and whistling.

"This day is full of promise and adventure," she sang out to Maria Rosa in the cot next to her. "I can hardly wait for breakfast. Even the San Francisco food police would approve rice, beans, and tortillas." She stretched again. "You know that crew boss, Úrsula, that I was complaining about? She's not so bad. She fought under Rosalea Bandera. She was separated from her family at such an early age and grew up with a bunch of male *guerrilleros* in the mountains. If she's brusque, it's because she didn't have a mama to comb her hair and teach her softness."

Maria Rosa was already dressed. "Look at you, eager to jump out in the hot sun and obey orders from that pit bull Úrsula. What's going on?"

"I think it's your friend Guillermo. He'll back in a few days. He said he would get in touch with me."

"So for the next few days you'll be all sunshine and roses?" asked Maria Rosa, stuffing her gear into a backpack.

"Does he have a girlfriend?" Lorna asked.

"Not that I know of."

"Or is he living with someone?"

"He had a wife, but my understanding is she left him."

"Hmmm. Well, for now, my feet are firmly planted on a cloud."

"He's very idealistic, Lorna. I think he may be married to the revolution."

"Well, we'll form a ménage à trois, Guillermo, the revolution, and me."

"So this is what happens when a dirty old woman meets a pure young man," laughed Maria Rosa.

White-haired Polly passed them on her way to the shower. "What's all this laughing in the morning, before anyone has had any coffee?"

"Lorna is acting like your American musicals, she's all song and dance this morning," said Maria Rosa.

"Oh, for heaven's sake. Sober up," ordered Polly, sternly.

Lorna grabbed her towel and work clothes, and waltzed over to the shower behind Polly. It was a beautiful morning. The morning work shift ended quickly. Lorna showered again, changed into a tank top, jeans, and sandals, and was ready to board the trucks that had chugged into the parking area at the bottom of the hill. Lorna stood waiting with the other volunteers, thinking about the work experience. Shoveling and lifting boards was hard work, but being part of such a great crew rebuilding the clinic was rewarding. Lorna was sorry to say good-bye to the Abraham Lincoln Brigade folks and even to Úrsula. She had made new friends. Helping on this project made the loss of Rosalea and Grandfather less painful. Her elevated mood prevailed.

Úrsula was standing off to one side in her olive T-shirt and baggy pants. There is still a woman in there somewhere, Lorna thought. She recalled how much *Comandanta* Rosalea Bandera had enjoyed the bubble bath Lorna had drawn for her on Hill Street.

"Look, I have a *regalito* for you." She handed Úrsula her bottle of cucumber shampoo. "It makes your hair really nice!"

A wide smile broke out on Úrsula's face. She opened the bottle and sniffed it, then looked up.

"Thanks, *yanka,*" said Úrsula, still smiling.

Lorna turned to the French woman. "Can I give you a hug?"

"When I see you again, I'll be showing off my baby," Carla said.

"Don't take any wooden nickels, kid," advised Fred.

"And don't get lost in subjective romanticizing about this country," Jimmy growled. "There's a war going on. You're a soldier of social justice, sweetheart. Keep your eye on the prize."

"Emma Goldman said, 'If I can't dance, I don't want your revolution!'" Lorna fired back.

"Dance all you want, but remember the goal, girl, and keep your eyes open. I'll phone you back in San Francisco. You can help us get more ambulances," said Jimmy.

"I earn a very small salary!" Lorna protested.

"Not your money, kid. It's your organizing skills I want."

"I warned you," Polly laughed. "These guys are out to recruit you!"

"Polly, I hope to see you again," Lorna said, hugging her.

"So can I stay with you in San Francisco?" Rabbit asked quietly, his pale-blue eyes standing out in his sun-scorched skin, beneath almost white eyebrows. To Lorna, he looked like another lost kid.

"Phone me, Tom," she answered, congratulating herself for remembering his name and not his nickname. "Call me when you get to town. If I can't put you up, I can probably find someone who will." She knew she could lean on Rini's friends or the arts and culture crowd. He was sweet; surely one of them would help him.

"Let's go, Lorna," urged Maria Rosa. "We're riding in the red GMC pick-up." They lugged their gear over to the truck and Lorna looked back at the yellow-green hill with its scrubby brush and *guanacaste* tree. She had kept the faith with Rosalea, her red-headed poet. She felt so good she was almost skipping.

Maria Rosa slid into the cab, crowding the driver to make room on the seat for a third person. Lorna peered past her friend to examine their chauffeur.

It was Guillermo, in dark glasses, and a loose white *guayabera* shirt.

"Wait," Lorna stammered, "what happened? I thought you were in Havana."

"At the last minute my boss decided to go instead. The result being that I have three whole days cleared. I don't have to miss one exciting day of this revolution. I can drive my friends home and stop at a great place I know for some fresh boneless fish."

Lorna looked over at Maria Rosa, whose eyes were twinkling.

"The Tipitapa fish," Guillermo continued, "has no bones. We have saltwater fish living in sweet water because a long time ago they got trapped in Lake Managua and have been there ever since."

The restaurant was clean and pleasant, most of it outdoors in a patio around a dry fountain with a brilliantly colored parrot in a cage. Guillermo arranged with a boy about nine years old to watch the truck.

"*Buenos días*," said Lorna to the bird, glad to share her happiness.

"*Buenos días*," replied the parrot in a high-pitched harsh voice.

"All sound and no meaning," said Lorna.

"My grandmother had such a bird," said Guillermo. "It said 'Andres, darling, come inside.' That's what the neighbor used to say all day to her son."

They sat at a table with a view of the parrot. A very young waitress in worn out sandals appeared. "We have fresh fish, fried potatoes, and salad."

"Excellent," said Maria Rosa. "I'll have all three."

"So will I," said Guillermo. "Do you have any cold beer?"

"Only two beers left, we expect a delivery tomorrow."

Lorna and Maria Rosa ordered freshly squeezed orange juice. The food arrived fresh as promised and the drinks cold.

"First good meal in a week," said Maria Rosa. "We dug trenches in Jalapa so the contra tanks can't get through. Good work and bad food."

Guillermo swallowed the head off the beer and caught Lorna looking at him. For a moment their eyes held still.

Lorna stopped worrying about how much alcohol he drank when he asked the waitress for coffee, not the last beer. They ordered the caramel custard flan for dessert.

"It's a shame you've come at a time of scarcity," said Guillermo. "Our Nicaraguan cuisine is quite delicious, but it's hard now to get all the ingredients, thanks to Uncle Sam's embargo. The fuel shortage means deliveries of too many beans in one town and not enough in the next."

The waitress brought instant coffee. Guillermo continued, "Nicaragua grows such great coffee and yet most people use the powdered. Once again, Uncle Sam takes our coffee beans and sells them back to us in instant powder form. Capitalism teaches us to save time and lose flavor. They never told us what we should do with the extra seconds."

"Watch instant coffee commercials on TV," laughed Lorna, and then every remark after that set them off laughing until the table was cleared.

"Perhaps we can take a little stroll before we climb back in the truck," said Guillermo. They walked down the town's paved street for several blocks. Revolutionary red-and-black paper flags and pictures of Sandino hung about as they passed shops and houses. Graffiti and "FSLN" appeared everywhere. Lorna saw the faded slogan "*Abajo con el traidor*" on a wall. She knew that the literal translation, "Down with the traitor," referred to Edén Pastora, who had been a revolutionary war hero called Comandante Cero. Pastora had since hooked up with the contra. The slogan didn't name him because it was against Sandinista policy to refer to him by name.

"Look!" said Lorna, "'*¡No Pasarán!*' 'They shall not pass!' freshly painted on almost every corner. It must be moving for the Abraham Lincoln Brigade vets to see the Spanish Civil War slogan brought to life again in another context."

"You don't need an opinion poll to know what our people think," said Guillermo.

"But, sometimes graffiti can be cruel," commented Maria Rosa as they strolled along. "Someone painted 'contra' on one of our neighbor's houses. But they're not contras."

"People and their cruelties," said Guillermo. "The cruelest thing is cruelty in love. In comparison, cruelty in ideological warfare pales."

"I agree," said Lorna. "Love should be as gentle and as pain-free as possible, though I have never known it to be so."

"Nor I," said Guillermo

"Nor I," confirmed Maria Rosa.

They all burst into uproarious laughter again.

"The whole world is funny today," chuckled Guillermo. "That is the nature of stolen days and I have stolen three of them."

Guillermo handed the little boy who watched the truck some coins and ruffled the child's hair affectionately.

"Lorna, why are you frowning?" Guillermo asked.

"Oh, nothing. I was just thinking how quickly holidays pass," she answered.

"This one, Lorna, I will savor slowly and suck out every moment of its pleasure."

Lorna smiled and turned her face away to cover her unabashed delight in being swept off her feet in a cloud of romance, no longer caring about his age, his broken marriage, or anything else. They climbed into the truck and drove off.

As soon as they pulled up at Maria Rosa's house, Xiomara came out to meet them. "I am so glad you're back. I was getting lonely."

"Were there any messages?" asked Maria Rosa.

"No. But the nice lieutenant came by in a jeep asking when *Doña* Lorna was coming back."

Guillermo looked at Lorna, who tried to keep a noncommittal expression on her face.

"There were also messages on that telephone thing," continued Xiomara. "It beeped and sang and even talked in tongues."

"Xiomara, you are a poet like Lorna."

"I did cook you a big pot of *vigorón*. It's in the refrigerator," said Xiomara and as she walked back into the house.

Maria Rosa went directly to the message machine, listened

to the messages, and reported. "There are many beeps and clicks as always. Very few people have phones and most people are too unaccustomed and scared to leave a message. But Rini left a message saying there's a problem in the dam construction and she won't be here for another three days."

"Rini is my daughter. She's an engineer," Lorna explained to Guillermo.

"So you mentioned. Now we both have three whole days, free. Let's go to the beach."

"Ah, stolen moments are like ripe fruit," said Maria Rosa. "Eat them now or they rot." She laughed wickedly at her own wit. "Go have fun. I have so much paperwork to catch up."

17

Day Trip

Lorna quickly threw a swimsuit, towel, and sunscreen into her blue nylon bag. She changed into a fresh tank top, slid on silver hoop earrings, and climbed into the GMC pick up. Guillermo started it up, saying, "Let's go! The only restriction is that this excursion must be very low budget. State workers earn small salaries."

"No problem. Is this your own truck?"

"No. I borrowed it from my brother to transport the shovels. He and his wife are driving my Mercedes for a few days."

"That's a fancy car for a modest salary."

"It came with the appointment to the Ministry. When the Somocistas left, we nationalized their property. So I drive a seven-year-old Mercedes."

"Nice," said Lorna.

"Just to be clear," Guillermo said earnestly, "most of the property that we nationalized is for schools, orphanages, or government offices. We placed some of the ministries in their mansions."

"And commandeered their Mercedes for outings? No problem," laughed Lorna. "So where we going?"

"To Xiloa. It is a lake created by a volcano. Mother Earth hates a hole, so she fills the crater with water."

Laguna de Xiloa lay a half-hour's drive northwest, in a peninsula formed by two volcanoes on the banks of Lake Managua. The beach was run-down and nearly empty, but the lake itself was inviting, full of reflections of the blue of the sky and the hills on the far side. As soon as they arrived, Lorna changed into her swimsuit in a cabaña with a pitted concrete floor, littered with Coke cans and cigarette butts. She wriggled into her bathing suit, pulling and tugging her fifty-two year old flesh to keep it from sagging out the bottom.

Guillermo was lying on his towel by the water's edge, as tan and smoothly muscled as an Aztec warrior in a San Francisco Mission Street Mexican bakery calendar. Working in a ministry hadn't made him go soft. Seeing her emerge, he waved.

She felt a little self-conscious about her aging body, but his admiring glance somehow allowed her to accept herself, putting away all thoughts of plastic surgery or liposuction.

"Can you swim?" Guillermo asked. "I never learned."

"Don't worry, I spent one summer as a lifeguard. I love to swim. I was on my swim team in high school. I swam, even when it meant going home with wet hair in those horrible, cold, windy Chicago winters."

"Horrible cold, windy winters?" Guillermo asked. "What are those? Here we have hot, rainy winters. And hot dry summers."

"Compared to Nicaragua, Chicago might as well be in the Arctic," Lorna said.

Guillermo leaped up and ran to the water, throwing himself in, splashing wildly and happily, and then stood. "Come in!" urged Guillermo. "It's perfect."

Lorna ran down the sandy beach into the water, walking carefully over the shells and rocks at the bottom, then swam to his side.

"My mermaid captain," he quipped, frolicking and splashing in the water. They tugged and tripped each other like children playing, then waded back to the shore and sat on their towels. Guillermo leaned back on his hands and looked at her.

"Are you married?" she asked. The blunt question just popped out.

"I was married for six years."

"Divorced?"

His face clouded. "My wife and her parents left the country

for Miami soon after the triumph."

"Do you have children?" she asked.

"I have a son. He was born abroad." Guillermo paused, adding, "I've never seen him. But I'm sure one day he'll look for me. Yes! We'll ride around the rancho, we'll go fishing." He stopped. Lorna was struck again by his sensual mouth, so finely carved, and capable of sad, tragic bitterness, as he spoke of his son.

"You have a rancho?" asked Lorna.

He brightened. "It is our family's. El Rancho Villanova. It's just a little place. We grow almonds, and make almond wine. You will taste it when you come to visit," said Guillermo with a smile. Lorna marveled at how his expressions passed across his face like clouds in the sky.

"You know that is my last name. Almendros. But I have never heard of almond wine."

"Lorna Almendros, you will love the almond wine of our rancho. It will be as if it was made only for you. It is an old family recipe. We add certain herbs and the very essence of almonds, to a dry white wine. Our almond wine has the *amara* aftertaste. I will serve it to you iced, with a curling peel of orange rind."

"How far is this rancho?"

"A few hours' drive. You can drive across our whole country in a few hours. We will go there together."

She lay back. How good the sun felt. Snuggling her body deeper and deeper into the warm, dark volcanic sand, she felt her shoulders finally relax, still faintly sore from yesterday's labors. She closed her eyes. The moment seemed perfect.

When she opened them, she found Guillermo leaning on one elbow and staring at her.

"Beautiful," he was murmuring. "You're just beautiful."

Lorna smiled, sat up, and reached for her sunglasses. "Oh, you just say that to all the girls," said Lorna, feeling secretly beautiful. "Thanks for the compliment," she said after a pause. For a few more moments neither of them spoke.

Walking toward them along the water's edge was a young

barefoot boy holding a sparkling fish dangling on a string. Guillermo rose, caught up with him, and started to negotiate. The child nodded, turned, and raced away. Guillermo sat back down next to Lorna. Not long after, the boy returned, carrying a plate wrapped in a clean cloth napkin. The boy lifted the napkin to show them the grilled fish cut up into pieces.

Guillermo paid him and watched him run off. "Help yourself," he said. The fish was crisp on the outside, flavored with lemon juice and chopped tomatoes. They began eating.

"His mother's a great cook, don't you think?" said Guillermo. He stretched his back, lifted his arms lazily. "This is the first real rest I've had in months. The revolution hasn't left us much personal time."

"Do you live alone?"

"When my wife left, I built a tiny place behind my brother's, just a little cabin, really, although I put in indoor plumbing."

"But what about the rancho? Is your family rich?"

"No! The opposite! These days my father manages a state-owned fruit-dehydration project. We state workers get only a small salary. My brother and his wife work at the Ministry of Culture. He's a musician and she's a dancer."

"So you are a family of artists!"

"After the break-up with my wife," he said, "I decided to take on my own domestic responsibilities. Of course, I cheat. I eat out a lot. A neighbor lady does my laundry. Me, I sweep and mop. Today, for instance, I put fresh sheets on my bed."

Lorna let the clean sheets pass without comment.

In the extended silence, Lorna looked at Guillermo as he turned over on his stomach, pillowing his head on his forearms. There were fine black hairs on the backs of his thighs, she noticed. He smelled of the lagoon, his warmth, the scent rising from his dark golden back, forearms, and armpits. Something sweet but very strong. They were so different. Her, with her *chele* coloring, red-gold hair, very light skin, and green eyes. Yet both Nicaraguan. Who knew what European adventurer or immigrant ancestor had sought his fortune in Nicaragua more than a hundred years ago? She would ask Angélica when she returned to Pueblo Azul.

In the cabaña, Lorna showered under a thin stream of cold water. She rolled her wet swimsuit into her towel, poked at her auburn curls, and emerged to find Guillermo in the parking lot returning napkin and utensils to the little boy. She saw how his eyes followed the boy as he walked away, thinking he must miss knowing his own son.

"You know why I love this revolution?" Guillermo said, as she approached. "It's because the kids go to school. You can't imagine how it was. Hordes of homeless children on every street corner, selling or begging or stealing."

"For me it's still a shock to see children working or begging."

"We've only just begun. Imagine where we will be in the twenty-first century! We're going to reverse the old trends. We have a plan. This isn't just a revolution of people. The lakes, the rivers, the trees and the animals are with us. Already the bird population has tripled. I've seen the most tremendous changes, Lorna, in such a short time. Even the way people wait for buses has changed. We now form a line. Everywhere there's a whole new feeling, people spontaneously pulling together. So inspiring!"

A slow sun slipped behind the volcanic hills. Quietly, they watched it sink. Guillermo finally opened the truck doors. They climbed in silently. He pulled the doors closed, and leaned over her to pick up a newspaper from the truck floor. Lorna held her breath, aware how close he was, and slowly let it out. For a moment, they sat silently, breathing. Guillermo opened the paper.

"There's a funny old Spanish movie, *Don Quixote*, starring Cantinflas," Guillermo said, reading from the entertainment page. "Would you like to go?

"I visit Don Quixote regularly in Golden Gate Park in San Francisco," replied Lorna.

Guillermo looked at her in surprise.

"They're park statues!" Lorna laughed. "Don Quixote and Sancho Panza, respectfully kneeling in front of the bust of

Cervantes!"

"So is Spanish literature respected?"

"Spanish literature? Maybe. Still, not that much Latin American literature has been translated. Though there is more of it being published. My friend Eddie discovered Latin American literature a few years before the revolution. He read all the greats, in Spanish!"

Guillermo's voice sharpened. "Who's this Eddie? Is he that lieutenant with the jeep that Xiomara mentioned?" He looked at her and burst out, "Is he your lover?"

"Not my lover. He's my friend. He got me started by introducing me to the *compas* in a San Francisco storefront. They called it El Chipote. After Sandino."

"El Chipote?" laughed Guillermo. "That was the name of Sandino's headquarters."

"It was the meeting place for all who supported the Sandinista revolution. It's thanks to Eddie that I got involved in Nicaragua."

"No!" Guillermo said, suddenly angry. "It wasn't him. It was your ancestors calling you. That, and your own deep sense of justice." He looked away; then looking back at her, said, "So where is this person?"

"Eddie?" she asked, trying to sound casual, "He's here in Managua."

He looked out the truck window. After a moment, he turned back to Lorna, "There's so much ground to cover in only three days." His voice softened. "Look, I know I suggested the movies, but let's just go somewhere and talk."

Relieved, she leaned back. "What's this three days, the end of the world?"

"No, it's the end of time that's not consumed by work. Right now, we're surrounded by US naval ships on maneuvers on both coasts. Planes are spotted over Nicaragua daily. No one knows what will happen. On Thursday, my life returns to being on call twenty-four hours a day."

"And I am conveniently nearby?"

He turned to face her. "No, Lorna, not conveniently. Not

from the aspect of my gas ration card, nor the tank of gas I'm using. At this moment, I would say, you're magically near. You walked into my life on the food line, when I was hungry for love but overstuffed with work. Suddenly, now, three days have been offered to me on a platter."

"And you think I'm hungry for love too?"

"Yes, I do! I see the loneliness in your eyes." He turned, looking out the window.

"I'm not desperate, Guillermo," she said. "I do have a daughter, a job, my poetry, and my political work.

"Your daughter's far away and grown. The rest of your life is three thousand miles away." He let that float for a second, and then added, "Besides, you might get bombed here, right alongside us."

"That is not my plan. I plan to live," she said.

"We all plan to live," he sighed.

"I hate this undeclared war between our countries. I hate being seen as an aggressor when my heart's with the victim. I can't handle the confusion."

"You're confused? Ah! That's a good sign. It means you're open to the big question." He paused and touched her wrist. "Are you one of us?"

Lorna reeled with the surprise of it! "That is the same question Eddie asked me when he discovered I was Latina, that my maiden name was Almendros. Eddie was the one who urged me to drop my married name, Sevens, and become Lorna Almendros again.

"This Eddie again . . ." Guillermo said, annoyed and pulling away. "Forget him! The real question is, will you stay at my side and be part of building our new society?"

Lorna felt alarm and deep pleasure at the same time. "We don't even know each other."

"I've always known you." He took her hand. "I could feel the doors to my soul opening when we met. I saw your soul in the clear light in your eyes."

She swallowed, gathering her thoughts. They sat in the truck, watching the sky change color. Her hand felt so comfortable in his, so natural. Twilight came quickly, then, darkness, and they still had not said a word. Suddenly, a beam of blinding light cut into the cab of the truck.

Lorna gripped Guillermo's hand harder, shielding her eyes with the other hand.

"What are you doing here?" demanded a male voice. The light slid from their faces and moved around the truck's interior.

Guillermo's voice remained calm, but she could feel his body go on alert. "Good evening, *compa*. Doing the night watch tonight?"

"Yes. Show me your IDs," the man replied briskly.

Their hands separated as they reached for their papers.

The man examined Guillermo's laminated card carefully. "You're with the Ministry." He shone the flashlight on Lorna's I. D. and snorted, "A foreigner! I knew you two weren't from around here."

"We're leaving," Guillermo said. The man stepped back from the truck. "Good night, *compa*. Have a safe evening." He started the truck up. "Sorry, Lorna. I should have remembered about the *vigilancia*. He's just a neighbor taking his turn at the neighborhood watch. You never know what the *contras* will do. Also it cuts down on neighborhood crime."

"I was startled, but not frightened."

"Brave woman!" he pronounced. Leaning over, still driving, his lips quickly brushed her cheek.

Lorna sat silently, wondering if she could she trust this man, this Guillermo, whom she had known barely a day.

Guillermo looked at her, concerned. "Lorna, you slipped away so fast again. Come back," he said, gently squeezing her hand. "Where have you been?"

After a pause, she replied, "Lost in the past."

"Forget the past," he said, pulling her hand to his heart. "Move up here to the present. If you're too distracted to notice, love may float right past you," Guillermo smiled, "or, Contras or *compas* might shoot you."

"I was remembering problems."

"Problems? We can solve problems," he said. "Think of the pleasure. I've been smiling since we met. As a matter of fact, I feel invincible."

He pulled over to the side of the road. Reaching for her, Guillermo kissed a spot by her ear.

"Guillermo, when my marriage ended, I thought my romantic life was over," Lorna whispered.

"And you've lived a lifetime since then. Well, there's more living to be done, beginning right now, with me." He revved up the truck and drove off again. "We're going somewhere for a cool drink and dancing."

"Can I go dressed like this?" she asked looking down at herself.

"In revolution, anything goes!" he assured her.

18

Dance of Life

Live music was spilling out of *Club Caribe*, an open-air night-club on the road back to Managua. A dirt path led to the entrance.

Guillermo and Lorna entered, snaking around the crowded dance floor to a table. Guillermo pulled out a chair, leaning close. His attentiveness made her feel beautiful. She held her head high and glided into the seat.

The waiter arrived almost at once, dressed in an embroidered folkloric shirt, the *cotona*. He nodded, "Good evening, *enginero*. How are you and the lovely lady tonight?"

"Very well, Nico, thank you. We'd like something cold to drink." Lorna wondered who else he brought here.

Nico ticked off the offerings—*cervezas, margaritas*, rum-and-Cokes, *tamarindo* juice.

"*Margaritas* for us both, Nico." When the drinks arrived Guillermo looked at her as he raised his cold salted glass. "To a very beautiful woman whose friendship I hope to deserve forever."

"And to Nicaragua," said Lorna. "May this revolution prevail."

"I know so little about you, *Compañera* Lorna. Yet I feel as if I have always known you. Do you feel that?" he asked, his eyes intent, under straight brows.

"We come from very different places," said Lorna. "Our countries have been at war one way or another for a hundred years. Much as I try to undo the harm my country has done, I am constantly reminded that Nicaragua does not forgive us."

Guillermo's eyes held hers. "Lorna. *Comandante* Che

Guevara said the true revolutionary does not recognize borders. We are moved by feelings of great love. I know you are with us, *Compañera* Lorna. You could be Xilonen, the corn goddess, with your light skin and green eyes. There are many who have your coloring up in the northern mountains. Around Matagalpa and further north."

"Yes, my mother came from the north," said Lorna. "Doña Angélica told me that."

"You see? Your mother was the corn goddess, and you are her daughter."

Lorna trembled silently, but her mind said, "Beware!"

"What are you thinking, *Compañera* Lorna?"

Lorna shook her head. She wanted to laugh because she could hardly tell him. She raised her glass and said, "To life!"

"To life! And to love!" toasted Guillermo.

Dancers were skirting around their table.

"Care to dance?"

Lorna put down her margarita and took Guillermo's hand. On the dance floor, the heat from the dancers caressed her bare arms. Amid the dense group of moving bodies, a space opened. They filled it. It was theirs.

They faced each other. She lifted her arm until her hand clasped the back of his neck, feeling his soft curling hair. Her other arm slid out, hand slipping into his. He touched her waist and off they sailed on waves of music, effortlessly adjusting to each other's steps. At the song's end, Lorna applauded enthusiastically.

The music began again with a slow intense introduction, setting the mood for *Cuando Venga la Paz*. A deep quiet embraced the dancers. The music flowed through them. The vibration of ancient bells went tingling up her back, as Indigenous instruments blended familiar jazz, blues, soul, Latin rhythms and melodies.

The lights dimmed to blue. The dancing couples rocked together, swaying slowly, all moving as one. The song ended with an epiphany of hope. Applause began strong and steady; then speeding up, creating its own unified rhythm, finding its own crescendo. It wound down, ending in perfect unison all at once.

The lights brightened as the band took a break. An informal promenade of table-hopping began. People greeted friends, stopping to chat, or pulling up a chair.

A young woman appeared behind Guillermo and covered his eyes playfully. She winked at Lorna. She looked younger than Rini, and seemed so at ease with Guillermo that Lorna wouldn't let herself imagine who she might be in his life.

"Guess," said the woman. A silver clasp was holding her straight black hair, pulled back away from her face with ballerina-like tautness. Her red-painted nails rested along the left side of his eyes and cheek.

"Who else," Guillermo guessed, "but my outrageous, impudent, sister-in-law, Nicolasa?" Nicolasa fell into the seat next to him, laughing. "He is the most handsome of the brothers!" she said to Lorna.

Guillermo turned to face her. "I'm so glad you're here. I want you to meet my dear friend, Lorna Alma Almendros. She's from California, but her family comes from Pueblo Azul."

Nicolasa looked at Lorna with interest. "I know Pueblo Azul well. I go there every month collecting folk dances for our archives!"

"Do you record the dances with a video camera?" Lorna asked.

"Sadly, video cameras for dance are not a priority for the national budget. I record the dances with a pen and paper using Labanotation."

The band was reassembling. "Here comes the band again," said Nicolasa. "Maybe they'll play the song we danced to at the front."

"You danced on the battlefield?" Lorna asked.

"We're part of an artists' brigade program, *brigades culturales.* Ours is called *Brigada German Pomares,*" Nicolasa said. "We troupe our show to the war zones, traveling to areas where the *contras* frequently attack. People are afraid to leave their houses, even to feed their animals, so we invade each town with live popular music. They hear us and peek out their windows. When they see clowns, prancing, and tumbling, everyone comes. Once a crowd is assembled, we start dancing."

The amplifier gave a shriek and a squawk as the band emitted tuning up sounds, and people covered their ears.

When it quieted down, Nicolasa continued. "If we're lucky, when the *Contras* see people out in full force, they go away without attacking or they hide to watch our show from a safe distance. When they hear the revolutionary slogans we shout at the end, they slink away."

Nicolasa laughed at the memory. "Other times we stop sooner than planned because the *contras* start shooting. We dive into the bushes and try to protect our musical instruments, but we save our own hides first."

A man joined their table, and Guillermo broke into a big laugh, hugging and slapping him on the back. "Lorna, meet my little brother, Javier." Javier was shorter than Guillermo, more studious-looking, but he smiled with some of the same incandescent warmth.

Soon they were all out on the dance floor, throbbing with the syncopated *cumbia* and *merengue* beats.

Guillermo's moves were subtle, as if he were barely moving on a small bit of the floor, his weight shifting with his feet. His hands touched Lorna's back and waist as he sent her out into a spin, and to her surprise, reeled her in, dipping her back in a Fred Astaire/Ginger Rogers motion. She tossed her head back still further with abandon, sure that she wouldn't fall with his arm around her. With a flourish, she raised her right arm behind her head, leaning way back, her torso supported by Guillermo. Her left hand around his neck, she looked straight into his brown eyes.

Too quickly, the song ended and applause broke out. But no one left the dance floor. The marimba played a familiar folk melody that was rapidly picked up by a jazzy saxophone, then by two electric guitars and a percussion section, including cowbells, claves, and a conga drum. The whole room throbbed. Dancers were a swaying, gyrating, and pulsing mass.

At the end of the set, everyone stamped and cheered: "*Otra! Otra!* One more! One more!" The musicians set down their instruments, waving regretfully. The lights came on. Dancers returned reluctantly to their tables.

Guillermo steered Lorna to their seats. "I'm so thirsty," he declared, sipping the melted ice from his glass with one hand and still holding Lorna's hand with the other.

Now the band's saxophonist walked over to their table and greeted Guillermo. "I'm glad I found you. I've been leaving messages at your office all afternoon. But your secretary told me you were gone for three days."

"What is so urgent, Jorge? Tell me about it, but make it short. As you can see, I am with a beautiful woman."

"We played at the new housing settlement as you requested, yesterday afternoon, but there was no electricity. We sounded terrible. I wanted you to know that it wasn't our fault in case anyone should complain. It was OK for me—a saxophonist needs only breath power. But others were lost without electricity."

Guillermo didn't look upset. His skin was glowing from dancing.

"Without electricity, it was a lot like the old days," Jorge explained to Lorna, recognizing that she was a foreigner. "Before the revolution, musicians, and dancers would perform in the streets to gather a crowd, then one of us would get up and preach revolution."

"One of the most popular songs was about how to take apart an M1 rifle. People learned those lyrics in a hurry," Guillermo interjected.

Jorge added, "And by the time we'd taught the crowd the song, the *Guardia* would show up and we would run like crazy!"

He turned, addressing Guillermo. "One of things I like about state power and being a state cultural worker is having rehearsal time and electric instruments. Our audience deserves the best sound."

"Things happen. I thought the electricity was supposed to be hooked up last Friday. I know you did the best you could." Guillermo's tone indicated the conversation was over.

"Nice meeting you, *compañera*. Our next song will be for you," said Jorge.

"What is it?" asked Lorna

"Solidarity is the Tenderness of the People."

"Thank you!" said Lorna. "I'll take this song back to San Francisco and our Friends of Nicaraguan Culture solidarity group."

"Thanks to you and to the solidarity movement!" said Jorge as he returned to the bandstand.

"The Ministry of Housing hires bands?" Lorna asked.

"I wanted some music for the moving-in day ceremonies at the new low-income housing project," Guillermo explained. "I asked ASTC for this band because they're so good."

"What's ASTC?"

"We're becoming a country of initials. ASTC is the Association of Sandinista Cultural Workers, an artists' union mostly for painters and performing artists."

"Is it part of the Ministry of Culture?" asked Lorna.

"No. Some say the ASTC and the Ministry are redundant and overlapping. Don't hold it against us. The ASTC also works as a kind of booking agency under First Lady Rosario Murillo. Ernesto Cardenal heads up the Ministry."

"I translated Rosario Murillo's poetry to read at a rally in San Francisco."

"She is also the mother of eight."

"Do you know her?"

"Yes, very well," said Guillermo.

"How does someone in housing know all the poets, all the dancers, and all the musicians?"

"Lorna, we're all artists. That's who Sandinistas are. We're not ideologues. Even those who tend to be ideologues also write poems and novels. Take our vice-president, Sergio Ramirez, for example. He's also a novelist and short story writer. The president writes poems. The first lady is a prominent poet. Even a lowly functionary like me has been known to scribble."

"You write?"

"A few articles, now and then, on culture and architecture. Lorna, you've asked a lot about me," Guillermo paused and leaned forward. "But who are you?"

"I told you. I'm a poet, a teacher, and a mother. My daughter lives here in Nicaragua as an engineer."

"That tells me little. Do you live alone?"

"Yes," Lorna nodded.

"How long were you married?"

"Rini was four when he left."

"Why did you get divorced?" Guillermo persisted.

The words froze in her throat. The dreaded past came bounding to the surface. All those years, she found herself looking out the window as if at any moment Carl would walk in and say, 'Lorna. I still love you.' But it never happened. She had searched the child support check envelopes for a reply to her repeated inquiries about why he left and what happened to their love.

"Lorna, you're gone again," she heard Guillermo saying. "I miss you when you go away like this. Fortunately I still have your hand in mine as a souvenir."

"I'm here . . . I'm here," she said, fumbling for words. "When you asked about my marriage, the past just loomed up like a thick fog."

Guillermo's hold on her hand tightened.

"Feel my hand Lorna," he urged. "This is the present. This has never existed before. This will never exist again. I am here for you, now."

A sudden, sweet note from the saxophone drew her back. The tune sounded familiar. She'd heard people singing it only this morning at the construction site. It seemed like a long time ago.

"He's playing your song, Lorna. Come on." With open arms, he motioned to the dance floor.

She danced with Guillermo's shirt button pressed on her

ear.

After the final song, it was time to go. Guillermo paid the bill and led her out into the starry night.

"I'm driving to my house, unless you object."

"I don't object," she said as they climbed into the truck.

After a silence, he asked, "Did you find what you were seeking in Pueblo Azul?"

"Yes and no," Lorna said. "I was thrilled to meet a friend of my grandfather, who was godmother to my father, a lovely poet named Angélica. But I was not happy to see that my grandfather's house was occupied by a mean-spirited old contra battle-axe. I hated her. I left Pueblo Azul covered with red dust."

"The rains are late. When it rains again, those red dusty roads will turn to mud."

Lorna looked out toward the dark road, with no idea where they were.

"Why did your marriage end?" he asked.

"I was married for many years. I don't really know why he left. He said he felt old and cold in the relationship and said our love was dead."

"But is it, Lorna?"

"Is it dead?" In the silence, she could hear the truck wheels winding down a narrow road. She sighed, "Yes, it is dead now."

"And do you go back to him when you're lost to me, thinking of your past?"

"Not to him. But to the feelings of rejection and abandonment. To my loneliness. Starting from when Grandfather left me to visit Nicaragua. He died here and never returned."

"And so you fear it will happen again?"

She didn't answer.

A strong wind was shaking the branches of the trees that they passed.

"My knee tells me it's going to rain," Guillermo said. "This knee put itself in the way of a bullet once. Ever since, it predicts the weather for me." Almost immediately, raindrops spotted the windshield, and within two or three minutes, sheets of rain were flowing over the glass.

The truck rolled through deepening puddles, splashing noisy water up along the passenger window. Overhead a tremendous clap of thunder boomed. Lorna slid as close to Guillermo as the gearshift would allow. He peered intently through the busy windshield wipers. Dim lights shone from the houses they passed. In one yard, two children and their father pulled on a goat, trying to force the animal into a shed. Her arm was resting on the top of his thigh. A smile passed across his face, but then he swerved to avoid a cow that appeared out of nowhere.

"Cows. That's the trouble with this road." He was almost shouting to be heard above the pelting rain.

"It feels like a biblical flood," said Lorna. "Your knee is very accurate."

"This will be a short one. The skies will clear in just a little while."

"That's hard to believe, but so far your knee has been right about the weather."

Guillermo stopped. Through the buckets of rain, Lorna saw a low stucco wall and a curly-leafed tree hanging over it, its leaves smashed against a gate. Bushes were whipping wildly back and forth in the storm.

"Where are we?" she asked.

"Bello Horizonte," said Guillermo, leaving the truck running as he rushed to open the gate. Jumping back in, he drove through the gate and parked in front of the house. As he ran back to close the gate, lightning cracked overhead, followed by a thunderclap. Lorna slid out the passenger side door, barefooted, carrying her sandals. With her first step, she was up to her ankles in a rivulet that came gushing down the driveway. She was slipping in mud. Rain soaked her T-shirt and jeans. Fat drops streamed down their faces.

"Amazing," Lorna breathed, looking at the sheets of rain. Stepping into a small gully, the water rose to her calves.

He brushed wet curls from her eyes, helping her out of the gully. He pulled her to him, hard and urgently, kissing her on the mouth. Her legs were entwined against his wet trouser leg, his belt buckle pressing into her ribs. Guillermo grasped her hand to pull her across luminous puddles toward the front door of his house.

Inside, they embraced again, as rain pounded on the zinc roof.

"Tenderness. I have found tenderness," she murmured, looking into his eyes in the dark house. The phone rang. They both ignored it. Then at the fifteenth ring, Guillermo cursed, and stepped across the unlit room.

"Hello?" he barked and then listened. "All right, I'll be there," Guillermo said, angrily slamming down the receiver. "These damn telephones! You can never get a call through when you want–but they work perfectly when you would prefer to be left alone."

He snapped on a small table lamp. In the sudden glow, Lorna noticed handcrafted masks adorning white plaster walls. The rest of the room was still in shadow.

"What's happening? Is everything OK?" Lorna asked, alarmed.

"Not OK. The storm took out the electricity again at the new housing project. The roof is leaking. The place is flooded. And there are two hundred kids in those units. I've got to go. Will you wait for me?" A raindrop rolled off his hair and down the side of his face like a tear.

He drew her close. "I'll be back as fast as I can. *Aquí tienes tu casa*. Make yourself comfortable," he said, waving toward the rest of the house. "I heard Javier and Nicolasa drive up. They live in the house in front. If you get frightened, knock on their door."

"I'm a grown-up, I don't scare easily. I'll wait for you."

He kissed her eyelids, nose, and lips. Then he left.

Lorna turned on another lamp. The top shelf of a bricks-and-board bookcase displayed Pre-Columbian statues and clay pots with animal figures. Underneath sat a portable tape deck and cassettes. Two mattresses stacked on the floor and covered with a heavy woven Mexican blanket and oversize pillows served as a couch facing a large ceramic elephant that carried a small TV on its back.

She was too wet to sit down, so she made her way to the bathroom. Amazingly, Guillermo had hot water in the small shower. She dropped her wet, muddy clothes in a heap and stepped in. She let the warm water run sensuously though her hair, down her face, over her breasts and belly. Wrapped in a towel after her shower, she had nothing to change into, and so went looking for Guillermo's clothes. She opened a door and found his bedroom.

The bed was made up with pale-blue sheets and freshly ironed white pillowcases. A small table supported a bed lamp, a book, a pen and a pad. She turned on the bed lamp, and opened the middle drawer of a chest. Clean white T-shirts were folded one on top of another, and in the bottom drawer, she found a pair of shorts. Lorna slipped into the T-shirt and pulled the shorts up around her slender waist.

Guillermo's clean sheets remark came echoing back. She regarded the pristine bed, sheets tautly pulled, the pillows plumped up. This bed seems to be inviting a guest. The man is bold! She folded the blue sheet back and lay down. The storm had washed away her doubts. Nature spoke louder than reason. She turned off the little lamp, and within seconds fell asleep.

She awoke to a gray pre-dawn light. Guillermo was climbing in next to her, naked, his clothes, heaped on a chair. The rain had stopped. It was very quiet. His warm breath caressed her neck. His hands began searching for her, and sleepily she pulled off the T-shirt and let him tug off her shorts. His hands found her breasts and thighs. They made love until the cool dawn gave way to sunlight and humidity. They showered together, quickly, soaping one another and laughing, then dried off and climbed back into bed. Their bodies nestled into each other.

"You've made me very happy, Lorna. We're good together,

very good. We fit so perfectly," he told her.

"Yes, we do."

"I love you, Lorna."

"I love you, too." The moment she said it, her fears returned. How can anyone love a stranger?

But Guillermo sat up abruptly, shouting, gesturing grandly toward the ceiling. "Hello, God! Do you hear that? She loves me. I can't believe it! With all her doubts and her bad memories. She loves me."

Ignoring her doubts, she stretched out luxuriantly, happily. "Good-bye, loneliness," she shouted to the ceiling.

He lay back down and reached for her, and they fell asleep curled in each other's arms.

19

First Breakfast and Last Supper

"*Tortillas, tortillas, tortillas,*" sang a woman's voice from the street.

"Hungry?" Guillermo murmured.

"Mmmmmm?" Lorna stirred sleepily as the sun crept though the edges of the window shade.

"If we're very quiet, maybe she'll shut up and go away."

"*Tortillas, tortillas, tortillas,*" sang the outside voice.

"*¡Váyate!*" said Guillermo.

"*Tortillas, tortillas, tortillas,*" sang the outside voice again. Now she seemed directly below the window.

"She doesn't hear you," said Lorna.

"All right, all right, I'm coming," shouted Guillermo at the window. Pulling his pants on, he fumbled for his wallet.

She watched him as he moved toward the bedroom door, thinking how handsome he was with his sculpted amber skin, the dark hairs peeking out from the armpits.

"Look," he said, minutes later, returning with his purchase, "*¡Quesillos!* Fresh and warm, with homemade cheese and cream on a tortilla. Shall I make some coffee?"

"You mean you're going to force me to get up?" murmured Lorna. "Come here."

Obediently, he bent over her to nuzzle her cheek, when a new sound filled the room. A man was strolling past their window, selling brooms, and he had barely moved on before two boys could be heard offering liquid bleach.

"Ah, no hope for it," said Lorna. She hunted for the T-shirt and shorts and wriggled into them, aware of Guillermo's eyes feasting on her naked body. "Maybe we should have that coffee."

"Sorry for the interruptions, it's our desperate economy," Guillermo apologized.

After some puttering and rattling, he came to the door of the bedroom. *"Coffee's ready!"* And indeed she could smell the strong, good coffee aroma filling the entire little house. They sat on the mattress-sofa, stirring the coffee in gaily decorated ceramic cups. The *quesillos* were arranged nicely on another colorful ceramic plate, and Guillermo had put out papaya slices, orange sections, and chunks of yellow mango.

"Good coffee, Guillermo. How sweet the sound of our clinking spoons."

How sweet the sound. She flashed back to the song lyric she'd first heard standing with Carl in a candle-lit civil rights vigil in Chicago decades ago, while Joan Baez sang "Amazing Grace," thrilling everyone to the bone. "I once was lost, till I found you, Lorna," Carl had whispered, taking her hand. His breath had warmed Lorna's cold ear.

Guillermo's spoon clinked against the coffee cup commandingly, startling her out of her reverie.

"Will you be my wife, Lorna Alma? I'm a good breakfast provider," said Guillermo.

"There's more to life than breakfast," she answered. "As we both well know."

"You should try my lunch . . . or shall we live on love?" he continued with a smile.

"Love Is All You Need." Lorna's thoughts drifted back again to the time in San Francisco when she and Carl were dancing wildly under pulsing strobe lights to the Beatle's tune, and Carl caught her in a dizzying turn. He had said, "You and Rini are all I'll ever need." And she had believed him. How quickly after that she'd heard him saying, "I don't need you, Lorna. You don't need me. The movement needs both of us, and I have to be free to do my work." She had not believed that.

As if reading her mind, Guillermo placed his hand on her knee. "I need you, Lorna. Come back. Let me pull you out of the past." He raised his coffee cup. "Here's to love. To love, and the revolution," amended Guillermo.

"Ah, yes, the revolution. The one that called you away last night," Lorna teased.

Guillermo refilled her coffee cup, saying, seriously, "You know, Mother Earth was too generous last night with her water. Her rain ruined the mattresses in many of the apartments. The construction's not always the best. Fortunately, last night we were able to find the leak in the roof and fix it . . . at least for now."

"Grandfather used to tell me of rain up to his knees," remembered Lorna.

"This rain wasn't the worst. It was relatively light. Sometimes after days of heavy rain, the floods come, and sweep everything away, houses, crops, possessions, hillsides. Everything. Sometimes entire towns. Then we have no choice. We build again. That is the history of Nicaragua. People find reeds, lumber, cardboard, and use these scraps to build up again. In the face of disasters, we never give up, and life goes on."

"I thought my life was over when Carl left. That was a disaster for me. If it had not been for Rini, I couldn't have gone on." Then Lorna felt self-conscious.

Guillermo was silent. Then he confided, "When my wife left, pregnant with our son, I felt that too. The morning her brothers came in a truck to pick up her things, they looked at me with such contempt, ordering their hired helpers around. I'll never forget that. How I hated them for being rich bastards, running off to Miami just as fast as they could. Fucking *Somocistas.*"

"I can't imagine you marrying into that kind of family," said Lorna.

"She was a student. Very pretty. She played at revolution; it was a game for her, although I didn't see that. Her beauty blinded me. I was young. I was in love. I didn't understand the pressure her family could exert. They felt she had married beneath her. And in the end, she couldn't live without the money and lifestyle they provided. She betrayed the revolution. She betrayed me."

"I know how that feels," said Lorna.

"And she wasn't the only one," he added, bitterly. "Way too many of the *compas* have been bought out by the CIA. Jaime Pasquier. We actually sent him to the United Nations as our first ambassador. He denounced us as Communists and sought exile in Miami. He was followed by Arturo Cruz, whom we foolishly trusted to serve as our ambassador to the United States." His face hardened. "I buried those feeling by re-committing myself to our revolution. Somoza and his pals fled the country with every last cent they could steal, running off to their cronies in Miami. They think they can wait us out and take over again. But Nicaragua will prove them wrong!"

"It's already happening," Lorna said.

"At first I was filled with dreams of rebuilt cities and towns, a whole nation rebuilt with respect for Mother Earth, solar energy, roof top cupolas to catch the breezes. I was burning to create a whole new architecture for Nicaragua."

"Aren't you still?" asked Lorna.

He smiled, ruefully. "I got caught up writing grants to Sweden, to France, to anywhere, just to get supplies! I'm nothing more than a damn bureaucrat. The US embargo makes materials much more expensive. We have to buy them from new suppliers at a higher price. You know how it goes. We compromise and compromise and meanwhile the need is so great. The people want housing now. So we build the cheapest, fastest structures, and they aren't among the Seven Wonders of this World, I can assure you. So much for my dreams of beauty."

"But you work so hard," said Lorna soothingly.

"I work hard at patching leaks, fixing generators, supervising repairs and finding housing for the homeless. The reality is that we can't, in months or even years, undo the decades of Somoza's total corruption. It took me a long time to overcome the sorrow I felt when my wife left. Inside, I felt homeless, my wife gone, pregnant with my son, who is still now lost to me. I wept until finally my self-pity became boring.

Repairing and remodeling this house brought me out of it."

He turned, putting his arms around her, kissing the back of her neck. "But now I have you, Lornita. It's a whole new day." He moved to the tape recorder. "Listen to this cassette of Andean flute music. Here in my little house in sultry Managua, we'll transport ourselves to the clear, cold *altiplano*."

Andean flute, guitar, and drum music soared from the tape recorder, bright, imaginative, intensely innocent. Guillermo was right. It spoke of chilled, high places. He got to his feet and pulled her up close to him. His feet found little rhythmic steps and she fell into them, his arms encircling her as they padded and danced on the cool tiles until they fell back down on the couch.

Lorna silently traced the woven patterns in the Mexican blanket covering the couch with her forefinger. "Grandfather must know I am in his homeland now. His old bones must be stirring in the graveyard behind the church. Not under an almond tree, as I used to think. I learned so much sitting with Angélica in those carved rocking chairs in that hot afternoon. I could easily imagine Abuelo in Angélica's house, catching flies in mid-air without losing a beat of the conversation, the way he did when I was a child. Abuelo would tell me, 'Put on your sandals, *amorcita*. Never go barefoot. How many times do I have to explain it to you?'" Lorna looked down at her bare feet.

Guillermo jumped up to study his tape collection, and then inserted another tape. "You'll love this one. Javier produced it with the band we heard last night."

He settled back on the couch. "Do you understand the words to this song? They're very idiomatic. It's a protest against the US trade embargo. It says we are all the children of the corn and describes the ways our ancestors used corn. Since your government prevents us importing wheat, we are forced to return to our roots. Corn! This song is for the corn goddess. Xilonen. She is the goddess of up-sprouting corn, and of happiness."

He looked at her tenderly. "You resemble our corn goddess,

Lornita, with reddish-gold hair, green eyes, and light skin. A *chelita*. This song lists all the dishes she makes possible: corn stews, corn soups, corn casseroles, corn stuffing, corn bread, corn puddings, and corn drinks."

Guillermo looked happy. "You know, Lornita, they've made me a judge at the corn festival. Nicaragua's best cooks present their corn dishes, and then, lucky me, I get to eat all the dishes, and decide which is best."

"I'm surprised you're not fat," teased Lorna, running her finger down his lean chest and belly, down to the hair below. "All this corn cookery you're stuffing yourself with!"

"No plastic containers are allowed, only our own clay bowls and plate," said Guillermo. "Slowly we are ending our dependency on foreign products. The United States may want to drive us to our knees. But thanks to the corn goddess we will survive!"

Guillermo stood up and walked toward the bookshelves. "Look!" he said, pulling out an old photo framed in silver-bordered, gray cardboard from a photographer's shop and handing it to her. "These are my grandparents on their honeymoon in Mexico City."

Lorna studied the photo of a man with a big mustache standing behind a woman seated gracefully in front of him, her soft dress flowing. It was a faded stylized portrait. The man looked fierce, and the woman submissive.

"I loved them very much," he confided tenderly. "You see, I understand your love for your *abuelo*."

Guillermo put the photo back and turned to her. Taking her hand, he led her to the bedroom, where he slipped off her T-shirt and shorts, then threw off his own clothing and lay down beside her. "Beautiful, beautiful!" he breathed, running his hands over her erect breasts and rounded belly.

"I love being beautiful to you," Lorna said, feeling happier than she could remember for years.

Now it was Lorna's turn to run her hands over his neck and down his back, feeling the strength of his body. Within his strong embrace, she was soft and luscious, like a quivering *flan.* She was in love, and she couldn't deny it, even to her most vigilante self. Her world dissolved into a kaleidoscope of colors, images, sensations.

Guillermo had just moved on top of her, when there was a furious pounding at the door. They froze. Lorna looked at Guillermo. The urgent pounding outside persisted.

"It must be my brother or Nicolasa," he said.

Bang, bang, bang, the knocks slammed through the house. He drew her closer. The pounding grew louder and more insistent. Then they heard a male voice, an angry, incomprehensible shout.

"Shit," said Guillermo, groping for his pants and sliding them up over his hips. "Wait here."

The knocking stopped for a second, then resumed even louder. Guillermo left, shutting the bedroom door firmly behind him. As soon as the door closed, Lorna scrambled back into T-shirt and shorts. Outside, she heard the sound of the front door opening.

"Who are you?" Guillermo asked angrily.

"Where's Lorna?" a familiar voice shouted. Lorna recognized Eddie's voice.

Lorna pushed open the bedroom door, her heart filled with foreboding that something had happened to Rini.

Eddie Flores stood in the doorway in full uniform. His .45 in its holster against his hip.

"Lieutenant Eduardo Flores," he spit out, pushing into the room. "Now where is Lorna Almendros?"

Guillermo stood with clenched jaw and fists. "Get the fuck out of here, Lieutenant," he said. "No one invited you in, and no one is breaking the law."

"Hello, Eddie," Lorna managed to say from the bedroom door, alarmed and shaking. "Has something happened to Rini?"

"There's nothing wrong with Rini," Eddie barked.

She was aware of Eddie's eyes scanning her, the thin T-shirt and shorts hitched up with a tie, her bare feet and naked legs. Guillermo had answered the door, barefoot, wearing nothing but his trousers. The scene spoke for itself.

Eddie and Guillermo were glaring at each another.

"Eddie, this is my friend, Guillermo Villanova. He's with the Ministry of Housing."

"He is, is he?" said Eddie. "Another upper-class bureaucrat riding the wave of the revolution?"

"Guillermo, this is my very good friend, Lieutenant Eddie Flores. Eddie was with the Southern Front," said Lorna, hurriedly to Guillermo. "He spent months fighting in the mountains."

"Ah, the Southern Front," sneered Guillermo, drawing himself to his full height, like a snake, uncoiling, looking at Eddie. "I know you internationalist types. You spent minutes in the mountains, and got out just as fast as a plane could jet your ass to the next all-expense paid international conference."

Eddie turned white with shock. Lorna knew that no one had ever accused him of not giving his all for this revolution. She felt the situation was rapidly exceeding her diplomatic skills. Guillermo took a step forward as if he were about to push Eddie back out the door.

Eddie, in turn, was bristling.

Lorna moved quickly between them. "What's going on, Eddie? Why are you here?"

"For Chrissake, Lorna," Eddie said in English, "you've been gone for two fucking days! Maria Rosa has been worried sick about you. She told us the last she knew, you had gone swimming with this . . . this architect, and that you never phoned or returned."

"Maybe I should have phoned her," Lorna said. "But Maria Rosa and Guillermo are friends and she has his number. Maria Rosa knows exactly what's going on. The reason she hasn't phoned is that she didn't want to disturb us."

"I borrowed the jeep today because I thought you wanted to go back to see your grandfather's house and that old lady, Angélica," Eddie said.

"Did we have some date to go back to Pueblo Azul today?" Lorna replied angrily. "If we did, I don't remember it. And now you come barging in here? You're not thinking of me. If you were thinking of me, you would be happy for me and not making this scene."

"But the jeep . . ." Eddie blurted out.

"I can't go to Pueblo Azul today, Eddie," Lorna said, cutting him off, trying to use her most pleasant and tactful tones. "I have other plans. But I do appreciate your offering."

"Excuse me, Lieutenant," interrupted Guillermo, speaking in Spanish. "It's time for you to go. You're not welcome here."

"I'm not leaving unless I take Lorna with me. I don't have any idea who the hell you are."

"Eddie, stop. I'm not going with you. I am fine. If I misunderstood about Pueblo Azul, I'm sorry. We can talk about it later. Please thank Maria Rosa for her concern, I'll phone her. You should leave now."

The phone rang. They all looked at one another. On the third ring Guillermo picked up the receiver.

"It's for you," he announced handing it to Lorna. Both men stood by the doorway, glaring at each other.

"Hello?" said Lorna tentatively.

"Lorna, how are you?" It was Maria Rosa.

"Fine, Maria Rosa" she replied, looking back at both men. "How are you?" She felt she was playing out a ridiculously polite charade.

"Fine, thank you. Eddie came by in the jeep looking for you. When I told him where you were, he threw a fit and took off straight to find you. He's sure Guillermo is an evil Don Juan out to take advantage of you. I just wanted to give you a heads-up."

"Uh, thanks, but it's a little late. He's already here, now."

"That must be a cozy scene! So how's it going?" Maria Rosa asked.

"Not well," Lorna said after a long pause, hoping Maria Rosa would get what was going on.

"Well, if he's there, let me talk to him," said Maria Rosa. "*Comandante* Camilo just called for him. They need the jeep returned right away. Eddie isn't supposed to be using it on his day off."

Neither Guillermo nor Eddie had moved, both still focused on her at the telephone.

"Eddie, Maria Rosa wants to talk to you." Lorna held out the receiver in the direction of the door, but looked questioningly at Guillermo. He nodded, but his face was set and angry.

Eddie stepped forward and took the receiver from Lorna.

"Yes?" Eddie said. "What's up? No, nothing. She's fine. OK. OK." Eddie ended his conversation and turned to Lorna. "Something urgent has come up. I have to leave. I'll see you soon. Give Rini a kiss for me." And he was out the door.

20

Thorns in the Roses

Guillermo locked the door after Eddie. "Well now, what was that about?"

"I don't know what to tell you," said Lorna. "How can you explain an old friend's behavior? He's seen me through a million situations, though our relationship these last years has been going downhill. He is probably jealous. But Eddie's still my friend."

"What a friend! What nerve," said Guillermo.

"Eddie's been so important to me, Guillermo," said Lorna. "He got me involved in Nicaragua. Eddie loves to quote Che Guevara's line about how, if you're tired you should rest, but then don't call yourself a revolutionary. That's Eddie, actually. He's been tireless, organizing in the States and fighting down here on the Southern Front. He's a very good person, Guillermo, and one of my oldest friends. It's just, well, sometimes, well, he gets carried away with himself." She was stumbling and stammering. "He was born in Nicaragua. He moved to San Francisco when he was three."

"I know there were many internationalists fighting with us but I never heard of this warrior *gringo* from San Francisco," said Guillermo.

"He wasn't the only one. Several men in our community fought in the revolution. Everyone had a pseudonym. Maybe you just didn't know them."

"Lorna, it's all right. You don't need to explain," Guillermo said softly, putting his arms around her.

She was silent.

"Lorna, can we pick up where we left off?"

"I'm trying to explain to myself what just happened."

"It couldn't be clearer. You're a beautiful woman, and your friend is stupidly jealous. Well, I'm assuming he had his chances, and whatever happened happened. In any case, with him, it's the past. Where we left off was, I want you to marry me and want you to stay in Nicaragua."

"I feel so bad that Eddie just acted that way," said Lorna. "I've known him for years."

"It's funny, I never ran into the tiresome lieutenant before," said Guillermo.

"Eddie was an important organizer in the exterior. He recruited me to work on Non-intervention in Nicaragua to stop US aid to Somoza. The amazing thing about that is that we did help stop it."

"Why do think this lieutenant of yours came to my house? How could he be sure I wouldn't shoot him?"

"Eddie acts on his feelings. That's his charisma. He has strong passions."

"I didn't notice any charisma. Does your daughter follow him too?"

"No, he's my friend, not Rini's. She's never liked him. She thought he was totally macho. A womanizer. She hated his cheating on his wife."

"Look, Lorna, frankly it struck me as pretty silly, him showing up at my house. You're here with me! He can just take his jeep and shove off." A dog began barking somewhere outside.

Lorna sighed. "In his own way, he cares for me and wants to protect me. He drove me to Pueblo Azul to help me connect with my family."

The telephone rang. "Damn that phone! I'm privileged to have one, but the damn thing is hyperactive." Guillermo jumped up and yanked the receiver.

"Hello?" he said irritably. "Oh, hello, Maria Rosa. Yes. Fine, thank you. She's right here. Quite all right." He handed the receiver to Lorna. Lorna looked at him quizzically as she accepted the phone.

"Hello, Maria Rosa?"

"Oh, Lorna, I'm so sorry to interrupt yet again, but Rini got a ride earlier than she expected. She'll be here tonight in three or four hours. I said you weren't home, but that I would let you know. She said there's been another contra attack around Ocotal. It's quiet now. We ran them off. But people were hurt, and two were killed.

Lorna gasped. Her heart lurched. "Is Rini passing near Ocotal?"

"Yes, but don't worry. The contras fled. No one thinks they'll return right away."

"Maria Rosa, I'll be back before Rini arrives. Thanks for telling me."

"Now what?" asked Guillermo, as Lorna hung up.

"The contras attacked Ocotal. My daughter's passing through there on her way to Managua. It's dangerous. She's due home tonight."

"Does that mean our three days have shrunk?"

"We have three hours before I have to be back."

"Three more hours, and then I chase your glass slipper and meet your daughter. And she comes to our wedding!" He lifted her face and kissed her on the forehead. "They lived happily ever after," he said, kissing her on the mouth.

"Grandfather died here in Nicaragua, but I haven't seen his grave yet."

"I suppose that's where this Lieutenant was planning to take you?"

"Yes, it was," she said. Lorna looked around the room, at the hand-formed pottery, rustic weavings, and handmade rugs. She felt at home. "It's so peaceful here. I don't want the outside world to intrude on our last moments together, but I also want to hear if there's any news from Ocotal. I'm so torn."

"I'll put on the radio," Guillermo offered.

Lorna shook her head. "Please don't. I know Rini will make it back safely. My grandfather is protecting her."

"You have some interesting beliefs. Yesterday, you told me that two people can stand under a cloud and experience love, because love lies outside them and rains down like a shower. Is that why you feel you can just walk away from love? Because it lies outside you, and you can walk into it any time you want? You can't, Lorna. If you ignore it, love will be buried alive inside you."

Lorna looked up, still not believing he was serious about getting married.

Guillermo pressed on. "We're a country of three million, just a few thousand miles or a short plane ride from the mightiest country in the world, determined to keep us as a little colonial satellite. Yet we think we can lead an uneducated people, in poor health, with short life spans, with high infant mortality, and take back our country. Only incurable optimists can do that, because it demands vision, not simply eyesight. Lorna, I think you're an incurable optimist too. I think you should join us. I want you to join me."

"I have joined you, but in my own way," Lorna said, emphatically. "I'm still thinking about what you said to Eddie. Did you fight on the Southern Front?"

He fondled her hair. "Yes, I did. That was real culture shock, living on the land, not in a house. Especially for the city guys, it was really rough. They were unfamiliar with everything. If they encountered a cow, they'd be scared it was a bull."

"Is that when you were wounded?"

"Yes. It was a little ambush. Happened quickly with lots of noise, gun shots, and shouts. I got hit in the right leg. I went down, falling on Chombo's dead body. I couldn't feel his breathing. I picked up his grenade and threw it. My brother, Javier, dragged me over to the medic, a Costa Rican medical student, who treated me."

"Is this the leg?" asked Lorna. She gently kneaded it, feeling the knee cap and the sinewy thigh muscle.

"Yes, that's the leg," Guillermo continued. "I had excellent medical attention in Spain, through the solidarity network. When the Cuban doctor, Dr. Daisy, recently checked me out, she told me that my leg will last as long as the rest of me."

Lorna stopped rubbing his leg. An irritation ran through her body. She removed her other arm from his shoulder and sat up.

Guillermo pleaded, "Don't stop! It feels so good." He looked up at her face, alarmed. "What's the matter?"

"Oh, nothing. I just didn't realize you and the doctor were such good friends."

"She's a fine doctor and has a very gentle touch."

"That's nice," Lorna said, a bit coldly. She stood up. "I think I want to leave now." As soon as the words came out, she was sorry. He was looking at her with so much concern. She hadn't wanted to stop the flow of his story, but she couldn't control her rising urge to flee. Dr. Daisy was the last straw.

Guillermo stood up slowly. "I can't argue with a mother's intuition. My own mother knew what was happening to me before I did myself. She knew I was sick when I came down with dengue fever. I thought I was just tired, but I was sick for ten days, fever, aching joints, the whole works. Now, we have evidence that the CIA introduced dengue in Cuba in the seventies and it spread. Nice guys, the CIA. That piece of germ warfare was another present from your Uncle Sam."

"He's not my Uncle Sam." Her irritation was increasing.

"I'm sorry, of course not," he apologized.

"I'll get ready to go," she said, feeling foolish and much too old to be in this situation so quickly and with someone so new in her life. She tried to keep the testiness out of her voice. "Will you be able to take me home in a few minutes?"

"Certainly, but I wish we could stay like this forever."

"Forever is a long time, Guillermo." He tried to pull her close, but Lorna was already opening her purse, reaching for the little mirror, comb, and brush in her cosmetic bag. He watched her brush her hair, smiling at her through the mirror.

The call from Maria Rosa about Rini was pulling her away from Guillermo. She couldn't focus on her own reflection with envy and the thoughts of being old and unlovable filling her head. She didn't care if a parade of women had been through this house. No matter how complicated love had become, it had been wonderful. She loved Abuelo's old friend, Doña Angélica on their very first meeting, but with Guillermo, it was romantic love, lust, and pure hunger. Her bad feelings faded a little as she brushed her hair more vigorously. She shook her curls free and tried to return Guillermo's smile through the mirror. She slowly turned to him, moving a little closer.

"This house will miss you," he said. "It hopes you will come back soon."

Their last kiss was slow and soft, but Lorna was intent on leaving. At first, they didn't talk in the truck. She relaxed back again into their romantic mood. He dropped his hand into her lap, and she held it, looking out the windows. The outside world appeared as fresh and new as if she had been away for a long time. The many shades of deep green trees and foliage delighted her eyes. Then her thoughts turned to Rini. She hoped she wouldn't be this unsettled when she saw her.

"I feel Rini's really close," said Lorna. "How odd it would be if we passed her on the road."

"They'd be coming on the other road," he said. A truck full of avocados was ahead of them. Several military vehicles passed in the other direction. Traffic grew heavier. Billboards became more frequent, mostly revolutionary slogans and some commercial advertising. Guillermo reached for the radio dial. "We've held the world at bay for two days. We need to prepare for reentry."

Radio Sandino blasted. Norma Elena Gadea was singing *Cuando Venga la Paz.* Guillermo turned down the volume. He said quietly over the music, "We need peace so badly. This contra war is a distraction from all the other urgent activities we should be doing. So many mothers hate President Ortega for instituting the draft."

They heard radio static and then the song dissolved into a jazz piece by a local group. Guillermo adjusted the volume again. "It's Igni Tawanka! We didn't have our own jazz groups before the revolution, or if we did, the radio never played them. It only played foreign music. Now eighty percent of music played has to be Nicaraguan. You can see how the music scene is flowering. Nica music is a big export item to Europe and the rest of Latin America. Even to the United States."

Lorna moved as close to him as the gearshift allowed, squeezing his hand in agreement, "I've developed a collection of Nicaraguan music myself. My friends and I trade tapes because they're hard to find."

"Radio Sandino is my favorite station," he said. "No ads. The old stations sold religious or commercial products every few minutes. I don't miss the ads."

"Once, Rini called me in San Francisco from Nicaragua," Lorna recounted. "She said they needed two hundred cassette players because they were setting up community radio stations to play the top forty from Mexico City and Spain. She said the CIA was blocking out Radio Sandino by beaming interference from Honduras and Costa Rica."

Guillermo freed his hand again and placed it on her thigh. Lorna covered his hand with hers and continued, "I couldn't imagine what pop songs had to do with international relations, or how two hundred tape recorders could help, not to mention how we would ever get them. Rini explained that popular music is everything in a country of young people who want to hear the latest hit tunes. Luis, one of our solidarity *compas,* had stumbled onto two hundred audiocassette recorders, retired from a university language lab. All we had to do was pack them and pay for the shipping. And we did it!"

"Rini was right," Guillermo said. "If we want the support of young people, we have to give them music. My brother was involved with that project; he may even know your daughter. They set up hundreds of small stations in different communities, playing the newest songs and serving as a telephone bulletin board. People in the countryside and the remote villages went to the local marketplace and left messages for each other to be read on the air."

Lorna leaned her head on his shoulder as he continued,

"Not everybody has phones or TVs, but everyone has a radio. The small stations have a very local broadcast range. When the contras jam our big station, the small ones keep on playing."

"How did those two hundred cassette recorders fit into the scheme?"

"We had only five old cassette recorders to copy the songs for hundreds of stations. We used those two hundred machines to make copies. They made all the difference."

They were quiet again. Maria Elena Gadea's throaty contralto filled the cab. Now the news came on. Guillermo turned up the volume. The US Navy was doing practice maneuvers with warships off both coasts. US spy planes were spotted in Nicaraguan airspace. The Swedes were donating raw materials. The president of Mozambique planned a diplomatic visit. The contras had attacked Ocotal, and two people were dead, a teacher and a social worker; several more were wounded. World boxing champion Panamanian Roberto Duran successfully defended his title. A Honduran school principal denounced the presence of the US military in Honduras.

"Please, turn it off, Guillermo. The world is rushing in too fast."

"No, the news is over, Lornita. Listen to this." Now the cab of the truck was filled with reggae-style Atlantic coast music. The program was called *The Spirit of the Caribe* and the infectious, insistent beat carried them into the flow of Managua traffic. Lorna settled back, against Guillermo's body, her doubts dissipating. Lorna felt protected by a caressing cocoon, undisturbed even when young men and children rushed toward their open windows at traffic lights, hawking newspapers and candy.

They arrived on Maria Rosa's street as evening was settling over the houses. TV and radio sounds drifted out of open doors and windows. A small group sat on a neighbor's steps, talking and laughing. A dog wandered alone, causing other dogs to bark.

"Are you going to marry me?" he asked, breaking the silence

between them.

"I'm not going to marry you. At least not tonight or tomorrow."

"Good, then perhaps this coming weekend?"

"No," laughed Lorna. "Getting married is not what I had in mind for myself. Forget marriage! I don't want any part of it."

"So where does that leave us? I go back to work and you visit with your daughter? When are you scheduled to leave the country?"

"My return flight's not for two weeks."

"Will you phone me in the morning?" he asked softly.

"Will you be there to answer?" she murmured.

"Yes, because I have one last day." He took her hand.

"Then, maybe you can meet Rini."

"I would love to. I'm sure she's as admirable as her mother."

Guillermo stopped in front of Maria Rosa's house. The neighbors on the porch next door were watching them. He held her hand and squeezed it, before getting out and walking to her side of the truck, opening the door, and helping her down. He shook her hand formally for the neighbors' sake. "Goodnight, *compa*," he said, with a slight bow of his head.

She replied formally, "Goodnight, Guillermo. Thank you for the meals and the time we shared."

"Call me please when Rini arrives. I'm worrying about her like a father."

Lorna waved at Guillermo as he drove off. She turned toward Maria Rosa's door, her blue nylon bag in her left hand, knocking with her right, as a lone dog on the street howled.

21

News the Night Brings

Maria Rosa was waiting. Lorna blurted out, "I shouldn't have let him go. At least I should have invited him to come in."

"I wish you had. Xiomara made a pitcher of lemonade before she left, and a lot of food. We thought you might arrive hungry."

"Thanks, Maria Rosa. We ate up all the food in Guillermo's refrigerator." She plopped into a rocking chair. "Any word from Rini?"

"No word yet. But the two deaths were tragic," said Maria Rosa.

"Horrible. We heard it on the radio."

Maria Rosa took a seat in the other rocking chair, and the two women sat rocking in unison.

"Lorna, what's wrong? You look sad."

"Guillermo!" she moaned. "Two days ago I didn't know him. Now I'm upset that he's driven away."

"He'll be back, if you want him to be," said Maria Rosa.

"That's just the problem," wailed Lorna. "I don't know what I want."

Maria Rosa shook her head with its crown of heavy braids.

"What do you think I should do?" asked Lorna.

Maria Rosa smiled. "What your heart tells you. Rini will be here soon."

"Rini's so different from me! Even as a teenager, I knew I was a poet. Rini was all math. Her mind was filled with equations. In high school, she had it figured out. 'Engineering's what I really want. Think of all the neat things you can do with bridges and robots.'"

"So Rini takes after her father?" asked Maria Rosa.

Lorna stopped rocking. "I don't know. Not exactly. Sometimes I worry that Rini has gone to great lengths just to make sure she would be different from me."

They heard a vehicle pull up. Maria Rosa rose from the chair.

"It's *Señorita* Smarty Pants. I know it," cried Lorna, jumping up.

Maria Rosa opened the front door and looked out. "It's Rini," she announced from over her shoulder. Lorna ran out the door.

Rini was pulling a faded flowered backpack out of the cab of the truck. She wore sandals, jeans, and a white T-shirt that proclaimed, "*¡No Pasarán!* They shall not pass."

"It's my beautiful daughter," exclaimed Lorna, hugging her. She noticed subtle changes in Rini. She was still slim, but there was a new roundness.

"Mom, you look great! How are you?"

"I can breathe now that you're safely here," she replied.

"We heard the bad news from Ocotal," said Maria Rosa. She picked up the flowered backpack. "It's terrible about the killings."

"I knew the two people who died. We worked together a few years ago. Pancho and I are so glad to be here. It was a grisly trip," said Rini.

A tall young man in a baseball cap with dark hair who looked about Rini's age emerged from the pickup truck. Lorna watched the man closely as he unloaded gear from the back of the truck, setting down a big dusty bag with a hand-embroidered elephant on its side.

"Mom," said Rini, "this is my friend, Pancho."

"Francisco Altamirano Ibarra," Pancho said. "Glad to meet you." His handshake was firm, his voice gentle. Lorna smiled at him with the dubiousness of a mother examining a daughter's boyfriend. Pancho picked up the elephant duffle bag again.

"Put the bag anywhere, Pancho," Maria Rosa directed as

they followed her in.

Lorna realized that Maria Rosa already knew him.

"Have you two eaten?" Maria Rosa asked. "Xiomara made fresh tortillas, beef, squash, and cabbage salad with lemon meringue pie for dessert." Pancho's face lit up.

"Yuck," said Rini, "I can't bear the thought of food after that ride. But I'm sure Pancho's hungry."

Maria Rosa laughed. "I'll heat it for you."

Lorna watched Rini waiting on this man, laying out a place mat, fork, knife, spoon, and cloth napkin. From the kitchen came the sound of a metal spoon scraping a pan, then sizzling and sputtering sounds of food being reheated.

"I'm stepping into the patio for a minute," said Rini. "I'm feeling queasy, the smell of food frying."

Pancho looked concerned. "I don't have to eat now," he said to Rini.

"Stay, enjoy your meal. I'm just stepping outside to get some air," she replied.

"I'll keep you company, Rini," volunteered Lorna.

The two women sat on a bench in the portico, looking out at the garden. Small lemon trees were growing in stone urns, and jasmine twined over a trellis, along with bougainvilleas. It was very peaceful in the cooler air of evening. Maria Rosa's parakeet made a harsh squawk.

"Are you OK, Rini?"

"Mom, I can't be around the smell of frying food. The reason I don't want to eat is I'm pregnant." She turned to face her mother to see her reaction.

Lorna jolted forward. "You're having a baby? When? With Pancho?"

"Yes, a baby, in February. But I'm not sure about Pancho."

"You don't know who's the father?" Lorna's voice quavered as she tried to suppress any note of disapproval.

"I'm sure he's the father, Mom. I just don't know if I want to share this baby experience with him. I'm considering raising my own baby."

Lorna looked at Rini, standing taller than her and now

going to have her own baby. Lorna was falling into the third age, becoming a crone, a grandmother. But she didn't feel any serenity or wisdom, only doubts and longings.

"Are you sure you want to go through with this, Rini?"

"I've never been surer," said Rini.

"What about Pancho? What does he feel?"

"Pancho wants to get married."

"Is it because of his political opinions? Is that why you don't want to marry the father of your baby?"

"I love Pancho. But he's one of those married-to-the-revolution types, Mom. You know. Like Dad. And that didn't work so well."

Rini's remark pained Lorna.

"I'm not sure I want to get married," Rini explained. "Pancho and I have slight political differences. But my real objection is that I don't feel right about marriage as an institution. Marriage is phony and patriarchal. Look at you and Dad. Marriage is for suckers. I want my individuality, my freedom, and I want my baby. Why should I compromise?"

"Rini, do you realize that single-handed child rearing is a major challenge? Shouldn't you come home to have the baby?"

"I have come home. I belong here. I'm in the land of my ancestors," Rini said.

"You want to have your baby here?"

"Yes. Although I'm scared by the infant mortality rate. There's a woman in the village where I worked who named her third baby Timoteo. She'd already named two other babies Timoteo, but they didn't survive their first year."

"So, you are afraid."

"Mom, I'm scared shitless. Scared of giving birth, and scared of raising a child. But I'm not scared enough not to do it."

"If you're planning to do it alone, I wish you would come home."

"That's non-negotiable, Mom," Rini said, giving her mother a look, a Carl look, of absolute determination. "I have projects I want to finish."

"You mean the electrification project?"

"There's that, and then I want to see how this whole Sandinista revolution works out. Will it follow the path of other revolutions? Or be crushed by imperialism, and the same old guys ultimately take over again? Or will it be like Cuba, and bring real change to the people and the continent?"

Lorna sighed. "I was hoping you and I might go look for Grandfather's grave." The breeze picked up in the little patio, and the white trumpet vines shuddered.

Rini, who had been looking so serious, brightened. "Sounds good, Mom! Let's do it!"

Through a grilled window facing the patio, the voices of Maria Rosa and Pancho could be heard, along with the glug, glug, glug of a liquid being poured from a pitcher.

"Shall we go in, Mom? I think I'll be OK now."

At the dining room table, Pancho was carefully pouring lemonade into tall blue glasses.

"Oh yes," exclaimed Rini, "I'll have some of that, please."

"Are you feeling better?" Pancho asked.

"I am," she said, throwing him a big smile.

Maria Rosa entered from the small kitchen with a lemon meringue pie and a pile of small plates. "Xiomara made this." Pancho helped clear a space on the table. Maria Rosa plunged a knife through fluffy white billows of meringue and cut a large slice which she placed in front of Pancho. Then she served Lorna and herself. Rini just shook her head no.

Pancho took a hearty bite. "This stuff can kill you. The cholesterol in the egg yolks and the lard in the pie crust clog the arteries." He didn't seem fazed by his own announcement.

"Pancho is a doctor," Rini announced.

Maria Rosa said, "Yes, Pancho attended one of my community-health workshops."

Lorna put her fork down in surprise and looked at him again. He looked so young, just like Dr. Daisy. Young or not, Lorna was glad he would know how to take care of Rini during her pregnancy. That is, if Rini would allow it.

"Well, Dr. Pancho," Lorna said, "you have finished the

deadly pie in a flash. Can I offer you seconds?"

"Oh, absolutely!"

"What kind of a doctor are you?" asked Lorna, getting up to slice him another piece.

"I'm a general practitioner now, but I would like to be a pediatrician. My family was exiled in Mexico for ten years. I had been about to enter my pediatrics training when the revolution triumphed."

"Are you still working in clinics in the north?" asked Maria Rosa. "If only children weren't dying of curable diseases."

"There's a lot of education to be done. We teach mothers about nutrition and the importance of sanitation. I urge them to boil the water, and to breast feed the babies. The mothers are diluting the canned baby formulas with impure water."

"That's the problem," said Maria Rosa. "Instead of nursing, they use imported baby formula that costs more. Poor women are victims of advertising which tells them the baby formula is safer and better. But it's not easy to boil water if you're a *campesina*. Boiling water means first fetching the water, then chopping and gathering firewood. Nursing makes much more sense."

"A Cuban doctor told me some mothers are mixing Coca Cola with the formula, because that's easier to get than water."

Lorna was instantly on the alert. "A Cuban doctor?" she asked. "Is her name Daisy Varela?"

"Yes!" Pancho said. "She's an expert in pregnancy. She trained in a maternity hospital in Havana. Do you know her?" He seemed excited.

"Yes, we've met," Lorna said.

Maria Rosa added, "Just last week, Lorna and I worked on the reconstruction of the Rosalea Bandera Clinic. Dr. Daisy works there."

Lorna's attention wandered while Pancho and Maria Rosa continued their excited exchange about Nicaraguan public health education. Lorna noticed that Pancho had quietly taken Rini's hand and was holding it under the table.

Watching her daughter with Pancho left Lorna lonely and

longing for Guillermo. With everyone absorbed in the conversation about the clinic, she quietly excused herself to use the phone. Lorna hoped her call would go through on Managua's unreliable telephones and let her escape these matriarchal feelings of a grandmother rising within her.

She dialed and listened to the sound of the phone ringing distantly, and imagined him in his kitchen or lying on the sofa with the big colorful pillows, listening to the music of the *alto plano*. She flicked on the nearby fan so its hum could cover their conversation. She felt its breeze on her face as Guillermo answered.

"Hello?" he said.

"Guillermo, it's Lorna."

"Our first phone call. Your voice is so charming on the phone. So is Rini there? Safe?"

"Everyone's fine," she said, without explaining further. The sound of his voice evoked the smell of his skin with its faint spicy aftershave, and the feel of his thick, curly black hair. "Rini and I might go to Pueblo Azul in the morning."

"I wish I could go with you," said Guillermo. "But I got called into work in the morning."

"It's OK. Rini and I will be fine," said Lorna, knowing it was important to share this experience alone with her daughter. She hadn't yet said a word to Rini about her new friend.

"I'll miss you," he said.

"I miss you too."

They made a date for the following evening after her return from Pueblo Azul. "I'll phone you tomorrow night," promised Guillermo.

"I'll be waiting. Bye."

Lorna held the telephone receiver a long time after hanging up. She stepped back into the dining room. Rini sat alone, resting her head on her folded arms on the table. Pancho was in the kitchen, washing the dishes with Maria Rosa.

"Tired?" Lorna asked. She stroked Rini's long hair which now spilled out over her shoulders. Lorna recalled scenes from

Rini's childhood, brushing out tangles so she could braid her hair for school. Rini would be howling and sobbing. "Owwww! Stop, Mom! It hurts!" No tangles now in her daughter's heavy, silky mane.

"My baby is having a baby," said Lorna. "Rini, I can hardly believe it."

Rini turned her head sideways. "I can hardly believe it either, Mom. I look and feel the same, but I'm different. Are there two of me? One houses this other me, who's not me."

Pancho came in from the kitchen, drying his hands on a dish towel. "I have to go now," he said to Rini. Turning to Lorna, he added, "It was such a pleasure to meet you, Lorna. Rini has told me so many wonderful stories about you. She is so proud of you!"

"And I am so proud of her," said Lorna, hiding her relief that Pancho would not be spending the night. "I'm sure we'll meet again soon," said Lorna pleasantly.

"But of course!" Pancho said. "I would stay, but my aunt is expecting me tonight. She's bound to be worried, with this bad news from the Ocotal attack."

"Your aunt? So your parents don't live in Managua?" Lorna said.

"No. They remained in Mexico City. My father opened a clinic there. I returned alone."

Maria Rosa walked Pancho to the door. "My house is always open to you."

Lorna watched him go, relieved she would have one night for herself and Rini. She knew there would be time enough for her to get to know Dr. Pancho.

Rini followed Pancho out the door to his truck. "I'll see you tomorrow," she said slipping her arm around his waist.

Lorna stood in front of the fan listening to its hum. The night had turned cooler. She switched it off, and then was startled by the sudden silence and the realization that Rini was an immigrant in Nicaragua now, like Grandfather had been in the United States. Over the generations they had traded countries.

"Lorna, you're daydreaming, staring at the fan," Maria Rosa said. Lorna snapped back to the present.

"Rini is pregnant."

"That explains why she didn't want to be around food cooking. No wonder Dr. Pancho treated her so tenderly. Congratulations, Grandmother."

"Thank you. Rini and I may go to Pueblo Azul tomorrow if we can figure out a ride."

"My neighbor, Jacinto, is not adverse to making a little money. There's been no work for months. I'll see if you could pay him to drive you," offered Maria Rosa.

Rini drifted through the living room, smiling dreamily.

"Well, Señorita Smarty Pants," teased Maria Rosa, "Pancho is very nice, and he even helps wash the dishes. He's the best one you've brought home so far."

"He'll probably last for the duration. We're having a baby together."

"I am so relieved. Does this mean you are not doing this alone?" asked Lorna.

"Yes. We are doing this together," said Rini.

"Congratulations, darling! When's the wedding?" said Maria Rosa.

"There will be no wedding. We're going to be like Simone de Beauvoir and Jean-Paul Sartre, or like President Daniel Ortega and Rosario Murillo."

"Not like Rosario Murillo, please, Rini. She has eight children," said Maria Rosa.

"Yes, but she writes poems and runs the ASTC Cultural Workers Union. Like Rosario, I want to use my talents at every level, from intimacy in the bedroom to fighting the contras."

Maria Rosa was beaming. "Spoken like a true Sandinista, Rini, the 'New Woman.' Then at least allow me to be the godmother!"

"I wouldn't have it any other way," said Rini, giving Maria Rosa a big hug. "But I'm very tired and need to go to bed. We had a hard drive."

Maria Rosa pointed to the guest bedroom. "Xiomara made

up a bed for you in your mother's room. Will you be comfortable?"

"Thank you. I'll be very comfortable," she said. "So are we going to Pueblo Azul tomorrow, Mom?"

"I think so. Maria Rosa's neighbor might be available to drive us."

"*¡Patria libre o morir!*" said Rini, giving her mother a hug and raising her fist, marching off to bed.

"How wonderful, Maria Rosa," said Lorna after Rini had closed the door. "Rini is back safely, she's expecting a baby, and we are going to Pueblo Azul in the morning."

"I'm happy for you and Rini," said Maria Rosa, giving her a good-night hug.

The house grew quiet. Lorna resisted the urge to call Guillermo again, and fell asleep listening to the Nicaraguan night sounds. She dreamed in two languages. Luis was speaking English to her on the phone from San Francisco. His voice was calm and reassuring, although in the background Doña Milagro screamed epithets, cursing the Sandinistas, in Spanish.

22

Flourish and Multiply

The next morning, a distant chorus of roosters and the sound of a church bell woke Lorna into the dawn of a new day. The smells of coffee and freshly made tortillas wafted in from the kitchen. Xiomara had been busy and Maria Rosa had already gone to work. Rini was still sleeping, her golden hair flared out against the quilt.

Quietly, Lorna arose and wandered into the kitchen. She poured herself a cup of coffee, adding some of the heated milk warming in a small copper pan on the stove. In the freshness of the morning, her new identity as *abuela*-to-be seemed more comfortable. Then she remembered her dream and realized that she often dreamed of Luis.

Rini wandered in, yawning and stretching. "Good morning, Mom. How did you sleep?"

"OK. I dreamed in two languages. Doña Milagro screaming at me in Spanish."

"That used to happen to me all the time. Now I think I'm losing my English. I only use it when you visit." Rini poured herself a cup of coffee. "I need to get away from the smell of those tortillas." She turned toward the door to the patio, and Lorna looked at her daughter, framed in the rectangle of light, a new generation growing in her belly, in the chain of life. Each link begetting the next. She idly wondered how Carl would react to the news of his impending grandfatherhood.

By 9 a.m. they were ready to leave for Pueblo Azul. A toot-toot-toot from Maria Rosa's neighbor, Jacinto's old Chevy announced that their ride was ready. Heading out, the two women grabbed packed lunches and water bottles, stuffing them into Lorna's blue bag. The sun was making its full presence felt, with a blinding shimmery glare. Jacinto held the back door open for them. He insisted he sit in front alone, like a chauffeur. He drove silently. Lorna and Rini conversing in English in the back.

"I'm excited to meet Arminda and Doña Angélica," Rini said, "but I'm not ready for Doña Milagro."

"So how do you and Pancho differ politically?" asked Lorna.

"Not much. But we disagreed about some Sandinista official policy decisions. I think that the Sandinistas are going too fast in trying to impose their socialist order."

Lorna asked, "For example?"

Rini swept her hair up with one hand to cool her neck. "For example, Pancho agreed with the official line that everyone should think of themselves as Nicaraguan. Many Indigenous people on the Atlantic coast identify with their own English-speaking people, especially the Miskitos. They self-identify as Miskito, not as Nicaraguan. They want self-rule and political power. I think, first, Nicaragua has to create a national consciousness."

"What do you mean?"

"During the literacy campaign, our brigade taught people the national anthem, what the Nicaraguan flag looked like. We promoted the national folklore. The Sandinista line was 'Everyone who lives in Nicaragua is a Nicaraguan.' That really alienated the Atlantic coast people. The literacy campaign accepted diversity, so we gave out books printed in Miskito, Suma, and Rama. But the Sandinista National Directorate didn't follow through with multiculturalism, and today we're paying the price. The CIA has lured the Miskitos across the Rio Coco into Honduras. Now some of the Miskitos are working with the contras. It's a huge problem for the Sandinistas."

Rini paused, and a smile crossed her face. "At first Pancho was a hard liner, all *mano dura, corazón ardiente*/hard hand, burning heart. But after we talked, he began to see I was right. He ended up supporting the call for autonomy for the Atlantic

236

coast. Now the slogan is 'The Atlantic Coast—A Sleeping Giant!' A lot of energy is going into improving conditions there. I'm sometimes called to help on electrical projects because I speak English. But it's a too-little-too-late policy. The Atlantic coast is still a security problem."

Jacinto was turning off the highway and Lorna reminded everyone to roll up their windows. "There's an incredible amount of red dust ahead on this road," she warned. And soon the Chevy was lurching and rattling over the bumps and potholes, occasionally striking a rock so hard Lorna felt her hair brush the top of the car. Their teeth were chattering so hard that further conversation came to a halt.

After thirty minutes, Jacinto came to a stop. "So which way is Pueblo Azul?" he asked.

Lorna pointed straight ahead. "I think we go toward those houses over there," she said. Then pointing to the left, "Or maybe, it's those over there."

At that moment, before having to decide, a boy riding bareback on a lanky gray horse approached them down the dusty road.

Lorna rolled down the window and smiled in greeting. "Hello."

"Good afternoon, lady," said the boy. He was carrying a large tablet of paper.

"We're looking for Doña Milagro's house—the old Almendros place," she told him.

"That's where my cousin, Arminda lives," he said. "We don't go there very much though. That old lady is mean. Doña Angélica sent me for this paper."

The boy took the tablet under his arm and held it up to Lorna for her inspection. She could see it was the lowest grade of paper that ink bleeds right through.

"Doña Angélica is my great-grandmother. She is going to fill this book with stories for me," said the child proudly.

Rini had stepped out and was patting the horse fearlessly.

"Can you show us the way to your cousin Arminda's house?" asked Rini.

"No, miss. I have to give a reading lesson at the cooperative. But it's right over there. See it?" he said pointing the way.

A short time later, they came upon a valley with squares of green and yellow fields, jagged blue mountains to the west, and flowering trees, illuminated by blazing sunshine, just as Lorna had seen it two weeks earlier.

"I remember this! There's the yard! There's the pump with the cool water, the sweet flowers and fruit trees," said Lorna.

A ginger-colored dog Lorna hadn't seen before wandered out to greet them, followed by Arminda, looking more pregnant than before, carrying a large fine meshed strainer filled with rice. She smiled, seeing the old Chevy and the two women getting out of the backseat.

"Doña Lorna, I am so happy to see you again," greeted Arminda. "I was coming out to wash the rice, when I heard a car. I was sad because Doña Milagro wouldn't let me go to the class at the cooperative. She says my husband has to have a hot lunch every day. But now I'm glad I stayed, now, because we have special company!"

Lorna introduced everyone, including Jacinto, who immediately excused himself to go wait in the car. Tilting the driver's seat as far back as it would go, he appeared to be settling in for a long nap. Arminda poured water from a clay jar into glasses for the guests. Lorna took a glass back to Jacinto, but already his eyes were closed and he was softly snoring.

Rini and Arminda were laughing, discussing their pregnancies as Arminda drew in the dirt with a long stick, explaining to Rini, "They say if your stomach is pointy, you'll have a boy. That's what my husband and Doña Milagro want."

"What do you want?" asked Rini.

"A girl, to keep me company," Arminda answered. She picked up the sieve of rice again and began sorting through the grains. "She could sit with me and help pick the stones out of the rice, and I would tell her stories."

The water splashed through the rice colander. Rini was helping Arminda. The dog licked Lorna's hand, and she noticed that even the dog was pregnant. Sadly thinking of her age, she wondered if Guillermo would want a young, fertile woman, not a woman like herself who could no longer have children.

Doña Milagro appeared at the window. "Arminda! Who are you wasting time with now?"

Rini turned to look at Doña Milagro.

Arminda pointed to Lorna and Rini. "Doña," she said in a loud voice, "This is Don Gabriel Almendros' granddaughter. She has returned with her daughter."

Doña Milagro screeched, "Whores, both of them! Whores, bandits, and thieves—all of them! They were always a no-good bunch, and they always will be, the lot of them, *desgraciados*, outcasts." She spat into the dirt outside the window.

Rini jumped up and shouted back at Doña Milagro. "I take great offense, madam, at your insults to my family. You have no business insulting my sainted great-grandfather, Gabriel Almendros, nor my mother, nor myself, nor my unborn child."

Doña Milagro's eyes sparkled. It was obvious she loved a good fight. She raised her shriveled fist and shook it at Rini.

"Typical. This is how the youth are today, no respect for their elders. No respect. You are a bunch of heathens and Communists." Doña Milagro was just warming up. She shook a gnarled dry finger toward Arminda. "This lazy slut Arminda is the same. She barely has my poor boy's lunch ready when he comes in from the fields, but here she is, dawdling with riff raff instead of getting her chores done. I'm waiting for her to prepare my juice. The doctor wants me to have my pills between meals and to take them with juice. Does she care? No, she jaws all afternoon with no-accounts."

"Doña," Arminda interjected softly. "Don't upset yourself."

Doña Milagro directed her rant at the heavens. "It's enough that these crazy Sandinistas want to draft the young men and drag the young women off to reading lessons when it's time to prepare a meal, or to militia training when they should be washing clothes." Doña Milagro pointed to Arminda again, accusingly. "This one wanted to join the militia, but I wouldn't let her. She even had my son convinced she should join, but I told him to put his foot down. The poor boy is so easy to lead. The girl hardly earns her keep as it is. Here I've been waiting for my juice and I find her passing the time of day."

Rini had balled her hands into fists, but Arminda gently put her hand over them. "*Ya voy.* I'm coming, *doña.* I wanted to get the rice ready first. Don't worry, I'll bring the juice to you in a minute."

"I wish that old witch would shut up," Rini hissed to Lorna.

"Hurry up," said Doña Milagro. "My legs are hurting standing here. They need massaging."

"Lie down, *doña.* I'll bring you the juice and your pills, and then I'll rub your legs." Arminda seemed unshaken and calm.

"Well, hurry up about it," grumbled Doña Milagro. "I can't wait all day."

Arminda worked the pump, and Rini, standing between Lorna and Arminda, said under her breath, "Thank god, the pump drowns out that voice. I could beat the old bitch to death."

"God forgive you for saying that," whispered Arminda. "She's old."

"Old or not," said Rini, "she's vile and hateful."

Doña Milagro cocked her head back out the window. "What are you two whispering about? There you go like Angélica, a sleazy slut, sneaking around. She lured my sweetheart away and then she killed him with her rotten care and bad cooking. I hope she has a slow, painful death."

Rini stepped toward the window. "Watch your mouth, old lady. Your hate spills out like bile."

Doña Milagro pulled herself up as far as her shrunken height would allow, shouting, "What? You dare to threaten an old woman?"

Lorna took Rini's arm. "Come on, Rini. Let's go," she said in English.

Rini shook her arm free. "I want to see Great-grandfather's

house, Mom. That's why I've come so far. The old bitch can't stop us. Don't you have the deed to the place in your purse?"

"I do, but let's not deal with that now, Rini. The more we upset the old woman, the harder she'll be on Arminda."

"Come with us," Rini commanded in Spanish, turning to Arminda at the pump.

"You go on to Mama Abuela's house. I'll meet you there later," she said.

"You two tramps better leave at once," Doña Milagro shouted angrily at Lorna and Rini from the window. "Arminda, drive this scum off my property."

"It's not your property!" shouted Rini over her shoulder, as Lorna hurriedly led her to the car. "It belongs to my great-grandfather."

Lorna quickened their pace. "We can't deal with this right now, Rini. To take possession, we'll probably have to get a lawyer."

"I know, Mom, but she's such a monster. Can't we do something now?"

"Let's talk on the way back. Right now, I want you to meet Doña Angélica."

"What a poor old woman has to put up with!" moaned Doña Milagro. They could hear her, incanting a long list of sufferings, and the farther Rini and Lorna walked, the louder her incantations got.

Lorna opened the car door and in they climbed. Rini slammed the door hard. "What a fucking bitch!"

Jacinto lifted his head. "Where to?" he asked.

"To the left, please, Jacinto. But go slowly, so I can recognize the house," Lorna answered.

"Mom," said Rini, "Do you have the house deed with you? Lorna nodded affirmatively.

"Let's give it to Arminda."

"You don't want it for yourself and Pancho and the baby?"

"Mom, we'll never live here. Of that I'm sure."

Lorna smiled. "Rini, Arminda may not know what to do with it. She may need us to help her get a legal advisor. We'll talk on the way home. Young women like Arminda have been told what to do for so long, they don't yet know their own strength."

Jacinto started the engine. Doña Milagro's litany of insults continued, taking such a bizarre turn that both women had to laugh.

"I could've wrung Doña Milagro's neck," announced Rini. "I don't usually go off like that."

"Hormonal madness, Rini. The early months of pregnancy are an emotional roller coaster."

"Forget pregnancy, that's every day for me."

"Me too," Lorna admitted. "This menopause thing is taking me for a ride. I haven't had a period in over three months."

"I can hardly wait for menopause," said Rini. "No more birth control."

"It doesn't look like you've been too concerned about birth control."

They laughed. Lorna felt at home, laughing with Rini, feeling whole and belonging again. "Rini, if you really don't want the deed to Grandfather's house for your baby, I like your idea of giving it to Arminda."

"That works for me. I came here to be part of a revolution, not to be an absentee landowner. I don't even want to own a house. Pancho's family still owns a ranch in San Jorge that his cousins are renting. But that is not what we're about. It's our work that compels us, not property. We need to live where our work is and our work moves around. Let's figure out how to give the house to Arminda."

The deed, slightly yellowed and brittle, was in Lorna's purse, in the same envelope the downtown Chicago lawyer had handed to her more than forty years ago. Somehow she had always known neither she nor Rini would live in Grandfather's house.

"Arminda's been a slave in that house," declared Rini. "She deserves it. And besides that, giving it to her is like the agrarian reform slogan, 'The land belongs to those who work it.' Though I really think she should get out of Pueblo Azul.

She's too good for domestic drudgery. Have you met her husband?"

"No. And I don't think I will now; I get the impression we're not welcome there."

"Maybe, Mom. That Doña Milagro loves to fight and complain. We're a good excuse for that. She's probably wishing we would come back right now so she could unleash her insults again." Rini laughed, "You have to admit she's good at it."

Lorna recognized Angélica's house. "This is the place," she said to Jacinto in Spanish. Jacinto pulled up in front, and Rini and Lorna piled out. Jacinto indicated he would wait again in the car.

A toddler climbed out of a swinging hammock to look at the visitors, as Dora, Arminda's mother, came out of the door, carrying an infant.

"Hello," she said, showing her missing front teeth. "Welcome, Doña Lorna. *Estás en tu casa*. Make yourself at home. Abuela hasn't stopped talking about you since you left." Dora looked to Lorna like she was barely thirty.

"This is my daughter, Irene Gabriela Sevens Almendros," said Lorna.

She noticed Rini looked wilted, no longer animated by anger or laughter. Rini rested her hand on the little boy's head. "I'm Rini, what's your name?"

"Anselmo," the boy answered.

"Anselmo, can you lead me to the bathroom?" Rini asked and followed him to the outhouse. In just a few minutes Rini returned with a worried look on her face.

"Mom," she said in alarm. "I'm spotting blood. Do you think I could lose the baby?"

23

Blood

They were in the car in a flash and nearing the rebuilt Rosalea Bandera clinic. Rini lay on her back with her head on Lorna's lap, her knees bent. "I wish Pancho was here." Rini said. "Could we try sending a messenger to his aunt's house?"

"How?" asked Lorna.

Before Rini could answer, Jacinto pulled up to the clinic. No longer a construction site, the clinic had a new sign. A new guard smiled at them as they entered. Lorna thought of his predecessor who had given his life so that everyone in that poor little community could receive medical care.

Rini headed straight for the reception desk and received a number. She and Lorna took a seat on one of the crude benches that Lorna had helped build. Rini gave Lorna a frightened smile and reached for her hand. Lorna squeezed it, trying to be reassuring.

"What a miracle the clinic is open again, so quickly," Lorna murmured to Rini.

Women crowded the plain benches around the room, slouching against the wall or learning forward, anxiously holding infants and toddlers. An old woman with straggly gray hair and bony shoulders seemed half-asleep. A young woman with the clear gaze of a Madonna held a squirming boy baby in striped pants. Two women with shiny fat cheeks covered their mouths, whispering to one another. The one male in the waiting room stood with his legs far apart, his belly flowing over his belt.

To Lorna's relief, the consulting room door opened, framing Dr. Daisy Varela, once again in white jeans, a white low-cut top, and high-heeled white sandals. She held a child in her arms, who was playing with her dangling stethoscope. The Cuban handed the child to its mother, then looked up, catching sight of Lorna.

"Compañera Lorna! I'm so pleased to see you. Did you come with Eddie?"

"No," said Lorna a bit sharply, thinking that Dr. Daisy and Eddie were still in touch. "We've come because my daughter may be having a miscarriage."

"I'm pregnant and spotting," said Rini, worriedly.

Daisy checked Rini's patient number. "It's almost your turn," she told her. "I'll see you in just a few minutes." She disappeared into the consulting room.

"How do you know her? She's so beautiful," Rini asked Lorna.

"Well, Pancho knows her too," responded Lorna. "Remember? He talked about her last night, the Cuban doctor who trained at a maternity hospital in Havana. But to cut a long story short, I met her with Eddie about a month ago, when he drove me out to Pueblo Azul the first time. Then I met her again last week, when Maria Rosa and I came back to help with the clinic reconstruction."

"I'm proud that you helped with the rebuilding."

"A pregnant Frenchwoman on our crew said Dr. Daisy saved her baby. She said she has gentle hands."

"Gentle hands? That reminds me to breathe," said Rini, relaxing some.

The receptionist called, "Number six."

"Don't worry, Mom," said Rini as she got up to go into examining room

Dr. Daisy came out, her dazzling smile so white in her dark face. "Lorna, my friend! Your daughter will be fine. Come on in, Rini."

The two young women disappeared into the clinic office. Ten minutes later they were back.

Daisy instructed Rini, "Get this prescription filled. Go home and get your legs up on a pillow. Set an ice pack on your tummy for good measure. Keep off your feet. If you feel you need to, check with a doctor in Managua. But I think you're going to be fine."

Jacinto looked relieved when he saw them walking toward the car. "Drive home? That means you're going to be fine, *mi reina*. Otherwise, they'd have sent you to a hospital. I'll drive very carefully. You won't feel the smallest bump!"

Rini dozed in the backseat, her head again on Lorna's lap. Lorna's hand idly stroked Rini's hair. It was clear that Rini really wanted to have this baby.

"We're here!" announced Lorna an hour later when Maria Rosa's house came into view.

Rini woke up. "I feel better, Mom!"

"You're going to have to rest! Doctor's orders," Lorna reminded her.

"Well, *mi reina*," said Jacinto to Rini, "I hope you had a smooth ride."

"I didn't feel a single pothole. It was like gliding on ice. Thanks, Jacinto."

That evening, Rini was lying on the wicker couch in Maria Rosa's living room, her head and knees propped up with pillows. Pancho hovered over her. Maria Rosa sat at a small table, surrounded by texts, drafts, and pamphlets on Nicaragua's banana industry. She was in charge of drafting up a new trade agreement.

At a knock on the front door, everyone looked up. Maria Rosa pushed back her chair and rose to open the door. Framed in the entry alcove, Daisy Varela's dark skin glistened against her white clothes. "Dr. Daisy! Come in, come in!"

"I had to be in town tonight, so I thought I would check in on my patient," explained Dr. Daisy. As always, she radiated total vitality, exuberance, and joy in living.

"Doctor!" cried Rini, rising to a sitting position. "I'm so glad to see you. I can't believe you're here to check on me! I'm flying high as a kite on all this attention."

"*Cálmate, hermana!*" laughed Dr. Daisy. "Don't get up! Remember, I advised rest!"

Rini reached for Daisy's hands. "You brought these gentle hands with you."

Pancho seemed less pleased than the others at the interruption. He stood now, with his arms crossed on his chest.

"Pancho, this is my new-found friend and savior, Dr. Daisy. Pancho is my *compañero*," Rini added, tugging on the doctor's hands. "Sit by me, sit by me!"

Pancho extended his hand, formally. "Dr. Francisco Altamirano Ibarra. Actually, we met at the conference here in Managua. I thank you for your kind attentions this afternoon to my *compañera* and our baby," said Pancho with a proprietary air. Lorna could see he wanted that baby too and he wanted to take care of Rini.

"The pleasure is all mine, *compañero*," Daisy told him. "I hope I haven't taken too much liberty in coming by. I feel especially close to this patient. I am a friend of Eddie Flores, and my patient's mother spent a week up north helping rebuild our clinic. We internationalists have a strong bond. We're all away from home," Daisy smiled warmly at Lorna.

Pancho moved a step closer toward Daisy. "Your prescription was only for vitamins." His tone was a bit truculent.

"Yes, rest and nutrition are very important. Many doctors try everything under the sun to save embryos in the first trimester, but I believe a baby has to make it on its own in that period. Most spontaneous miscarriages in the first three months indicate there's a serious problem. It's probably a fetus that wasn't meant to be."

"Our baby was meant to be," declared Pancho firmly.

Silently, Lorna cheered.

"I'm sure that's true," Daisy said, soothingly. "May I have a very brief private consultation with my patient?"

"No problem," said Maria Rosa. "We'll go out on the patio to enjoy the jasmine and the *sacuanjoche*. It is very fragrant tonight."

Pancho looked as if he would remain at Rini's side, but she

reached up to him, blowing him a kiss. "Go, *amorcito*," she said. "I would welcome a few minutes alone with my doctor." Grudgingly, he moved with the others toward the open door.

Outside fireflies glimmered along the clothesline. Lorna swatted a mosquito, absent-mindedly. Maria Rosa lit a citronella candle. "This should discourage mosquitoes," she said.

Pancho appeared to be brooding. "We always give women in this situation diethylstilbestrol. DES," he said.

"You know, *Panchito*," responded Maria Rosa, softly, taking a seat on one of the wooden benches, "in the States there's been a big scandal that women prescribed DES during pregnancy have been shown to have an increased risk of breast cancer, and it can cause malformations of the fetus. Daughters of these women show an increased risk of abnormalities associated with the reproductive tract. These pharmaceuticals are not allowed in the States anymore."

Maria Rosa added, "Dr. Daisy may never have used DES because of the US trade embargo against Cuba. That embargo is almost as old as she is."

"DES can be very effective in preventing miscarriage," Pancho insisted.

"Yes, in the short term," Maria Rosa replied, "but it can affect the children later, especially daughters. And researchers are still studying the effects on subsequent generations—grandsons and granddaughters."

"I should read the literature. My father prescribed DES all the time."

"It's another sad facet of imperialism, that a drug banned in the US is still made available by US manufacturers in Third World countries."

"The health-care solidarity group from San Francisco is coming next month. I'll ask them to bring reprints of the article," said Maria Rosa.

"So did you train in medicine?" asked Pancho respectfully.

"I wanted to. I studied here in Managua," said Maria Rosa. But I went to work as a researcher for several years while my husband completed medical school. When he was killed, I was able to get out of Nicaragua, to San Francisco, with my mother and my sister's two sons. I did work in women's health education for Spanish-speaking women at San Francisco General Hospital. Since returning, I've become a cog in the bureaucratic machinery of Nicaragua's diplomatic corps. But I still find time to volunteer in health education."

"You're hardly a cog!" exclaimed Lorna.

"No wonder you're so interested in my work," said Pancho. "Rini never told me you worked in the hospital. Your ideas are so interesting."

"What I'm telling you about the problems with DES took a lot of organizing and protesting to get the attention of the medical establishment. I'm shocked at the attitude in mainstream medicine. Important work is done in the alternative medicine field and it's growing."

"Look, the fireflies have left," said Lorna.

"As a child, I had to go to bed when the fireflies left," said Pancho. "I hated that! I wanted to stay up and be part of what was going on."

"As a child, Rini never wanted to go to bed," said Lorna. "You must be very compatible."

"Rini and I have our best times late at night, planning, reading, talking. Our village goes to sleep at sundown, but we carry on!"

Daisy emerged onto the patio, her white jeans and blouse catching the remaining light. "Our patient is doing fine. The bleeding's stopped. But she says she's lonely, hearing you all outside while she has been sentenced to the couch for the evening. Please return. Your queen awaits her subjects."

Inside, Rini lifted her head from the pile of pillows. "If I am queen for a night, then I demand that we all play canasta. Pancho taught me to play, and I adore it."

"Oh, I love that game," cried Daisy. "An older Argentinian taught it to me in Cuba. He was so interesting. He had gone to medical school with Che Guevara."

"Do you get homesick, Daisy?" Lorna asked.

Daisy looked down at her ten beautifully polished fingernails. "I miss my mother the most. My mother cleans at a *círculo infantil*, a childcare center. Before the revolution, she was illiterate. Something about you reminds me of her."

Something inside Lorna melted as she reached out to hold Dr. Daisy's hands in hers. Dr. Daisy and Rini were both the same, she realized. Far from home and in constant danger. Lorna let the superficial jealousy dissolve, replaced by maternal feelings and fear for her safety. The contra targeted internationalist volunteers, especially the Cuban doctors and technicians. "I am so grateful to you for what you are doing for Rini and my grandchild, " Lorna said.

Lorna released Dr. Daisy's hands at the sound of a sharp tap at the door.

Maria Rosa rushed to the door. It was Eddie, saying in his most charming voice, saying, "Hola, can I come in?"

"Come in," said Maria Rosa, opening the door.

"*Hola,*" Eddie said. His bearing was jaunty, cocky, as always, and he looked impressively fit in his well-pressed military fatigues and shiny boots.

"Long time no see, Eddie," said Lorna sarcastically, in English, remembering his intrusion into Guillermo's house the day before.

"See me no sees," Eddie answered, also in English. He turned to the group and said in Spanish, "I came to pick up Dr. Daisy." Eddie addressed Pancho, "I don't think I've met you, I am Lieutenant Eduardo Flores. And you?"

"Dr. Francisco Altamirano Ibarra. I am Rini's *compañero.*"

"My pleasure," said Eddie. "Rini, how are you? Daisy tells me you're pregnant."

Lorna bristled hearing that Dr. Daisy had talked about her patient and stolen her thunder to tell Eddie Rini's news herself.

"Yes," confessed Rini happily. "I'm going to have a baby."

Eddie turned to Lorna, "*Felicidades,* Grandma. Or do you prefer *abuelita?* Either way, let me congratulate you." Lorna felt her cheeks burning, either from a hot flash or from her annoyance at being called Grandma.

Daisy interrupted. "We're on our way to go dancing. Eddie suggested he pick me up here, since I was checking on Rini."

Eddie couldn't leave fast enough as far as Lorna was concerned. She turned her back on him and poured a glass of lemonade for her daughter.

"Good" Daisy approved. "It's very important to keep up her liquids."

Lorna headed toward the kitchen to refill the pitcher and Maria Rosa followed her. "Lorna, I forgot to tell you, Guillermo called. He phoned three times today. I promised him you would telephone as soon as you got home. Call him now. I'll take over the lemonade pitcher."

Lorna stepped into the hallway and dialed his number, marveling at how quickly her fingers had learned it. As the phone rang, she pictured Guillermo's small house, the sofa, and Guillermo himself.

"Hello," came Guillermo's voice.

"It's me, Lorna."

"Lorna, I'm dying to speak to you. I've so much to tell you. Only right now I have guests, my brother's family."

"The same," said Lorna.

"Tell you what . . . I'll phone you back, or better yet, I'll come by and pick you up in an hour."

Lorna surveyed the scene in the living room. Between Pancho and Maria Rosa, Rini had plenty of care. "An excellent plan. I'll see you soon."

"A date?" Eddie inquired when she had hung up. "And where's granny going? The new young boyfriend, perhaps?"

Lorna could have swatted him. Eddie was getting under her skin two days in row. She was infuriated by his teasing about dating younger people and hoped Dr. Daisy wasn't going to get hurt hanging out with Eddie.

Lorna felt all eyes turning toward her, especially Eddie's. He persisted, "So, *abuelita*, when you bring your basket of goodies to grandmother's house, watch out for the big bad wolf."

Everyone chuckled, except for Rini. "The only wolf around

here is you, Eddie," Rini said, tartly from the couch.

"A wolf? Yes," acknowledged Daisy, "but not a bad one. A rather charming one who gives English lessons and draws the funniest doodles. The whole clinic was laughing at the one you drew yesterday, Eddie."

"You're cartooning again?" Lorna found herself interested, as her anger settled into annoyance. This side of Eddie had always attracted her, making it worth having him as a friend.

"Just doodles," Eddie said, modestly.

"Everyone loves his drawings," Daisy said. "He put Mickey Mouse ears on Ronald Reagan!"

"M-I-C," sang Rini.

"K-E-Y," sang Lorna.

"M-O-U-S-E-," they sang, Eddie joining in, in a thunderous baritone.

"What is this?" asked Pancho "The US national anthem?"

"It might as well be," said Eddie, amidst more laughter.

Lorna excused herself and went to the bedroom to prepare for Guillermo's arrival. She had two big questions. What answer would she give Guillermo about their relationship? And what would she wear? She decided to put off thinking about the relationship question for the more immediate wardrobe question. She opened the suitcase from under the bed. The dark clothes that she'd rejected during the heat of the day stared back at her, with their aura of San Francisco's brisk air and fog. Managua cooled off in the evening. The black cotton pants will do just fine, she thought.

Back at the closet, she pulled out the white blouse with the low neckline bordered with colorful green and red flowers. Critically, she held it against the black pants as her thoughts returned to the granny business. Maybe it bothered her because of Guillermo being younger and they had gotten too close too fast. She reached for her strappy sandals under the bed. Now her outfit was complete.

Undressing for the shower, she looked in the mirror. Her body looked healthy and strong. Guillermo had liked what he saw.

Freshly showered and dressed, Lorna joined the others in the living room. Dr. Daisy and Eddie hadn't left yet. She felt Eddie's eyes on her, interested and approving. She knew that Eddie's belittling granny talk was just his way of needling her, so she would not get too buoyant and float out of his orbit. At that moment, she didn't appreciate his jealousy of Guillermo.

Eddie turned back to the doctor, drinking lemonade and chatting with Rini. Pancho and Maria Rosa were back on the topic of DES.

"This is such an outrage," Pancho was saying. "To think DES is banned in the United States, yet the pharmaceuticals sell it in Nicaragua. It's just like the banned pesticides that have been dumped here for years. Maria Rosa, I wonder if you would give a talk about this to our health team?"

"I would love to, Pancho, but diplomatic duty calls. I have to finish this draft banana trade agreement tonight."

"All de nations love bananas," sang Eddie, throwing himself into the song. "That's an old Atlantic coast song," he explained, jumping up and swinging his arms wide open. "All de nations love bananas," he sang, showing off for Dr. Daisy.

"It's a good thing they love bananas," said Maria Rosa acerbically. "What would a banana republic like Nicaragua do without them?"

"There's always coffee," suggested Pancho.

"The whole world seems to love that too," said Lorna.

"Or maybe Nicaragua should just grow the basic staples the people need?" said Rini from her couch. "Bananas are a totally exploitative crop. And so is coffee."

"And the conquistadors made off with all the gold," said Pancho.

"Right now our best export is our culture," said Maria Rosa. "Our music, our poetry, and our primitivist art. The whole world is interested in our revolution. Who could blame them?"

"That's no exaggeration!" Eddie continued. "At the InterContinental hotel, I saw some *gringo* buy a primitivist painting, a small one for $1,500 US dollars from a

253

Solentiname painter. A few years ago that guy was a barefoot islander, tending a few banana trees and fishing. Now he's an artist, with a beret, even on the hottest days."

Lorna thought about the crowds at their Friends of Nicaraguan Culture solidarity table at the San Francisco benefit concert events. It had been Luis's idea to sell Nicaraguan cultural goods, and it had turned out to be a source of steady revenue. The tape cassettes of politicized folk music sold like hotcakes. T-shirts made of the flimsiest cotton sold out because of the dynamic graphics printed on them.

Now Rini took notice of Lorna. "Mom, you look nice. Where are you going?"

"My friend, Guillermo, is coming by. I'm not sure where we're going."

"Oh, Mom, why haven't told me about him! Now who's keeping secrets? Who is he, Mom?"

"A snooty architect," said Eddie. "He has an equally snooty brother at the Ministry of Culture who turned down my poster design."

"If you don't like him, he must be a decent guy," said Rini, never missing an opportunity to deflate Eddie.

"Hey, wait a minute, Rini. I've known you since you were wet behind the ears. How can you come down on a poor soldier who just wants a little respect for his art?" said Eddie fondly.

"Mom, I am looking forward to meeting your friend," said Rini, changing the subject.

Eddie picked up a spoon and tapped out a rhythm, bellowing out, "All de nations love bananas" again. Then he danced across the room and grabbed Dr. Daisy around the waist. "Come on, come on, come on!" he shouted. "Conga line!" Maria Rosa fell in behind Dr. Daisy. But Lorna sat it out.

"If you can't beat 'em join, 'em," said Rini, clinking away with her spoon on the lemonade glass, providing the 1-2/1-2-3 clave beat. Pancho snapped his fingers. Maria Rosa grabbed a bunch of bananas from the fruit bowl and held them over her head with one hand, the other hand clutching Eddie's waist. No one heard Guillermo's knock on the screen door.

"Hello," he shouted more loudly. Lorna stood up and opened the door. Guillermo laughed, seeing a roomful of people dancing, and put his hands on Lorna's waist, pushing her to form a second conga line.

The two lines, led by Eddie and Lorna, met in the center of the room. Eddie veered to the left. Lorna veered to the right.

Maria Rosa was the first to fall back down on a chair, and the conga lines broke apart.

"You must be Rini. I'm Guillermo Villanova," Guillermo said to Rini on the couch. Rini introduced Pancho. Eddie and Guillermo barely acknowledged each other. But Guillermo smiled and acknowledged Daisy.

Lorna picked up her bag. "I'm ready, Guillermo," she announced.

"I'm sorry I can't get up to say good-bye, but my doctor," Rini said, looking at Daisy, "insists I stay off my feet till tomorrow."

"Nothing serious, I hope," asked Guillermo.

"Fortunately, I think I'm fine."

"We're having a baby," said Pancho, looking at Rini.

"Congratulations," Guillermo said, offering his hand to Pancho. "Congratulations to both of you," he nodded, smiling to Rini.

"We're off," Lorna said waving.

"Goodnight, all," said Guillermo. "Nice meeting you." And they walked out the front door.

In the car, Guillermo kissed her and snapped on the tape deck. "Listen to this, Lorna, it's from Iceland. My brother copied it for me, and I've been waiting eighteen whole hours to share it with you." Strange instrumental music with beating drums and chanting male voices filled the truck cab.

"Here we are listening to music from Iceland, while basking in a warm Nicaraguan night," said Lorna.

Guillermo snapped it off. "I have some complicated

information to tell you," he was saying. "I was hoping we could go to my house."

"What's up?"

"We'll talk at my house. Tell me how you spent our time apart. You never mentioned that your daughter was having a baby. That's very exciting."

"I didn't know until last night."

"You must be very proud."

"Don't you realize this makes me a grandmother, an old lady?"

"Not an old lady, but a blessed lady. Your grandchild will be beautiful, and a Nicaraguan. What a great combination," he said.

"I love your enthusiasm. It makes me feel beautiful, optimistic and very un-grandmotherly."

Once again they were in Guillermo's neighborhood, Bello Horizonte, and without the rain, Lorna could see the low green stucco wall and the gate more clearly. Guillermo unlocked the gate and drove in. When they entered his house, he turned on a light, and the little room sprang into view, with its scratchy Mexican blanket, and bookshelves. It was much more modest than Maria Rosa's house in Los Robles, but everything was orderly and colorful.

Guillermo offered her a drink. "Just rum, lemon, and sugar," said Lorna. She took her glass to the couch and they sat down on the rough woven covering. She shuddered, as a chill ran through her from the ice cubes.

Guillermo noticed the shiver. "Thinking of the dead?" Guillermo asked.

"Not consciously. I think I was remembering my grandfather."

"He's probably throwing a big party in heaven to celebrate the news of your Nicaraguan grandchild."

"A new baby is very good news," she said.

"Whenever I hear laments about overpopulation, I think to myself that if the world's resources were distributed fairly, there would be enough for everyone. Your new grandchild might be the one to figure out how to save our little planet."

"You're very global tonight."

He turned to look at her, intently. "Because I'm leaving on an assignment to India. That is what I wanted to tell you. I've been assigned to the diplomatic staff at our Indian Embassy. I leave tomorrow. I want you to come with me."

The ice in her glass tinkled as she put it down, abruptly.

"If I had agreed to marry you two days ago, you would now be telling me you were leaving? Is this a game?"

"It's not a game, Lorna. It's a revolution. Listen, please. Someone else was supposed to go, but it turns out she couldn't travel. My boss said the replacement meeting went on for hours. Many names came up. Mine was the one that stayed through all the rounds of discussion. I'm basically a pawn; the National Directorate places people like me wherever they think we are most useful."

"When do you have to decide?" asked Lorna.

"I already accepted the post."

"You accepted?"

"To be honest, they decided for me. I didn't have a choice. India won't be forever, Lorna. You could come with me."

"When I met you, you said the worst thing would be having to leave Nicaragua. What happened to that? You were talking about the ancestors. Your ancestors, my ancestors. I can't believe this."

"I have to go where I am sent. Where I am needed," he replied.

Her thoughts were racing. "You're leaving me. I'm not going to India, Guillermo. Marriage is out."

Lorna saw the stricken look on his face and was moved by it. "Guillermo, maybe this doesn't really change anything. We shared something very wonderful. It's just going to end sooner than we hoped."

"We still have the whole night before it does," whispered Guillermo, nuzzling her neck and caressing her hand. She turned totally liquid as he touched her.

They spent the night making bittersweet love.

24

Where Is the Silver Lining?

The next morning, Guillermo and Lorna pulled up in front of Maria Rosa's house in his truck. He left the motor running, gazing at her with his penetrating dark eyes.

"Come with me, Lorna," he urged.

A rooster crowed in the distance.

"I can't," said Lorna, regretfully, and she quietly opened the truck door and slipped out. Without looking back she walked to the front door. She heard Guillermo take off.

Fresh coffee smells floated from the kitchen, and Lorna realized Maria Rosa was already up. "Good morning, Lorna, there's coffee on the stove."

Maria Rosa glanced at her. Lorna found her look too searching. She busied herself at the stove, pouring the coffee and hot milk, stirring it, carefully avoiding eye contact with her friend. She felt totally drained. The tears were ready to stream out of her eyes at any moment, if she was not careful. She carried her coffee into the dining room. Maria Rosa followed her and set her own coffee cup down and took a chair. "Helen phoned from San Francisco and woke us all up early," said Maria Rosa, cheerfully. "She wanted to talk to you."

"What did she say?" Lorna asked vacantly, walking back into the kitchen for a saucer and spoon.

"Helen said a letter came for you from Three Rivers Press," Maria Rosa called out to her. "She thought it might be important, so she opened it. Guess what? They've accepted your book proposal! Isn't that great?"

Lorna stared at the ceramic counter tiles. She was having trouble focusing on what Maria Rosa was telling her. Instead she found herself thinking of Guillermo's face, of his body and their passionate night.

Lorna willed herself to pay attention to Maria Rosa's voice coming at her from the dining room. "Oh, yes, that's my book proposal for the interviews with Nicaraguan women about the revolution," she called mechanically in a flat tone. "When did Helen call?"

"About thirty minutes ago. She said it was about nine in California. Aren't you going to come sit down?"

Lorna was holding on to the edge of the counter as if it were the sole support of her life. Then she heard footsteps, and Rini emerged, wearing the *No pasarán* T-shirt and shorts which seemed to be her nighttime costume. Rini was grinning wickedly.

"Hi, Mom. At four thirty this morning, I noticed you weren't home. You must find this Guillermo pretty interesting." She gave her mother a knowing look.

"I do," Lorna said, without embellishing. She was dying to sleep, so she could forget Guillermo, forget everything. "He's very interesting, but he's leaving for India today."

"How exciting," said Rini, still smiling. Maria Rosa picked up the thread.

"India?" Maria Rosa chirped brightly. "He's been assigned to the Nicaraguan Embassy?" Lorna nodded. "He's such a good choice," Maria Rosa commented. Lorna could hear the clink of her spoon as she swirled the foam in her coffee.

"He's a natural for the job, Lorna. With his interests in history, architecture and foreign cultures, he'll be perfect. You must be very happy for him."

"I am," said Lorna, so unconvincingly that she was surprised Maria Rosa took no notice.

"Foreign diplomacy for me is a great strain. I would much rather be doing health education in Dr. Daisy's clinic," said Maria Rosa.

"I'm sure he'll be great," Lorna said without enthusiasm, walking into the dining room and sitting down at the table.

"Something I forgot to mention Maria Rosa," Lorna

continued, changing the subject. "Rini and I have decided to transfer the deed to Grandfather's house in Pueblo Azul to Arminda. But she's so under the thumb of this Doña Milagro, she'll need assistance in getting it registered with the proper authorities. Do you have a friend who could help her with the legal stuff? I would be happy to pay whatever this person would charge."

"Guillermo would be the perfect person to help you," said Maria Rosa. Lorna felt like screaming, but Maria Rosa was continuing to talk. "Sadly, he's leaving. It's too bad. Deeds, land titles and all that sort of thing are exactly what he's been doing in the Ministry of Housing. In any case, you are generous, my friend. This makes me very happy. I am sure I can find someone who will help the young woman, although she may need more than legal help. From what you tell me, she needs a woman's support group to help her learn to be assertive."

"Well, one thing at a time," said Lorna. "So did Helen say anything more?" she sidetracked, hoping to keep Guillermo out of the conversation.

"You should phone Helen for details," said Maria Rosa.

Suddenly the implications of Helen's message hit home. Lorna felt a jolt of recognition. "Oh my god! This is huge! My book will be published! I can hardly believe this news!" she said. "This is the first book proposal I've ever had accepted!"

"Congratulations, Mom!" Rini said. She draped herself around Lorna's chair and threw her arms around her mother. "I'm so proud of you, Mom!"

Lorna walked to the phone and dialed the long distance operator. "All circuits are busy; please try your call again later," she heard. Frustrated, Lorna took a seat at the table again.

Lorna inhaled the steam from her *café con leche* as if she were inhaling inner strength.

"Are you going to tell your new beau?" asked Rini.

"Guillermo's flying off this very morning," she said, trying to sound matter-of-fact. "So that is the end of that."

"Ouch!" said Maria Rosa. But that was all she could say

before Rini jumped in.

"Mom, this is stupendous news. You've always wanted to publish another book. How marvelous can life get?" Seeing her daughter's happiness, Lorna tried as hard as she could to smile. Maria Rosa, too, was smiling at her, as if somehow this news of the book should trump any disappointment about a weekend romance.

Lorna smiled back at them until her face hurt. All she wanted was to go to bed and cry.

"Let's party tonight to celebrate!" Rini was saying. "Girls' night out."

Maria Rosa laughed. "Good idea, Rini, but your poor mother looks exhausted. Give her a chance to rest first. I'll make reservations for dinner at the Intercontinental hotel for eight thirty tonight. It's a good place to make international telephone calls too, Lorna, if you don't reach Helen sooner."

"Thanks, ladies," said Lorna. "You are both wonderful. I don't deserve you!" Swilling down the remainder of her coffee, she headed straight for her bedroom.

Alone at last to sort out her confused feelings and lick her wounds, Lorna flopped onto the bed. She fell asleep at once without a tear. She woke up just before the sun went down, sensing that Guillermo was gone. He'd flown off, just like Grandfather.

At seven in the evening, the three women stood in Maria Rosa's bedroom amid a heap of clothes, preparing for their outing. They had tried on many outfits, rejecting them, trying them on again, and discarding them on the bed or haphazardly over the closet doors.

Maria Rosa pirouetted in a red taffeta dress with a short, flouncy skirt that flared out around her knees as she turned. The bodice was tight and low cut. She'd piled all her hair on her head in an Empress Josephine look and colored her lips in bright-red lipstick.

"I didn't even think you owned something like this," said Lorna. The Maria Rosa she knew was relentlessly practical, always attired in clean pressed jeans or business suits.

"Perhaps this is the real me!" sang out Maria Rosa. Reaching for a bottle from an array on the dresser top, she squirted the bulb, filling the entire room with the scent of Tabu as she sprayed her cleavage and behind her ears.

Rini, meanwhile, was squeezing into a yellow satin halter top and matching mini-skirt, leaving her tanned midriff and long tanned thighs exposed. She had found glittery high-heeled sandals, and her long, honey-colored blonde hair streamed over both shoulders. "My god, Rini, you look like the blonde bombshell in La Dolce Vita!" exclaimed Lorna.

Rini did a couple of wiggly rumba steps. "Watch out, *compañeros*, here I come!" she laughed. Then she swiveled her hips in a complete bump-and-grind.

"Oh my heavens," said Lorna. "Aren't we veering dangerously close to the outrageous, the disreputable, and the disgraceful?"

"That's the point!" cried Rini, wiggling again. "Girls' night out! If you've got it, flaunt it!" Lorna's suitcase lay open on Maria Rosa's bed.

"Here, Mom, try this!" Rini said over her shoulder. She'd found a garment Lorna had thrown in at the last minute, a rayon sheath with blue-and-green flowers. Lorna slipped it over her head. In the mirror, her eyes stared back at her, a bit haunted. "I look old and tired," she commented.

"Sit, Mom. Just a little under-eye makeup, and some blusher," commanded Rini. Lorna sat dutifully on the edge of the bed while her daughter smudged a dab of concealer under Lorna's lower eyelids, and whisked sienna powder on her cheeks. "A little lipstick, a squirt of cologne..."

"Not Tabu!" admonished Lorna.

"So which one? Mom, this is not a garden party we're going to—we're going to a bar! We kinda want the guys to sit up and take notice!"

"Maybe some Yardley's lavender," said Lorna weakly. "Look in my bag."

When she was done with Lorna's makeup, Rini said, "There, go look at yourself now," pushing her to the mirror.

The face that stared back at Lorna looked passable.

"How about a belt, Mom?" suggested Rini. "You have a fantastic figure for a woman of your age."

"A woman over the hill is more like it," Lorna answered.

"And high heels?" added Rini.

"Like these," said Maria Rosa, prancing about, kicking out her feet in high-heeled, open-toed shoes that revealed crimson toenails.

"No! No high heels," said Lorna. "I don't want to be tottering around. I'm wearing my flat gold sandals." Lorna took a last glance at her reflection. She thought her smile in the mirror looked a little forced, but it would have to do.

Rini did a few more dance steps, moving her arms and hips, as if drying off her backside on a big towel. "The only places we can go in these outfits," she said, happily, "are the most bourgeois and reactionary hangouts!"

Lorna noted that her revolutionary daughter seemed ecstatic at the prospect of bourgeois and reactionary hangouts, looking as she did at that moment exactly like a Swedish sex starlet.

"Yes, that's why I made us reservations at the Intercontinental hotel," said Maria Rosa. "We'll give the big shots and rich tourists a thrill."

A taxi took them to the Intercontinental hotel. It was a tall building, nine stories high, in the affluent *barrio* south of Lake Tiscapa. The driver pulled up under the massive beige-colored portico flanked by swaying palm trees, where a uniformed doorman greeted them.

The cabbie was pleased with Maria Rosa's large tip. "Have a good time, ladies," he called out with a wide smile as he pulled away.

Maria Rosa led the way through the lobby, her red ruffles bouncing into the crowd of well-dressed males in snowy shirts and their female companions, in skimpy outfits like those of Maria Rosa and Rini. The lobby itself was tasteless, a faux Art Deco carpeted in crimson patterned with bright yellow flowers, and adorned with massive leather furniture. The only redeeming charm came from fresh flowers in stone planters, and six-foot high potted palms.

Maria Rosa sashayed forward to be greeted warmly with kisses on the cheek and appreciative compliments from her acquaintances in the lobby. The men were eager to be introduced to beautiful Rini. Clearly Maria Rosa had found a place in this world. Lorna had not known this side of her serious friend. In her green-and-blue sheath and flat sandals, Lorna felt a bit invisible.

Through an open door of filigree iron, the restaurant was lit by a two-tiered crystal chandelier. One whole wall was open to the terrace. Soft candlelight on the tables created a discreet, luxurious sense of privacy.

The headwaiter unctuously greeted Maria Rosa and led the party to a table near the wall open to the garden. In the low light, Lorna couldn't see the other diners clearly, but her heart stopped when she thought she spied Guillermo himself in a far corner. She peered through the moody half-light. No, it was not Guillermo, she decided. But her heart had lurched.

As they took their seats, she had another sighting. This one was not a mirage. Eddie and Dr. Daisy were coming toward them. Eddie, as always, had that confident, in-charge way of carrying himself. Dr. Daisy, walking next to him, appeared beautiful, her soft Afro a halo around her wide smile. She was wearing a tight, low-cut white dress and sexy white high-heeled sandals.

Eddie greeted them with, "Three beautiful women, and without male companionship! Fortunately Lieutenant Flores is here to remedy that." Daisy continued to smile, broadly, totally unfazed by his flirtatious manner.

Eddie bowed before Maria Rosa. "Splendid! Splendid! *Compañera,* you should always wear red."

He took Rini's hand and brought it to his lips. "And you, my *reina de oro!* The men of Managua are fortunate to have such a goddess in their midst." Rini, who usually had no use for Eddie, did not yank her hand back.

Lorna took a deep breath to maintain her composure.

Despite the "concealer," she felt her tired eyes and the tears she had been suppressing.

He brushed her cheek with his lips, and she heard his voice, in her ear. "Beautiful. Beautiful, *mi Lornita*. I hope that young man appreciates what he's getting." As he raised his head, his eyes met hers again, and Lorna was struck by his kindness.

Dr. Daisy watched Eddie's courtship of females in total equilibrium, even amusement.

"So what brings the three beauties out tonight?" asked Eddie.

"Mom got a book contract this morning!" cried Rini. "We're celebrating. Her book proposal for *Daughters of Silence* just got accepted by Three Rivers Press! Maria Rosa and I are taking her out to celebrate!"

"Bravo!" cried Eddie. "So, *Compañera* Lorna, you've outgrown our little *Unidos*/Together publishing collective? You've moved on, and you're leaving it in your dust! A *New York Times* best seller is next? A National Book Award perhaps?" Turning to Maria Rosa, in a serious tone, he went on, "Lorna is one of my oldest friends. Of course I am totally happy for her, and for myself that I encouraged her as a writer in the first place."

Rini rolled her eyes. "This is so like you, Eddie. Mom is the one with the book contract, and somehow you take all the credit."

"Rini, I'm the biggest supporter Lorna will ever have," objected Eddie.

"We're just leaving," Daisy said quickly, taking Eddie's hand and pulling him away playfully. "We had to come over to say hello! But we've got more places to go."

Lorna was relieved, despite Eddie's unexpected sweetness toward her.

After they ordered, Lorna excused herself to find the phone booths in the lobby to call Helen. While she waited for the call to go through, she looked at the exhibition of primitivist Solentiname paintings. Lorna gazed at the oil paintings of turquoise skies and cobalt-blue waters with enormous white birds in the foreground. Colorful small figures of men tilled the soil or pulled fish out of wooden boats on the shore in the background. The small primitivist paintings on display, just as Eddie had said, had price tags for $1,500 US dollars. She imagined Guillermo's plane flying midway across the cobalt-blue Pacific, by now high, and far, and out of sight, flying into a future she would not share with him. The lobby international phone lines crackled and Helen's phone began ringing. "Oh, Helen, please be home," she whispered.

"Hello?" came Helen's voice. This was followed by silence.

"Hello?" Helen repeated a little louder.

"Helen, it's Lorna."

"Lorna! Oh, I'm so glad it's you. Guess what? Your book proposal has been accepted!"

"I heard!" said Lorna.

"I'm thrilled for you. They want two hundred pages of interviews, double-spaced. A cross-section of women from all walks of life. The draft manuscript is due in February. This is so exciting, Lorna! Congratulations! How are you? How's Rini?"

"I'm well," she said, noncommittally. She was tempted to let it all hang out, to tell Helen how bereft and rotten she felt, but she did not. "The big news here is that Rini is pregnant. Pregnant, and she's due in February."

"Like your book," laughed Helen. "Is there a father?"

"Yes. She met a young *Nica* doctor out in the boonies where she works."

"Are they getting married?" Helen asked.

"Rini says it's out of style."

"Oh?" Over the humming, crackling international phone line, Lorna could sense lifted eyebrows.

"So, Lorna, how do you feel about becoming a grandmother?"

"I guess I like it. In fact, I look forward to it."

"Congratulations!" said Helen.

"Thanks, but Rini's pregnancy also reminds me of how old I am. Heaviness mixes with the happiness."

She was almost about to mention the affair with Guillermo when Helen asked, "Is it safe there, Lorna?"

"Totally safe where we are right this moment. Rini, Maria Rosa, and I are out celebrating the book tonight. We're at the swankiest hotel in Nicaragua—the InterContinental. Nothing to fear here."

"I mean, about Rini."

"The contra action is mostly along the Honduran border. I asked her if she wanted to come home to have the baby, but she said no. You know how she is—very independent."

"So you're living it up at a swank hotel? What are you wearing?"

"I'm wearing that dress you insisted I buy when Joseph Magnin went out of business."

"So have you met someone?" asked Helen.

"What do you mean, met someone?" Lorna asked defensively.

"What do you mean, what do I mean? I mean a man, of course."

"I did meet someone, but he left the country this morning." Lorna took a matter-of-fact tone.

"Do I hear disappointment in your voice?"

So that hadn't worked. "Helen, you're like a bloodhound on the scent. We can talk about it when I get back."

"I suppose Eddie's up to his old tricks?"

"Yes, he's met a beautiful Cuban doctor. We just ran into them, in fact."

"Interesting. Oh, by the way, Three Rivers Press wants you to respond to the letter. Shall I phone them to say you're out in the field?"

"Give me their number, and I'll call from here to thank them."

"Don't thank them, Lorna. You're doing them the favor."

"I am grateful. Or have you forgotten my folder full of rejection letters? So how are you?" Lorna asked.

"I've had a week off from politics. Larry and I are going up to Tahoe. Well, this is costing you. Give Rini a big hug for me and take care of yourself."

Before they could say good-bye, the connection broke off. Lorna stood thinking it was good to talk with Helen, reassuring herself that she did have a life in San Francisco.

The sound of Spanish being spoken jolted Lorna back to her immediate situation, and she rejoined Maria Rosa and Rini at their table. The party had expanded. Two young men who seemed to know Maria Rosa had pulled up chairs and were talking and laughing with the two women.

Maria Rosa introduced Olaf and Wolfgang, from Sweden and Germany, delegates to a geothermal energy conference being held at the hotel. Olaf was tall, his fair hair almost white. Wolfgang had darting, quick eyes, like a fox. Both seemed quite drawn to Rini, and when they learned she was very familiar with the geothermal project at Momotombo, they could hardly believe their good fortune. A beautiful blonde in a skimpy gold outfit who was also an engineer. Lorna was thinking this might be her last glimpse of Rini's smooth midriff without stretch marks.

Her eye traveled to Maria Rosa, glowing in her red taffeta dress, her small hands moving as she told a story from her recent militia training.

"Well," said Maria Rosa, looking around, "I was by far the oldest of the volunteers. Our training maneuvers took place on the hottest, muggiest day, and I was lugging my backpack up and down hills, battling thorns, and mosquitoes. I was thinking,'I'm too old for this. I can't keep up.' Just then the unit leader called out '¡Formación!' and I rushed to my place in the front row. The sun was beating down. I was so tired I could hardly stand as she shouted instructions about cleaning our rifles. My mind wandered, regretting I was too out of condition and too middle-aged to defend my country. I forced myself to stand up as straight as I could. Then a mosquito buzzed around me, and as I slapped it, I turned my head and saw that I was the only one left standing. All those young people behind me? They were sitting on the ground, leaning on their backpacks."

Everyone around the table laughed. The next food course arrived, and the musicians, an accordionist, a vocalist, and a man with a marimba, began tuning up. Lorna raised her glass, "To this evening of international friendship, which has just begun!"

There were cheers and clinks. Then Rini raised her glass "To your book, *Daughters of the Silence*, Mom," she said.

The others raised their glasses with more cheers and clinking of glasses.

Wolfgang turned to Rini. "To your electrification, *Señorita* Rini!"

Rini giggled as she lifted her glass in response. "That's a toast with a charge!" she said.

Olaf cried, "To Maria Rosa's militia unit. Long live the revolution!"

The first notes of a *cumbia* swept through the dining room. Wolfgang reached out his hand to Rini. "Shall we?" Lorna watched her tall daughter and the German make their way to a space in front of the musicians. Others were coming forward also, and within minutes a throbbing crowd was moving to the music.

Lorna found it all very beautiful in spite of Guillermo's absence. Two days ago they'd been part of a crowd like this. She'd better get used to it, she thought. She was making a valiant effort, but sadness still crouched in the shadows.

Part Three

San Francisco & Managua

25

Climate Change

Back in San Francisco four months later, it was four o'clock in the afternoon and, to Lorna, the November sunlight seemed tired of the day's task of lighting the hemisphere. These last months home dragged on miserably for her. She worked doggedly on the *Daughters of the Silence* manuscript as a prisoner of self-imposed writer's loneliness. She looked up from her desk, feeling the pressure of the soon-to-end quarter's leave of absence from her job at New College that she had taken to complete the book. But with her continuing regrets over Guillermo and bouts of writer's block, the job in front of her dragged on.

Concentrating on her writing was even harder because of international political events. In October, the Sandinistas had brought down a contra cargo plane full of weapons. The sole survivor, an ex-marine mercenary by the name of Eugene Hasenfus, had implicated the CIA. Hasenfus publicly claimed that Vice-President George Bush was running a covert arms supply operation, in total defiance of the Boland Amendment limiting US government assistance to the contras. This illegal escalation of the contra war made Lorna more concerned than ever for Rini's safety. Public opinion was turning against Reagan and the contras, making it a moment for the Nicaraguan solidarity movement to press forward. But in order to finish her book, Lorna had to step back, giving up her leadership and reducing the number of meetings she attended. Luis and a new recruit, a young choreographer by the name of Jackie St. John, stepped forward to take over her role in Friends of Nicaraguan Culture. Helen, too, continued to be involved, despite her city supervisor post.

Beautiful, complex rhythms came down from her neighbor's apartment, as he practiced his sitar, which he did every afternoon and again at night. The fog floated in, obliterating what was left of the weak winter sun. The strange, vibrating melodies from India underscored her longing for her lost lover and set the entire day adrift. She'd spent August, September, and October mourning Guillermo. Now she understood the harsh cries of flamenco singers. He might as well have gone to another planet.

The sense of being abandoned by someone who had loved her grew as the days shortened and autumn turned into early winter. But had he really loved her? she often wondered. Always her deeper sorrow would come back to her broken marriage and the loss of Abuelo. Replaying these old themes of loneliness bogged down her writing.

The phone rang. She was happy to be interrupted. It was Helen. Lorna launched into a gloomy litany of complaints.

"Lorna, sounds like you're still not over Guillermo. You're still mourning your boy toy." Madonna had recently made this expression famous, but Lorna did not like it.

"Helen, I feel so bad. Why? It's been over three months. The relationship, if that's what it was, hardly lasted three days."

"Life is full of sorrow. This will pass. Get over it."

"I feel so empty," Lorna said. "I'm crying all the time."

"You have to empty yourself before you can fill up again."

"I whine to you on the phone every day. How do you stand it?"

"You've got lots of credit with me, Lorna. Besides, I have a favor to ask. I need your help editing. Can we get together tomorrow?"

"OK. Where? I promise not to moan."

They set the date, and Lorna hung up. Usually at five o'clock she ran out the door into the darkening day to seek her fortune, do some grocery shopping, meet a friend for coffee or a movie. But not today. Luis was coming at five to present her with his old computer. She had been using the

New College computer lab to transcribe the interviews for her book. A computer here at home would save a lot of trips up and down the hill to campus.

Lorna ran a comb through her unruly curls and studied her face in the mirror. The Nicaraguan color had long since faded from her face. She looked old and tired, she decided, and quickly applied a streak of pink lipstick and blotted it. She was about to change out of her sweatpants and old sweater when the doorbell rang. Luis stood in the doorway, looking up over a big carton.

"Hello there," she called. "That box looks heavy."

Luis bounded up the stairs and placed the carton on the dining room table. Then he ran down again and returned carrying up a second box.

"The printer," he explained. "What's wrong, Lorna? You look wistful."

"I always feel this way after working on the interviews. They're such a reminder of the harsh realities of Nicaraguan women's lives."

"There's one woman who has just left her reality with me behind. She seems to thinks she's creating something better."

Luis set the second box next to the first and turned to face her.

"There is?" asked Lorna, instantly alert, thinking about his wife, Jennifer.

"Jennifer left me. She's been involved with the senior partner in her firm for some time. He's married too. They've made quite a mess of it." But Luis didn't appear at all sad.

"That's big news. How do you feel about it?" Lorna asked. "I'll put up some tea."

"To be honest, all I could think was that I'd be arriving at your house at five a single man."

Following her into the kitchen, Luis continued, "I guess you're not surprised. Probably everyone saw it coming except me. I've been so wrapped up with the business, and working on Nicaraguan issues. But honestly, Lorna, I am delighted to be a free man. My relationship with Jennifer has been dead for years."

While making the tea, Lorna said, "That's what Carl said when he left. 'Dead for years.' It must be how couples finally break up. I've let the past hold me back too long. Now Rini's going to be a mother. I'm going to be a grandmother. And if Grandfather were alive, he'd soon be a great-great grandpa. We have to live in the now, Luis."

"Agreed. How about forgetting the tea and letting me take you out to dinner? Then, single man that I am, I'll set up the computer afterward."

Lorna turned and saw Luis flopped onto a chair looking at her. Suddenly she felt self conscious, tired, a bit frazzled, in the sweat suit and athletic shoes. Luis was long and elegant, in a Shetland sweater and pressed khakis. She wondered if the room was spinning or just her emotions. She had not been expecting his announcement, though she'd often hoped for it.

She put down the kettle. "That would be nice. I should change my clothes, since this is a dinner date. I'll be right back," she said, smiling.

Her one and only romantic outfit, a black lace dress with long sleeves, was still wrapped in dry cleaner plastic. Lorna shook it out. The lace was sheer, but an interior black silk slip with spaghetti straps provided the requisite modesty. Did it even still fit? Shoes? Her happiness and excitement quickened as she hurried through a shower and dabbed a tropical flowery perfume behind her ears, reminding her of Nicaragua. She slipped on her dress. Amazingly, it not only still fit, it fit very well. With her fingers, she fanned out her auburn curls. The shower made her face look pink and radiant. When she entered the dining room, Luis whistled. The computer and printer were already unpacked.

"You look great!" he said appreciatively. "From hardworking authoress to *femme fatale*."

"Thank you, Mr. Jaramillo," said Lorna, doing a quick twirl. "And thank you so much for the computer. I'll be able to finish the book in no time!" A surge of optimism flooded

Lorna, even euphoria, as she waltzed over to the coat closet. Too bad, but the old trench coat would have to do. Luis helped her on with it.

"You look so beautiful," he remarked, laughing. "So I'll take you to the new Peruvian place over on Valencia Street. They have a decor worthy of your outfit. It's quite nice."

At a highly polished wood table on the restaurant's balcony, overlooking the dining room below, they shared a bottle of wine. They were discussing the latest Hasenfus news that the CIA-backed contras were trading cocaine for guns.

Lorna said, "I'll be finished with *Daughters of the Silence* in time to help more with FNC work for our big fundraiser in December."

"This event is going to be big," said Luis.

"You and Jackie did a great job lining up some impressive performers," said Lorna.

"Yeah, we have movie stars, a famous author, and your Nicaraguan poet, Lionel Ruben, coming from Nicaragua to read."

"I gave Lionel a draft of my translation when I was in Nicaragua a few months ago, but I haven't heard from him yet," said Lorna. "There are still a few bird names I have to find English counterparts for. I need a better scientific dictionary."

"We have you on the program, with Lionel Ruben reading the original on stage. You will read your translation and then translate for him in the question-and-answer session after," said Luis.

They continued to talk through dinner, with the candlelight quietly flickering. The subject of his wife, Jennifer, never came up. Finally, Luis said, "Let's get back to your place so I can boot up your new computer and printer."

When they returned to Hill Street, the apartment was very dark. Lorna turned on a lamp so Luis could set the computer up on her desk. He moved her typewriter aside, placed the printer on her typing table, and plugged everything in.

"I have the word processing program all installed," he said, "and I put in your book manuscript from your floppy disk. It's ready to use, Lorna, but I hope you can wait because, right now, there's so much I have to say."

They moved into the living room, sitting down on the sofa and looking out at the lights sparkling in the Mission and the dark hills beyond. Luis had uncorked a bottle of wine from her cupboard and poured wine into two glasses Lorna had placed on the coffee table. A bluish-white full moon had risen high in the sky, a reminder of winter to come. They sat close, but Lorna couldn't think of anything to say.

"How about it, Lorna?" he said. His face was so serious, so close to hers. "To us?" He stretched his glass forward in a toast. "We talked so easily in the restaurant, with candlelight flickering over your face, but I never mentioned Jennifer. I want to tell you Jennifer and I are finished."

Luis's moved closer to her. She could smell the wool of his sweater, Old Spice aftershave, and another fragrance, perhaps that of Luis himself, as he leaned toward her. This moment was new and yet familiar. They had been close to it many times before, sharing armrests in an auditorium, passing each other too closely in a doorway, his hand, helping her out of a vehicle, lingering a moment longer. She had never allowed herself to fully imagine their first kiss. Luis drew her close and they kissed deeply and long.

Luis's warmth, his thigh alongside hers, her shoulder comfortably pressing into his, were becoming much more immediate than old memories. That was then, Lorna thought, and this is now. Luis was raising his glass, and she did the same.

"To Lorna and Luis," she said, clinking his glass.

Luis's body was strong and developed. She knew it from watching him over many years, hauling boxes of art supplies, folding up chairs after meetings, sitting beside her at concerts and events. She could feel the muscles now, the sinews, and the fine hairs covering his arms. He was holding her tightly and pulling her up so they could embrace front to front.

Downstairs the neighbor was practicing his sitar again. Its

melodies suggested a very ancient erotic knowledge that pulled Lorna closer to Luis.

"Indian music?" he asked.

"My neighbor plays sitar for hours, beginning in the late afternoon," Lorna explained.

"Beautiful," he murmured, squeezing her tightly. They had waited so long, now there was no need to rush, as they shared words of love and headed to her bedroom.

The next morning Luis jumped out of bed, rejoicing, "It's Saturday and I am in love."

Lorna slid into the warm spot he had just vacated, deeply happy and relaxed. She heard him singing a Beatles song loudly, above the roar of the running shower, "Love, love me, do! You know I love you." Chorus after chorus. Deep down she knew they had crossed a border, no passports needed. She would never have to wonder if they were compatible. In her heart, she knew that Luis would be totally committed and that they were already proven friends. She wished Grandfather could have met Luis.

Luis sauntered in, naked, grinning and toweling his hair. "Lorna, come down to New Mexico for Thanksgiving and meet my family. My mother has always wanted to meet you."

"She has?" asked Lorna, surprised.

"Sure. She loves your poetry. I gave her your book."

"Oh, yes. I remember you said she used it in her class."

"You'll like her. All my brothers and sisters and their families will be there too."

"Won't they be upset to see me so soon after Jennifer?"

"Probably more like relieved," Luis said. "They said she was so cold."

26

Nesting

Lorna and Luis were riding in a rented pickup truck two weeks later with Cisco Kid checking out neighborhood garage sales for furniture for Luis's new apartment. Jennifer had taken all of the old furniture and Luis let her have it without an argument. "I never liked Danish modern anyway," he said.

At the first garage sale, they found a leather living room set on the sidewalk. Luis jumped out, and negotiated a good deal.

Cisco Kid confided to Lorna, "Wow! It so great being around you two since you got together. You're so upbeat." Then he leapt from the truck to help Luis lift the couch while Lorna grabbed the cushions.

A few hours later Lorna, happy but hungry, checked the list. "We got almost everything, but let's pick up some tacos before we unload."

One night a week later, Lorna sat cross-legged on Luis's couch in his new bachelor apartment in the Mission. She looked around, enjoying the decor and said, "Hanging out at your place feels so natural. I'm here more than in my own home. Helen says I'm always smiling and laughing. Even the dean at work mentioned it. Being in love with you suits me, Luis."

"I'm pretty happy myself," said Luis, leaning over to give her a kiss.

She was working on the translation of Lionel Ruben's poem for the upcoming "Stop Contra Aid" fundraiser. And for a change, she was writing without suffering. "Life is a joy!" she said to Luis as he left the room.

She underlined a word on her yellow pad and placed her

pen down on the coffee table. It was littered with an uneven tower of her many dictionaries, including a fat heavy new botanical dictionary. She felt excited that she would read her translation at the beautiful San Francisco Palace of Fine Arts.

She stood up and stretched as Luis walked back in from the bedroom. She loved the sight of him, the height of him, his kind eyes, and those shoulders.

"Hi, stranger. I missed you. I haven't seen you for at least ten minutes."

Luis laughed. "We're turning into companionship addicts."

"I've been working on this translation until I'm stiff and cross-eyed."

He rubbed her neck with his fingers. "I can feel a little knot right here."

"Ahhhh," she murmured as he instinctively rubbed the right spot and it loosened. "You know, I've been at your house every night this week."

"Yes, we're cooking together. I'm eating better meals. No wonder I'm happy. And I get more work done with you here too. We have a good thing." He delicately planted a kiss behind her ear.

"Oh, yes. It feels like a very good thing," she said, shuddering.

She began shedding her clothes, dropping them onto the floor in a pile and then, watching him strip to his muscular frame. Leaning forward, he pushed her down onto the couch. The yellow legal pad glided silently onto the floor as the pen rolled to a gentle stop by the table leg.

Luis turned off the lamp, and she felt his full weight on her. Skin to skin, they made love, knocking over the piled dictionaries on the coffee table. The tower of books crashed down with a loud thud.

Later that evening, Luis was glancing again at the yellow pad. He asked, "Can I read the translation?"

"I'm still polishing it," Lorna apologized.

She scrutinized his face as he read it, looking for even the smallest expression of disapproval. "What do you think? Tell me."

"I'm still reading. I read quite slowly." Finally, finishing, he looked up.

"Do you like it?" She anticipated the worst.

"Yes, I love it. It doesn't sound like a translation. It sounds like regular English."

She was first relieved, and then elated. "I'm so happy you like it. I still need translations for some of the birds and plants that aren't in these dictionaries." She was picking up the books from the floor, smiling to remember how they fell.

He crouched down and helped her, saying "My cousin Rudy in Los Angeles phoned me."

"What did he say?" She was full of curiosity. She hadn't met Rudy yet.

"First, he teased me about having a new girlfriend so fast. I told him that it doesn't feel fast. It's like we waited forever."

They laughed knowingly.

Luis stood. "But then he told me about how the recent flow of cocaine into the streets of the East Los Angeles barrio is coming from the contras. He'd heard it has been showing up here in the San Francisco Bay Area."

"How does he know it's really from the contras?"

"Rudy is a DEA agent and that's what he told me. Reagan's so-called Freedom Fighters fly arms down to Honduras and come back with plane-loads of coke. Especially this new form of cocaine, crack cocaine, that's smoked and not sniffed. It's stronger and more lethal. Rudy says it's spreading through Central and East Los Angeles. Barrio kids are dying from cocaine-related gang violence and overdosing and now we're hearing about it here in the Mission, Hunter's Point and the Tenderloin. Thank you, American taxpayer."

Lorna rose to her feet. "If only we could stop this! I hate it."

"Shutting off aid to the contras may be the best way to stop it. So we are on the right track with this big event," he replied, giving her a strong hug. "I want this event to succeed as never before."

"Jeanne at the national office in US says we're starting to get some congressional support," Lorna said.

"I wonder if we can add Rudy's information to our *San Francisco Chronicle* op ed piece? I'm writing the first draft, maybe I can squeeze it in."

"Good idea," she agreed. "Can Rudy get you some hot quotes from the Drug Enforcement Agency people?"

"I'll ask. It's a major threat to our youth, all over California," he said, drifting toward his computer in the bedroom.

Lorna picked up her legal pad, "I need to work a short while more on the translation."

Adrenaline surged as she imagined herself before an enormous audience on the Palace of Fine Arts stage. She felt nervous, but confident. So much depended on the success of the "Stop Contra Aid" event. This contra/drug news linked their cause directly to their local communities.

Just a few more plant names, she thought, and I'll be finished. It would be her biggest poetry event ever.

27

Red Roses in December

On the night of the December event, at six-thirty, Lorna stood backstage at the Palace of Fine Arts, holding a clipboard, an hour before the performance. Posters hung all over town. Tickets had sold out. They were on-track to raise thousands of dollars. Reagan's covert aid to the contras, in defiance of Congress's Boland Amendment, became daily fare in the headlines. Friends of Nicaraguan Culture was doing its best to turn up the heat and prevent Reagan from getting away with this.

With the curtains open to the still empty auditorium, the stage and backstage area were one large chilly space. Lorna was wearing her black lace dress, with the red earrings and bracelet Luis's mother had given her. But she'd thrown a bulky Mexican cardigan over it, which she planned to leave behind when it was time to address the crowd.

She looked up to see Luis with a big bouquet of long-stemmed red American Beauty roses in his hand.

"Luis, how wonderful of you. I'm actually so nervous I can hardly breathe." She kissed him, then inhaled the flowers' fragrance, taking slower, deeper breaths.

"You know, Lionel Ruben's dressing room is so bare, I'm going to set these flowers in there, so he'll feel really welcome in San Francisco."

Luis looked crestfallen. "Lorna, I bought them for you."

"Let me place them in his dressing room for ninety minutes, until his press conference is over. Then I'll snatch them back."

"Do you think he'll even notice them, Lorna?"

"No. But reporters at the press conference will."

"I wish you would take them for yourself. You're a poet! You should stop coordinating others and read your own poems and translations more often."

"This event isn't just about poetry. We have a whole voting public to reach. We need media attention."

Cisco Kid came running up. "Luis, come on! We're supposed to be stationed in the lobby."

Luis turned on his walkie-talkie as he headed off with Cisco Kid. Lorna could see he was slightly upset with her.

Lorna placed the roses in Lionel's dressing room and returned backstage, putting on her headset. Through the headset she could hear the sound man in the balcony talking to the light booth woman.

"Backstage hospitality is connected," Lorna announced crisply into the mouthpiece, consulting her clipboard one more time. "The dressing rooms are almost ready."

She checked off her list: hot tea for the novelist; grapefruit juice for the vocalist; sandwiches for the musicians; bottled water for the movie stars. She plugged in a coffeepot and put out cookies for the press conference in the poet's dressing room. Luis' roses made the dressing room look very celebratory. She had seen Luis's disappointment, but she would be sure to take them home later to the best and tallest vase.

The headset crackled. "This is Jackie in the box office to Lorna. The performers have all arrived, except Lionel Ruben. Even the movie stars and the novelist are already here. Over and out."

"This is Lorna, backstage, to Jackie. The poet's coming at the last minute. He's finishing a Spanish-language TV interview first. Ask Helen to show him to his dressing room when he arrives. Over and out."

Luis and Jackie had done a great job with Friends of Nicaraguan Culture while Lorna had dedicated herself to finishing *Daughters of the Silence*. Jackie, an innovative choreographer, and a few other new recruits made a good addition to the team.

Excitement and nervousness rushed through Lorna's body. She forced herself to take deep, even breaths and review her translation. The voice on the headset interrupted. "This is Jackie again, at the box office. Lionel Ruben has arrived with two bodyguards, a driver, and a translator. Over and out."

"This is Lorna. Send them backstage. We're all set. Over and out." Lorna responded. She found herself wondering who the translator would be.

Jackie's voice came on again. "They're leaving some books for sale on the sales table in the lobby and are heading backstage."

"The dressing room's ready," said Lorna.

Helen passed by, showing the movie stars to their dressing rooms. They seemed distracted, although the one Lorna had seen on a late-night movie gave her a nice smile. Helen did a thumbs-up as she passed. Everything was on track. The stage manager flipped a lever and the auditorium curtains closed, reconstituting the backstage area into its own world. "The audience is arriving," he informed Lorna.

Lorna moved toward the point where the poet and his entourage would enter. Suddenly the backstage area plunged into total darkness.

"Ooops—sorry!" said a woman's voice through the headset. "I hit the wrong switch."

Lorna became aware of a group approaching. She smelled the spicy scent of Florida Water. Then she felt a familiar touch. She turned sharply as the lights went on.

There stood Eddie Flores. "Hello, Lorna."

"What are you doing here, Eddie? I thought you were in Managua," she said.

"I'm here to translate for the poet. We need to know where his dressing room is." Eddie was smartly dressed, as always. This time in an embroidered guayabera shirt, and cowboy boots that made him taller.

Lionel Ruben nodded to Lorna shyly, his well-groomed white hair and fine Panama hat giving him an air of dignity. The two bodyguards looked on impassively.

"Lorna Almendros, so nice to see you again," Lionel said in Spanish. "I wasn't sure you would be here. I read your translation of my poem and like it very much."

"Oh, thank you," said Lorna. "The dressing room is right this way." Lorna led the entourage to the dressing room, but she was bristling with anger.

"So, tell me, Lorna, did you find the English translation for the birds' and plants' names?" asked Lionel, on the way to the dressing room.

"Yes, they are all in the final translation, which I'll be reading on stage tonight with you," said Lorna. "The movie star will introduce you. You will read the original poem, and when you are finished, I will read the translation." Lionel nodded as they stepped into the dressing room.

Helen poked her head in the door. "House lights are on and the audience is being seated," she said, looking around the dressing room. "Beautiful flowers."

Lorna smiled and addressed the poet in Spanish, "My compañero gave me the roses, but I wanted to share them with you, to welcome you to San Francisco. There will be a short press conference right here after the show." Lionel smiled but turned to Eddie looking confused.

Eddie turned to Lorna and said in English, "There's been some miscommunication, Lorna. Using your draft translation, Lionel and I worked it out on the plane. He'll read a section in Spanish, and I'll then read the same section in English. In tandem, as they say. He's used to me. You'll just upset him if we make a change. So give me your final translation with the new words in it."

Helen looked to Lorna for a response. Lionel stopped smiling, irritation beginning to show. His two bodyguards stood expressionless.

"Eddie, the program is all set. We didn't even know you were coming," Lorna said.

Eddie smiled. "Know me no knowings. It all happened at the last minute. I thought I could be of help. Everyone in the Ministry of Culture agreed because I'm so familiar with the

San Francisco scene. The poet counts on me." He explained briefly to the poet and bodyguards in Spanish.

Lionel looked at Eddie, then at Lorna.

"Eddie, I am prepared to do the translation. I'm named on the program." She did not enjoy challenging Eddie, and he seemed truly startled by what was happening. She held her ground.

"No way!" said Eddie. He was showing a flash of anger. "Lionel and I worked it out. Don't create problems now, Lorna."

"No, Eddie, Friends of Nicaraguan Culture worked it out. You weren't part of our planning committee," said Lorna.

Lionel continued to glance from one to the other, with a look of concern.

"What should we do?" Helen asked Lorna nervously. "The program is starting." They could hear the movie star, welcoming the crowd, warming them up, mocking Ronald Reagan, George H. W. Bush, William Casey, and John Negroponte. Each time he made a point, he raised his fist. "Are we going to stand for this?" he would yell, and the crowd would yell back, "No!"

"You can't do this to me, Lorna." Eddie was glowering at her.

"Yes, I can," replied Lorna.

"You're not in charge here, Lorna. The poet asked me to accompany him."

"No, Eddie. You're not in charge here. The poet is our guest."

Helen burst in. "Guys, work it out. The audience is waiting! It's almost time to go on!"

"I didn't fly all the way up here to be pushed aside," said Eddie, his face turning red.

Helen intervened. "Eddie, we're incredibly grateful for all you do. Look, we have to stay with the program. But after the intermission, you can be the one who takes the questions from the audience, translates them for the poet, and then translates his answers."

Luis ran up, almost out of breath, and stood in the doorway. "It's starting. What's going on?"

Lorna took him aside. "Eddie wants to be the translator. He says the poet is accustomed to him. He wants me to give him my translation to read on stage."

"That's bullshit. Lorna, stand up for yourself!" he told her.

Just then, Jackie rushed in, carrying a flashlight. She stood next to Luis and Helen. "What is the delay, Lorna? You and the poet should be ready in the wings right now."

Everyone waited for Lorna's reply.

She glanced down at her clipboard for a second. Then, she slid out of her bulky sweater, looking up with a small smile, and said, "I like Helen's idea. First, I'll read my translation with the poet. Eddie will go on after the intermission to translate the questions and answers for him."

Lionel, who had been watching the proceedings, lifted his hand. "Peace, friends," he said in Spanish. "I will be honored if the lovely lady will translate my work. We worked on it this summer and it was good."

Eddie nodded consent, looking deflated.

When it came time for Lorna to step out onto the stage with Lionel, she was nervous and excited as she always was before performing. He read in a musical Spanish; his voice was low, yet compelling, and very well received. She smiled at the poet and audience before she began. Then she read her translation. She knew she had aced it from the enthusiastic applause, so many in the audience glad of the English.

During the intermission, she found Eddie in the poet's dressing room, elbows on knees, head in hands. He looked up mournfully as she passed by. "Shit, Lorna, I sure didn't see that coming. Why did you have to embarrass me that way in front of Lionel? I thought we were on the same team." Eddie was pressing his hands to his forehead, shaking his head.

"We are," said Lorna.

"Sure feels like no, Eddie, no . . . to me."

"Come on, Eddie. We're working together on this and it's time for you to stand in the wings with Lionel for the audience questions." He stood up and Lorna walked him to the wings.

After the intermission, there were many questions about what was going on in Nicaragua. Eddie charmed the audience, reverting to his old self, cocky, light on his feet, quick with the humor and repartee, explaining in English what was really happening inside Nicaragua. Eddie was happy again. The movie star's pitch brought in a pile of cash and checks that the volunteer ushers collected.

The big event they worked so hard for was a success. Lorna scooped up the flowers on her way out.

28

Political Is Personal

Lorna was deplaning at Augusto C. Sandino International Airport. The February heat and humidity of Managua smacked her in the face with its visceral tropical sensuality, its floral and vegetable smells mixed with odors of metal and exhaust. It took forever to clear customs, but finally she was free, and she saw Pancho waiting for her in a faded blue T-shirt. Pancho looked durable, like she hoped her grand-child would be.

"Where's Rini?" she asked, anxiously, as he pulled her into a hug.

"Rini's waiting for you at home. Don't worry. Your unborn grandchild refuses to come out unless you're present."

"You are such a welcome sight, Pancho. Let's hurry home so the baby can come," replied Lorna.

Managua was always shockingly poor, after San Francisco. Pancho drove into town on the Carretera Norte, where the improvements, if there had been any, were undetectable. Low houses of chipped stucco with cement pads for front yards, animals, and horse-drawn carts had not changed. The city's desolate empty spaces created by the 1972 earthquake were still not rebuilt.

"How is it working out, staying with Maria Rosa?" Lorna asked. Rini and Pancho had come down from the countryside for this last month until the baby was born, which was going to be any day now.

"She couldn't be kinder to us, although she's awfully busy. We don't really see her until dinnertime and sometimes not even then. Right now she's out of town for a few days. We were hoping Luis would come with you."

"He wanted to come, Pancho, but they've just launched some new software. He's doing awfully well. Money is finally not a problem!"

"I wish we could say the same," said Pancho. "Here, everything is a problem. Blackouts. Food shortages. Even water. This is a hard place to raise a child."

"Do you and Rini want to come home?" asked Lorna quickly.

"If you're talking about California," said Pancho, "I think Rini feels Nicaragua is her home now."

For the rest of the ride they chatted about the Joint Congressional Committee on Iran-Contra which had been formed in January to get to the bottom of the arms-for-hostages scandal. Only two days earlier, CIA director William Casey had submitted his somewhat overdue resignation. He had been incapable of speech since December, when he had been operated on for an alleged brain tumor. His medical condition would certainly prevent him from participating in the upcoming hearings.

"Oh, my god!" gasped Lorna upon seeing Rini. "You are enormous!" The cool, dark house welcomed her with its familiar smells of spice, flowers and cleaning agents. The tall lovely young woman flying toward her was the main welcome Lorna sought. Rini's belly had expanded and hung low; her face a little changed. Rini was more beautiful than ever, her hair and skin glowing.

"How are you, honey?"

"Mom, I'm so ready for him to come out. I swear, he feels like he's going to fall out. He's so active, kicking and moving around."

"So you think your baby is a he?" said Lorna.

"I know he's a he," said Rini, laughing. "No girl baby would be kicking as hard as he is."

"And what are you going to name him?" asked Lorna.

"Gabriel Nazario!" said Rini proudly.

"And if he's a girl?"

"Mom. He's not going to be a girl."

That night Lorna awakened to the familiar crowing of roosters. But there was an additional sound of pacing in the hall. Rini was pacing with animal intensity in the hallway.

"I'm having contractions, Mom. He was waiting for you to be here."

"How much time between your contractions?"

Rini strode back and forth fiercely. "Every five minutes."

"I'll get dressed," said Lorna as she raced to the bathroom to change.

Pancho appeared with a small suitcase packed for the hospital. "Let's go!"

He raced ahead of them to start the car, and Lorna and Rini followed, with Xiomara opening the door for them and watching anxiously. Pancho's old Plymouth was often hard to start, but this time it caught on the first try.

Six hours later, Dr. Daisy walked into the waiting room of the hospital with a huge smile. "It's a boy!" she exclaimed.

Pancho clapped his hands. "A son!" he cried. "I knew it!"

"How is Rini?" Lorna asked the Cuban doctor.

"She's fine," she said. "The mother will be back in her room a bit later, but you may see the baby now."

Pancho was racing ahead to the nursery, and Lorna followed him, a few steps behind. The care at the hospital felt like the 1950s all over again to Lorna. Fathers were not permitted to be present at the birth. They were standing now with their noses pressed against the glass of the nursery. An array of small bassinets faced them, each with a tiny human being, most with tightly closed eyes and a bit of damp hair on their craniums. Only one bassinet was empty, and as they watched, a nurse entered the room, carrying a newborn she gently placed in the empty bassinet by the window. She looked up at them, smiling and pointed to the little red package of life she had just set down.

"It's him!" Pancho said, almost as in prayer.

"Gabriel Nazario Altamirano," Lorna said. "A new life."

Three days later, with the new baby, they drove back to Maria Rosa's, where they planned to stay for a few more weeks until Rini regained her strength. Lorna would stay until then.

"It's so good to be out of the hospital," said Rini, as they walked in the door. They settled the baby into the waiting folkloric woven straw cradle next to the bed. While Xiomara finished lunch preparations, Rini lay down on the bed and Pancho went out to unpack the car. Lorna and Maria Rosa began setting up the diaper-changing area on top of the bureau.

While folding the freshly washed baby clothes, Lorna asked Rini, "Are Pancho's parents coming for the naming ceremony?"

"No, they're coming later when we hold the baptism at the church," said Rini. "I think the naming ceremony might upset them because it is outside the church and a little too Indigenous for their conservative tastes. But don't get me wrong, I think they're wonderful."

"How should we set it up?" asked Maria Rosa.

"It will be a party for about thirty people to welcome Gabriel to the community, announce his name and his godparents. Pancho is looking forward to roasting a suckling pig," said Rini. "Later at the baptism, we will do the same without the pig."

"I will be so honored to be the godmother," said Maria Rosa. "I love him already."

Two weeks later in Maria Rosa's patio, baby Gabriel lay peacefully cradled in Rini's arms, wearing the elaborately stitched and embroidered baptismal gown Pancho's mother had sent from Mexico. Rini was standing amid party decorations and a crowd of guests. The odors of roasting suckling pig and burning copal wafted through the air, mixing with the heavy fragrance of tropical flowers. Rini looked radiant, her long hair flowing forward over her shoulders, almost touching little Gabriel. She wore a loose blouse that opened in the front so she could nurse the baby whenever she wanted, and a long white skirt. Pancho wore a simple white cotona and white pants, beaming with pride. Maria Rosa wore red and black satin ribbons interwoven into her dark braids and fastened on top of her head. She stood slim and erect in a white dress of very fine silk, with appliquéd bright-red roses on an embroidered black silk background.

Most of the other guests were dressed entirely in white, without other colorful adornments. Pancho's best friend, Gato, would conduct the ceremony and had established certain rules drawn from his knowledge of Central American Indigenous traditions. "All the principals must be dressed in white," he had proclaimed in the planning meeting with Rini, Pancho, Lorna, Maria Rosa, and Xiomara. But Maria Rosa had gone her own way. "*La madrina* must be very special," she had said, and insisted on her colorful, ornate outfit that included the Sandinista colors. Lorna agreed because she wanted *la madrina* to stand out as a sacred figure, a sorceress, in this white-attired crowd. Everyone was happy to have Sandinista colors represented.

Maria Rosa took Lorna's hand. "I am so happy for you, Lorna. You are blessed, you have the baby grandchild and Luis Jaramillo in you life."

"I feel blessed, especially having you for a friend," said Lorna. "I feel the presence of Abuelo here. I wish Doña Angélica had lived a few months longer to be here, and I wish Dr. Daisy hadn't gone back to Cuba so soon."

The master of ceremonies stood behind a cloth-covered table on which was arranged an earthenware water jug decorated with the image of a jaguar. A clay bowl held chunks of fragrant burning *copal* resin. "Oh, great Goddess, and you ancient spirits of mountains and waters! We call on you to protect and guide this child, Gabriel Nazario Altamirano Sevens. Let those present bring forth an offering."

A young man stepped forward, his dark eyes burning intensely. "I bring a polished stone from the Rio Coco, where Sandino fought. May it protect Gabrielito."

Marcos, Maria Rosa's cousin who had visited the Rosalea Bandera Clinic worksite the summer before from the Ministry of Foreign Relations, came forward. "I offer this jar of honey collected from the sweetest beehives of Palacaquina, in the Segovia Mountains," he announced.

Arminda handed her baby to her husband and stepped forward. "I offer this handmade story book written by my great grandmother, Doña Angélica, a friend of baby Gabriel's great-grandfather, Gabriel Almendros." She placed the hand-stitched book with its beautifully decorated cardboard cover on the table.

Jacinto, who had driven Lorna and Rini to Pueblo Azul in July, stepped forward. "My wife sends these embroidered clothes, with crocheted blue edgings. She began sewing the night I returned from Pueblo Azul with Rini and her mother. She was afraid he might not be born, so she prayed over her needles. 'It will be a boy, Jacinto,' she told me. And so he is.'" Jacinto placed the little blue-and-white suit, bib, and booties on the table. They were wrapped in a clear, worn, plastic bag. He appeared embarrassed and self-conscious, perhaps because it was a non–Roman Catholic spiritual event.

Offerings filled the table. An ear of corn, symbolizing the corn goddess gift, lay in a woven basket. Someone had brought a package of disposable diapers. A framed photo of Pancho and Rini, visibly pregnant, standing at the edge of the Masaya volcano, smoke billowing behind them, was placed at one end.

When all the offerings had been made, Gato handed a feathered shaker to Maria Rosa, the godmother, to represent the female element. A second feathered shaker was handed to the godfather, Pancho's cousin, to represent the male element. Gato gripped a more elaborate feathered and painted gourd, and all three began shaking their instruments in a slow, steady rhythm. Then Gato raised the pot of burning copal over his head, moving it in small circles. The burning resin mixed with the aroma of roasting pig. He raised his eyes heavenward.

"I call on all those here, all those above and below, and all those still unborn, to protect and guide little Gabrielito."

Lorna looked at baby Gabriel's sweet face. He was sleeping obliviously in Rini's arms, unaware of the powerful invocations being chanted on his behalf. His small head looked tiny and vulnerable, with its damp black hair. Rini's hand caressed his forehead and little face.

Lorna leaned over to Gabrielito and murmured, "Are you from the cosmos where Abuelo is? Has Grandfather asked you to take good care of his little girl Lorna? Who is the oldest one here, you or me?" Rini smiled at Lorna.

Lorna put her arm around Rini and said, "So much history is being passed on. I can physically feel it."

When the ceremony was over, Xiomara set out the food and pitchers of tamarindo on a long table. The guests dropped their air of solemnity and the mood turned festive as the men popped bottles of beer and Jacinto opened the bottle of Flor de Caña rum. "¡Salud!" he announced loudly, pouring himself half a glass and adding a squeeze of lemon. "To the baby!"

Rini was sitting in the shade in the patio, nursing little Gabriel. Lorna sat down next to Rini, feeling an up-welling of love and pride in her daughter.

"May Gabrielito know a lifetime of peace," said Maria Rosa, sitting down next to them.

"Peace seems even more urgent to me now since Gabriel's birth," said Lorna. "Do you think that is what is meant by 'the personal is political'?"

"I thought it was the other way around, 'the political is personal,'" said Maria Rosa.

"Is there a difference?" Lorna mused.

29

Tenth Anniversary

Two years later, Lorna, Helen, and Jackie were together on a flight to Miami on their way to Managua. Lorna was beginning to feel like a commuter. Helen sat next to her, reading Board of Supervisors briefing papers intently. Jackie, as the co chair with Lorna of Friends of Nicaraguan Culture, sat on the aisle, studying conference papers in a big binder and scribbling notes on her clipboard. The three women were the official Friends of Nicaraguan Culture delegates to the 1989 tenth anniversary celebration of the Revolution. They were also delegates to the International Conference on Revolution and Democracy. Lorna also looked forward to attending the events of the International Book fair being held at the same time.

Helen nudged Lorna abruptly. She was glancing over at Jackie's clipboard. "We have our first meeting of the North American delegation tonight about two hours after we arrive," said Helen. "Jackie thinks we better be prepared for a fight."

Lorna and Helen were in their mid fifties now, fully middle-aged women. Lorna's graying hair hid behind auburn monthly color supplementation, while Helen's formerly brown bob was now a champagne beauty parlor blonde. Jackie, twenty-five years younger with a very fit dancer's body, looked up from the clipboard.

"That's right. I phoned Jeannie Giacomelli, the DC contingent leader, two nights ago. We're going to meet briefly before the meeting to draw up the agenda. Jeannie's also going to help me arrange the room assignments. Jeannie said there's a delegation from Philadelphia planning to make a big stink about how the movement is drifting toward the center. They want to pull it back."

"Jeannie Giacomelli?" said Lorna. "I haven't seen her since I was in Washington, DC, years ago." Lorna suspected that, unlike herself and Helen, Jeannie would now be unabashedly gray-haired.

"Please make sure I'm rooming with you and Helen tonight, Jackie. I don't want to be with a stranger, and I don't like rooming alone," Lorna begged.

Jackie's face turned a little stern. "Please understand that I can't be giving my friends special privileges. Jeannie Giacomelli and I will be rooming together to make it easier to coordinate the US delegation. The Nicaraguans call us the *responsables*."

Helen patted Lorna's hand. "Don't worry, I'll room with you, Lorna. We can spend the whole night gossiping and catching up."

"You have to be up very early every day," Jackie cautioned them. "We want to be sure our people are appointed to the key committees. We mustn't let the Philadelphia group dominate, or make the official US delegation statements. We don't want Philadelphia deciding the follow-up action plans for back home."

"To be honest, Jackie," said Lorna, "I don't get it. I hate these internal power struggles. We're all basically on the same side. I know Jeannie, she's a very good person. I might have to miss a few meetings because I'm delivering copies of my book to the women I interviewed. I'll also be spending some time at the book-fair."

Jackie checked something in her binder. "Lorna, don't give me a hard time. Some of these ultra-leftists object to our focus on legislative work. We don't want them grabbing the leadership."

"So what if they do? The main way to grab power is to do all the work. I'm willing to let Philadelphia do some of the work. We've had more than enough on our plate."

Jackie rolled her eyes. "They are tricky. That's why I'm doing all this advance planning. Eddie Flores is going to be an important link for us. I'm counting on your friendship with him, Lorna."

"Well, don't," said Lorna, sharply. "Eddie and I have not been close since the Palace of Fine Arts reading, in case you don't remember."

Jackie leaned across Helen. "You're being very individualistic and subjective, Lorna. Get over it! He could be very helpful in positioning us."

"That's the problem, Jackie, I don't think we need to be positioned. Our work speaks for us."

"Girls, girls, girls!" said Helen. "What's this all about? Come on, we're here to have a good time, celebrate the revolution, celebrate all that Nicaragua has accomplished in ten years. Could we stop this bickering?"

Jackie made a face and snapped her binder closed. Helen turned toward Lorna. "Long time friendships can be difficult, can't they? But you and Eddie have been political buddies for so long. I'm sure if you needed him, he would turn over heaven and earth to help you."

Lorna frowned, remembering Eddie's intrusion into her brief relationship with Guillermo. "Well, maybe," she allowed. "But I wouldn't count on it."

Jackie sighed. "OK, so Eddie Flores can be a problem. But we still might need his help, Lorna."

Lorna smiled, taking in Jackie's youthful good looks, and said, "I'll leave that to you."

Lorna turned her thoughts to her planned journey to see Rini and her beautiful family up north after the conference. Maria Rosa would be there too.

The women had a four-hour layover at the Miami airport, so they loaded up on drugstore items, Tampax, Pepto-Bismol, hand cream, and sunblock. Jackie bought herself a Miami Dolphins bill cap and some dark glasses.

"Enough shopping! Let's sit down and eat!" Helen cried.

"Helen, do you remember Rosalea Bandera? The poet I picked up for one of our first readings? She told me the best

Cuban food she ever had in her life was the Cuban food at the Miami airport. Let me show you—there's a great little eatery here, with the most fantastic *batidos,* and grilled pork and cheese sandwiches. Cuban coffee to die for. Mmmmm mmmmm!"

"Hmmm," said Jackie. "Are we sure we want those calories?"

"I'm sure I want those calories!" said Lorna.

"Sounds like a cholesterol bomb to me," complained Jackie.

"You should worry!" exclaimed Helen. "You don't have a spare ounce on you, my dear."

"I should get some credit for watching what I eat!" said Jackie.

As they pressed up to the Cuban food counter, the dancer ordered a salad.

The Miami–Managua flight was a short one. As always, Lorna's heart beat a little faster as the plane descended toward the green fields, the clumps of forest, the low buildings with zinc roofs backed up against dark trees. The irregular shoreline of Lake Xolotlán glistened. It was the rainy season, and threatening blackish-blue cumulus clouds had piled up in the big tropical sky. The tarmac was shiny with puddles. Soon they were trudging with their carry-on bags across the wet pavement into Managua's heat and intense humidity. There was the familiar, yet always endless, walk through the narrow white corridors leading to passport control, immigration, and then customs. At the end of the customs counter, Lorna was pleased to see Maria Rosa's cousin Marcos, from the Foreign Ministry, waiting for them, holding a clipboard just like Jackie's. As always, he looked crisp and business-like in a white shirt and khaki slacks. Before he could approach them, another uniformed official standing at a booth said, "Excuse me, ladies, please step over here to pay the tourism tax."

Lorna, Helen, and Jackie looked at one another. Jackie said, "What tax is this?"

Now Marcos slipped into the situation, with suave diplomatic grace. "It's a new tourism tax, but it doesn't apply to you." He flipped open his wallet and showed his credentials to the official. "These *compañeras* are special guests of the government."

"Go ahead then, *señoras!*" declared the agent. His official expression relaxed into a smile.

"You saved us, *Compañero* Marcos. I brought just enough money to buy a few souvenirs," said Jackie.

"We see tourism as a promising new revenue source," Marcos said calmly. "The whole world is curious about Nicaragua's Sandinista revolution. But you ladies are our honored guests." With Marcos leading the way, they marched through a lobby filled with duty-free liquor, watches, perfumes, and jewelry. Marcos apologized, "After the splendors of Miami International, this must be a pathetic imitation."

"Not at all," Jackie said. "It's a pleasure to be here, after the insane consumerism and waste of America." Marcos looked pleased with her response.

To Lorna's eyes, little had changed except for the new commercial-style posters depicting touristic white beaches and waving palm trees of Nicaragua's Pacific coast, or reminding newcomers of one of Nicaragua's major exports, Flor de Caña rum. The "Tenth Anniversary of the Revolution" banners hung everywhere with their slogan: "Nicaragua was never more in my heart."

"So they don't pose models in skimpy bikinis lying on the beach anymore. I've read that it's been recently outlawed to use women's bodies in advertising to sell products," said Helen approvingly. "I wonder if I could get the Board of Supervisors to adopt a similar ordinance for San Francisco."

"In San Francisco, you'd have to outlaw beefcake as well as cheesecake," commented Jackie.

"The Mercedes Hotel is just across the road. I'll take your luggage over in the van and meet you in the hotel driveway to unload." The van was filled with all the visiting delegates' luggage.

A slight breeze relieved the heavy humid air and played with the blue-and-white Nicaraguan flag. Next to it waved the red-and-black Sandinista banner. With the 1990 election looming, Sandinista political posters announced, "We'll do it again!" Under the photo of President Daniel Ortega was written his nickname, "El Gallo," the rooster. The cement walls lining the highway were emblazoned with graffiti, in the form of a simple black and red stripe, without any words. Those two colors, red and black, simply signified, "Vote Sandinista."

"That's a great campaign idea," noted Helen, pointing at the red and black stripes, "considering how many Nicaraguans are semi literate."

They could see Las Mercedes Hotel across the Carretera Norte as they walked through the airport parking lot. The hotel was a complex of low stucco buildings with red clay tile roofs, sitting in a grove of palm trees. The challenge was to cross the highway. They stood at the carratera curb, evaluating the traffic and awaiting their chance. Jackie jumped back as a taxi veered too close to the airport curb. Lorna inhaled the familiar warm tropical air mixed with gas fumes and dust. "Managua," she sighed.

Helen boldly led the way. "The only way to do this is to step off the curb and run like hell when I give the signal." She waited while a truck full of chickens passed, then yelled, "Run!"

Lorna took Jackie's hand and pulled, but Jackie, usually fleet of feet, was glued to the curb. "Faster, women, faster!" shouted Helen, who had already made it to the other side of the road. Uneasily Lorna and Jackie made it to the center of the highway. The hotel was only a few more feet away, but now a slow-moving car and a man on horseback had to be allowed to pass. Behind their backs cars zoomed west toward Managua.

"We can do it," Lorna urged Jackie. Pulling the dancer's hand, she ran across the eastbound lane and stepped up safely in front of the hotel.

Helen applauded them. "Here we are, the very special guests of the government, all sweaty and gritty."

"I can hardly wait for a shower," sighed Lorna. They walked across the hotel parking lot to the lobby.

"No water," Lorna heard a woman saying distinctly at the crescent-shaped, light wood reception desk.

"Oh no," groaned Helen, who had heard it too.

"I'm sure it's a small plumbing problem, easily fixed," said Jackie, an incorrigible optimist about all things revolutionary.

"Nothing here is easily fixed," said Lorna sadly. "Thanks to the embargo, there's a shortage of plumbing supplies." Lorna's spirits sank as she looked around the lobby.

It resembled an atrium, brightly lit with high ceilings and large floor-to-ceiling windows with views of the greenery surrounding the hotel. It was full of guests trying to sign in. Others filled the armchairs and benches arranged around potted palms on the highly polished floors. Delegates of all races, ages, and nationalities, conversing in many different languages, created a buzz, like the droning of bees.

Marcos pulled into the driveway and up to the front door with the van. He started unloading luggage on the sidewalk and a hotel staffer pulled them into the lobby. Marcos moved the truck, returning quickly.

"How do you like this hotel?" he asked the three women. "It took a lot of arranging to get you installed here. But it puts you in the center of the action."

"We love it, Marcos. Thank you!" said Helen. Marcos's face flushed with pleasure.

"It's wonderful," said Lorna, following Helen's gracious example, without mentioning the water problem.

"I'm so excited to be here," said Jackie. "This is my first time out of my country." She turned to Marcos. "I remember when I first met you in San Francisco. We talked of a conference like this. Now it's really happening! In fact, I have a meeting with the North American delegation leaders in half an hour."

"All the North American delegation meetings will be held at here at Las Mercedes," said Marcos happily. "That's why I wanted you lodging here." Jackie beamed back at him.

The women lugged their bags across the lobby to the line at the registration desk. The guest who had said "No water" was still arguing with the desk clerk who said, "I'm sorry. You'll have to be patient. We've let management know, and they're doing their best."

Lorna interrupted the woman to ask the clerk for a room key.

"You're rooming with Helen Hart in cabin 7," said the clerk, sliding a big key across the counter toward Lorna.

Marcos jumped in. "A little change, I forgot to mention. We're putting Helen in cabin 18 with the New York City councilwoman just for tonight. She's doesn't speak Spanish, and the rest of her delegation arrives tomorrow. She didn't want to be alone in a strange place and since they are both US urban officials, I arranged for Helen to stay with her for this one night."

Marcos turned to Helen. "I hope this is all right. She wanted someone who knew both the US political scene and the situation in Nicaragua. You'll go back to Cabin 7 with Lorna tomorrow night. OK?"

Lorna, very disappointed, said nothing.

Helen threw Lorna a what-can-I-do look. "Of course, no problem," she said, smiling to Marcos.

Jackie pulled the clipboard out of her big purse and made the room-adjustment note. Lorna glumly carried her heavy bag to cabin 7.

It was one of many rooms on a wing of the hotel, off a red-tiled corridor. At one end, the corridor opened up into a garden, with wrought-iron patio furniture and a fountain that was not working. Not a good sign, thought Lorna.

In the room, she turned on the tap water first thing. A little stream trickled out and then stopped.

30

Dragon Slayer

Lorna dragged her heavy suitcase into the room with a heavy heart. The wood-ceiling room seemed clean but drab. One window opened onto the hallway, and another opened onto a patio. Lorna could hear all the traffic of the Carretera Norte highway careening by through the patio window. She sat down on the twin bed and kicked off her sandals, wondering how she would ever go to sleep with all the noise in the stifling room. The air conditioner was unplugged. She plugged it in and set the control on high. The air conditioner sound drowned out the highway. Lorna lay down on the bed and looked up at the rustic wood ceiling, thinking back to summer camp and her longing for someone to take her home, to Abuelo.

She heard a knock on the door. "It's me, Helen." Lorna let her in. She sat down on the other twin bed.

"What a cute room, so clean and woodsy," said Helen.

"It's terribly hot," said Lorna, sulking in spite of herself.

Helen maintained a cheerful tone. "Your air conditioner's humming. It looks like a new one," said Helen. "This room will cool off in no time. And guess what—water's coming on in an hour."

"Believe that, and they'll tell you another one," grumped Lorna.

"No, really! I saw the crew working on it. I talked to the crew chief."

"Even when and if the water comes, I'm going to be miserable here alone."

Helen looked surprised. "Lorna, why are you being such a

big baby? This isn't like you. It's only for one night. Look on the pluses. You won't have to wait until I'm finished in the bathroom. You have a private bathroom, all to yourself."

"I don't like being alone anymore. I've had enough of it," whined Lorna.

"Oh, for heaven's sake," said Helen. "How old are you? This is a tiny thing. We've handled so much more."

"You promised me," said Lorna sulkily. "I can act like a twelve-year old if I want!"

"And you certainly are, Lorna," replied Helen. "I'm sorry, but how could I let Marcos down? You know how helpful Ed Koch has been on this contra thing; and this woman has important connections to him. We need New York, with all its money and media."

"I know. But I'm hot, exhausted, and disappointed," Lorna admitted.

"Look, let's go get a cold fruit drink on the patio. I saw everyone out there. It's fun! Come on."

"I don't know why I'm being such a brat," Lorna said. "When I get this tired, I revert to the child missing her grandfather. If Luis were here, I probably would be the brave, mature person you want."

"We all have our down times," said Helen briskly. "Come on. Let's go. You'll feel better."

"OK, maybe there will be water when I get back," said Lorna. She stood up, looked at her hair in the mirror and ran a comb through it.

Lorna followed Helen out to the main patio and they took refuge at a table in a covered cabaña open to the swimming pool. Lorna looked around. The rain had been threatening to return and now the first drops were falling. The little garden was charming, with feathery potted palms, a breadfruit tree with its gigantic leaves, and several fruit trees and tangles of fragrant vines. The sky was darkening overhead, and a white-jacketed waiter scurried to and fro, lighting candles at each table.

"The hotel grounds are lovely," said Lorna. "Thanks, Helen,

for dragging me out of the room. That pool looks inviting. If the water doesn't come on soon, we can swim."

"We'll smell of chlorine all night," laughed Helen.

Now the waiter appeared, standing between their two chairs.

"*Buenas tardes*," he said, handing them each a menu. "How are you ladies?" he added in English.

"We're so happy to be here," Helen told him.

"The pleasure is ours," he said. "What can I bring you? A cool drink?"

"Yes," Helen requested, "a soda, please."

"I'll have the same," Lorna added.

"And an appetizer? Something to eat?" he prompted.

Helen consulted the long menu. "I'd like the shrimp cocktail," she replied.

The waiter looked sad. "*No hay*. We didn't receive any shrimp today."

"Well then, I'll have the *ceviche*."

The waiter looked even sadder. "*No hay*," he said. "We don't have any fish today."

Helen referred back to the menu. "Fruit salad?" she asked hopefully.

"*No hay*," said the waiter.

"Can we have a plate of tortillas and fried cheese?" Lorna asked.

They looked at the waiter, and he nodded, brightening at once.

"*Sí, sí, no hay problema*," he said with a big grin. Soon he had returned with sodas, tortillas, and fried cheese.

The music floating out over the sound system was an old country western hit. "I'm crazy, crazy for thinking that my love could hold you," sang Patsy Cline, with a well-rehearsed quaver. The second tune was a Mexican hit, "Juana, La Cubana," with a loud jazzy saxophone. Lorna preferred the Nicaraguan folk-based jazz-fusion music.

"I feel a cultural shifting coming on," said Helen, with a grimace. "Seems like this music is an attempt to please us *gringo* tourists." Over Helen's shoulder, Lorna could see musicians rolling in their electronic equipment. To her surprise, she realized she recognized one of them. The fair-haired musician was the saxophonist who had been playing with Mancotal at that outdoor club, the place she and Guillermo had gone to after their swim in Lake Xiloa, years ago. Instead of the *cotona* and jeans he had been wearing then, he was wearing a pink ruffled tuxedo shirt and shiny black trousers. Years ago, he had dedicated a song to her: "Solidarity is the tenderness of the people."

"Helen, I know the saxophonist, Jorge, that's his name. He's setting up the amps. The drummer looks familiar too."

"How do you know them?" Helen asked.

"Jorge was with Grupo Mancotal. The drummer too. I heard them when I was here the summer of 1986, the summer the clinic got bombed. It's strange to see them here tonight in pink ruffled shirts instead of the folkloric garb." Lorna found she did not want to mention Guillermo's name, even though she was being inundated with memories of that evening.

Helen turned around. "I think he recognizes you too, the way he's looking over here."

"Oh, I don't think he'd remember me," Lorna said, but the man was putting down the cables and walking over to their table with a big grin.

"Hola, *compañera*. How have you been?"

"Very well," said Lorna. "You are Jorge, no? I am Lorna Almendros. I remember listening to you at the little club."

"Yes, yes," said Jorge enthusiastically. "*Compañera* Lorna. Yes, I remember you very well. I always remember the beautiful ladies. You came with Guillermo Villanova, the brother of Javier at the Ministry of Culture. How is Guillermo?"

"He took a post with the Nicaraguan Embassy in New Delhi. I've not seen him for three years."

"Javier mentioned that Guillermo might be coming for the Tenth Anniversary," said Jorge, smoothly.

Lorna was startled. "I just arrived in Nicaragua this afternoon," she added weakly.

"Welcome! Did you come from New York?" asked Jorge quickly.

"From California," Lorna said. She pointed to Helen. "Jorge, this is my good friend, Helen Hart from Friends of Nicaraguan Culture. She's a San Francisco city supervisor. We're here to help celebrate the tenth anniversary of the revolution."

"I hope you are going to enjoy our music, *compañera* Helen," said Jorge, smiling. "I know *compañera* Lorna enjoyed our music from the New Song movement when I last saw her. We used to play *volcanto* music, the Nicaraguan version of Latin American protest music. Her friend Guillermo told me that she performed her poetry with the famous Chilean *nueva canción* group, Quilapayún."

"Oh, that was a very long time ago!" said Lorna, startled to hear Guillermo's name on his lips again. It brought a memory back she had carefully put away. She couldn't imagine having to see him now.

"I would love to hear the Nicaraguan *nueva canción*," said Helen enthusiastically.

"Unfortunately, tonight we'll be playing standard background dinner music. And a bit later, when it's really dark, we'll switch to popular dance tunes."

"You are no longer with Mancotal?" asked Lorna.

"No, sadly, and unfortunately. We had to disband when the government defunded the arts. It was good-bye to long, intense, exploratory rehearsals. Hello, again, to clubs and tourist hotels, wearing these frilly pink shirts." He plucked one of the ruffles with a dismayed look.

"Oh, I'm so sorry. Grupo Mancotal is one of my favorites."

"We did recently make a recording for the election, a little song for Daniel," Jorge told her.

"Will you play it tonight?"

"No, Las Mercedes hires us to amuse the guests, not bombard them with political messages."

"How do you think the election campaigns are going?" Helen asked.

"Conditions are very bad with the *compactación,* the government spending cutbacks. Fighting the contras is very expensive. The cutbacks have left thousands jobless. Like me, last year. And the people are so impatient, so tired of the blackouts, the food shortages, the high prices. It is very, very sad. Violetta Chamorro may stand a chance in her bid for the presidency."

"We hear that inflation is high," said Helen.

"It is hyper-inflation," said Jorge, sadly. "The rate is thirty-three thousand percent. With the trade embargo, the contras, and Nicaragua's inability to get international loans, we're now the poorest country in Latin America. It's all the fault of the imperialists, their embargo and their contra war. But people blame their troubles and hardships on the revolution. Some say if there were no *Sandinistas,* there would be no war. People are sick of war."

Jorge shook his head, sadly. "But most can see our free schools, our free medical care, and they understand the pressure Nicaragua is under. I hope they express that at election time in November. Above everything, we treasure our sovereignty. Everyone has heard of Nicaragua now."

"Especially my husband, Larry. He loves your recording of *All de Nations Love Bananas,*" Helen told him, "and always sings it."

"I'll play that tonight and dedicate it to my California *compañeras,*" said Jorge, looking happier. "Management won't have a problem with the banana song."

They listened to the squawks and whines as the musicians tested their monitors. Others were taking seats at the tables. The rain that had threatened to dampen the evening was holding off, and Lorna could see a bright star above her. She felt excited, sad, and lonely, all at once. She had so firmly put memories of Guillermo in a special remote box in her heart. Now, seeing Jorge, it was as if the memories threatened to escape.

Draining her Coke glass, Lorna said to Helen, "If only Luis were here."

The band began to play, and Lorna recognized the usual bar tunes, *The Girl from Impamena*, *Body and Soul*, and *Summertime*. The musicians did not seem inspired, and their music sounded very standard. Lorna felt she could have been anywhere. Then Jorge took the microphone and announced a special request from the *compañeras* from California, and to some laughter from the audience, they launched into *All de Nations Love Bananas* which they performed with considerably more spirit. That broke the ice.

The waiter was clearing their table when Lorna noticed a tall woman with a clipboard approaching them. "Do you speak English?" she asked.

They nodded.

"I'm Roberta Nickelberger from Philadelphia. I'm on the US delegation steering committee. I came to tell you the water's been turned on, now. We'll hold a quick welcome meeting in an hour in the dining room."

Lorna saw that streams of water were now spouting from the three porpoises that formed the central sculpture of the fountain. "Thanks," said Lorna, "these are glad tidings!"

Roberta Nickelberger moved on to another table. As soon as she was out of earshot, Lorna asked Helen, "Do you think she's part of that ultra-leftist group Jackie is so worried about?"

"Probably. But she certainly brought good news. Let's go shower before this welcome meeting."

On the way back to their rooms, they met Jackie. She looked worried.

"How was the steering committee meeting?" asked Lorna.

"Very disappointing," said Jackie. "Your friend, Eddie Flores, was paying so much attention to one of the woman delegates, he didn't even hear my questions. I'd been counting on his help, but he was useless. I guess you were right, Lorna."

"Eddie will be Eddie," said Lorna. "He's a good guy but he has that problem."

"We met one of the Philadelphians, a tall woman named Roberta Nickelberger," Helen said. "She said the water's been turned on. We're on our way to take a shower."

"That damned group wheedled themselves into several key positions," said Jackie. "Roberta was supposed to be making hand copies of the agenda for tonight's big meeting. She's probably using the water issue to get to know all the other delegates so she can lobby them later for support." Jackie looked very glum.

"Don't worry about it, Jackie," said Helen. "We had better shower before the water's gone."

Helen went off to her own room. As Lorna opened the door to cabin 7, she was met by a blast of cold air. "Ah!" she said out loud. She stepped into the bathroom and turned the shower faucet. Only cold water. But cold was just fine, she thought. Helen was right, it was nice not to have to wait her turn for the shower.

Lorna opened her suitcase and hung a pretty white dress in the closet that she planned to wear for for her big speech, "Inside the Belly of the Beast: International Solidarity against Imperialism," at the conference plenary session. She put other things in drawers, and arranged her lotions and potions on the dresser, leaving space for Helen. After showering and changing clothes, she joined the other delegates congregating in the dining room for the US delegation's welcome session. A mood of excitement was tangible in the room.

Jackie stood at the entrance to the conference room, freshly showered, wearing the latest in fashionable fitness clothes, in turquoise and white.

Lorna greeted her. "You look great, ready to work."

"Who's working?" Jackie asked happily, as she marked Lorna present on her list. "This is fun."

Lorna entered the conference room and glanced around. Sixty chairs were set up looking toward a long table draped in green cloth, with three chairs behind it, facing the audience. Next to it was a podium and microphone. Delegates formed small groups here and there. Some had taken seats already and were staring straight ahead or ruffling papers. She recognized no one. She stepped over to a small table on which were arrayed plastic name badges. She found hers: "Lorna

Almendros, USA." The safety pin was thick and cumbersome.

"Native manufacturer," said a scornful voice in English. She looked up to see a big-boned man in a white suit watching her fumble with the pin. He couldn't very well assist her with it, she realized, without having his big hand all over her breast. She was irritated.

"Who are you?" she asked, looking down as she attempted to slide the sharp pin into the fabric of her blouse.

"Leif Larsson, from Sweden," he said, pointing to his badge. He had a cadaverous face and light hair that was almost white and a ruddy complexion.

"This is the welcoming session for the North American delegation," she said, still struggling.

"I'm crashing it," said the Swede. "There are too few of us Scandinavians to have our own reception." He looked again at her name tag. "Until the Sandinista Ministry of Economics learns to implement quality control, their manufacturing sector is going absolutely nowhere," he said.

Lorna felt a flush of anger toward the Scandinavian. She wanted to defend Nicaragua, but before any words came out, she managed to jab the pin into her thumb. A small smear of blood appeared. Finding a paper napkin on the table, she wrapped it around her thumb. She turned away from the obnoxious stranger and walked across the room to where she recognized Jeannie Giacomelli talking to Jimmy Greene, one of the old Lincoln Brigade guys.

"Lorna! Oh my god, it's been so long! How are you?" said Jeannie.

Jeannie was the same warm-spirited person Lorna remembered from the congressional hearings, now a little plumper, and her brown curls were heavily mixed with gray.

"Let me introduce Jim Greene. He's been active with our group for so long."

"Oh, we've met!" said Jimmy Greene, bowing deeply to Lorna. "Beautiful Lorna graced our construction site three years ago when the Rosalea Bandera clinic was bombed. She was one tough lady, let me tell you!"

Lorna smiled, remembering how she had fallen asleep on her shovel. "I was not as tough as Jimmy Greene, let me tell you!" laughed Lorna.

"Lorna! How are you?" Jeannie suddenly saw Lorna's thumb, wrapped in a bloody tissue. "Oh my god, what happened? You've hurt yourself!"

"I'm fine. Some man made a disparaging crack about what poor quality these Nicaraguan pins are, and I got so mad, I jabbed my thumb with the pin on the back of the badge trying to put it on."

"Given all the good that the Sandinistas have done for Nicaragua, he is ridiculous to attack them for these name tags. You should go take care of that thumb," said Jimmy.

Marcos was approaching them. He examined Lorna's thumb with solicitude. "I'm so sorry," he said. "People from the neighborhood block committee stayed up all last night making badges for hundreds of delegates. These were not professionally made."

"I'll help you with that finger," Jeannie said. "Let's go to the bathroom in the lobby."

There were four metal stalls, a pink Formica sink with four bowls, and a long mirror. Jeannie turned on the water and tested it. "See, we're in luck, now the water is working, even the hot!" Gingerly, Lorna unfolded the bloody napkin and stretched her thumb out under the faucet.

"Wash it well. Use some soap. Germs grow so easily in the tropics."

Lorna enjoyed being taken care of. She washed her finger and dried it carefully on a fresh paper towel.

"See, I found a Band-Aid in my purse," said Jeannie.

"So, Jeannie," said Lorna. "What's this stuff about the Philadelphia group trying to take over the conference? What do you they want, anyway? Something the San Francisco group is opposed to? I keep hearing from Jackie about this East Coast–West Coast warfare, and I'm totally confused."

"Oh, Lorna," sighed Jeannie. "Come sit down." There were several large cushioned chairs and a sofa in the ladies room lounge. Lorna and Jeannie sat down on the sofa, next to a tall potted palm.

"What I've found," said Jeannie, "is that there are always egos involved. I swear it's easier to get along with the enemy sometimes than to get along with the members of your own team. There are turf battles, ego battles, and ridiculous issues no one cares about. There's always someone in a power struggle with someone else. Philadelphia doesn't want anything San Francisco doesn't want."

"That is what I thought. I don't know why Jackie takes it so seriously," said Lorna.

"She's young," said Jeannie. "I like her. Jackie's very efficient. She understands the effectiveness of lobbying in Washington. You know the Philadelphians only want to organize mass rallies and pickets to end contra aid. But are we on different sides, ultimately? Absolutely not. We need both. I tell you, this is just a very personal power struggle between Jackie and Roberta Nickelberger. They're competing to see who is going to set the line for the national organization."

"Anyway," Jeannie added, "it's harder and harder to get attention about Nicaragua. All the attention is flowing to El Salvador these days because of the civil war there."

"We don't get the big crowds we used to," admitted Lorna. "You're right. The solidarity movement is turning toward El Salvador."

"One thing is certain," said Jeannie reaching over and taking Lorna's uninjured hand. "We old Wisdom Women will continue to work together in solidarity and we'll keep our organizations from destroying each other, *compañera!*"

"Say, do you know this Scandinavian character, Leif Larsson?" asked Lorna. "He was rude and unpleasant to me when I first entered."

"I know who you're talking about," said Jeannie, standing up. "I don't know much about him, but I don't trust that guy. We better be getting back."

During a break, Lorna tried to reach Luis from the telephone booth in the lobby. Disappointingly, there was no answer. She was dying to talk to him and was already starting to miss him despite the flood of activity, people and intense shifting emotions. There was already so much to tell. With only a few minutes of break left, she headed out to the patio to get a breath of fresh air and took a seat on one of the wrought-iron patio benches. She remembered the scent of the tropical Nicaraguan night, like it had been that night with Guillermo.

Much had changed for Lorna in three years. Her hair had gone from mostly brown to mostly gray under her continuing color treatments. Little Gabrielito had arrived. Her new book, *Daughters of the Silence,* had been published and received some nice reviews. She had finally made a commitment to a wonderful man she even hoped to marry.

Yet she wondered where Guillermo was right this minute. Was he still in India? Did he ever think of her? Maria Rosa never had any news of him, even though they were both in the Ministry of Foreign Affairs. Just then, Jackie passed by the bench and said, "Come on, Lorna. Break's over." They went back into the conference hall.

The remainder of the welcome session was short. Lorna caught sight of Leif Larsson leaning against a wall, watching the proceedings with his arms folded. She didn't see Helen anywhere and dreaded going back alone to the empty cabin, with only the air conditioner and her worries for company. But she needed to rest. Her speech was the next day at the conference opening. The butterflies in her stomach were arising from their cocoons. Grandfather had always said, "When a butterfly comes in the house you will have a visitor," making Lorna wonder who she might meet.

When the welcome session was over, the rest of the day was spent in small group meetings, sharing experiences and planning future solidarity campaigns. After the group dinner, no one seemed to notice when she slipped away to cabin 7. A blast of cool air hit her as she opened the door. The air conditioner was humming loudly, and now there was hot water as well as cold water in the shower. Lorna undressed, examining her body in the mirror. She still had the voluptuous figure of her youth, but it wasn't only Jeannie who was a bit plumper. Lorna was also definitely rounder in the belly and thighs. Slipping on a nightgown, she climbed into a hard hotel bed that felt halfway around the world from home.

For a while, she read, but soon found herself staring up at the wood-paneled ceiling thinking about the awful time in summer camp decades ago when she arose from her bunk bed to be told her grandfather was dead. As a grandmother, a published author and a respected journalist, this childhood experience still brought tears to her eyes. She wiped them off with the edge of her sheet. Lorna realized it was time to make peace with Abuelo's death. She had to come to terms with her own aging. Almost instantly her mind wandered to Rini, the upcoming elections, and the hyperinflation. She hoped she could reach Luis by phone the next day. She thought about Guillermo and how he would probably say that the Sandinista economy would work if the US would withdraw the contra forces and allow Nicaragua to borrow money from global financial institutions.

She could not hold off her confrontation with her old fears. Helen was right to call her a self-centered baby. Her loneliness-and-abandonment dragon might return again and again, but as an active grandmother instead of a grieving child, she would shoo it away. Maybe someday it would disappear. It would have been nice, however, to have a sleeping pill.

By morning, the room was chilly. She had slept soundly and felt ready to give her speech. "It's morning," she said out loud, putting aside her old ghosts and congratulating herself. Another dragon slain. She bounded from the bed in a single leap.

31

Who's Listening?

Lorna turned on the hot water and hung out the white summer dress for the plenary session. Under the shower spray, she squirted a little of her cucumber shampoo into her palms and into her hair. Luis had stopped teasing her about smelling like a vegetable. His line now was that he adored cucumbers, because they smelled like Lorna. She began singing "Solidarity Forever." The old trade union song always made her feel part of some grand and unbeatable tradition. While she was dressing, there was a knock at the door.

It was Jackie, calling from outside. "I'm coming," Lorna called back, searching for her other sandal. As she opened the door, the heavy, steamy outside air hit her. This dress could wilt before breakfast, Lorna thought. Jackie was dressed in a sleeveless yellow jersey with a low V neckline and bright-blue printed skirt. She looked cool and prepared for action.

"Ready for your speech?" said Jackie, holding her clipboard.

"As ready as I'll ever be for an international audience," replied Lorna.

"I want to make sure everything goes well for your speech. Everyone has to be on the bus to the Olaf Palme Center by eight forty-five. It's good we're getting an early start. The restaurant opens for breakfast in five minutes."

"Mmmmm," agreed Lorna. "*Café con leche*, made just the way I want it."

"Where's your speech?" Jackie asked, as they hurried into the garden.

"In my head."

"You've got to be kidding. This isn't art, Lorna. This is

politics. You have to have a plan. We didn't hold all those meetings deciding what the points you should cover just to have you wing it."

"I don't wing it, Jackie. I number the points in my mind and then I move from one to the next with a few poetic flourishes and what's called thesis development in between."

"Please go back and get your speech. You have to give a copy to the interpreter anyway. People will be listening in Spanish, English, French, and Russian, on different headset channels."

Lorna sighed in acquiescence and reopened the door. The room was still cool. She picked up two copies of the speech, neatly word-processed and printed on the fancy new home computer Luis had bought her.

Jackie took a copy, almost pushing Lorna down the garden path toward the restaurant. "Thanks. You go eat. I'll drop this off at the translation booth."

Early risers were lined up before the patio breakfast buffet. Lorna looked at her watch. It was not yet seven a.m. Two large silver urns contained fresh black coffee and warmed milk. Lorna poured herself a cup, half coffee, half milk, and took a roll from a woven basket, along with a small plate of fresh orange slices, honeydew melon, and banana.

As she savored her coffee, she thought Jackie was right. She knew the speech so well, but the interpreter didn't. She'd read it slowly and clearly for the interpreter to translate, giving Lorna plenty of opportunity for looking up at the audience.

She could see Jackie hurrying back. "I just want to warn you, Lorna, don't go off on some poetic tangent. You're representing all of us, not just yourself."

"Jackie, don't worry. Please let me relax and get centered. This is not the occasion for a bunch of criticism. I haven't even finished my morning coffee."

"I'm sorry, Lorna, but your speech is one of my responsibilities."

"Stop it! I am not one of your responsibilities. Go away—go check up on another one of your duties. I've been doing this a whole lot longer than you."

"I'm sorry, Lorna. I know I tend to get carried away with my responsibilities. But I'm worried. There's so much to handle, like getting everyone onto that bus on time."

"Jackie, don't worry about me. I can get myself on a bus. I'll board five minutes early so you won't have to worry. How's that, my friend?"

Jackie left her in the silence she was craving. Lorna took out her speech, not to review it, but to use as a barrier against further socializing. Nonetheless, Lorna could not help but look at what she had written, although something like stage fright kept her from seeing the words.

"Can I join you?" It was Helen, balancing a full tray. She was wearing white slacks and a red-and-black blouse, with a colorful white shawl with red-and-black poppies. "Gorgeous shawl!" said Lorna. "You don't normally wear anything so wild! What happened?"

"Oh, Larry bought this for me when we were in Jamaica. I certainly wouldn't wear it in San Francisco, but red and black seems just right, and it will help with the air conditioning."

"I'd lost all hope of finding you," said Lorna.

"Well, here I am." Helen unloaded her tray. "The councilwoman is all taken care of, so I'm free. How's the room? I move back in tonight. Did you save me some drawer space?"

"Yes. Of course. There's always a space for you."

"So how's the speech coming along?"

"Well, it's amazing that I'm giving the speech at all. I think the organizers have very reluctantly allowed a *gringa*, an 'enemy of the human race,' to quote their anthem. It's generous that we get to play a part in their celebration."

"Well, we *gringas* aren't all cut out of the same cloth," laughed Helen. "They know that. The National Directorate is very aware of all we've done to try to cut off funding to the contras."

"I know, Helen, but I get whiffs of suspicion too. What with the contras, and political intrigue, it's like you never can be sure who your friends really are. But you were right, it was good having the room to myself last night. That doesn't mean I'm not looking forward to our all-night gabfest."

After breakfast Lorna and Helen found Jackie in the driveway of the hotel, surrounded by delegates who were all asking her questions at once.

"Why don't I help Jackie?" Helen said, "You wait in the air-conditioned lobby. You've got to keep your cool for that speech, Lorna. You can see through the glass wall when the bus arrives to take us to the Olaf Palme Conference Center. I'll hold seats for us."

Lorna took the same seat she had taken the night before, on a wooden sofa with gaudy floral cushions. Around her the entire atrium was filled with delegates. Some were standing in a long line waiting to use the lobby telephone. Her phone call to Luis would have to wait. To her dismay, coming toward her was Leif Larsson, in a beige polo shirt and pleated pants. He sat down right beside her, and Lorna squeezed against the arm of the sofa to avoid having to make physical contact with him.

"Good morning," he said. "All ready to lead the cheering for the Sandinistas this morning?"

"Cheering?"

"You know. Rah rah for the Sandinista saints that can do no wrong."

A woman on a chair facing them looked up. "They really are saints and I can certify it. I have an advanced degree in theology." She had short-cropped gray curls dancing about her plain face. With her short-sleeved cotton blouse, gray pastel skirt that hung to her calves, and sturdy sandals, she was no different from many other middle-aged American women, including Lorna. However, a heavy wooden cross hung around her neck.

"Our Maryknoll Order has been developing low-cost housing since before the revolution. I can tell you, what the Sandinista government is accomplishing in the face of incredible American pressure constitutes a miracle."

Leif Larsson laughed. "Miracle? Total debacle, I'd say.

Nicaragua is nothing but a geopolitical pawn, with Cuba and the Soviet Union on one side, and international capitalism on the other. Ortega's making such an enemy out of the United States hasn't won him any friends. No one trusts his brand of socialism."

"If you find Nicaragua so dismaying, why did you even come?" Lorna said. "This is, after all, a celebration of the revolution. It's like you didn't come to praise Nicaragua, but to bury it."

"I guess you might say I like a good joke," said Larsson.

Lorna stood up. She could not bear to hear him speak one more word.

The other woman stood up also. As they moved away, the nun turned and gave her a hug. Just then Lorna caught a glimpse of Helen waving to her. A big bus was rolling up to the hotel. "Are you going to the conference? They're boarding the buses now."

"Oh, no," said the nun. I'm waiting for my sister from St. Louis. She's flying in today. I haven't seen her for ten years. She's been afraid to visit me because of all the violence."

"Yes, there is so much violence in the north. I'm always afraid for my daughter and her family. She works up north."

"And what does she do?" asked the nun.

"She's an engineer developing hydraulic projects. But after the contras killed Ben Linder, my heart is always shaking."

"Don't worry, dear. God protects his angels."

As Lorna boarded the bus, she was still smiling. She turned toward the window, imagining angels watching over Rini and baby Gabriel as Rini installed her micro-hydro electrical systems. Lorna was so nervous ever since Ben Linder, the young Portland engineer's murder two years earlier in April 1987. She had wished for Rini to come home, or at least to move back to Managua. Rini continued to work close to the area where the contras had shot him. She, Gabrielito, and Pancho needed all the angels they could get. Lorna hoped one of the angels had time to keep an eye out for her during her speech as well. She wished Rini and Maria Rosa could have come down to hear it.

Helen dropped down alongside her, wiping her forehead with a handkerchief. "It was hot out there!" She turned to her friend. "But you, my dear Lorna, are as fresh and cool as a cucumber!"

The bus pulled into the Olaf Palme Conference Center parking lot. The building was the work of the minister of tourism, Herty Lewites, and was a huge success. Everything worked and the building gleamed all new and fresh. As Lorna and Helen stepped down from the bus, Jackie was waiting for them.

"I took your advice, Lorna," she said. "I'm letting Roberta Nickelberger and her Philadelphia people take care of registration. Those who do the work get the power, but then, they also get the work! Great, let Philadelphia do the work. I'm ready to kick back a little. We're all three going to sit together, in the front row, so you can reach the stage easily when it's time for your speech."

Lorna happily linked her arms with Jackie and Helen, and the three entered the lobby, arms entwined.

"So many people," marveled Helen, looking around. "There must be two thousand delegates here. I want someone to take our picture. Lorna and I will each put up four fingers. You, Jackie, put up two, showing it is the tenth anniversary."

Helen caught the eye of a young man striding and held up her camera. "Will you?" He eagerly took the camera and the brilliant flash went off. Lorna hoped she had not been squinting.

"History is preserved!" Lorna cried. "A history that began fourteen years ago when I walked into Eddie Flores's closet."

"You never told me that story. What in the world were you doing in Eddie Flores' closet?" screamed Jackie.

Lorna shook her head. The sense of excitement and exhilaration around them had her skin tingling. "Let's just say it's a long story."

"You'll have to do better than that, Lorna," said Jackie.

"Later," promised Lorna. The multinational crowd milled

around them. "It's a tower of Babel!" Lorna cried. "I'm hearing languages I don't even have a clue as to what they are!"

The large lobby was filled with the registration tables of the various national delegations, information booths staffed by peace organizations and NGOs, and tables of Sandinista literature, banners, and T-shirts.

Helen pointed. "There's Charlie Ryan, selling the English-language version of *Barricada*." Lorna looked. A small man with sandy hair was stacking newspapers on a table. Lorna was excited to see the special international edition of *Barricada*. It had accepted her article on the Bay Area solidarity movement's history. It would appear in the July 19 issue for this tenth anniversary commemorative issue. *Barricada* was published in Spanish, but they were planning to publish it in six other language editions. She wondered if Guillermo would be reading her article today.

Lorna excused herself to use the ladies room. The butterflies in her stomach recalled memories of the stage fright she'd had in the fourth grade while reciting her own spontaneous speech, "Abraham Lincoln Was a Poor Lad," in the school assembly. She'd said the words to herself the night before as she went to bed. The next morning in the assembly, the principal on stage asked if there were any students who had anything to say about Abraham Lincoln. She raised her hand and walked onto the stage. In a strong and clear voice, she said that first line, "Abraham Lincoln was a poor lad," which unleashed her unwritten thoughts about the humble boy who grew up to be president and abolish slavery. Lorna still practiced this strange inner path to the spoken word.

Washing her hands, she looked in the mirror at the row of women studying their reflections, applying makeup, and tucking in strands of hair. All were young and pretty, it seemed. She was older than most of them. Behind her, women bent upside down, with their hair unpinned, so Lorna had a view of high-heeled legs and manes of hair, brushed out and flowing. One woman was spraying her hair, leaving an unpleasant smell that blended chemicals and perfume, probably mousse or hair gel.

Beside her, a woman caught Lorna's attention. She had an oval face and her tumbled mane of brown hair was parted in the middle. Her lipstick was applied flawlessly, her eyes were flashing and dark. Lorna was struck by the quick, reassured glance the woman gave her reflection. She did not study herself endlessly, dabbing at this and redoing that, as so many other women did. It was one quick glance, a look that said, yes, I'm perfect. The woman turned away from her reflection, striding out in impossibly high heels. Her skirt was swirling gently below her pretty knees and well-turned calves. Lorna followed her out, scanning the lobby for Helen and Jackie.

There stood Guillermo.

He was beaming a heartbreaking smile in her direction. Following the lovely woman, Lorna moved closer as he opened his arms. She could not breathe. She took another step forward, toward those arms. The lovely woman ahead of her floated into his embrace. Guillermo's arms wrapped tightly around her, his eyes closed, his face flooded with happiness.

Lorna stopped abruptly, her face burning.

Had he seen her?

32

Two Thousand Strong

Lorna stood frozen, continuing to stare at the couple.

Guillermo glanced up and their eyes locked. His face changed color, his expression of beatific happiness fading the way clouds float across a windy sky. A look of alarm arose, combined with surprise, and then pleasure.

Removing his arm from the woman's waist, he stepped forward, that elegant profile and chiseled mouth unchanged. The woman he had been holding was looking at her too, with a mixed expression, her eyes slightly narrowing.

He stepped toward her and said, "Lorna! What a pleasure to see you again!" smiling that enchantingly irresistible smile. He stepped closer to her, putting his hands on her shoulders. He kissed her on the cheek. "I was hoping you would be here! I have heard you have a grandson. Congratulations!"

"Yes," Lorna stammered. "He's two."

"You are as beautiful as ever!" said Guillermo, scanning her with his eyes. "I want to introduce you to my wife, Vida." He turned to his wife and said, "Vida, I want you to meet Lorna Almendros, an old, dear friend."

Vida smiled at Lorna. Lorna smiled back. Vida looked young, forthright, and guileless.

"I am so pleased to meet you," Vida said gaily and charmingly. "Guillermo makes sure we always know what Lorna Almendros is writing. He must have every book and pamphlet you have ever written! Just this morning at breakfast he pointed out your *Barricada* article on the international solidarity movement. I never guessed how strong the San Francisco one had been. So interesting!"

"Oh, thank you!" said Lorna, keeping a polite face while the earth wobbled under her feet. "So you are still in India?" she said to Guillermo, looking at his dark intense eyes.

"We're still on our honeymoon," Guillermo said. "We were married six months ago in New Delhi."

"Congratulations!" she said, forcing another smile, wondering if their relationship began in India or if Guillermo was involved with her all along.

"Yes, we met in India," said Vida. "I was an English-language major in college so the ministry sent me to India."

Guillermo took Vida's hand. "You see how the National Directorate just moves us around as if we were pawns," said Guillermo, giving Lorna a rueful smile.

Lorna felt a tugging on her arm. Jackie had appeared, holding her eternal clipboard. "Here you are, Lorna. It's time for us to take our seats." She spoke in English and smiled apologetically at Guillermo and Vida. "They want all the speakers to take their places now, so we can get started."

"This is Compañera Jackie," Lorna explained in Spanish. "She's a leader in the San Francisco solidarity organization. Please excuse me, I have to go now."

"We are so looking forward to your speech," said Vida as Lorna and Jackie moved away. Lorna glanced over her shoulder at Guillermo, who was still staring at her.

Jackie and Lorna entered the auditorium with row upon row of theater chairs sloped toward a far-distant stage. The ceiling was very high and paneled with acoustic tiles. The auditorium was slowly filling up, mostly with men, some in African dashikis, or in turbans, some in military uniform, some in *guayaberas* and *cotonas,* some, especially the North Americans and Europeans, in T-shirts with inflammatory or ironic left-wing slogans. Others were more conservatively dressed in open-necked white shirts and even some in lightweight tropical suits.

As they made their way down the carpeted aisle toward the front row of seats, Jackie said to her, "Who were you talking to? I hope I wasn't interrupting, but I didn't want you to be late."

"You weren't interrupting. It was just a small shock before the big event."

"Small shock?" asked Jackie curiously.

"Just an old friend," answered Lorna.

"Here's Helen, holding our seats."

Helen had spread her lovely shawl across their seats, but now tugged it free and drew it across her shoulders.

"This is so exciting," said Jackie. "My first international event. I think we stick out, being women."

"Well, there are a lot more of us than there would've been a decade ago," said Helen.

Lorna rearranged her hair around her seat's headphones, fiddling with the dial until she found the English-language channel. Loud hissing and crackling almost blasted her out of her seat. She quickly lowered the sound level as the words, "The conference will officially come to order" announced the beginning of the meeting. Lorna put Guillermo out of her mind, turning instead to what she was hearing through her headset, channeling her focus into her ears. She felt the energy of two thousand people in this auditorium who were there because they cared about human rights, revolution, and changing a world where only corporations and big money ruled. So much effort had gone into bringing them all together in this one place, some slipping incognito through dangerous borders to get here.

Through the headset she heard the translation of the words being spoken by the Polish delegate, who was listed on the program to speak before her. The English interpreter sounded as if she were reading from a script. Lorna was glad Jackie had insisted she do that too. She gathered up the pages of her speech one more time, rechecking that the pages were right side up and in the correct order.

Looking up from her papers, she heard the applause and knew she was about to be introduced. Lorna stood up to walk to the stage. Jackie shifted in her chair as Lorna negotiated her way past Jackie's long legs and messenger bag. She passed below the stage, remembering to breathe deeply, to hold her head high, and to mount the steps one at a time. She did not know whether she was experiencing total confidence or total terror. Her hand holding the speech was not shaking. One foot after the other carried her calmly to the stage, then three steps to the podium. She set her papers down and looked out. With a slight nod and a smile, she acknowledged the polite applause that greeted her. The clapping died as Lorna paused briefly, looking at the audience slowly from right to left, from the top rows down to the front. The silence was becoming a palpable entity.

"*Compañeras y compañeros,*" she began, hearing her own voice large and full returning through the amplification system. "Brothers and sisters, we are here today to celebrate a revolution. I come to bring you greetings from the solidarity movement of North America, inside the belly of the beast."

Her voice had found its root. She glanced down at her speech, looking up again at the audience, as she delivered the first lines. Soon came the first laugh, the first applause, and then an easy force carried her through, until she was speaking the last word on the final page.

"*¡Compañeras y compañeros! ¡Venceremos!*"

The applause came back at her, a strong pulse, heartfelt, powerful. Lorna applauded back in the customary manner, nodding her thanks, and, holding her head high again, returned to her seat.

It had been good. Excellent. She could feel that.

Jackie hugged her. "Good job."

Helen beamed. "As Larry would say, 'Way to go!' How do you feel?"

"I feel good. I did it! Whew!" Lorna let her breath out completely as she sank back into her chair. The butterflies in her stomach flew away. She felt normal, even triumphant. She was done, and she had been a success.

Later that morning, at the break, Lorna, Helen, and Jackie made their way into the lobby. The lobby hummed with languages, handshakes, and embraces. When strangers' eyes met Lorna's, she felt their warm approval. They liked her! She was not the gringa, the hateful *yanka*. She was one of them.

Jackie steered them to the refreshment table with its big jugs of ice water. Helen looked around. "This is incredible, so many old friends and new friends, all of us linked by our hopes for Nicaragua."

Soon, flickering lobby lights reminded them it was time to hurry back to their seats.

After lunch Lorna found the table with the stacks of *Barricada*, in Spanish and English. She found her article in both languages. Then she looked for other-language editions. She wanted to see her words reproduced in Arabic, Russian, Italian, and German. "Where are the other language editions?" she asked Charlie Ryan, who was manning the table.

"They weren't able to publish more than the Spanish and the English."

"But we were told it would come out in six languages!"

"The price of newsprint has gone up tenfold," he said, shrugging. She tried to hide her disappointment. Lorna would have to content herself with reading the Spanish translation of her article. She paid for a Spanish and an English newspaper, and looked around for a place to sit. All the lobby benches were filled. Outside the lobby was a garden, and she found a spot on a cool cement step in the shade. Hidden behind the newspaper, she savored every word of her own piece. The translator had added some more precise details, making the article crisper than her original. She was grateful to her unknown collaborator as she finished the article, then noticed her hands were black with newsprint stains. She would have to go wash her hands.

"Lorna!" Jackie called. She was talking to a tall Black man. "I want you to meet Gregory Allen. He's a poet from Bluefields."

"Charmed to meet you," said the man. "Can we borrow some pages of your newspaper? My friend wants me to cut this up, but she's afraid we'll make a mess." The Bluefields poet, with dreadlocks, beads, and a soft Atlantic coast

Caribbean lilt to his English, was holding a mango.

"Oh, no, I'm not giving this away," said Lorna. "It has my article in it."

"This mango is perfectly ripe," Gregory declared. His bass voice was resonant as a drum. He passed the fruit under Lorna's nose. "Smell," he commanded.

Lorna tucked the newspapers protectively under her arm. "No way I'll give up this paper! It's historic!"

Gregory Allen burst into a deep, rich laugh that seemed to come almost from his toes. "Miss Lorna, you are a true believer. For you, this issue of *Barricada* is historic. For the rest of us in Nicaragua, when torn into neat strips it's toilet paper. It's also excellent for wrapping fish or patching a hole in a shoe. But I'm a writer myself, Miss Lorna, so I know how you feel about your published work."

"Are you the poet who performs in the Atlantic coast video my friend Eddie Flores made?" Lorna asked.

"You've seen my video?" the poet cried.

"But in the video, you're not only a poet. You are also drumming and singing," Lorna said.

He looked ecstatic. "Yes, I sing my poetry! And I drum as well. It is all one spirit, as you know. So you know Mr. Eddie?"

"We go way back. He is the one who got me into Nicaraguan politics."

"Splendid!" he exclaimed. "He wants me to do a poetry reading in your beautiful city of San Francisco, followed by a Northern California tour."

Lorna winced, looking at Jackie. Friends of Nicaraguan Culture had a shrinking base of volunteers; funds were tight. Almost all the progressive Bay Area activists had shifted over to the El Salvador issue.

"We would love to bring you to the States!" Jackie crooned, her brown eyes shining. "It would offer a great outreach to the African American community. I will make sure we'll take it up at our steering committee when we get back." Gregory Allen looked pleased. Pressing his palms together, he gave Jackie a little bow.

"Look, there's a copy of *La Prensa*." He swooped down and grabbed the newspaper laying it on the floor with his large hand. A photo of Mikhail Gorbachev appeared above the fold. "Comrade Gorbachev smiles upon the slicing of this mango, and he can be sure we slice it in the spirit of *glasnost*! Thus the tenth anniversary issue of *Barricada* is preserved for history!" He pulled a pocketknife from his jeans pocket and sliced the mango with deft strokes, offering pieces to Jackie and Lorna. "This is the baptism of our friendship."

Mango juice ran down Jackie's chin and she wiped it off with her fist. Jackie looked so happy, Lorna thought. Two artists, one a dancer, and the other a poet-musician-drummer. How wonderful to find Jackie dropping her customary seriousness. Lorna silently thanked Gregory Allen for that.

"We better clean up," Lorna said, holding up her hands. "We have to get ready for the afternoon session." Jackie nodded agreement but gave Gregory Allen a last flirtatious look before following Lorna to the ladies room. Inside, there was a line, and as Helen came out of a stall, the three women greeted one another, inadvertently blocking the entrance to it.

"This conference is so thrilling!" Jackie was gushing. "I've met so many extraordinary people today! The whole world is here! Helen, I met your poet friend Gregory Allen. He's fascinating!"

A woman was maneuvering to take the stall Helen had vacated. "Out of the way, *gringas*." she snapped.

There it was again. The trio fell silent.

"I'll wait for you outside," Helen said in a subdued voice.

Jackie mopped her face with a wet towel. Lorna scrubbed her hands. Joining Helen in the hallway, Lorna could see Helen was upset.

"Anti-American feeling is understandable, given our government's foreign policy, but it's no fun," said Lorna.

"It feels like reverse racism," said Helen.

"But it's not," said Jackie. "Reverse racism is prejudice, not racism. With racism, there's an institutional power to reinforce the inequality. That's why African-Americans can't be racist. They can only be prejudiced."

"Prejudice, racism, whatever," said Helen, "it hurts to be mistaken for the people we are working against."

The lobby lights flickered on and off. "Hurry, they're closing the doors. We may lose our good seats," urged Jackie.

The plenary came to order. Two thousand people were facing the podium. As the first speaker began, Lorna took notes as fast as she could. If the speaker spoke in English or Spanish, she did not bother with the headset. Ideas reverberated over the microphone. She hoped she could make sense of her scribbles later: mixed economy, open market, nationalized models, revolution and democracy.

"A mixed economy is what the *Sandinistas* had wanted a decade ago in their first economic plan," Lorna whispered quickly to Helen. "Why is everyone treating this as such a new idea?"

Before Helen could respond, the Cuban delegate began speaking at the podium. The atmosphere in the room changed perceptibly. There was a heightened tension, as if the audience feared a challenge might arise. Lorna jotted down notes:"Cuba stands for socialism. Opposed to laissez-faire capitalism. Opposed to private accumulation of capital." Lorna took more notes."Cuba is beginning a rectification program. Cuban society is undergoing more self-criticism. The US low intensity war and blockade against Nicaragua must end."

Jackie nudged Lorna, "He's over there."

"Who?"

"Your friend. The one with the wife."

"Where?"

"Three aisles over. See the man in the blue turban? Behind him. Next to the man in the yellow shirt."

Lorna turned her head very cautiously, letting her eyes slide toward the direction Jackie indicated. About twenty rows back, and to her left, Guillermo was sitting with Vida. She tried not to stare, turning to steel her attention to the speakers on stage. A middle-aged Mexican man in a dark business suit and tightly-knotted tie was next. He looked like he was perspiring. When he was introduced as a director of a government human rights program, the mood in the room shifted again.

"Marcos told me he's very important," whispered Jackie to Lorna and Helen.

"Shh!" said a woman behind them. Jackie ignored her.

"It's a prestige factor for Nicaragua that Mexico sent a representative," she continued whispering. "Marcos says if Mexico defies the US embargo and sends oil, other Latin American counties may do the same."

"Have you heard the saying, 'Poor Mexico, so far from God and so close to the United States'?" whispered Helen.

The woman behind them groaned. "Shhhh!" she commanded.

Now the Mexican was beginning his speech. He was finishing the formalities and beginning to describe Mexico's commitment to human rights when there was a stir at the back of the auditorium on the other side. Someone was shouting in Spanish.

"What's going on?" whispered Jackie.

"It's a woman, across the room," reported Lorna "I can't make out what she's saying."

A woman was standing up in the very back row. It was hard to see her face in the vast auditorium. She stretched out her arm, pointing at the speaker. "Fraud! Liar! Not only is Mexico not sending Nicaragua any oil, it is disappearing its own citizens."

The Mexican official tried to speak over her, but she raised her voice, bellowing accusations. "My son was a political prisoner. Now he's missing! He's one of the disappeared!"

"What's she saying?" Jackie asked. "The English interpreter on my headset has gone silent."

"She says the Mexican government is disappearing political dissidents," Lorna said.

The speaker dropped his prepared notes. Looking very angry, he addressed the gathering. "I am Mexican. This is an outrage! My country is honorable. I know this person; she is a lunatic!"

"Now what's going on?" asked Jackie.

"The Mexican man says she's crazy."

"This woman is mad!" the speaker said. "Mexico has an impeccable record of human rights!"

The room was in an uproar. Everyone was talking, trying to understand what was happening. The Mexican continued to speak, but in the babble, his remarks were hard to discern. No official explanation seemed forthcoming from the headsets. Lorna whispered to Jackie, "This woman's white scarf signals her connection with the *Madres de la Plaza de Mayo*. She's expressing solidarity with the Argentinian women whose children have been disappeared. But the speaker says she's a mad woman and it's no wonder her son doesn't tell her where he is. He says Mexico has a perfect human rights record. That's a lie, and everyone in this room knows it. Everyone in this room remembers Tlateloco."

"Tlateloco?" asked Jackie.

"The plaza in Mexico City where eight hundred students were killed in 1968. The square was stained in blood. Eddie made a silkscreen print of it."

Jackie straightened in her seat. "Well, I think she's acting very irresponsibly. She could even be a provocateur. I'll bet the *Sandinistas* don't appreciate it. Marcos says Mexico's support is very important."

Helen whispered back, "It's so confusing. We don't know if she even has a son. Why doesn't anyone officially acknowledge what's happening? Maybe she is crazy."

"We're here to lend support, not cause more trouble. Our government has done enough harm," said Jackie, back to her more politically correct self.

Lorna said, "I feel compromised by our collective silence. What if the woman is telling the truth, and her son is disappeared? Mexico's human rights record is a farce, and everyone here knows it, yet no one says anything. Silence in the face of evil is complicity."

Several individuals had approached the Mexican woman.

It appeared they were placating her. Then the woman jumped up again. "It will be the Mexican solidarity movement, not the Mexican government, that will send an oil tanker to Nicaragua!" she shouted. Then she sat down. The Mexican representative repeated again that Mexico had a perfect human rights record. The translators' voices could be heard on the headsets again as if nothing had happened. People settled back in their seats and the Mexican official droned on.

Lorna recognized the photographer strolling quietly up and down the aisles, taking photographs of the delegates. She caught his eye and gestured toward the Mexican woman. He returned a questioning look. Lorna beckoned to him, and he worked his way over to her, kneeling in the aisle by her seat. Lorna scribbled off a note.

> Sister,
>
> I send you greetings and a strong embrace full of the hope that you find your son.
>
> In Solidarity,
>
> Lorna Almendros
> Friends of Nicaraguan Culture
> San Francisco, California USA

The photographer read her note, then, surprised her by adding his own name—Danilo del Solar, Caracas, Venezuela Solidarity Committee. Lorna watched him make his way across the room and up the aisles to hand the paper to the Mexican woman, who unfolded it and read it. The photographer pointed across the room. Lorna waved. The woman waved her white scarf to acknowledge her.

The session ended in the late afternoon. Tired delegates poured into the lobby. Lorna was exhausted. Her head was throbbing with information and languages as she walked out of the hall. She lost track of Helen and Jackie. Seeing a free bench half-hidden by a potted palm, she slumped down into it, taking time to think, and reorganize her thoughts. She longed for a cold drink of water. She covered her eyes with one hand, rested her elbow on the bench armrest. It had been an intense opening day.

"Lorna?"

She looked up. It was Guillermo. He was alone.

"I saw how upset you were," he said. "I'm glad you didn't say anything. Your face said everything. May I sit down?"

She nodded. He sat down beside her, stretching out his legs. She felt a blazing warmth where their thighs were almost touching. But what was he talking about? "You mean you're glad I said nothing about—" but he interrupted her before she could say, "us?"

"The moment the Mexican woman started, I was expecting you to speak out. I remembered your sense of justice. I just wanted to say that you did the right thing to be silent. Daniel Ortega is under a lot of pressure. He has enemies everywhere, many of them pretending to be friends. We can't know who may have sent her. Our enemies will do almost anything to discredit us."

"So is that why you've come over?" asked Lorna.

He looked away. "No," he said. "There is something else."

She waited.

He turned back to her, looked away again. Then looked back at her.

"I wanted to tell you," he said slowly, "that you were and are and will always be important to me. In those first lonely months in India, you were my muse, you were my light. You were a beacon to me."

Now he turned back to face her. "Meeting you this morning was incredibly awkward for both of us. I could see in your eyes you were upset. I want you to know I met Vida in India a few months after arriving."

Lorna said nothing. An aching sensation was filling her chest.

"You know, I have followed your writing career," said Guillermo. "I am so proud of you. I admire you more than any woman I have ever known."

"I am with someone now too," said Lorna.

"This man is very, very fortunate," said Guillermo.

"I was too old for you," said Lorna.

"A beautiful woman is timeless. As is love."

"Are you happy, Guillermo?" she asked.

"Like you, Vida has a career and is very independent. We are happy and hope to have children."

"And your son in Florida?"

"I have still never seen him," he said.

Around them, delegates streamed and milled on their way out of the Olaf Palme Conference Center. Some could be heard making dinner arrangements; others exchanged cards, or wrote information on slips of paper. Outside the large glass doors of the entrance to the lobby, Managua shimmered in late afternoon heat. Lorna saw the Mercedes Hotel bus pulling into the driveway.

"I have to go," Guillermo said. "We may not see each another again, but our souls will be connected, Lorna Alma. Your place in my heart is yours alone." Seeing he was bending over to kiss her, she offered her cheek. But he kissed her on the mouth, and was gone.

Lorna's heart was swirling; she was swimming in memories, reflections, sensations.

"Lorna!" Jackie called. "So there you are! The bus is here." She and Helen were standing beside the Bluefields poet, Gregory Allen.

"Jackie says you were upset that no one supported the Mexican woman," Gregory Allen said in his deep rich bass. "You did the right thing. Politics is like that. It's impossible to know in Nicaragua these days who is with you and who is against you. People are not always who they seem."

"I tried to explain that to her," said Jackie, "but I don't have a way with words like you poets." Jackie put her clipboard and notes into her messenger bag. "You and Helen go ahead. Gregory and I are going to discuss the details of his tour. I'll get a ride with Marcos later if I miss the next bus."

As Lorna and Helen boarded the bus, Lorna said, "How quickly feminist Jackie turned herself into an eyelash-batting flirt. The dance of life is eternal."

"It certainly is. I saw you talking to someone just now," said Helen. "A very attractive someone. One of the delegates?"

"That was Guillermo," said Lorna.

"So that was Guillermo?" asked Helen. "The famous Guillermo?"

"Yes. What did you think of him?"

"He's hot. That must have been some weekend, even if it was three years ago."

Lorna smiled.

"I understand now why you were so sad when you came back that year. So what did he want?"

"He told me he thought it was right to be silent when that Mexican woman spoke out. He said the *Sandinista* government is under all kinds of pressure."

"Is that all?" asked Helen, giving Lorna her don't-try-to-fool-me look.

"Well, that was the gist of it," Lorna said. "I forgive myself for my silence. But we didn't have enough information, even though everyone in that room knew Mexico has an abysmal human rights record. And still we were quiet! I am glad I sent her a note anyway."

She looked out the bus window at Managua. A barefoot man stood at a crosswalk. He was holding a heavy plastic bag, waiting patiently for the light to turn. She noticed again how wide the human foot developed, with big spaces between the toes, when people go barefoot for a lifetime. Lorna forced her attention back to Helen.

"Do you think protocol won out over principle? To speak out wouldn't have been polite," said Helen. "Strange that etiquette can trump our core beliefs, we who stand for revolution and social change."

"Maybe Nicaragua is at the end of the revolutionary period," said Lorna.

The bus rolled past a construction site. Two workers were perched on a scaffold ten stories up. They wore no safety belts. Helen was saying, "Basically, revolution is limited in time. Sooner or later the need to retain political power sets in, and that means concessions to the global economy."

Helen went on in her world-weary voice, "Ortega is deluding himself if he thinks the compromises the *Sandinistas* have made by tightening the economic belt will get US loans. He will never get such loans, no matter what he does."

"This horrible contra war has to end if the Sandinistas are going to win this election," said Lorna.

"The Sandinistas have pretty much won the war, militarily, if Daniel Ortega feels it's safe enough to hold an election."

"Some people think that if Violetta Chamorro wins, the US will stop funding the contras," said Lorna.

"Do you think she is qualified to be president?" asked Helen.

"She's a figurehead. She was asked if she was ready to be president. She said that she had enormous faith in God, and he would show her how to govern."

"That's scary, but the polls show Ortega ahead. Millions of US dollars are being funneled for the opposition party through secret channels," said Helen, gathering up her Jamaican shawl and bag as the bus arrived at Las Mercedes.

"Remember, it ain't over till it's over," quipped Lorna.

"I'll get my things and check into cabin 7. Then we can go to dinner together," said Helen, wickedly. "We don't need to wait for Jackie. I have no idea when we might see her again, with her newfound interest in Atlantic coast poetry."

33

Nicaragua, Nicaragüita

Lorna opened the door to the welcoming cool air of cabin 7. Kicking off her sandals, she checked the bathroom water situation; the hot water was still working. She undressed and rushed to enjoy the shower. She put her entire head under the stream of water, lathering with her cucumber shampoo. As the water washed over her scalp, forehead, and face, she smiled to herself with thoughts of Luis and how he preferred flower-smelling fragrances for her. The water streamed wonderfully down her body with just the perfect force. Seeing Guillermo gave Lorna closure. It was bittersweet, so much to remember and so much left unsaid. She felt the nagging need to phone Luis and the frustration of never finding an available phone.

As much as Lorna loved this private room, her private oasis, she was glad when she heard a knock at the door, thinking it was Helen. She wrapped herself hastily in a large towel, and her hair turban-style in a smaller one, and opened the door.

There stood Eddie.

"Very elegant, Lorna. I like your tropical glamour."

She clutched at her towel. "Glamour me no glamour. I was expecting Helen."

"That's not much of a greeting, old friend. You haven't seen me for a year. How about a hug?"

He quickly grabbed her, pressing Lorna, towel and all, against his trousers, belt, and camouflage T-shirt. He smelled of Florida Water, and his chin was bristly. Lorna felt her towel coming undone and quickly stepped back. "That's enough!" she warned, clutching the towel tightly. "Have a seat while I get dressed."

"Don't change your costume on my account," he said, with feigned innocence.

She offered the desk chair, but he ignored it and sat down on her bed.

She grabbed her clothes. "I'll be right out. Helen will be here any minute."

"Good, I'd love to talk to Helen too. This is an unofficial visit on my way to some official business."

Retreating to the privacy of the bathroom, Lorna wiped the steamy mirror with her towel, combed out her wet hair, and dressed hurriedly in the cramped space.

When she came out, Eddie was still sitting on the bed. "No shoes?" he asked. "How many times have I told you . . . ?"

"So, what's the official business? Or the unofficial business?"

"I've been shifted around in my post. They've assigned me to international support for the elections and I have a dinner date here at the hotel to ask for contributions. That's the official business." Eddie looked up with a sly smile, rubbing his knuckles against his mouth. "In addition, I've been seeing this other lady. Her husband is trying to kill me. That's the unofficial business."

"Who's the other lady?" asked Lorna, alarmed.

"You wouldn't know her. By the way, congratulations. I heard you gave a great talk at the conference."

"Thanks." Lorna waited. "So what's really the official business?"

"In fact, I'm officially dining with a beautiful Hollywood star tonight, and afterward I am unofficially meeting the other lady."

"Official me no officials, Eddie. If you're asking me for money, Friends of Nicaraguan Culture is broke. And you're making things worse by offering this poet, Gregory Allen, a California poetry reading tour without even consulting with us. He's marvelous, but we are broke. What were you thinking?"

"The guy is talented. You and Helen will find the money somewhere. Helen has tons of connections."

"Her connections haven't made Friends of Nicaraguan Culture rich. You'll have to get your election-campaign money from your movie star."

"I'm not here about your money. I am here about my unofficial problem. I need this room for tonight," Eddie announced.

"You what?" she exclaimed, outraged. "Eddie, you're going too far." She couldn't forget the Palace of Fine Arts incident.

"I need this room for tonight," he repeated.

"So what are Helen and I supposed to do? You have all of Managua for your clandestine romances. What? Are you also planning to seduce the cash-cow star, after she makes the big donation? Just check off the boxes? Money. Check. Sex. Check."

Eddie raised his hands, palms toward Lorna. "Lorna, Lorna. Don't do this to me. Sometimes things are complicated. The movie star is a separate work issue. The room thing is personal."

"I'll bet. Maybe you should try simplifying."

"It is simple. Let me use this room tonight. It's important, Lorna."

"Why?"

"I can't say why."

"Then I say no!"

He stood up. "Come on, Lorna. We've had our ups and downs. But you've always been there for me when I needed you. You've never let me down."

"I'm not letting you down. Letting you down is if I promised you something. I have no idea what you're up to. This is crazy. I'm saying no."

Eddie took a step toward her. He looked angry. "Well, it sure feels like you're letting me down. There's a hell of a lot riding on this election. You don't understand all the stuff going on, and you shouldn't even try. You and Helen come down here, two do-gooders. You want all the excitement of a revolution, but I ask you one little tiny favor, something that would cost you almost nothing, and it's no, Eddie, no."

"For god's sake, if you need a hotel room, go rent one. Why

are you dragging us into this?"

He moved closer, looking into her eyes. He had little crow's feet around his penetrating green eyes, now, she noticed. Long folds were forming in his cheeks. He is getting old, as am I, she thought. She could see their last fourteen years reflected in his eyes.

"Look, Lorna," he wheedled, putting his hand on her shoulder. "A lot's at stake for me, personally. The higher-ups are watching my performance. If they find out about my unofficial business, I'm screwed. All I need is a little help from my friends."

"So go rent yourself a room if you need one," said Lorna.

Eddie shook his head. "Don't you get it, Lorna? I need you to cover for me. The room can't be in my name."

She wavered. She and Helen might be able to rent a room somewhere else. The Mercedes Hotel is full. And how could they explain to Jackie and the delegation when they couldn't easily get to the constant meetings and activities? "No, Eddie."

"You're saying no to Eddie? Who led you here to Nicaragua? Who linked you up to your ancestors? Oh, come on, Lorna, you've always been my own personal corn goddess. Always been able to do a favor for little old Eddie."

There was a loud thud. Lorna and Eddie jumped apart. Helen's suitcase had just landed against the outside door. Now Helen pushed the door open.

"Am I interrupting something? I could leave my suitcase and come back later."

"No. Not at all," said Eddie, rushing to help her. "I'm here to talk to both of you. Daniel has asked me to raise some campaign funds."

Helen lifted the suitcase onto the bed and snapped open the lock. With her back to them, she said, "The last of our funds went into our Stop Contra Aid campaign."

"So, Helen Hart you're saying no too?" said Eddie.

"We don't have any funds," Helen said.

"Well, there's one thing you lovely women could do for me and it doesn't involve writing a check."

"And what is that, Eddie?" Helen was rummaging through her suitcase.

"I need this room for the evening. Don't ask me why."

Helen turned around. "This is a very strange request, Eddie. What did Lorna say?"

Lorna shook her head. "I said no,"

"I love you muchly, Eddie but I say no too," said Helen.

Eddie's brows drew together, his lips pursed. He looked first at Lorna, then at Helen. He bowed deeply. "So, dear ladies, it's been lovely. But I have to run now. I'll see you around some year, some continent."

Giving them a snappy salute, he stepped out, slamming the door shut behind him.

"So, what was that all about?" said Helen, sitting down on the bed.

"I have no idea." But Lorna felt troubled. "What *was* that all about?"

"I'm going to take a shower," Helen said to Lorna, gathering her toiletry kit and robe. "I like this room!"

The next morning, Lorna had a hasty breakfast of coffee and a roll before the big July 19 event. After the meeting of the North American delegation, she headed straight for the book fair. The Managua International Book fair was occurring in a vacant lot a few doors down from the hotel. The Ministry of Culture had thrown up a big canopy to house the trade show, with cables and wires to power the tall circulating fans that provided some breeze. The space was set up with aisles upon aisles of white-skirted tables, with banners pinned to their fronts, announcing this publisher or that. All the major Spanish and Latin American publishing houses were there, and several European ones: Deutsche Verlag, Penguin, Oxford University Press and others she didn't know. The US Embassy had an immensely popular booth since they were giving away free books and posters.

The booth that most interested Lorna was the Alternative Presses USA bookstall. Charlie Ryan had persuaded a number of small presses and writers to donate books for the stall.

Lorna was proud to see that Three Rivers Press had sent a dozen copies of *Daughters of the Silence*. The book cover, with its colorful, primitivist, Solentiname painting, made her cheer inwardly, even if the extra cost would be debited against her royalty payments. It would have been nice to think that her royalties would help recover the plane fare that came out of her instructor's salary at New College.

Seeing the book on the table was so satisfying, knowing she had given Arminda, Nicolasa, Xiomara, even the terse Ursula, an opportunity to tell their stories to the world. And there had been other women whom Rini had introduced her to from up north, and others Maria Rosa had suggested. A few were well known, like the poet Carlota Pérez, but most were not. The back cover, with a very flattering head shot, made reference to Lorna as a prize-winning San Francisco poet. While she had not written a single poem during the time she worked on the book, these stories were poetic. They were cries of life.

"I've already sold two copies of *Daughters of the Silence* this morning," Charlie told her. Lorna was disappointed. "A few people said they would buy their copies later," he said to cheer her.

Lorna mumbled a thanks and walked over to the performance area where Carlota Pérez was scheduled to read her poetry. Empty folding chairs faced an impromptu wood platform placed on the dirt floor. She sat down with a sigh, wondering if Guillermo would buy a copy of her book. After last night's confrontation, she couldn't imagine Eddie doing anything to help her with sales.

Slowly the chairs filled. Whole families were taking seats, perhaps expecting entertainment. Among the crowd were Nicaraguan intelligentsia, writers, musicians, artists, and foreigners. Behind her, a group of North Koreans sat primly facing forward. Lorna had visited their red and gold bookstall. A six-foot color portrait of President Kim Il-sung hung on the wall. The table contained only a bound series of his political tracts. "Where are works of the other North Korean writers and poets?" she'd asked. The North Korean attendant had merely smiled.

The program began with a Ministry of Culture representative, poet Lionel Ruben, introducing Carlota Pérez as one of Nicaragua's foremost women poets. She read poems from her books, looking lovely and confident, with her rippling long dark hair beautifully combed out. Her poetry spoke of love and grief, of the revolutionary process, of her fallen comrades, her personal loss, and her hopes for the end of Nicaraguan *machismo*. Her reading ended with thunderous applause.

After the reading, Lorna joined a circle of people congratulating Carlota. She acknowledged Lorna at once, kissing her and speaking effusively. "Lorna Almendros, I am so glad you're here. I love *Daughters of the Silence*. I am overjoyed that you have put our voices out there." In Lorna's interview for *Daughters of the Silence*, Carlota had been outspoken about the ongoing struggle against the deeply ingrown machismo of Nicaraguan males—including the revolutionary *comandantes.*

"Thanks, Carlota," Lorna said. "Really I did nothing but transcribe, translate, and edit. The women of Nicaragua did all the work. But your reading just now had me spellbound. I am impressed that, with so many responsibilities, you still find time to write."

Carlota shook her head and made a face. "Well, since I started my novel I hardly write any poetry. Today I read only older poems."

"I understand that," answered Lorna.

Leif Larsson, who'd been standing behind Lorna, whipped out a pad and pen and brushed Lorna aside.

"Leif Larsson, with the *Stockholm Weekly Review*," he said. Lorna moved away slightly. He was addressing Carlota in perfect Spanish. "When can we expect this novel to appear in publication?"

Carlota threw back her cascading dark long hair and

laughed. "When I finish it!"

"What do you think about the elections?" he asked, writing in his pad.

"Win or lose, women's issues must be part of the national agenda. We can't keep burying questions of abortion, birth control, domestic violence, and homosexuality. Women's rights are human rights. This is the revolution within the revolution."

"Do you think women are ready for political office? The National Opposition Party will be running Violetta Chamorro for president, the widow of the slain publisher of *La Prensa*," said Larsson.

"Of course, women are ready," said Carlota.

"Specifically, do you think Violetta Chamorro is qualified to be president?" he persisted.

"I am pleased to see a Nicaraguan woman willing to throw her hat in the ring for the top office in the country. It takes courage," answered Carlota.

"So you are not among those who feel she is unqualified?"

"I am among those who will vote for Daniel Ortega," said Carlota calmly.

To Lorna's relief, Leif closed his notebook and pushed his way out of the group.

A gay activist, Theodore, who Lorna recognized from San Francisco's Castro District, came forward. "Congratulations on your novel, *Compañera* Carlota," he said. "I'm writing a novel too. It's about the gay scene here in Managua."

"Is there a gay scene in Managua?" interrupted Lorna. "I hadn't noticed."

"Hidden in plain sight, dearie," Theodore said. "There's none so blind as she who will not see. The *machismo* that you women so detest also includes a very powerful dose of homophobia. There's no greater insult to a Nicaraguan male than to be called a *maricón*."

Carlota Pérez shook her head. "Good luck with the novel, brother. The struggle against machismo and homophobia are the same struggle. It will be years before Nicaragua will overcome these patriarchal prejudices. The National Opposition Party uses homophobia to discredit our women's movement, claiming we invite foreign homosexual delegations, like yours, to corrupt our morals."

Theodore laughed. "I'm corrupting as many beautiful Nica men as I can get my hands on!"

Lorna was startled, as she looked back and forth between Carlota and Theodore.

"In my novel, dearie! In my novel! You don't have to be alarmed! And all my characters practice safe sex too," Theodore said to Lorna. He pulled a battered notebook out of his shoulder bag. "Carlota, darling, scribble a line for good luck. I tested HIV positive. I want to finish this novel fast."

Carlota solemnly signed his notebook and wished him well. As Lorna returned to the book exhibit area, she reflected on the situation in San Francisco, where so many were dying of AIDS, especially in the arts community. She hoped Theodore would survive.

The morning was becoming warmer and stickier, despite the moving air beneath the rotating fans under the cloth canopy. Lorna looked at her watch. It was almost lunchtime.

On her way out of the book-fair, she spied a small booth of Basque publications. The staffer had a portable boom box and was playing a CD that caught Lorna's attention. On a whim, she asked if he had any for sale. He reached under the table and produced one. She bought it as a souvenir for Luis, smiling at the idea.

She wanted to call him. She walked back to the hotel in hopes of passing a telephone booth. Two public telephones near a busy intersection were broken. At Las Mercedes Hotel, she waited patiently for a turn at the lobby telephones. Finally it was Lorna's turn to dial the hotel operator and request international long distance. She heard the familiar clicks and squawks as the operator put the call through, then the telephone ringing in Luis's apartment, bringing up self-defeating fears that his ex-wife had returned while she was away and they had reunited.

"Hello?" Luis said.

"Hooray, you're home! Hello!" she said, feeling a rush of excitement on hearing his voice.

"Lorna, I was hoping it was you."

"It's me! I've got some news."

"You haven't met someone else, have you?" said Luis.

"No such luck. You're stuck with me. The news is, my speech yesterday was a success. I was so nervous ahead of time but it went really well."

"I expect no less from you," said Luis, so far away in San Francisco. "I miss you. How are Rini and the baby?"

"I'll be seeing them and Maria Rosa the day after tomorrow."

"Give them my hugs."

"I will. How are you?"

"I'm working on a new software design that will revolutionize the building-construction process."

"That's great Luis! How's—" The line suddenly filled with clicks and static. Then nothing. After shouting "hello" a few times and hearing only her own echo, she hung up in frustration. They had talked for less than a minute.

Back at cabin 7, she found Helen sitting on the bed, reading a book with little reading spectacles perched on her nose. She looked up as Lorna fell across her bed.

"I phoned Luis, but the call broke off. I'm feeling homesick."

"Hang in there. There's a thrilling two weeks more before you're on the plane home."

"Charlie Ryan said he sold two copies of my book this morning."

"It's only the first day of the book fair. Tomorrow will be better."

"I saw Carlota Pérez."

"How was she?"

"Beautiful. So sensual. I wish I looked like her."

"Stop it, Lorna! We're grand old Wisdom Women. Who wants to be a hormonal-driven sex pot?"

"Me!" said Lorna. "This Wisdom Woman thing gets a bit

old."

"Tell me about it," Helen concurred, laughing and went back to her book.

The next morning was the nineteenth of July, the tenth anniversary of the revolution. Lorna woke while it was still dark and jumped out of bed. She could hear water running in the bathroom. Helen's bed was empty; she was already in the shower. The air conditioner was off.

Through the open window, Lorna could hear the *Carretera Norte,* noisier than usual. People had been streaming into the capitol on foot, horse, wagon, and bus throughout the night, and they were still moving in the dawn's light. Lorna felt alive with excitement. The US delegation had been invited to sit on the guest platform at the Plaza de la Revolución, a few blocks from the shores of Lake Managua. After a quick shower, Lorna grabbed a big hat, sunglasses, and her straw bag with a water bottle in it. She and Helen were out the door as the sun rose.

Jackie was checking off names as the delegates boarded the bus. Along the Carretera, it seemed every available space—houses, utility poles, and stucco walls—were festooned with red-and-black banners. Their delegation arrived early. From high on the guest platform Lorna could see an ocean of hundreds of thousands of people filling the huge plaza and more arriving.

The morning breeze off the lake fluttered blue-and-white Nicaraguan flags and the red and black Sandinista banners. A huge poster behind the grandstand announced *Un futuro camino.* The crowd was a sea of heads: men, women, children, tall and short, and all the different shades of people that made up the population. There were straw hats, bill caps, and visors as shade against the rising sun. Some groups carried small plastic flags; others held up homemade cloth banners attached to long poles. A sea of red and black everywhere. The humidity and sunlight were already intense.

"If all these people vote Sandinista, this election's won," Lorna said.

Jackie looked out. "I've never seen so many people in one place."

"I wouldn't be surprised if there were half a million people in this square," said Helen, who was used to estimating crowds.

Now, popular musicians Carlos Mejía Godoy and his brother Luis Enrique were setting up with their bands. As soon as they appeared on the grandstand, the crowd roared with approval. The musicians tuned up, looking at one another, laughing and slapping their thighs, giving high-fives to the crowd. Then the first notes filled the air. They were playing "No Pasarán," and the crowd began a rhythmic clapping. Thousands upon thousands of voices sang along, clearly knowing all the words, verse after verse. Helen translated some of the lyrics for Jackie: "It's as if their hearts as well as their banners are red and black."

Lorna became aware of Leif Larsson standing directly behind them. He broke in. "This crowd may look impressive, but it's all been staged. Ortega decreed today was a holiday for all government workers. They had to attend, or lose their jobs. I don't know what color their hearts are, but I think they're ready to say uncle and vote for Violetta Chamorro."

Lorna whispered to Helen and Jackie. "He's so irritating, always riding my bumper. Let's shake him." They hooked arms and moved away from him to another section of the crowded guest platform.

Now the Mejía Godoy brothers had broken into "Nicaragua, Nicaragüita." Hearing the opening chords, the crowds started swaying, arms around one another.

> Ay Nicaragua, Nicaragüita
> La flor mas linda de mi querer

Lorna joined in on the lyrics, singing with all her heart. She sang for Abuelo, for Angélica, for Rosalea, for Rini, for little Gabrielito, and for Maria Rosa.

"Not even 'We Shall Overcome' or 'This Land is My Land' has left me with so many goose-bumps," marveled Helen. "This is a love song to their ten years of struggle and sacrifice."

"I can't understand a word, but I can feel it, too," Jackie said.

> *Pero ahora que ya sos libre, Nicaragüita,*
> *Yo te quiero mucho más*

As the song ended, Lorna translated it for Jackie.

> But now that you are free, dear little Nicaragua,
> I love you even more.

34

Agree to Disagree

"I am too tired to even take off my clothes," Lorna said, flinging herself on the bed. The day had been amazing, hot, inspirational, incredible. Daniel Ortega's speech alone had the crowd screaming, "Daniel! Daniel! Daniel!" as he roared that the Sandinista Front had changed the tide of history. They had withstood ten years of attacks by *Tío* Sam. They had survived everything the United States had thrown at them: contra warfare, trade embargoes, and even the mining of Nicaraguan ports. The shouts continued, "Daniel! Daniel! Daniel!" as he said that for the sake of Nicaragua, all factions must now work together, putting aside ideological differences. He promised that the Sandinistas were offering a transparent political electoral campaign and that opposition was welcomed. The response of the crowd was visceral.

Helen groaned with fatigue as she sunk into the other bed. "I'll take a shower in a few minutes," she mumbled and stretched out. Soon her light snoring lulled Lorna to sleep.

That was the last thing she remembered before an insistent knocking on the door woke her up. Still dressed, she stumbled toward the door. "Who's there?" she asked. Helen stirred and snapped on the bedside lamp.

"Telephone call for Lorna Almendros," said the night desk clerk. "She says to wake you up, it's an emergency." He handed Lorna a slip of paper. She recognized Rini's number.

"Stay calm," she mumbled to herself, following the clerk down the red-tiled corridor and through the nighttime garden. The air was fresh and the garden redolent with the odor of night-blooming plants and flowers. Little Gabrielito is fine. Don't panic. Wait until you talk to Rini. The hotel lobby glowed an empty beige. The clerk handed her the desk phone. "Use this."

She phoned Rini but Maria Rosa picked up immediately.

"Has something happened to Rini? Or little Gabrielito?"

"They are fine, Lorna," said Maria Rosa. "It's Eddie. Eddie is wounded, shot."

"Eddie?" said Lorna. Her voice was trembling, but it was cold in the lobby. She felt chilled to the bone, even under her shawl. "No. I saw him Tuesday night. He was fine."

"He's in the hospital, Lorna."

"That's not possible," said Lorna, filled with disbelief. "He asked a favor, and I turned him down. Eddie always lands on his feet. What happened? Can he talk? Where was he hit? How bad is it?"

"Eddie landed on his feet in someone else's garden, apparently. Somewhere he wasn't welcome."

"What are you talking about? What is going on?" Lorna was flooded with guilt. Had she somehow caused this?

"I'm getting very conflicting reports. Eddie was shot late Tuesday night or very early Wednesday morning before the celebration. He was taken to the Hospital Bautista. Someone from the Ministry just phoned me."

"But he was fund-raising for the Ortega election and having dinner with a movie star Tuesday night."

"It gets worse, Lorna. The police think Eddie may have been involved with the shooter's wife."

"Oh, my god, that's Eddie. He's great at the triangles, but he never gets caught." Lorna dropped the phone.

The desk clerk looked up. "Everything OK, señora?" he said.

"No! Everything is not OK!" snapped Lorna, picking up the phone.

"Lorna, stop it! Get a grip," she could hear Maria Rosa saying. "We don't know everything yet. I'm still up north with Pancho and Rini. I have a lot of phone calls in to the hospital but I haven't been able to get anyone yet. It's three a.m. You won't even find a taxi this time of night. But go to the hospital as early as you can in the morning and tell me what is happening."

Back in their room, Helen was waiting. "Lorna, is Rini OK? The baby?"

Lorna was shaking. "Yes, they are OK. But I can't understand this, Helen. It makes no sense." She sat down on the edge of Helen's bed, trembling.

Helen took Lorna's hand. "Your hand is like ice. What is it, Lorna?"

"Eddie's been shot. He was shot by a jealous husband."

"No," said Helen, sitting upright. "He was just here asking us to let him use our room."

"We should have done it. He even mentioned a jealous husband wanting to kill him. I thought it was just a metaphor. It's all my fault. You always forgave Eddie everything. You turned him down for me, me and my injured ego. Eddie was here in this room, healthy, full of hope. I was so rotten, unleashing all my anger, and thinking how good it felt. I was so self-righteous, shouting all those ugly things."

"You didn't shout any ugly things that I heard. You just said no. He wanted us to vacate. Do you think . . ." Helen let her voice trail. "Lorna. I wonder what happened and how he is now? Where was he hit?"

"I don't know," said Lorna.

An hour and a half later, the desk clerk found them a taxi in the first dim rays of morning light. Speeding down the *Carretera Norte*, Lorna felt shaky. How would she explain all this to his kids and his mother in San Francisco if it turned out to be really bad for Eddie? If she hadn't refused to help him, maybe it could have been avoided.

They were at the hospital in record time. No traffic. They found Eddie in the emergency ward, sitting up in bed, bare-chested, with a bandage on his arm and three giggling nurses in attendance. The nurses made an opening for Lorna and Helen and soon left with promises to return.

"Hi ladies. See," he said pointing to his left arm, "just a graze. I'm fine. I'll be out of here in a few hours."

"Graze me no grazes, Eddie," answered Lorna. "We were worried sick when we heard, and so is Maria Rosa. I felt so bad that we quarreled."

"Don't even think about it. I know who my friends are. You're both here now."

Helen tried to read his dangling hospital chart. "What happened Eddie?"

"Remember the jealous husband I mentioned? Well, he interrupted me when I was hunting down this CIA agent. Maybe you met him, a so-called 'Scandinavian journalist.'"

Lorna nodded. "I think I know who you mean."

Eddie continued, "Well, I was trying to squeeze in his capture *en route* to meeting the movie star. But I got interrupted by that crazy husband. I had to break the date with the actress to come to the hospital. But she's already promised to donate some big money. Guess she was alarmed at my being shot. And the CIA guy is under arrest."

"All in a revolutionary day's work?" Lorna said, feeling relieved.

"You know, it's good I didn't use your room," he said, letting down his bravado, slumping slightly on the bed. "He would have shot me at the hotel and then you'd be implicated. We'd all be humiliated. I mean, I still have to explain to the higher-ups how the situation came about. And some of them get so puritanical about romance, especially the women."

Lorna put her hand on his good shoulder. The room was silent. Lorna saw the sadness in his face.

"I am sorry you are hurt," said Lorna. "But your constant womanizing always leads to pain, injured feelings, and broken hearts."

He looked at them squarely and, putting his hand over his wound, said in a low voice, "I've been thinking that I have to change. Maybe this is the wake-up call."

Just then, a nurse returned with a medication tray. She looked disapprovingly at Lorna's hand on Eddie's bare shoulder. She turned to them briskly and said, "It's time for you to leave now."

35

Home

When Lorna arrived at the San Francisco airport ten days later, Luis murmured into her hair, "I was so worried about you. I missed you so much."

"I stood in the multitudes, missing you," she murmured back, inhaling the scent of him.

"After the news of Eddie's wounding, what a relief to have you back, safe and sound, Lorna."

After picking up her baggage, they took off in Luis's Volvo. "I'm in culture shock," she mused, peering out at the fog and traffic. "No sun. No horses. No potholes. So many late-model cars."

She slipped the cassette from her purse into the tape deck. "I brought you this cassette from a Basque separatist booth at the book fair," she told him. The van filled with electronic music, rich and sensuous. She leaned her head on his shoulder, feeling how much she had missed him.

"The fog will lift soon," he noted. "You know our San Francisco summers. Morning fog, followed by late morning sun. I've spent every foggy morning you were gone thinking of you. Especially when you called me at five a.m."

"I phoned whenever and wherever I found a telephone actually working."

"Don't apologize, Lorna. I loved your calls."

They were silent, but only for a moment. Lorna overflowed with news. "Jackie invited an Afro-Nicaraguan poet to tour the Bay Area. He's from Bluefields, wears dreadlocks."

"You aren't even home from the airport, and already you're wanting to talk about working. I had another agenda for us entirely. Like going to my place for pillow talk."

"Great agenda! I just need to stop a second at my house first."

"OK. How was Rini and family?"

"They're doing very well. Gabrielito is so cute. I miss him already. But by the end of my visit, Rini's house felt like a series of old-fashioned mother-in-law jokes. Maria Rosa is busy as always, and last I heard of Eddie, he was mending well and, like everyone, working on the election."

Taking one arm off the wheel, he placed it lightly across her shoulder. "How good it is to be home," she said.

"Lorna, I want to move our vague getting-married plans forward . . . to this weekend!"

She placed her hand over his, letting her fingers run along his to reestablish the feel of each one. "We should wait until spring. But, maybe you are right. If the Sandinistas lose the election in November, we might get too discouraged to take the plunge."

"You know my favorite saying," he teased. "'You're not having fun unless you're scared.' But seriously, do you think the Sandinistas are going to lose?"

"I hope not. Not after that show of support in the *Plaza de la Revolución*. But the country is hurting so badly, and the opposition is taking advantage of that. No water half the days of the week. Electricity blackouts. Wages way down."

Even in profile Luis looked worried. But she continued in earnest to answer his question.

"Half the women of Managua seem to be wearing black because they've lost their sons in the contra war. But win or lose the women's movement will continue and I believe a progressive consciousness is in place."

"It sounds like you think they might lose."

"It's a hard call, Luis. Even if the funding for the contra war ends, there's still so much covert stuff going on. So many dollars have been channeled into supporting Violetta Chamorro. The mood there's intense. People are polarized. I fear anything could happen."

Luis sighed. "That's not the reassuring sort of answer I was hoping for."

"The Sandinistas admit they've made mistakes. Ten years in power is a long time, and the people blame them now when things go wrong. And I worry about Rini, Pancho, and little Gabrielito. If the opposition wins, will it be like the coup in Chile in 1973 when foreigners were rounded up if they supported the Allende government? It frightens me."

Luis patted her hand. "Despite American bucks, this is still an election; it's not a coup. That's one permanent change the revolution made. Democratic elections. Violetta Chamorro is conservative and pro-business, but she's not a monster. Rini has a good head on her shoulders. She will know what to do."

His arm over her shoulder gave her a light squeeze. "It's us I'm thinking about, Lorna. I'd like us to be there for each other, come hell or high water, in sickness and in health, till death do us part."

"Yes, in health, lots of health! Let's not even think of any bad possibilities anymore. But getting married feels like . . ." Lorna paused. They were approaching Hill Street.

Luis turned his head toward her, still looking at her, waiting for her to say more.

"I love it!" she exclaimed. "San Francisco, I love you!"

"And me? Do you love me?" Luis asked shyly.

"Luis, I love you!"

"That's courage," he said. "Courage means heart. With courage, win or lose, we can still keep on going."

"Commitment," said Lorna slowly. "Feels like . . . when I'm driving at the top of Hill Street. The first moment, when I can't see the street below beyond the hood, I hold my breath fearfully. Putting my foot lightly on the brake, I steer forward. Even though I'm scared, I find myself trusting that the earth is still underneath me as I sail down to my destination." She fell silent.

Luis reached the turn at the top of Hill Street, braking smoothly for the steep downhill road ahead.

"I can't see the road, but I know we'll arrive safely," Lorna said.

He smiled. "Glad to hear it."

"I'm going to keep on going and live until I die," she said, inhaling deeply and letting out a long slow breath.

Epilogue

In February 1990, the Sandinistas lost the election, receiving 41 per cent of the vote, to the national opposition party headed by Violetta Chamorro, who was sworn in as Nicaragua's first woman president. Free elections have continued to the present. The Somoza dictatorship and his Guardia never returned. The Sandinista army was not dismantled. When the contra war ended, the contra army was disarmed and disbanded. Nicaragua, like everywhere, continues to struggle with the problems of democracy, ecological balance, and poverty.

Eddie left the army, remarried, and had two children in Nicaragua. He and his wife own a café/bookstore/gallery in Granada, that is very popular amid the new tourism and increased global interest in Nicaraguan culture.

Rini found new work in Nicaragua on geothermal projects funded by Scandinavian institutes. She lives with Pancho in Managua near his growing medical practice and clinic. They have three children.

Maria Rosa, left unemployed by the election of Chamorro, went back to medical school, graduated, and works as a doctor in the Maternal and Children's Hospital in Managua.

Helen served out her last term as a city supervisor and continues her activism working as the city art's commissioner. She and Lorna meet regularly for coffee and friendship.

Lorna continues to write and publish, giving active support to women's struggles, locally and internationally. She married Luis and they live in San Francisco. Her friendship with Helen and Maria Rosa remains strong.

Acknowledgements

Writing Nicaragua Way has been a long creative journey with many people aiding me and cheering me onward.

Thank you to my writer's group, guided and inspired by Rebecca Rona Spalten. They are Bill Compton, Diana Mansfield, Robert Roth, Susan Sherrell, and for a time, Bob Feinglass and Todd Fretter.

Thank you to the friends and family who encouraged me and/or read early drafts: Daniel del Solar, Diane Wang, Louise Music, Jack Hirschman, Mary Rudge, Claude Marks, Gloria Bacon, Nicole Landau, and Valerie Haynes Perry. The writing journey has been so long that there may have been others I have mistakenly omitted. But please know that I appreciate your efforts.

Thank you to the readers and their feedback on the last version of Nicaragua Way: Elaine Elinson, who lived through many of the events the book is based upon. Thanks also to Julieta Kusnir and Eileen McGregor for their helpful comments and on-going support.

Thank you to the editorial helpers, Hodee Edwards, Rose Richards, and most definitively Gail Chiarello of Workwomans Press and my publisher, Paul Richards.

Thank you to Anthony Holdsworth (www.anthonyholdsworth.com) for his memorable oil painting *Diramba Festival* that I always knew I wanted as the cover art, to Adrian Arias for his beautiful cover design, and to Paul Richards for the awesome book design and for making this book possible.

Thank you to Lincoln Bergman, Valerie Haynes Perry, and Marie Switzer Landau for proof reading. Any mistakes left in the text are my own.

Dear readers, I hope you enjoy this book.

nina@ninaserrano.com

Other Books by Nina Serrano

Heart Songs: The Collected Poems of Nina Serrano (1969–1979)
Heart's Journey: Selected Poems, 1980–1999
Heart Strong: Selected Poems, 2000–2012

Available from Estuary Press
www.estuaryress.com and from
www.ninaserrano.com